About Master S.

Mountain Masters & Dark Haven Book: 8

Opening the pages of each new book from the wonderfully talented pen of author Cherise Sinclair is like welcoming an old friend back into your life after a noted absence. You know you are going to laugh, cry and delight in the characters.

~ The Romance Studio

Since childhood, Mallory McCabe has dreamed of falling in love with a hero. And then one saves her life. He's honest…and blunt. Deadly, but filled with pain. Overpowering, yet ever so gentle with her. Oh yes, she's found her hero. Taking him to her bed is simply…right. As is losing her heart.

How could she have known he'd want nothing more to do with her?

His indifference hurts. She vows to forget him…then he buys the land next to hers.

Released early from prison, all Sawyer Ware wants is to move to the city and get his life back together. But when a violent gang targets his police detective brother, Sawyer puts his future on hold. After a decade as a Navy SEAL, he won't—can't—walk away when someone he loves is threatened.

His task might well be deadly. He sure can't afford to get involved with a woman—especially his captivating neighbor. Although he hungers to be near her, to enjoy her clear laugh, her easy friendship, and the peace she brings wherever she goes, a relationship is absolutely out of the question.

Why won't his heart obey orders?

Want to be notified of the next release?

Sent only on release day.
Sign up at:
www.CheriseSinclair.com/NewsletterForm

Master of Solitude

Mountain Masters & Dark Haven 8

Cherise Sinclair

VanScoy Publishing Group

Master of Solitude
Copyright © 2017 by Cherise Sinclair
Print Edition
ISBN: 978-0-9975529-9-7
Published by VanScoy Publishing Group
Cover Art: Hot Damn Designs

This book is a work of fiction. The names, characters, places, and incidents are products of the writer's imagination or have been used fictitiously and are not to be construed as real. Any resemblance to persons, living or dead, actual events, locales, business establishments, or organizations is entirely coincidental.

All rights reserved. This copy is intended for the original purchaser of this eBook only. No part of this eBook may be reproduced, scanned, or distributed in any manner whatsoever without prior written permission from the author, except in the case of brief quotations embodied in critical articles and reviews.

Warning: This book contains sexually explicit scenes and adult language and may be considered offensive to some readers. This book is for sale to adults only, as defined by the laws of the country in which you made your purchase.

Disclaimer: Please do not try any new sexual practice, without the guidance of an experienced practitioner. Neither the publisher nor the author will be responsible for any loss, harm, injury, or death resulting from use of the information contained in this book.

Author's Note

To my readers,

The books I write are fiction, not reality, and as in most romantic fiction, the romance is compressed into a very, very short time period.

You, my darlings, live in the real world, and I want you to take a little more time in your relationships. Good Doms don't grow on trees, and there are some strange people out there. So while you're looking for that special Dom, please, be careful.

When you find him, realize he can't read your mind. Yes, frightening as it might be, you're going to have to open up and talk to him. And you listen to him in return. Share your hopes and fears, what you want from him, what scares you spitless. Okay, he may try to push your boundaries a little—he's a Dom, after all—but you will have your safe word. You will have a safe word, am I clear? Use protection. Have a backup person. Communicate.

Remember: safe, sane, and consensual.

Know that I'm hoping you find that special, loving person who will understand your needs and hold you close.

And while you're looking or even if you've already found your dearheart, come and hang out with the Mountain Masters.

Love,
Cherise

Acknowledgments

OMG, this is my twenty-fifth book! So, to you all, thank you so much for all your support, for the handholding and encouragement, for the ideas, for the scoldings <g>, and the reviews. Y'all mean the world to me.

Speaking of scoldings, this story is for the lifestylers who reminded me that not every submissive has had a rough past. You're right. Although I love writing about heroines who've overcome adversity (and gone on to kick ass and take names), many submissives come to the lifestyle without a past trauma. So…here you go.

A huge shout-out goes to my awesome critique partners, Bianca Sommerland, Fiona Archer, and Monette Michaels. I am so very blessed to have you guys in my life.

Hugs and more hugs go to my magnificently sharp-eyed beta readers, Marian Shulman, Ruth Reid, and Barb Jack. You rock!

Thanks go to Red Quill Editing for their wonderful work. I have to say, I love our discussions.

Hugs to go Leagh and Lisa at Romance Novel Promotions for their valiant efforts in herding the Shadowkittens in the News & Discussion group. *muah!*

And finally, to my dearheart who protects me from giant wasps, kills hurt chickens when I can't face the task, and holds my hand during the scary parts of movies (and life), *I love you!*

Chapter One

S AWYER WARE HAD been out of prison for a whole five weeks and was still acclimating to freedom. Wasn't it interesting how a year in prison could give a man a whole new appreciation of life outside the walls?

In the ClaimJumper Tavern, he looked around and appreciated the hell out of everything. Like how the ice-cold, draft Budweiser tasted better than any specialty beer ever.

Like Johnny Cash on the jukebox. Women in tight jeans. Unlocked doors. Eating, drinking, and rolling out of bed anytime he felt like it.

And hanging out with his brother with no overbearing corrections officer nearby.

"I like this place," Sawyer told Atticus. Every breath was redolent with the aroma of beer and French fries. Antlers on the rough log wall served as coat hooks for jackets and hats. In front of the jukebox, two couples were country dancing.

The end of July was the height of the tourist season. On this Saturday night, the small tavern in Bear Flat, California, was packed with loggers and ranchers, most in jeans and plain T-shirts. The tourists visiting nearby Yosemite Park added color with brightly patterned clothing and sunburned faces.

As Sawyer looked around, many townspeople either avoided his gaze...or gave him the stink-eye. This was the downside of small towns—like cockleburs in a horse's mane, a bad reputation clung to a man forever.

Not that he particularly gave a fuck about the ugly stares. Unlike prison convicts, the law-abiding locals wouldn't come after him with fists and shivs. "I see the locals aren't setting out a welcome mat for ex-cons."

"'Fraid not. They're pretty resentful about the prison." Atticus took in the bitter glances toward Sawyer and rubbed his short beard thoughtfully. Although the two of them looked alike—over six feet, muscular, brown hair, blue eyes—Att wore his hair to shoulder-length whereas Sawyer'd never lost a military preference for short hair and being clean-shaven.

Sawyer figured he looked more like a cop than Att did.

"Why would they be resentful?" Sawyer asked. "Doesn't a prison boost the economy?"

"Bear Flat never wanted a prison located here...or the crime that accompanies one." Atticus's mouth curved into a grim smile. "The spotlight on the prison riot and breakout was very welcome."

"I bet." The investigation had exposed a multiplicity of bribery and kickbacks, beginning with how the private prison company acquired the building permits to the maneuvering for a state prison contract when its federal contract fell through. The suppression of failed environmental studies had been the kicker. California was very into the environment, and when the state EPA had seen the studies, the prison had been shut down so fast the warden was still probably in shock.

As of last Monday, Bear Flat no longer had a prison on the outskirts of town, and the citizens were damned happy. The locals also made it clear they wanted the prison riff-raff to leave just as fast as the prison staff had.

The noise in the tavern increased as three members of the tattooed, pierced, and over-muscled Neo-Nazi Aryan Hammers sauntered through the room. When the townspeople's disapproval switched to them, the gangbangers sneered back and took a table in the far corner. Looking around, they spotted Sawyer and Atticus.

Atticus noticed the waves of hate coming from the corner. "Ah, hell. Looks like the morons finally figured out who stopped their

MASTER OF SOLITUDE   3

buddies from escaping."

Sawyer snorted. "I didn't stop them, bro, hard as I tried. I just got stabbed. You were the one who actually took them out." In the process of rescuing two kidnapped social workers, his brother had killed the leader of the imprisoned Aryan Hammers.

"You killed one and flattened another. They won't forget it." Atticus's gaze turned serious. "It's barely been...what...five weeks since you were nearly gutted? I know the big bad SEAL could normally flatten a platoon of nasties, but right now, one punch to your gut and you'll be on the floor. Walk careful, frogman."

"Hooyah, jarhead. Same goes for you, in spades. You're at the top of their shit list." At least as a cop, Atticus was packing.

"Oh, yeah. That'll keep me up nights." Att grinned and asked, "Want another beer?"

"Nah." Sawyer hadn't had a night out since his hospital release or, come to think of it, since being imprisoned. He was tired, and all the animosity was getting to him. "I'm ready to call it a night."

"Sounds good. I'll—"

"Hey, Ware. Did you bring in the saddle you want me to repair?" The shout came from an older, leathery-faced man at a nearby table.

Atticus turned. "I did. It's in the pickup. Want me to toss it in your van?"

"Yeah. Door's not locked. Lock it when you're done." The man resumed his conversation with a short, round woman.

"Leaving a vehicle unlocked is either trust or laziness," Sawyer said.

"Actually, he probably doesn't want to leave his wife right now. It's their fortieth anniversary, and I'd say he's going to get lucky." Att chuckled. "I hope Gin and I still look like that in forty years."

Sawyer studied the silver-haired couple. Bottle of wine on the table, mostly gone. The woman was flushed and smiling, and her hand was on her husband's thigh, edging higher. The man laughed heartily before leaning forward to kiss her.

Evidently, some relationships worked out. "I'd say you and Gin've got good odds for success."

"I'm going to do my best to ensure that." Att rose. "Be back in a minute and we can head out. Gin's gathering should be finished by now."

Atticus's woman was the sociable sort and had some girl-thing planned tonight, which was why the Ware brothers were in the ClaimJumper. "Sounds good. I'll handle our bar tab."

Atticus had found himself a fine woman. Sawyer should know since Gin had been his counselor in the prison for a while and had helped him forgive himself for his massive screw-up.

Now he was out and needed to figure out what he wanted out of life.

Sawyer frowned at his empty beer glass. At one time, he'd planned a military career, but being wounded and a nice case of PTSD had put the skids to those hopes. For too long after his discharge from the service, he'd been buried in hallucinations and nightmares.

Although he'd worked through the PTSD while in prison, he'd also been forced to acknowledge—and mourn—that the path to his future had taken a sharp detour.

He needed to find new goals.

As soon as the stab wound in his gut healed, he'd give San Francisco a try and see what kind of a life he could make. The Navy SEAL teams had given him a home. Someday, maybe, he could find that sense of belonging again.

And he'd look for a woman he could love for forty years.

Last night, when Gin had teased his brother about his *"oh-so-macho"* movie choice, Att had pulled her onto his lap and kissed her to silence. Then they'd shared the chair, so immersed in each other they'd forgotten the movie. Yeah, Att had a good woman.

Sawyer was damned pleased for him…and a tad bit envious.

Up at the bar, he paid the tab and exchanged a few words with the grizzled Swede who owned the place.

As Sawyer turned to leave, a drunken logger the size of Godzilla stumbled into him.

Pain exploded in his side, and fuck, it felt as if every stitch had busted loose. He knew the incision would be all right, but *God. Damn.*

"Sorry, buddy." The logger slapped Sawyer's shoulder and lumbered on across the room.

As Sawyer held his side and tried to regain his breath, two more guys pushed past. One man, beefy with a receding hairline, said loudly, "Damn convicts need to get out of our town."

Sawyer straightened, his good mood soured.

Obviously having overheard the irate local, a slender blonde moved up to the bar and gave Sawyer a slow, predatory perusal. "You were in jail? A convict?" Her nipples made tiny points under her thin shirt.

He nodded without answering.

"I'm Candy." The slowness with which she said her name added a potent suggestion. "Want to buy me a beer...or join me for something else?" When she moved closer, the way she ran her hand down his chest indicated what *something* she had in mind.

"No." To hell with being polite. As he took a step away, disgust was a foul taste in his mouth. She wasn't the first woman he'd run into—in prison and out—who was aroused by the idea of fucking a convict. How freaking warped was that?

One hand on his aching side, he walked away. The stabbing pain was receding, and hey, he was standing upright, not hunched over like a ninety-year-old. Right after the surgery, he'd wondered if he'd end up with permanent curvature of the spine. Fortunately, he was getting better. And he was alive. Getting shanked trying to save women from escaping prisoners hadn't been fun...but had caused the politically shrewd governor to grant Sawyer an early release.

He was *free*.

As he made his way toward the door, he looked for his brother. Shouldn't Att have returned by now? Unless, of course, he'd gotten caught up in a conversation outside. The sociable bastard knew almost everyone in town—probably a side effect of being a police detective.

Nonetheless...

As Sawyer's instincts tap-danced a warning across his nape, he sped up. Gut tightening, he glanced around, trying to ID what'd set off his lizard brain. Nobody new had entered. The crowd hadn't changed except…

The Aryan Hammers' table was unoccupied. *Fuck.*

Sawyer shoved through a cluster of people to get out the door.

Darkness shrouded Main Street. The air was dry and cold as he sucked in a breath and looked up and down the street. The silence after the noisy bar throbbed in his ears—and then he heard a broken-off shout. Hand on his side, he dashed around the corner to the parking lot behind the tavern.

It was too fucking dark. As his eyes adjusted, he saw movement between two pickups. One man fighting three. Fear stabbed into his chest. *Atticus.*

A tire iron rose up, glinting in the dregs of light.

"Hey! What's going on!" Sawyer bellowed. "Call the cops, Harry!" He sprinted across the lot. The fight was too far, too fucking far away.

The tire iron swung down, fast and hard—and was blocked, thank fuck.

As the other two men punched the lone man, the first swung the tire iron like a baseball bat. The metal connected.

The grunt of pain was familiar. *Atticus, dammit.*

Att fell to his knees, and his attackers fled the parking lot.

Sawyer skidded to a stop beside the pickup.

His brother was already trying to get up.

Alive. The wave of relief was so intense, Sawyer's head spun.

One knee still on the ground, Att glanced around before squinting up at Sawyer. "Who the hell is Harry?"

"No clue. Just wanted them scared enough to drop the tire iron and leave." He put his hand on Att's shoulder, pulled out his phone for a light so he could assess the damage, and reconsidered. It wouldn't be wise to give the assholes a well-lit target. "How bad are you hurt?"

Att swiped a hand over his mouth and spat. "Caught some punches. No major damage." He used Sawyer's hand to pull himself to his feet, groaned, and pressed an arm to his side.

"Busted ribs?"

"Or cracked." Att straightened slowly.

"You're fucking lucky they didn't split your skull open."

"Oh, they tried, believe me."

Jesus. Sawyer turned on the phone Att had bought him last week.

"What're you doing?"

"Calling the cops."

Att laughed and winced. "No need, bro. Station's across the street. We'll walk over, and I'll report it."

"You don't want them rounded up fast?"

"Can't. I can't ID who attacked me—they wore ski masks." Atticus sighed. "I have no doubt it was the Aryan Hammers. Their new head honcho, Animal, got in my face the first week he was here. Slash was his cousin."

Atticus had killed Slash.

"No shit." Fury still snarling in his veins, Sawyer fought the urge to chase down the bastards. The law sure as fuck wasn't going to be any help.

Trouble was, he wasn't in any shape to battle gangbangers. *Dammit.* As Sawyer walked beside his brother, the image of the tire iron hitting Att kept flashing like a strobe light in his brain. His teeth ground together. If Sawyer had arrived a minute later, Att would've been dead, his brains splattered over the pavement.

Dammit, his brother should still be safely on the police force in Idaho, near the family ranch. He shouldn't be targeted by a gang known for its savagery.

All my fault. He should've gotten more help for his PTSD. Instead, he'd fallen asleep in a car, killed his best friend, and been sentenced to prison.

Att had abandoned everything and moved to California to support Sawyer. Damn idiot over-protective big brother. Hell, when their abusive stepfather had whipped them, Att would take the blows directed at his mother or siblings.

Sawyer wouldn't have made it to adulthood without Atticus.

As Att stumbled on the boardwalk and cursed, Sawyer gripped his brother's upper arm to steady him. "Easy, bro. Not much farther."

The Aryan Hammers wouldn't back off. The violent white supremacists were out for revenge—and to restore their damaged reputation. They couldn't afford to let Att live.

Sawyer's mouth tightened. He'd have to postpone his plans to find a city job. Until Atticus was safe, Bear Flat had just gotten itself another resident.

Chapter Two

BITING INTO A German pastry from Friede's bakery, Mallory McCabe ambled down the boardwalk, enjoying the sights and sounds of her small mountain town. Could any place in the world be more beautiful? With a nineteenth-century boardwalk, mining-town storefronts, and antique hanging signs, Bear Flat was a picturesque delight. Wooden barrels spaced along the railed boardwalk overflowed with bright orange marigolds and nasturtiums.

As the sun dropped behind the dark mountain peaks, the air was finally cooling. Such a relief. She'd spent the day running back and forth between two of her construction sites—and the early August weather had been exceedingly hot and dry. Her all-male crew often stripped off their shirts to keep cool. As a female—and their boss— she couldn't exactly do the same.

Life could be so unfair at times.

On this Saturday, Main Street was filled with activity. Some people, like her, were finishing up their weekend errands. Others, especially the tourists, were starting their evening early.

With a quick side-step, Mallory dodged a young man who was already drunk as a skunk. Thrown off his stride, the guy thumped into the boardwalk railing, apologized politely to the post, and staggered on.

Jeering at the young man, two skinheads swaggered across the street.

Mallory slowed to avoid intersecting them. One had horrible

racist tattoos everywhere. They both had dark...ugly...auras. A shudder ran up her spine.

Crossing the street, Mrs. Jenkins and Holly Simmons gave the skinheads a wide berth—and glares.

When the prison closed two weeks ago, some gangs had left. She hadn't seen the Crips in the last few days. However, Virgil Masterson, her neighbor who was a police detective, was worried the gangs with profitable drug distribution networks would stay.

Trailing after her mother, Holly's teenage daughter, Jasmine, turned her blue-eyed gaze on the skinheads...and smiled.

Now *that* wasn't good. How easily youngsters could be fooled by a macho façade, not perceiving the brutal nature beneath.

Noticing Jasmine's flirting, Holly took her daughter's arm and tugged her away quickly.

Mallory frowned. Drugs and violence had followed the gangs like winter followed autumn. Just last weekend, her other neighbor Atticus Ware had been attacked.

Surely there was something that could be done—that *she* could do. As frustration surged, she shook her head.

Stop. She knew better than to let events dictate her emotions. *She* was the one who decided how she would feel. Her childhood teacher in the commune would have been disappointed in her.

Pausing, Mallory collected herself, settled herself. Years ago, her instructor had taught her how to shift her focus to the shimmering light around each person—and to note how the clear colors of bighearted people far out-numbered the cruel ones. Peace swept through her at the reminder, and she continued on her way.

Half a block down, an aura outside the bookstore caught her attention. The beautiful golden color indicated a person who was charming, gregarious, artistic, and generous. Rebecca Hunt.

Smiling in delight, Mallory crossed the street toward the artist. Becca and her husband owned a wilderness lodge. When Mallory had remodeled the lodge's second floor, they'd become friends.

"Hey, Becca. Where's my favorite baby?"

"Hi, girl. Logan took Ansel so I could grab some reading materi-al." Tall, lushly curved, and redheaded, Becca tucked an arm around

Mallory for a quick squeeze before holding up a stack of paperback books. "Look at what Mrs. Reed has on sale."

Mallory glanced at the paperbacks and tried not to react, but...

"Your face!" Becca sputtered a laugh. "Haven't you ever seen a BDSM romance before?"

"Ah, I read mostly fantasy, and I don't think Aragorn is into bondage."

Becca blinked. "Oh, wow. Roleplaying *The Lord of the Rings*? How fun would that be? Especially with those horse lords. What was the bossy one's name?"

"Éomer?" *What was roleplaying?*

"Yes, him. Maybe he finds a pretty elf maiden on his lands and gets upset. Mmm. Yes, your rider of Rohan would get very upset with a trespasser. Plus, he has rope."

Mallory choked. "You can't turn Éomer into some pervert."

"Not a pervert, honey. Just a cranky, bossy, fighting man with a really big...sword."

The vision of Éomer getting all sexual and...bossy...made Mallory flush. What would he do with the rope? Maybe it would be fun to find a horse lord. A bossy one. "You're so twisted. Now, I'm going to have Éomer fantasies every time I read Tolkien."

Becca laughed. "Mal, you wouldn't have to daydream about him if you came to the BDSM parties here."

Mallory would have accused Rebecca of corrupting their little town, except the Hunt brothers' kinky parties had been a well-known "secret" long before the city girl had arrived. "I don't think so."

Sure Mallory had indulged in a few fantasies about kinky stuff. Even so, attending a BDSM party was a whole different box of tools. "I'm not much of a party girl."

"No? How come?"

Mallory laughed, although a trickle of wistfulness ran through her. "Get real, Becca. I'm quiet. No flash, no witty conversation."

"You're not shy, though." Becca studied her for a minute. "Although I've never heard you mention a guy. When's the last time you had a date?"

"It's been a while. Bear Flat is pretty small." Interesting, intelligent, kind men weren't plentiful here—let alone powerful, confident ones. And a real hero? He wouldn't even notice her.

She wasn't ugly, just...average. Her green eyes were pretty enough, but her face was a bit too long for beauty. Her hair was plain—long, straight, and brown. Working construction meant she rarely wore makeup or sexy attire.

Becca linked arms with her as they strolled down the boardwalk. "Hmm. Well, what about that cowboy in front of Vanessa's Antiques? He's cute."

Cute? So not her turn-on and never had been, even during her teenage years. Mallory followed Becca's gaze. "Oh, Eddie Nilsson." His orange aura said he was intelligent. Unfortunately, a brownish tinge revealed his laziness, as well. "When there's trouble on his ranch, he sends his hands out while he stays warm in bed."

"A slug, huh? Forget him, then. You can do much better."

Mallory rather doubted it. "I think my standards might be too high. My mom raised me on children's fantasy books—like *Narnia*—full of strong, save-the-damsel champions. I grew up wanting a hero, and I don't think they exist."

"Well, actually, they do," Becca said thoughtfully. "I married one, after all. And what about how Atticus rescued Gin after the prison break? And there's also his brother Sawyer."

The prison break had ended in a ghastly bloodbath. "You're right. I guess even Wyatt and Morgan Masterson deserve hero labels." Too bad she considered them the same as family.

"Exactly."

As they passed Eddie Nilsson, he glanced at Mallory, dismissed her, and gave Becca a long, appreciative stare with a wink.

Once past him, Mallory snorted. "See? Guys don't think of me as female." She glanced down at her attire and grinned. Jeans, blue short-sleeved work shirt, and boots. "You think it might be the work boots?"

"More like they're terrified of a female whose favorite toy is a power tool." Laughing, Becca steered them around a cluster of teenagers. "Now, listen to Mama Becca. You're an attractive woman, and the right guy is out there. When you do spot a hero, stop being all quiet and grab him."

Mallory broke out laughing. "You're talking to the wrong woman. I don't even know how to flirt."

"That is just so wrong." Becca pursed her lips. "Fine. If you can't manage to talk to him, screw his brains out instead. The rest will follow."

"You... I always think of you as so proper, then you say stuff like that."

Becca smirked and shoved a book into Mallory's hands. "While you're searching, give this story a try. It's super hot. And now, I need to go claim my champion." She hurried over to where Logan strolled with their son in his arms.

Yes, Logan Hunt was a walking, talking figure of a superman. Tall and muscular, hard-faced, gravel-voiced. Scary...but also an adorable softy with his one-year-old son. Becca was a lucky woman. Of course, Logan was pretty lucky, too. The two were incredible together.

That's what Mallory wanted—a strong, confident, protective man like Becca had.

Mallory sure didn't want to end up with losers like those her mother had found. Mom had been a sculptor, a Wiccan, seeing only the good in people—and far too trusting. Like aphids on broccoli, weak men had overrun her mother. *"Hey, Evelyn, got a few bucks to tide me over till payday?" "Evelyn, I got turned out of my place. S'okay if I crash here for a while?"* Financially and emotionally, Mom had supported boyfriend after boyfriend—and been dumped the minute each was stable.

Mallory shook her head. Despite her intelligence, her mother had a blind spot when it came to men. Look how her high school boyfriend had fled upon learning she was pregnant.

Of course, Gramps hadn't helped matters by losing his temper. After the blow-up, Mom had run off to a San Francisco commune and stayed away for over a decade...right up until she'd learned she had hepatitis. Back then, it was often a death sentence, and Mom had wanted more family for eleven-year-old Mallory than the transient commune members. For the five years until Mom died, Mallory had spent every summer with Gramps and Gramma.

At eleven, Mallory had barely understood the light she saw around each person. The strength and protectiveness in Gramps's aura had been a revelation.

She wanted a man like Gramps...like Logan. Sadly, men like them didn't chase after women like her. If she followed Becca's orders, would a man notice her? *"Screw his brains out."*

Oh, please. Her friend was crazy.

Grinning, Mallory glanced at the book Becca had given her.

And choked. The woman on the cover was *naked*. Rope was twined around her wrists, her arms pulled up over her head.

Flushing, Mallory shoved the book into her purse before anyone could see what she held. She glanced back at the little bookstore. Obviously, she'd been browsing the wrong shelves.

A SHORT TIME later, finished with errands, Mallory drove her pickup up her winding mountain road. As the tall evergreens cast shadows over the darkening road, loneliness trickled through her.

Seeing Becca had reminded her of Serena and Missy, her besties who'd moved to San Francisco earlier in the summer. When she'd spoken to them last night, she'd realized they loved living in the city—and weren't coming back. She had other friends, but she missed the ones she'd had for years.

And she was returning to a dark, empty house...because Gramps had died last year.

She sighed. Her life wasn't the same without him in it. The aching grief she'd anticipated, but not how often a missing sound or habit would stab at her heart. There was no longer a hoarse, raspy laugh in response to the cat's antics. There were no grumbles before a cup of coffee had cheered Gramps up. After work, she'd automatically check the cookie jar...and it hurt to see the container still full.

Her first summer in Bear Flat, he'd taught her how to hammer nails, saw boards, and...had taken the place of her nonexistent father.

Why did you have to die, Gramps? She pined for him the way a person longed for sunshine at winter's end. Only with death, the warmth was gone forever.

She wished he hadn't fretted so much about her before he'd passed on. He'd been proud she'd taken over his construction company, but he'd also wanted her to have the joy of sharing her life with someone.

Yes, Gramps, it would be nice to have a husband and children. To have someone to laugh—and grumble—with. Someone to cuddle her during the long snowy winters and to point out the first daffodils in spring.

But she didn't see a loving relationship in her future.

The last man she'd dated hadn't lasted a month. She'd overheard him tell a friend, "She's nice—and as boring as watching paint dry. I want to get smashed on weekends; she wants to garden. To hell with that."

Slowing for a curve, she huffed a laugh. Life was a balance, now wasn't it? Maybe she wasn't flashy, but she had plenty of friends. She loved her work—and loved making her clients happy. She liked who she was and wasn't about to twist herself up, trying to look all eye-catchingly feminine.

However…

She grinned, thinking of Becca's advice. *"…screw his brains out."* Considering she'd turn thirty in a couple of months, she was quite old enough for a fling, right?

Missy and Serena occasionally indulged in one-night stands they half regretted and half boasted about. "I knew it wouldn't go anywhere, but he was just too hot to ignore," Serena had said on the phone last week. "Oooh, girl, the sex was worth it."

What would a one-night stand be like?

Sex wasn't something she obsessed about. She did just fine with her own hand. Although she could climax if a man was talented with his fingers or mouth, it seemed a lot of effort for a mild orgasm. Especially since she took so long. Guys could pump a few times and be done. And boy, when they were finished, they were *finished*.

Each of her three lovers had been a friend first—and each had returned to being a friend after the fleeting romance. Steamy sex? It just wasn't in her DNA.

Would a one-night stand be different since she'd know she'd never see the man again? Would it be more exciting?

Hmm.

Mallory slowed the truck for the next sharp curve. Deer browsing at twilight would often dash across the road unexpectedly. As the road straightened, she spotted a couple of cars pulled off on the turnout.

Trunk open, one vehicle was jacked up with a tire off—and looked like young Zoe Larson's car. The teenager had just gotten her license last month. She might need help—or a ride home.

Mallory braked, parked in front of the jacked up car, and hopped out.

No one was working on the flat tire.

The encroaching forest stood in ominous darkness. As Mallory turned in a circle, trying to spot someone, uneasiness sent a shiver up her spine—and kept her from calling out. Instead, she reached into the door's side compartment for her heavy, foot-long flashlight.

As she walked to the other side of the cars—away from the road, a shimmer caught her attention. The flash of a bluish aura was gone too quickly to read. *No, wait.* Someone was upslope where the forest's shadows reigned. Squinting, she caught a glimpse of a shiny yellow fabric.

A man's low voice came from there.

Mallory hesitated. Was she interrupting a hot interlude? Well, too bad. Even if she embarrassed everyone, at least she'd know Zoe was all right.

Moving closer, she saw a man. Tall and beefy. In his early twenties. His chin-length hair was oily and tangled. Piercings studded his lips and nose—and his murky aura was ugly.

Zoe faced him, her yellow shirt half off.

Saying something too low to hear, the man shoved the girl against a tree trunk and slapped her. *Slapped* her.

Anger surged in Mallory, and she dashed toward them. "You *bastard.* Get away from her!"

The man spun around. "We're just talking. Beat it, bitch." When he straightened, and his hand covered Zoe's mouth, Mallory realized how big he was.

Don't be stupid. Mallory skidded to a stop, yanked out her phone so fast she almost dropped it, and punched in 911.

"911. What is your emergency?"

Mallory raised her voice. "A girl is being attacked up on Kestrel Mountain Road, the turnout on the north side. Before Whiskey Creek Lane. Hurry!" Leaving the phone on, she shoved it into her jeans as the operator continued to talk. Mallory took a firmer grip on her flashlight.

"You fucking bitch." The man turned toward Mallory, his hand closing into a fist.

Yanking her arm from his hold, Zoe lurched into a run toward Mallory. Blood streamed down her chin from a split lip.

The thug chased after the girl.

Hiss and spit, why didn't he leave? "Get behind me, hon."

Running past Mallory, Zoe tripped and fell to her knees.

The attacker was far too close; escape wasn't possible.

The flashlight seemed woefully inadequate for self-defense. With her free hand, Mallory snatched up a dead branch. Heart hammering, she took a step forward, planting herself squarely in front of Zoe. Her mouth felt too dry as she faced the man, and her voice creaked. "You'd better leave before the cops get here."

"You dumb bitch. Shouldn't have butted in." The last of the light glinted off his piercings, and an ugly sneer pulled his thick lips back. He kept coming.

Mallory gritted her teeth and set her stance. The Mastersons had taught her self-defense…years and years ago.

Why did this guy have to be so big?

He swung at her.

Ducking low, she smacked the long flashlight into his side so hard her hand went numb. As he shouted in pain, she poked him in the stomach with the branch.

It broke in two. *Stupid branch.* She dropped it and back-pedaled.

"Fucking *cunt*." He kept coming, swinging at her like an enraged grizzly.

Although she dodged one swing, the other slammed into her shoulder like a wrecking ball. Knocked onto the ground, she rolled and scrambled up—and threw a handful of dirt and gravel into his face.

As he scrubbed his hands over his eyes, Mallory danced away, looking for Zoe.

The girl had wormed her way under Mallory's pickup. Good. With the cops coming, that was the safest place for her.

Mallory'd have to keep the man away from Zoe until help arrived. Oh, *sure*. Fear had her breathing far too fast. She backed up farther and tightened her grip on the heavy metal flashlight.

Tears streamed from the man's reddened eyes as he blinked furiously. "Fucking, fucking bitch. I'm going to rip you to pieces." His aura was black with his rage.

He rushed her and swung one fist.

Mallory jumped to one side, whacked his forearm hard with the flashlight, and darted away.

Lunging, he snagged her loose work shirt and yanked her toward him.

Bending forward against his pull, she kicked backward. Her boot smashed into his shin.

"Shit!" He lost his grip on her shirt.

Off balance, she fell forward, clambered back to her feet. Even as she turned, he charged her.

And a big muscular stranger sprang from behind the car. He grabbed the thug's arm and used the momentum to slam the bastard against Zoe's battered Ford. The car toppled off the jack and bounced on creaking springs.

Heart hammering, Mallory retreated.

With a yell of pain, the thug whirled to face the other man. "I'll *gut* you, asshole." Pulling a switchblade, the brute attacked.

Mallory bit back a scream.

The rescuer dodged to the side and landed a solid punch to the thug's ribs.

"Fuck!" The thug backed away, then moved forward more cautiously. His blade weaved a defensive net, stabbing here and there, at the rescuer...who was weaponless.

Oh, *no*. Horrorstruck, Mallory searched for a weapon—and spotted Zoe's flat tire. The tire was heavy in her hands as she picked it up. Summoning up strength, she heaved it at the thug with all her might.

The solid tire hit his ass, knocked him forward—and right into the rescuer's big fist. With a terrible groan, the thug staggered back.

Following through, the good guy flattened him with the next punch.

Zoe's attacker landed on his back.

Mallory's trembling legs threatened to drop her to the ground beside him. Leaning against the truck, she stared at the unmoving attacker.

He was out cold.

Okay. As she tried to catch her breath, she glanced at the victor...and blinked.

His aura...oh, she'd never seen anything more lovely. In predominance was the clear, deep red of strength and determination. Grounded in reality, this man could take anything and survive. Green was his secondary color—he was probably a hard-working perfectionist. An outdoorsman. Generous. Loyal. Streaks of brilliant darkness spoke of pain, both physical and emotional—and called to her.

He noticed her watching and moved forward.

One hand on the truck, Mallory pushed herself upright. "Thank you so much."

"No problem." The way his black T-shirt stretched over his heavily muscled shoulders and chest distracted her for a moment before she noticed how he'd braced his hand against his side.

She didn't remember him getting hit or cut. "Have you been hu—"

Looking down at her, he frowned. "Are you all right, miss?" His hand curled around her upper arm, and his grip was powerful. Careful.

"I—" She realized she was trembling like an aspen during a high wind. She tried to straighten her spine…yet the unexpected sensation of being cared for and protected made her want to bury her head in his shoulder.

His brown hair was cut very short, and his face was all hard angles. "Miss?" In the shadowy light, his eyes were a dark, dark blue. His gaze appraised her, up and down, before returning to her face. "Are you hurt?"

Considering his size and the rugged lines of his face, she'd expected a deep, harsh voice. Instead, his voice was a smooth, dark velvet, reminding her of the guy in *Die Hard*.

The *hero* in *Die Hard*.

She had a hero here.

And he was waiting for her answer…

"I'm fine. Thanks to you." She patted his hand and pulled free. Ignoring the quivering of her legs, Mallory went down on one knee and looked under the truck. "Zoe."

The girl was curled into a ball in the gravel, shaking and crying.

The attacker was still out cold, or Mallory might've kicked him a few times. Despite the fury raging inside, she gentled her voice. "Let's get you out of there, honey."

Once she'd managed to coax Zoe from under the truck, Mallory pulled the trembling girl close…and watched two police cars come wailing around the bend.

The first patrol officer out of the black-and-white spotted her. "Mallory! What's going on? Are you hurt?"

"No, I'm fine." She gave the girl a squeeze. "I think Zoe could use a ride home, though…after you remove the garbage lying there."

To her delight, Zoe managed a tiny sputter of a laugh.

SAWYER RUBBED HIS bruised knuckles as he talked with the police officer. Ex-cons weren't always given the benefit of the doubt, but the young cop had recognized him—because of Atticus—and listened rather than automatically clapping on the cuffs.

Another officer had taken the two females to one side—because the terrified kid wasn't about to be separated from the woman—and apparently the females had confirmed his account.

The asshole assailant sealed his fate by cursing the cops and re-sisting arrest.

Although Sawyer's side throbbed from the action, he enjoyed when the bastard got cuffed and tossed into the patrol car. A fine finish. He didn't want to think of what would have happened if he hadn't driven by just then on his way to Atticus's house. Still...all good. The kid's only injury had been a slap and a huge fright. The woman would have some bruises but nothing more.

Full dark had fallen before one patrol car took the asshole away and another left to drive the girl to her parents. Sawyer let out a relieved sigh and climbed into his pickup. Amazing how quiet the night was without everyone around.

As he started the ignition, his headlights spotlighted the other vehicle parked at the end of the turnout. Melissa—no, the cop had called her *Mallory*—sat unmoving on the tailgate of her pickup.

Well, hell. Sawyer turned the key, got out, and walked over. "You okay?"

"Mmmhmm." Her gaze came up. "Did I thank you?"

"Several times." He frowned.

She'd wrapped her arms around her waist and was shaking hard enough to bust bones. Not surprising. Most civilians weren't used to violence. The young woman had fought well and afterward had kept herself together to comfort the girl. Now, everything had caught up with her.

Although she'd insisted she was fine, the cops should have made sure she was taken care of—but they were young, and what with tourist season and Saturday night, short-handed. "You got someone at home who could pick you up?"

"No. No one." Her big eyes darkened in a way that tugged at him.

"I'm sorry." Needing to extend comfort, Sawyer rested his hand on her shoulder—and realized he was far too close. She was female, and smart women ran from ex-convicts.

"How about I call someone else?" he asked. *Let go of her, fool.*

"No, thank you. I'm fine. I just need a moment to pull myself together." Her attempt at a smile was heartbreaking.

"All right, you take the time you need." Trouble was, the night was dark, and she was sitting on the side of the road. He'd be damned if he'd leave her here alone. "I'll wait with you."

She smiled at him. "Thank you. And thank you for the rescue. You were right in time."

The thought of her being hurt by the bastard was unsettling.

And he wanted to kiss her more than he wanted his next breath.

No. Just no. Come on, Ware.

But...damn...

She wasn't what some idiots would call classically beautiful; her face was lean and tanned, her mouth wide, her chin firm. This was a strong woman. Yet her big green eyes held vulnerability. The mixture was incredibly appealing.

He'd overheard the teen tell the cop how Mallory'd taken on the assailant to protect her. This woman was totally, crazily brave, and he was a sucker for courage. Not that he'd do anything about it. Nice girls and ex-cons didn't belong together.

Unable to help himself, he ran a finger down her cheek, finding her skin as soft as it looked, then brushed a strand of her long, sun-streaked, dark brown hair back. The surprise showed in her eyes. Yeah, he shouldn't have touched her. In fact, he braced himself, waiting to see her flinch away.

She didn't. Instead, her gaze dropped, and she bit her lip. And then shook her head. "I need to go home." Yeah, she did. Unfortunately, from the way her hands were shaking, she might not get there.

"I'm not sure you're up to driving."

With a rueful smile, she turned her hands over and watched them shake. "It's a good thing I live close."

No shit. Idiot cops to leave her here. "I'm going to follow you home and make sure you get there. You can call the police station and let them know, if you want."

She laughed, actually laughed. Her voice was crystal clear and fucking beautiful. "If you don't mind, I'd appreciate an escort. Thank you again."

A few minutes later, following the red taillights of her pickup,

Sawyer was startled to see her turn onto Whiskey Creek Lane—the gravel road his brother lived on. She drove past Atticus's acres to the end of the lane and turned into a private drive, which curved upward toward an older farmhouse.

When Sawyer stepped out of his pickup, he took a long breath of pine-scented air and looked out over the land. He'd seen it from Atticus's house, but it was even more stunning from this higher vantage point. Forested mountains encircled the wide valley. Moonlight bathed the creek-fed meadow and fenced pastureland.

Mallory stopped at the foot of the steps, her hand gripping the railing. Maybe unsure her legs would hold her.

No porch light. The house was dark. Not a comforting place after the violence she'd endured. Frowning, he walked over and put a hand under her arm. "Let's get you inside and put some lights on."

She let out a soft sigh. "Thank you."

He helped her up the steps, unlocked the front door for her, and flipped on the hallway lights.

She stepped inside and hesitated. "Um. Would you…would you like to come in for a drink?"

"Seriously?" In his far-too-extensive past, "come in for a drink" was usually code for "wanna have sex?" He shook his head. "Not a good idea. I don't think you realize who or what you're asking in, Mallory."

"I do. I know exactly what you are. You're a…" In the light from the hallway, he could see her face darken with her flush. She bit her lip, obviously unwilling to say the word.

Yeah, well, he knew the word. *Ex-con.* Fucking great. Another woman who got off on violence. This shit was getting old. In the Navy, he'd enjoyed the tag chasers who wanted to score with a uniform. At least, at first. After all, young men lived for sex. Then, he'd realized he wanted more than meaningless sex—and as a SEAL, he'd avoided the frog hogs who had competitions for the numbers of SEALs they'd fucked.

Now, he was getting hit on by women excited he'd served time. Last week, one had actually hoped he was a murderer. Earlier today, the local named Candy had flirted with him—again—and begged for stories about prison fights.

What with prison and surgery, he'd been celibate for a long while, although he'd been getting offers since the day he walked out of the hospital. He'd turned them all down. "I don't think a drink'd be a good idea."

She drew back. "Of course. You have things to do."

Although her expression hadn't changed, he could hear the disappointment—and hurt—in her voice.

He hesitated. Maybe she had poor taste in her fuck-buddies, but he had to respect her courage. She'd come to a girl's rescue when almost anyone else would have run away. Then she'd cared for the teen with not only common sense, but enough warmth to melt the hardest heart.

Hurting this woman didn't set right with him. Not at all.

Besides, maybe she only wanted to give him a drink. Have some conversation. He'd enjoy talking to her. Simply being with her made him realize how lonely he'd been.

He took her hand and ignored the way he wanted to pull her into his arms. "On second thought, I could use a drink."

THE MAN'S HAND was warm and strong, and Mallory could feel courage flowing into her from him. With a big breath, she led him into her empty, lonely house. Oh, boy, could she do this?

Becca's advice kept running through her head, but seriously? Going to bed with a man she'd barely met wasn't the kind of person she was.

Still… If he hadn't rescued her, she could have died tonight. The realization shook her…wakened her…simmered like a fire in her veins. Each moment was to be lived. This *life* was to be lived, and if she had second thoughts tomorrow, at least she wouldn't look back and wonder what she'd missed. Wonder what making love with this brave man would be like.

Not just because he'd saved her, but because he was who he was. She looked at her rescuer and…oh, she'd never felt this way about anyone. His aura was like a bonfire, radiating warmth she wanted to nestle against, to wrap around herself. She cleared her throat. "Do you like scotch?"

"How could anyone turn down scotch?"

"Oh, good." Wasn't it wonderful she had something he'd like? Every Christmas, one of Gramps's friends had gifted him with Glenfiddich. Gramps had stored the bottles away, admitting that without Gramma, drinking made him melancholy.

Mallory pulled out a bottle and glasses, then frowned and turned the kitchen lights to low, before pouring two hefty drinks.

When he lifted an eyebrow, she checked the glasses and remembered she hadn't been pouring wine. This was hard alcohol, and she'd probably dispensed about two shots apiece.

Oh well...

She handed him one and raised hers. "To life."

He tilted his head. "Good choice." He *clinked* his glass against hers and took a drink.

Although she rarely overindulged, right now, she needed what Gramps had called liquid courage. Because she'd used up all her bravery in the fight. So rather than sipping, she tipped her head back and drank the scotch down.

An explosion of fire burst in her belly and seared her throat.

"Boy, scotch sure isn't wine," she wheezed.

His laugh lightened his aura and made her smile.

Pulling in a breath, she leaned against the counter. "You were holding your side earlier. Did the thug get in a punch I didn't see?"

A corner of his mouth tilted up. "You were terrified and still noticing everything, weren't you?" When she nodded, his chuckle was warmly masculine. "I had surgery about six weeks ago. All healed up, although I still feel it if I exert myself."

"You just had surgery and jumped into a fight?"

He shrugged.

Why did he have to be so...amazing?

And why couldn't she think of any brilliant conversational subjects? He wasn't *that* intimidating...quite. They were about the same age, right? She studied him more closely. Laugh lines at the edges of his eyes, deeper creases bracketing his mouth. Well, he might have a few years on her. He not only sounded but kind of looked like the star of *Die Hard*.

But with better hair.

The giggle she tried to smother almost choked her.

Sun and stars, she was getting stupid. She started to push her glass away, saw how her hands still shook…and filled it instead.

Watching her, not appearing at all uncomfortable, the man took another sip. "You've got some nice land across the lane. You run cattle on it?"

"It's not my land. A few years ago, my grandfather split the property, keeping this farmhouse and a few acres on this side of the road. A big shot CEO bought the pastures and the original log cabin on the other side."

"The CEO doesn't use the pastures?"

Mallory shook her head. "He'd planned to retire here and died instead. Apparently, it took forever to settle his estate, and now his son is trying to sell the place, which is extremely bad timing. With the prison closure, houses are getting dumped on the market right and left. I doubt if he'll sell anytime soon."

"What a shame. It's beautiful land." After taking a sip of his drink, he studied her, not at all uncomfortable with the ensuing silence.

His eyes held a masculine appreciation—and heat—she wasn't used to seeing.

And oh, she wanted him to touch her. The desire ran through her, so disconcerting that her gaze dropped.

She groped for something to say and found a question rising. When he spoke of the land, it was of pastures and cattle. But he didn't have an outdoorsman's tan. "Do you raise cattle?"

"Nope. But I grew up on a horse ranch—with cattle on the side. Gotta say I miss the life."

Puzzled, she pushed her hair back behind her ear. "Then why don't you return to it?"

"That's a very good question." He started to smile and frowned instead. Cupping her chin, he tilted her head and touched the side of her jaw. "You acquired some bruises, baby."

She worked construction; bruises were common. Being touched

like this? Looked at like this? She tilted her face into his hand, seeing the way his eyes darkened. *Yes.* He wanted her.

After brushing a light kiss over her lips, he pulled back.

Disappointment streaked through her.

Trying to figure out how to seduce him, she lifted her glass. Her second drink—okay, another couple of shots or so—started down even more smoothly. At least before he removed the glass from her hand.

"Mallory, alcohol impairs judgment. Time to stop."

Meeting his firm gaze, she lifted her chin. "I wanted you long before I had the first sip. I haven't changed my mind." She reached for her drink.

"I see," he said thoughtfully. He set her glass out of reach and put his own down. "In that case, come here, pet."

She took a step forward—and he pulled her into his arms and kissed her.

Kissed her.

His lips were warm. Firm. Teasing over hers. When she didn't open to him immediately, his hand closed on her hair and pulled her head back. Her gasp was smothered by his mouth and his invading tongue. And he took her over, possessed her mouth, teasing her with his tongue, retreating to nibble and suck on her lips, and kiss her neck before returning for more.

A fire ignited low in her belly in a way she hadn't felt since she was...a teenager with her first kiss.

How was he—She heard a huffed laugh.

"You've got a busy brain, do you?" He pulled her against him even closer, his hand sliding into her jeans, massaging her bottom even as he pressed her against a rock-hard erection.

Between the alcohol and his kisses, her busy brain simply melted out of her.

"The bedroom down the hall?" he asked at one point.

"Mmmhmm."

He moved her backward, step by step, kissing her the entire time, and suddenly she felt the bed mattress against the back of her legs.

The *bed*.

Holy lady of cats, could she do this? Still…her body was on fire, her breasts aching, her pussy wet and tingling.

"Hands up, baby," he said.

She frowned at him, confused. Rather than unbuttoning her work shirt, he simply lifted her arms and pulled it over her head. Even in the dim light, she could see the hunger in his gaze as he looked at her bra-covered breasts—and then the bra wasn't there any longer either.

"Mmm, beautiful." His hands touched her, gently at first, cupping her breasts, weighing one in a huge palm, teasing her nipples to hard, aching points.

"But…" *Head in the game, Mallory.* "*You're* still wearing *your* shirt."

His smile changed his features from dangerous to captivating. "Guess I'd best catch up." Without any hesitation, he stripped off his T-shirt.

Oh. Wow. Her mouth went dry. His chest and shoulders seemed even bigger without the shirt. Wonderfully broad. He had a scattering of brown chest hair over his pectorals, not nearly enough to cover the tautness of the skin over solid musculature. She laid her palm over his chest, and her heart skipped a beat. She'd never felt anything so hard. Her other hand closed on his left biceps. Just as hard. An ugly red scar showed under his left ribs.

"It's barely healed." When she touched it, his jaw tightened. All right, he didn't want to talk about his surgery.

Moving on, she ran her hands down his chest and over his ridged abdomen, following what Serena referred to as the happy trail, until her fingers ran into the barrier of his jeans and leather belt.

When she looked up at him, his lips tilted up as he said, "Your turn again, baby." The smoothness of his voice had acquired a sexy edge.

Her turn. She became mesmerized by the blunt angle of his jaw, somehow more forbidding with a dark five o'clock shadow.

He snorted, and she felt his hands undo her belt and unzip her jeans. Without asking, he pushed—*pushed*—her onto her back on the bed. With quick tugs, her boots were gone, her jeans, and her briefs as well.

Before her head had stopped spinning—the second drink really *had* been a mistake—he'd stripped as well. He was fully erect and long and... Could a cock be called muscular? Like his chest and arms, his shaft seemed thick with muscle. His pubic hair was trimmed neatly. He gave her no more time to look before he joined her on the bed, coming down on top of her. He smelled of clean pine and citrus.

As he pressed her into the mattress, even his heavy weight seemed appallingly sexy.

"Look at me, Mallory," he said quietly.

Her gaze met his, and he studied her face for a long moment. "You with me? This is the time to say yes or no, pet."

Why did he call her *pet*? He held her gaze, his eyes steady and...controlled. Both of them were naked and yet, she knew if she said stop, he'd simply roll off and get dressed.

Right now, she understood why her friends indulged in quickie sex nights.

She didn't want to say no.

"Yes," she whispered. The humor of the situation caught up to her, and she laughed. "You rescued me. Ancient tradition demands I reward you."

He chuckled, the sound quiet and low. "Guess I'd best be about collecting my reward." His mouth covered hers, and even as he took possession there, his hand covered her breast.

Under his caress, her breast swelled, and when his thumb circled the nipple, her back arched for more.

He made a pleased sound, and his touch grew slightly rougher as he switched to the other breast.

A shiver ran through her—as well as surprise. She hadn't expected how much she'd like feeling his hard hands on her body, how disconcertingly exciting the abrasive calluses would feel on her sensitive skin.

Shifting to lie beside her, he propped up on his elbow and simply...looked at her.

Embarrassment lit within, and a flush covered her body like a hot blanket.

"You're not as thin as I thought." His hand stroked down her torso and over her hip. "Your loose shirt covered these pretty curves."

Like her wide hips. *Oh, hiss*, how humiliating. "Don't," she whispered.

An eyebrow rose, and the firm look he gave her made the shivers start in her belly. "Mallory, I'm going to enjoy myself—including looking my fill. Touching my fill. Taking my fill. You can always tell me no, and I'll stop and leave. Is that what *don't* means?"

She shook her head, not sure what she was feeling. Only…being naked and *looked* at was discomforting.

He made a gutturally annoyed sound. "Women." He hadn't stopped touching her, and now, he played with her breasts, teasing the nipples back to throbbing peaks. "You have adorable breasts. I like looking at them." He trailed his fingers to her belly, to her hips, then squeezed her bottom. "And you have a gorgeous ass. Men like to look, girl."

His touch brushed down the tops of her thighs and returned. So close to…there. As she held her breath, he rolled up, pushed her legs apart, and knelt between them.

She shut her eyes, wishing she'd closed the curtains. The full moon provided far too much light. Would he expect her to be…oh, as lovely as some romantic heroine? She wasn't.

But she didn't regret being able to see *him*. The man was beautiful in a terrifyingly lethal way, like her cat, Aslan, when on the hunt. He was all coiled power harnessed by an intimidating self-control—and his aura shimmered with it.

SAWYER DIDN'T THINK a woman had ever looked at him as Mallory did now—as if she could see past his skin and into his soul. And still liked what she saw.

He studied her expressive face and wide eyes. Every thought showed clearly, and when she spoke, her beautiful soprano voice revealed every emotion.

Most women he'd bedded watched him as if he were a challenge or a point in a game.

Mallory's eyes held a stunned pleasure. Delight.

And he felt his muscles pump up as if he were a teenaged boy trying to impress a pretty girl.

Dumbass.

She wanted sex, nothing more, or she'd have cooked him a meal for thanks instead. He'd have been fine with a home-cooked meal.

He'd be fine with sex, too.

He liked her. Her courage, her wry sense of humor, her warmth, and the way her eyes met his honestly.

And she had a sweetly curved body. Both muscular and tantalizingly soft. The extra couple of inches of height were nice. Her breasts weren't big, but were a pleasing handful, and her waist curved out to spectacular hips. He looked forward to rolling her over and taking her from the rear.

Meantime, he stroked over her plump mound and down to her pussy. Beautifully wet. Her face flushed to pink as he looked his fill. The neatly trimmed hair exposed dark, glistening labia.

Jesus, it'd been a long time since he'd played. Ignoring the urgent ache in his cock, he teased her pussy with one finger, taking his time as he moved from her entrance to circle her clit. Back and forth. The folds swelled, and her clit engorged until the hood couldn't conceal it any longer.

Her hips wiggled. "This isn't right. You shouldn't be... I mean, you're not getting any...stuff."

"Stuff," he repeated, managing—barely—to smother a laugh. For someone who went after convicts, she was adorably unsophisticated.

"Yes, stuff." She tried to sit up, reaching for him.

"Nope, I'm not done playing. I happen to enjoy this kind of...stuff." With a hand between her pretty breasts, he flattened her again and came down on her in exactly the right position to suck on one nipple.

Her gasp was entertaining, and the way her fingers convulsed in his hair was fucking painful. And satisfying. She was passionately responsive. Nothing was more tempting to a man like him.

He took his time, sucking and licking around the tight nub. When he teased the peak against the roof of his mouth, her fingertips dug into his skin. *Yeah, more here.*

With his free hand, he slid a finger into her cunt, thrusting slowly, as he used his teeth very lightly on one nipple tip.

Her cunt clamped around on his finger like a vise.

As she started to tremble, he stopped to kiss her, to gentle her back down as he would a skittish foal.

Shifting under him, she closed her hand around his cock, pumping lightly.

Fuck, her touch felt good. Too fucking good. He had to exert a fair amount of control to keep from just taking her.

Interesting move on her part, though. If she'd been a subbie he was topping, he'd conclude she was embarrassed and wanted to get it over with. Although Mallory's body was obviously loving his attention, her head might not be as far into the game.

Yet...she'd been the one who wanted him here. He'd expect her to want to draw this out and get as much pleasure from him as possible, but she wasn't acting that way.

Didn't matter. He liked playing with a woman's body, and this one was more fun than most. If she thought to hurry the sex along, she was in for a big fail.

"Uh-uh, baby." He pulled her hand off his dick. Lifting her to a sitting position, he pulled her arms behind her, bending her elbows so her arms crossed at her lower back. And then he laid her back down.

Her own weight would keep those busy hands buried beneath her.

"Hey!" When she struggled to pull her hands out, he leaned on her, ignoring the painful tug of his wound.

"Leave your hands there." He met her eyes and put an edge of command into his voice. "Can you stay still for me, Mallory?"

Damned if her expression didn't melt into the sweetest surrender he'd ever seen. Her body relaxed under his. Submissive—and lovely.

"Thank you, pet." He gave her a slow kiss to reward her, before starting again. After all, he might have missed something. Her mouth was perfect. Soft, velvety lips. Pointed chin. Long neck. Surprisingly muscled shoulders and upper arms. Breasts—so fucking nice. Narrow waist. Full hips.

Reaching her mound, he inhaled. Her lightly musky scent was compellingly feminine.

When he pulled open her outer labia, she shook her head and started to pull her hands out.

"Stay put, girl," he growled.

The way she froze was delightful. Her body wasn't tense, and he could feel her growing even wetter. This one liked being dominated.

Wasn't it convenient he just happened to be a Dom?

When he licked over her clit, the incredulous gasp she gave almost made him come like a boy.

FOR THE LOVE OF CATS, she was going to die. He had her legs pushed widely apart, was holding her folds wide open, and was...licking her. Oh, she'd had guys do that before, usually like it was something they were required to do before getting to the good stuff.

Not this man. He was enjoying himself. Every time she grew close to coming, he...backed off. Slowed down.

The first time, she'd thought it was an accident.

But he did it again. And again.

He was propped up with an arm over her pelvis, which held her down at the same time. She couldn't pull her arms out from under her back—not without fighting him—and the way he'd kept her from doing *anything* changed...*everything*.

His aura said she could trust him—and she did. The position she was in, his strength and control, his confidence and sure hands, all robbed her of the will to resist.

Ruthlessly, his warm, clever tongue teased her clit. Sometimes it was thin and hard and rubbing firmly along the sides, sometimes flat and soft right over the top. Circling, flicking, tapping. The nub grew tight and increasingly sensitive.

He pressed a finger inside her and woke a whole new array of nerves. When her hips gave an involuntary wiggle, he laughed—and continued.

One finger became two, gliding in and out in a slow, gentle rhythm, even as his tongue flicked hard and fast. Pressure grew in her core.

And—wild fling or not, she wasn't sure she wanted to climax. She didn't know him. Sharing sex was one thing; sharing an orgasm...

What had she been thinking? She stiffened. "List—"

Her objection died as he took her clit between his lips and sucked. His tongue flickered over her. His fingers plunged in and out, faster. Harder.

Everything inside her gathered as each touch of his tongue, each thrust of his fingers shoved her closer. Her hips tried to rise, and he pressed them down, sucked harder—and drove her right into a shocking climax.

Wave after wave of pleasure exploded inside her, and she clenched around his penetrating fingers, gasping for air.

His tongue continued until she grew too sensitive and moaned a protest.

He stopped. Didn't change positions. Even with her eyes shut, she could feel the intensity of his gaze. Watching her.

She'd never been the subject of such concentrated focus.

Blinking, she looked back.

He was still kneeling between her legs, and when he met her gaze, his lips curved. "I like watching you come, Mallory." He stroked her hip, his hand warm and hard. "Now, let's see how good your stamina is."

Still smiling slightly, he dragged his jeans closer, pulled a condom from his wallet, tore the wrapper open, and sheathed himself.

Moving up her body, he gently pulled her arms out from behind her and lifted them over her head.

She wanted to hold him, yet when she moved, he fixed her with a stern gaze. "Stay where I put you, pet." He braced himself, his arm next to her wrists, and came down on top of her.

As he guided himself to her pussy, she realized his erection was as hard and big as he was. Slowly, firmly, he penetrated her a few inches before halting to study her.

Even though she didn't try to resist, she was acutely aware of how she was being...taken. She closed her eyes.

His soft growl was an objection. "Uh-uh. Give me your eyes."

She looked up.

His blue gaze held hers as unyieldingly as his weight held her down and his command held her arms in place. After a second, he moved, gradually impaling her. As he stretched her, filled her, he kept her restrained, mentally and physically.

Nothing had ever felt so intimate.

As her insides throbbed around him, her body trembled. The shaking ran from deep in her core to the tips of her fingers.

When he was deep inside her, he nuzzled her temple. "You did well, pet. Damn, you feel fucking good."

The knowledge she'd pleased him was a warm hum inside her, and she smiled.

His eyes narrowed, and he made a thoughtful sound.

She didn't have a chance to think about what that meant before he pulled his cock back...and pressed in again even deeper. So big. She squirmed at the edge of discomfort.

His gaze ran over her face, her arms, her shoulders, as he continued the slow retreat and advance.

Then, as she adjusted to his size, the slick slide turned to pure pleasure. Everything inside her turned into a molten pool of lust. "Mmm."

His grin flashed, and he picked up the pace. Hard and fast. *Slam, slam, slam.*

As pressure thickened within her, her clit throbbed, demanding more. Her hips rose to meet his, trying to grind against him.

And...he pulled out.

No! "Wait. You're—"

He shifted to one side and rolled her over onto her belly.

The alcohol in her system was still there. Her head spun. "What are you *doing?*"

He pulled her onto her hands and knees. "Easy, girl. This position'll be better for you." With ruthless hands, he pushed her knees farther apart, found her entrance, and impaled her with one hard, long stroke.

"*Aaaah.*" His merciless entry was a shocking blast of pleasure—and she almost came in that moment. "Oh, more, please." Her clit throbbed, her breasts ached.

He bent over her, his left arm supporting him, his right around her waist, anchoring her in place. His chin rubbed the back of her neck as he whispered in her ear, "I'll give you more." He moved his right arm down, and his fingers slid over her clit.

At the exquisite sensation, her entire center clamped around his cock—and he laughed. "Nice. You can do that again." As he drove in and out, he worked her clit, rubbing firmly on one side and then the other.

As her core quivered, her arms gave out, sending her down to her elbows…tilting her ass upward.

He rumbled his pleasure as he went even deeper inside her.

Slam, slam, slam. As he hammered into her, his fingers rubbed and teased her clit until she felt swollen to the point of pain. Until her muscles clenched tightly around him with the torment, and she was desperate for more, thrumming with the impending release.

"Uhhhhh." She shook with the need. Each touch, each thrust was perfect. Wonderful.

And not…quite…enough.

Her hero—the bastard—laughed. "Go on over, baby." His teeth closed on her shoulder, even as he rubbed directly on top of her clit and slammed into her hard. The devastating mix of sensations blasted through her, engulfed her, and she was coming, the pleasure indescribable as the dazzling splendor rolled over and through her, again and again.

With a pleased growl, he increased his pace and finally pressed in, even deeper than before. She contracted tightly around him as his shaft jerked inside her.

After a long moment where there wasn't a millimeter of space between them, he eased back. "Nice." Gently, he rolled, landing them on their sides.

Even though her muscles were limp, she couldn't stop trembling. Everything he'd done... She'd never felt like this before. Controlled. Taken. Coming so hard.

"Easy, baby." He pulled her against him with her back against his chest and spooned her. He was warm against her, almost enfolding her. With one hand, he stroked her shoulder, her side, her breasts—petting her as she would her cat.

Safe and warm and petted. No wonder felines purred.

Chapter Three

A S MALLORY DRIFTED off to sleep, Sawyer reluctantly disentangled himself. The downside of condoms meant getting up before his dick shrank too far.

After cleaning up in the master bath, he returned to the bedroom…and hesitated. His body urged him to climb into bed, nap for a while, and enjoy her again. He wouldn't mind putting the fanciful iron scrollwork on the headboard to good use. She'd liked being held down. How would she react with some true bondage? He'd like to hear again those pretty cries she made when climaxing.

And dammit, he wanted to cuddle her for the rest of the night.

Part of his mind was onboard with the idea. She was a woman he'd like to know better. Especially after realizing she was not only submissive, but a submissive who loved to give. To please. She was someone special.

Nevertheless, he knew better than to linger here.

In the six weeks since his release from prison, he'd had ugly lessons about where he fit in the world, especially with females.

Even more to the point, he had a mission in this town. He had no business getting involved with a woman. Not now. Probably not ever.

Rather than crawling back in, he covered her with the soft throw from the foot of the bed.

Sighing softly, she curled around the blanket and pulled it to her front, much like she'd snuggled up to him. The room smelled of sex.

Bending to touch her soft, silky hair, he breathed in her clean, spring-grass scent, and fuck, he wanted to be inside her again.

Get a grip, Ware.

In the dim light of the kitchen, he scratched a note, left it on the counter, and walked out the front door.

A minute later, he was driving down the gravel lane. The full moon was directly overhead, streaming golden light over the wide pastures he'd admired. Across the valley and up the slope were the barns and huge house owned by the Masterson family. A long fence between the pastures glowed white in the moonlight, and then he was past the meadow and at his brother's property.

After parking beside the other two vehicles, Sawyer let himself into the house, toed off his boots, and padded across the hardwood floor. Much like the Ware ranch house in Idaho, his brother's place was decorated in what Sawyer considered practical western. Red, brown, and white colors predominated. The oversized furniture was sturdy. Native American accents and a stone fireplace added beauty. The sixty-inch, flat-screen TV was, of course, essential.

"It's late, bro." His brother was stretched out on the long leather couch, a book in his hand. "You okay?"

"Fine. I stopped to intervene in an assault. You'll probably hear about it from your fellow lawmen." Feeling the ache in his healing side, Sawyer eased down on a dark red armchair. Leaning back with a grunt of relief, he ran through the high points of the battle.

Satisfied, Atticus nodded. "Mallory and Zoe were lucky you happened by."

"Could've been ugly." Two innocents were all right because he'd been there. That felt damn fine. The sense of satisfaction faded as he studied his brother.

It'd only been a week since Att had taken a tire iron to his ribs. In the dim light, the lines in his face looked deeper, and his color was faded.

"You look like shit."

"Might've overdone a bit today." Att eased to a more comfortable position. "I swear my busted ribs didn't hurt so much when I got tossed by a bronco."

"You were eighteen that year, dumbass." Sawyer'd suffered his share of busted bones, too, back when they rode rodeo.

Att grinned. "True. The black-hearted, four-legged bastard would probably kill me now."

"Yeah." Last week, the two-legged bastards almost had. Fucking assholes. "Take a pain pill, dammit."

"Already did, thanks. Some ibuprofen. Gin insisted before she hit the rack. I'm just waiting for it to kick in before I join her." Att tilted his head. "How long are you going to be pissed at me for getting jumped?"

"A while." Sawyer scowled. "You knew those bastards were out to get you. Next time, check your six, jarhead."

"Yeah. I made a mistake." Att shrugged. "And I got thumped to remind me to do better. Ease up, bro."

Hard to do when his brother was hurting. But Att had a point. Sawyer tilted his head back and let the breeze coming through the open window cool him down.

Leaves rustled in the encroaching forest, and an owl hooted. Peaceful sounds. Very different from the clang of metal doors, the cursing of inmates, and the heavy tread of the prison guards making rounds. How long would it be before he stopped expecting to hear the sounds of imprisonment?

Atticus bookmarked his page and studied Sawyer. "Last week, you planned to talk with Jacob Wheeler about moving to San Francisco. I didn't get a chance to ask you about it."

Sawyer's prison counselor had served twenty in the Marines, and they spoke the same language. Since Wheeler also had a private practice, Sawyer had continued with him after being released.

"Yeah, we talked." He stared out the tall front window. Although it was dark outside, the curtains were open—because there wasn't anyone around. No neighbors. No traffic. Quiet night. Clean air. "Bear Flat's going to have a grudge against the prison for a while to come, and I figured a city would have more options for an ex-con."

Atticus's eyes sharpened. "But…?"

"Wheeler made me think twice." Actually, Sawyer'd been planning to leave…right up until Att had been attacked.

Atticus waited. They'd both learned patience on the ranch. The military had made it a necessity. Being Dominants had honed the skill to a sharp edge.

Sawyer ran a hand over his short hair and laid out some—honest—reasons to remain in Bear Flat. "I'm not sure I can live in a city. Although anonymity would be good, I don't like crowds or traffic."

"Got that. It's the side effect of being raised on a sprawling ranch."

Or a year in prison. "Maybe."

"If Hector hadn't sold the ranch so fast, you could've gone there," Atticus speculated. "You figure on joining him once he moves down here?"

"It's my second choice." Their little brother had operated their Ware Ranch up in Idaho until a polar blast froze half a herd of cattle. Fed up, Hector'd sold the ranch and was hoping to buy a spread in the Sierra foothills.

"Hector won't be far." Att set the book down. "It'd be nice to have you close, too."

"How close?" Sawyer asked slowly.

"Close as I can get you. If you want to live here, we can build on—like the Mastersons did with their place. All three brothers still live there."

Sawyer cleared the thickness from his throat. He'd always known Att loved him, but the confirmation was sweet. "I'm not going to live with you, bro. However…I hear the place to the west of you is for sale."

"Is it?" Att blinked. "Well, damn, that'd be fucking fantastic. What'll you do with it?"

"Got some thoughts." Sawyer rose. "Let me grab a beer and run them past you. Want one?"

"Damn right."

Sawyer headed into the kitchen. This might actually work.

Att had moved here to be close to Sawyer while he was in pris-on. Of course, being Atticus, he'd put down roots. He'd taken a job with the police force, bought enough acreage to pasture a couple of horses, made friends. Found a woman.

Bear Flat was Att's home.

Now…maybe…it'd be Sawyer's.

He had to find work. Even so, his counselor was right. He wouldn't do well being penned up in a building. He needed to be outside, to have space and solitude. Land and livestock were in his blood.

He also needed a base to operate out of as he drove the fucking Aryan Hammers right out of Atticus's town.

AS USUAL, MALLORY woke at dawn. Yawning, she sat upright and started to stretch.

Oh, *pain*. Her body felt like she'd fallen down a flight of stairs. And her *head*. *Spit and hiss*. Some evil entity named Scotch had crammed her brains into her skull in the same way Gramps had always overstuffed the washing machine.

Would Gramps come back to haunt her if she poured his precious Glenfiddich down the drain? Gingerly, she shook her head and remembered how she'd filled her glass. Twice.

Her lips curved up. Hangover or not, the sex had been worth it. Becca was so right.

After another yawn, she glanced around. Sunlight shone over the pale blue walls and across the hardwood floor. Covered by her chenille throw, she'd slept on top of the fluffy white bedspread.

Alone.

Where had her rescuer gone? She listened for a minute. Complete silence.

He'd left. Disappointment swept through her. She would have liked waking up beside him. Feeling his muscles against her. Hearing his smoky-smooth voice. He'd have a scratchy beard—and she'd be able to see the laughter that sometimes appeared in his eyes.

She'd see the way he'd watched her.

Pushed her.

Being pushed had been...exciting. She remembered how his weight had pinned her against the mattress. How amazing it had felt when she couldn't move her arms. Yet, he hadn't scared her. She'd known he'd stop if she objected, and having him...dominate...their time together had fulfilled an odd need inside her.

I want more.

Maybe she could meet him for coffee or lunch. Get to know him and see if he was as nice outside of bed as he was in it. Because—she smiled slightly—he had a hold on her. He was brave, honest, and protective. He had a sense of humor. Was polite. And, oh, his aura was beautiful.

Everything inside her said he could be someone special to her, but...okay, she wasn't a total fool. She should actually get to know him.

Talk to him. Light, flirtatious conversation wasn't her strength. Nonetheless, she was willing to give it a shot. Maybe she could call him.

Her thoughts sputtered to a halt. Call...*who?* She flopped backward, making her head hammer even harder. Talk about an idiot. She'd not only been to bed with—had fucked—a man she'd just met, she hadn't even asked him his name.

Oh, wow. Two demerits for bringing a stranger home. Two demerits for letting him into the house. Two more points lost for getting intoxicated. Two down for having sex on a first date—no, no, wait, it wasn't even a date. Four points, then. And at least a dozen demerits for not even learning his name.

Slut wasn't a word she tolerated, but she probably deserved a T-shirt with BAD, BAD GIRL on it. In flaming red letters.

Heaving a pitiful sigh, she slid out of bed and pulled on her robe. A pot of tea was calling her name.

In the kitchen, she noticed the note on the kitchen countertop.

"Thanks for the reward." No name. No number. His meaning was as clear as a slap in the face.

As the bottom dropped out of her stomach and tears welled in her eyes, she realized her mistake. She'd never tried a one-night stand with a stranger before...and she still hadn't.

He hadn't been a stranger to her—he was the man she'd waited for. And last night had been a dream come true.

For him, it'd been meaningless sex...with someone who meant nothing.

All the muscles around her heart ached as she pulled in a slow, careful breath. She'd made a mistake. It wasn't the first and wouldn't be the last.

Move on.

Her cat, Aslan, padded into the kitchen and jumped onto the blue stool at the kitchen island. Lion-like, he twitched his golden tail in a blatant expression of annoyance.

She managed a smile. "Yes, I brought a stranger into your house and didn't introduce you. However, you can relax. It won't happen again." Under his stern eyes, she tore up the note. "There. All gone."

Her lips quivered for a second before she lifted her chin. "Isn't it nice Becca gave me a new book to read?"

Chapter Four

FIVE WEEKS LATER, with his brother beside him, Sawyer walked the fence line. *His* fence line. Possessiveness and pride welled up inside him at the knowledge that every step was on his own land. The hot mid-September sun heated his shoulders, but within a couple of months, there would be snow. He couldn't wait to watch the seasons change from fall to winter—and in the spring, his pastures would fill with horses.

Atticus grinned. "I had the same reaction when I bought my place."

Sawyer pulled in a deep breath of the clean air and looked out over the long expanse of meadow. Four properties shared the mountain valley, which had the finest grass in the area. A year-round stream ran through the Masterson's pastures, across his, and around the edge of Mallory's place.

A hawk perched on a fence post gave him an assessing look before returning its gaze to the ditch beside the lane.

"Feels good to be back in California," Sawyer said. It'd been odd to realize that Idaho didn't feel like home any longer. They'd just spent a month on the newly sold Ware Ranch there, helping their little brother prepare to move.

"Yeah, I missed being here. Although if Gin hadn't joined us for a couple of weeks, I'd have returned sooner." Atticus lifted a cynical brow. "I also realized something. After I got attacked, you wanted me out of town until my ribs healed. I'm betting you talked Hector into calling and asking us for help shutting the ranch down. Am I right?"

"Yep." Sawyer grinned. "You're a pretty good detective, bro. Besides, Hector did need help."

Talking about help… Sawyer looked around at his own property and winced at the broken-down fences. "I get the impression your spread was in better shape when you bought it. Mine's going to take a shitload of work." The huge stable was run down, and the small log cabin wasn't much better. "At least the buildings are structurally sound."

Atticus nodded. "I thought you were overly optimistic when you proposed this, but the more I think about it, the more I like it." He nodded toward the Mastersons' massive house and barn upslope on the other side of the northern fence. "If you could talk them into letting you handle their stock, you'd have a good source of income."

"We'll see." Sawyer's plan was to raise, train, and rent out horses for the various guide businesses in the area. His neighbors over there ran the Masterson Wilderness Guides, and if they'd lease trail horses from him, he'd have a good leg up. The well-respected family had been here for generations.

As he and Atticus walked past the stable toward the house, his brother shook his head. "Your cabin is a fucking mess, bro. Stay with us until you get it fixed up."

"Nah. Long as it doesn't leak and the heat works, I'm good." A shame the fancy CEO hadn't put any money into maintaining the place.

Sawyer glanced down toward the end of the road, wondering if Mallory'd heard she had a new neighbor. Dammit, it'd be easier to forget her if she didn't live so close. If he didn't recall the feel of her every time he saw her house. He shook his head. *Focus, Ware.*

"I need to get shit repaired before I bring in horses next spring." Since real estate values in the area had nose-dived with the prison closure—and since the sale of the Idaho ranch meant he could offer cash—he'd gotten a hell of a deal. Now all he had to do was make it work. Starting with repairs. He frowned. Anything more than basic carpentry would be beyond his skill level. "Looks like I need a general contractor. Any suggestions?"

"There are only two in town, both competent. Probably hungry at this point, considering the economy." Atticus glanced at his watch. "We need to get going. Gin's off work now."

Sawyer nodded. They were meeting her at the ClaimJumper to celebrate the real estate closing.

His lips tightened. Last time they'd been at the tavern, Att had gotten his ass jumped. Now he'd be going back to work—which would put him at risk.

It was time to drive the Aryan Hammers out of Bear Flat.

Sawyer smiled slightly. Should be interesting, if nothing else.

Turning, Att slapped his shoulder. "Might be some pretty women at the tavern."

"Jesus, Att, you changing careers to matchmaking?" Sawyer shook his head. "Women run away from me." Or he'd get the ones who wanted a danger fuck like pretty Mallory. Trying to get her out of his mind, he'd indulged in a few since, but… She'd stuck in his mind. Didn't it just figure she'd be his neighbor? "At least the *nice* ones run."

Apparently hearing the edge in his voice, Atticus laid a hand on Sawyer's shoulder. "You know how small towns work. You'll be disreputable for a while, then the prison stint will turn into interesting past history. Takes time, though."

"Yeah." Atticus was right. Eventually, his past would be of less interest than the present and future.

Damned if he wouldn't make himself a shining future.

Chapter Five

O N FRIDAY EVENING, Mallory opened a second bottle of wine and crossed to her great room where Becca and Kallie lounged in front of the fire. It was her birthday, and her friends had shown up unexpectedly with wine and food to celebrate.

As Mallory filled the glasses, Kallie picked hers up. Curled into a corner of the white slipcovered couch, the tiny brunette looked like a contented kitten. Aslan sprawled over the other half of the couch. One giant, fluffy, orange cat.

Tossing her red hair out of her face, Becca drank some wine, resting her long legs on the coffee table. Her golden aura was a softly radiant glow around her. "So, Mallory, did you ever find yourself any hero material?" She glanced at Kallie. "She saw my kinky books and told me she was holding out for a hero."

"Ah." Kallie grinned. "The guys who come for hiking and climbing are pretty buff. Want me to bring some over here? You live close enough, after all."

The thought of Kallie tromping across the bottomland followed by a herd of males was enough to make Mallory choke. "What a…lovely…offer. No. Just no." After a second, she added a polite, "Thank you."

Becca had descended into giggles. "Such an expression. Like Kallie was offering to bring over a pack of…what were they called? Orcs."

Mallory gave Kallie a stern stare. "No Orcs. Bring me Aragorn—

or Éomer—or nothing."

"Yes, ma'am." Kallie waved her wine glass in a salute. "Request is noted. So is the difficulty. Have you ever found any man even close to your specifications?"

The memory of the man—the nameless man—swept through Mallory, followed by a wave of heat that went straight to her face.

"Oh my God, you *did*." Becca sat upright. "Who is he? Do we know him? Are you—"

"No." Mallory's flat statement silenced the enthusiasm. "Actually, he was just some guy passing through." She sure hadn't seen him in town since. "It was a while back and"—she tipped her head to Becca—"as ordered, I indulged in a one-night stand."

"As ordered?" Kallie looked at Becca in dismay. "You thought *Mallory* should have casual sex?"

Becca had an unhappy expression. "I didn't think you really would."

Mallory frowned. "Other women do, and it's not a big deal. It's not like I'm a virgin, so why are you shocked?"

Kallie shook her head. "You just—maybe it's me—but everything you do has...well, significance, I guess. I can't imagine you going for meaningless sex."

Because she didn't, and it hadn't been meaningless, at least for her. Though it had been for him.

"Are you okay? Was he nice? He didn't hurt you, did he?" Becca's mouth tightened.

Under their worried eyes, she shrugged. "It was fun and good sex, but no, not something I'll do again. I found something else instead." Her lips curved. "Remember the book you gave me, Becca? By the sun and stars, it was amazing. I have a whole shelf of kinky BDSM romances now."

Kallie's mouth fell open, then she giggled. "You're corrupting the natives, city girl."

"I'm doing my best." Becca waggled her glass at Mallory. "Let me know when you want to do more than read about BDSM."

"Mmmhmm." *When* would probably be *never*. Mallory leaned forward and refilled the glasses. "Drink and we can cut the cake."

Becca took a sip and—thankfully—found a new subject. "Did you get new furniture?" She patted the floral slipcovered chair. "No, I just slipcovered the couch and chairs. Although the upholstery was dingy, Gramma's furniture is sturdy enough." Mallory glanced around and grinned. "The last time Serena was here, she called this 'shabby chic'—which sounds rather insulting but at least implies I planned the décor this way."

"I love the way your house looks," Becca said. "French cottage décor, I'd say. The feel is so light and airy."

Mallory's smile faded. After Gramps died, she'd binged on remodeling, more to fill the empty silence than due to any artistic desire. She'd removed most of the downstairs walls...and had compulsively continued. "The decorating just kind of happened. When I added the sunroom and put in bigger living room windows, the increased light made the old brown couch look ugly. So I covered it in white linen. Then the brown plaid chairs looked wrong. So they went a pastel floral."

She looked at the overflowing foliage in the windows and corners ruefully. "The plants aren't my fault. Honestly. They just migrate in. I'm not sure how."

Kallie grinned. "Because every time you discover a new plant, you can't resist propagating it and end up with a dozen." She nodded at the line of African violets in one windowsill. "Like those."

"True. I expect you and Becca to take a couple with you, by the way."

"Always." Becca grinned. "Logan finally stopped glowering at the plants I put in the lodge. He's actually admitted the main room seems friendlier and the guests more comfortable."

Quite a concession for such a scary man. Just as friendly plants could turn the lodge into a cozier place, Becca's love had transformed the owner into being...somewhat...less intimidating. Nice, nice work.

"Time for cake, birthday girl." Setting her glass down, Kallie leaned forward and started pushing green candles into the white-frosted birthday cake—more and more candles.

Mallory rolled her eyes. "That's not a cake; it's a forest."

Becca snorted. "I know the feeling."

"Have you noticed how the mountain under the 'forest' had a landslide?" Kallie indicated the way the cake slumped to one side. "Morgan slammed the door so hard this morning it's a wonder only the cake fell."

Mallory frowned. "Slamming doors sounds more like Wyatt than Morgan." Morgan was a year younger and quieter than Wyatt.

"Not anymore. Morgan's mood has gone steadily downhill ever since Wyatt headed off to Ethiopia."

"I bet Morgan's still in shock." And lonely. The brothers were a year apart in age and, aside from when they led wilderness tours into the backcountry, they were rarely apart.

"He is, and also majorly grumpy." Kallie swiped up a stray piece of frosting and stuck it in her mouth before smiling at Mallory. "You'd better stay out of his reach. He blames you for encouraging Wyatt to join a volunteer corps."

"Wait a minute. I didn't encourage him. I told him he should talk with a counselor."

"Really? I thought—"

"Really. When he insisted on leaving, I checked around since I still have a contact from when I served in the Peace Corps. She recommended an organization able to process his application quickly and willing to accept a mere six months of his time. Otherwise, he'd be gone two years like I was."

"Oh, wow. I'll tell Morgan." Kallie shook her head. "I feel terrible for Wyatt…and it still pisses me off how he walked away in the middle of our busiest season. I want to hug him *and* wallop him, and I know Morgan feels the same."

Becca shook her head. "Poor Morgan…and poor Wyatt."

Poor Wyatt, indeed. Mallory's heart went out to him. During the jailbreak in June, the escaping convicts had headed into the mountains with two hostages. One of the social workers was Atticus's girlfriend, and since Wyatt and Morgan knew the backcountry like no one else, they'd gone with him. During the bloody rescue, Wyatt had killed one of the convicts.

Afterward, Wyatt had been…different. He'd come over to her

place often to sit in her meditation garden room. Looking for peace. The death had traumatized the big wilderness guide. She'd understood his need to make amends with the universe, although the tough guy would never admit to such a thing.

During her morning meditations these days, she included prayers he would find the peace he was searching for.

"There. Thirty candles." Kallie lit the candles, and Becca joined her in singing the obligatory birthday song.

Even as Mallory leaned forward to blow out the forest fire, her heart glowed with happiness. No birthday present could match the gift of friendship.

"Hey, make a wish first," Becca said.

"Right." A wish. What did she need?

I want Gramps back. Regrettably, such a wish wasn't one she could make.

So, what else? On the whole, she had a good life. She loved her work, loved her town, and loved her friends and her mountain home. Okay, maybe she was lonely now and then—and a bit envious of her friends who'd found men. And maybe she wanted a baby, one as adorable as Becca's Ansel.

Well, she had a wish, didn't she? Feeling like a traitor to feminists everywhere, she sent her desire wafting into the ether. *I want a protective, strong, confident husband, one who thinks I'm wonderful, and I want his children, too. I want a family to fill this house with laughter and love.*

As the longing grew strong enough to make her chest ache, she blew out the candles. Every single one.

Chapter Six

THE NEXT DAY, with a sack of cat food on her hip, Mallory walked through the feed store, breathing in the scent of leather from the corner filled with tack, and the dry fragrance of hay and grain from the back room.

Having no self-control whatsoever, she detoured to the room's center, where a clear enclosure held several kittens. *Free to a good home* was posted on the outside.

There were three yellow kittens along with two black-and-whites. All fluffy with tiny tails straight up in the air. At the surge of kitten craving, Mallory shook her head. Honestly, she knew better than to have come over to see them.

Aslan would have a fit if she took one home.

"Kitties!" Seven-year-old Heath Simmons ran up and pressed his nose against the glass. Kids always wanted to play with the puppies and kittens...which was why the glass enclosure had been elevated so high.

Mallory smiled at the boy. Brown tangled hair, freckles, and a snub nose. He was too cute for words. The purple hue of his aura said he'd be good with animals. "Want to hold one?"

The child's vigorous nod said it all.

Setting down the bag she carried, Mallory reached in and scooped up a yellow-striped ball of fluff. "Sit down."

Heath dropped and crossed his legs.

Mallory squatted and placed the kitten in his lap.

The kitten set its paws on the boy's stomach and looked up. *Mew, mew, mew.*

"He likes me." Giggling, Heath carefully stroked the tiny feline.

Approaching, Roger Simmons spotted his son and groaned. "Oh, hell no." The big gas station owner was a ruddy-faced man with a loud voice—and a tender heart for his children.

Heath looked up. "Da-a-a-ad, please?"

When Mallory laughed, Roger gave her a harassed look. "Mal, his mama would murder me."

"He looks pretty responsible."

"He is, actually." With a sigh, Roger set the kitten back in the enclosure and helped his son stand.

The look on Heath's face was heartbreaking.

His father harrumphed—and caved. "All right, boy, you can have a kitten *if* you take responsibility for feeding and cleaning up."

The yell of happiness made everyone in the store laugh.

Shaking his head, Roger grinned. "Come on, son. Guess we better get some kitten chow."

"And a dish. And toys." Heath gave Mallory a strangling hug and kiss on her cheek. "Thanks, Mallory."

Smiling, she watched the boy trot after his father. Children were so amazing. Her favorite times in the Peace Corps had been when helping the children.

As she bent to pick up her cat food, her ass thumped into someone passing by. "Sorry." Straightening too quickly, she lost her balance.

Hard hands closed on her waist to steady her. "Easy there."

That dark, smooth voice. She spun.

Tall and muscular. Cowboy hat and boots. And eyes the color of desert bluebells.

Those eyes had appeared in her dreams. "It's you!"

Happiness filled her, bouncing around like bubbles in her bloodstream. Moving closer to the compelling warmth of his aura, she closed her hands over his forearms, remembering the powerful feel of his muscles under her fingers.

And, hiss and spit, she was overreacting. What was she thinking?

She hastily let go of his arms.

"You okay?" He wasn't smiling.

Her own smile faded. She nodded.

He released her and stepped back. "Good." His voice held no warmth, and his aura had darkened to a muddy red. His eyes weren't cold, simply indifferent, as if he were a complete stranger and not someone who'd kissed her…everywhere. Who'd been inside her.

From his shuttered gaze, she could tell he recognized her—and didn't want anything more to do with her.

The excitement and wonder at seeing him shriveled away, leaving a heavy hollow of pain behind. However, she couldn't object. If this was how he wanted things to be between them, she had no place to say different. He was still amazing.

Certainly, she was fantastic in her own way, yet her experiences with other men had taught her she was too quiet and not stupendous enough for a man like him.

Embarrassment was something she rarely felt. What other people thought of her wasn't as important as what she thought of herself. Nevertheless, right now, yes, she could feel heat rising in her cheeks. She took another step back, pulled on Gramma's social manners, and inclined her head the proper degree. "Thank you for your assistance."

"No problem."

"Sawyer, let's go," someone called from the front.

"Coming," he yelled back. He glanced at her, touched his hat brim, and then her one-night stand walked away.

Well. She let out a breath, feeling as flattened as road-kill. At least she knew the first name of the man who had *fucked* her stupid. And stupid she'd been.

They sure hadn't made *love*, no matter what her feelings had told her.

Chapter Seven

WITH THE SEPTEMBER sun scorching his shoulders, Sawyer leaned against the wall of his run-down log cabin as the general contractor jotted down numbers on a clipboard.

Dressed in jeans and a work shirt, Larry Burns was tall, lean, and hollow-cheeked, with silvering hair. His construction company had built mostly new homes until the Bear Flat market had gone belly-up.

Sawyer hoped the contractor was eager for a new job.

The hum of a vehicle caught Sawyer's attention. In the dry air, dust rose from a pickup coming down the lane.

As the vehicle pulled into the drive, Sawyer glanced at his watch and frowned. If this was the second contractor, he was early by a good hour.

But the black-haired guy who jumped out of the cab and headed for Burns wasn't any contractor. Sawyer stiffened. The man had worked as a correctional officer in the prison—and was a complete asshole.

"Hey, boss. Got a situation at the house on Jackass Way. The fittings—" He glanced at Sawyer and halted abruptly. "Ware."

"Romero."

"I'm sorry for the interruption, Mr. Ware," the contractor said, moving toward the pickup. "Just give me a minute to settle what he needs."

As Burns and his man walked to the pickup, Romero's voice was all too audible. "…was one of the prisoners. Got out early. Yeah, a convict."

Sawyer's gut tightened. Yeah, he deserved all the fucking grief he got—after all, his best friend was dead because of his screw-up. Yet the derogatory labels used by the locals—*convict, felon, crook, prisoner*—scraped like sandpaper over open wounds.

After a few minutes, Romero jumped into the pickup and drove away.

Burns returned to Sawyer, the casual friendliness now replaced by stiff formality. "Sorry about the interruption. I didn't realize my cell's battery was dead. The crew needed answers before they could act."

"Not a problem." Sawyer glanced at the clipboard. "When will you have an estimate ready?"

"Shouldn't take more than a day or two." The man's mouth tightened. "I have to admit I'm backlogged right now. The crew wouldn't be able to start on the job for a couple of months."

"Months?" When they'd set up the appointment, Burns had sounded as if his current job would finish within two weeks. Sawyer gave him a hard look.

Although the contractor's cheeks darkened, he didn't back down.

"I see. Well, email me the estimate, and I'll let you know." Tamping down anger, Sawyer held out his hand.

After a hesitation, Burns shook his hand politely.

As the contractor drove away, Sawyer sighed and hoped to hell the other guy worked out.

LATE IN THE afternoon, Mallory turned off Kestrel Mountain Road onto Whiskey Creek Lane—her own road. Earlier, her answering service had relayed the request for an estimate. It'd been a shock to hear the property across the road had been sold. Then again, the owner lived—had lived—in Los Angeles, and the real estate listing had been out of Modesto rather than local.

Once again, she was behind on the news. She rolled her eyes at the teasing Gramps would have dealt out. A total extrovert, he'd never understood her lack of interest in gossip.

These days, she did try to pay attention to the news, but hey, she'd been busting ass over the past few weeks to add a new room to the Conleys' house before their new baby arrived. Then she'd scored a contract with a property management firm to upgrade the rental houses vacated by the prison staff.

So…she had a new neighbor—Mr. Ware. Had Atticus Ware or one of his relatives bought the property? She hoped the new owner wasn't another city guy. Gramps hadn't liked selling to the CEO and had complained loudly. *"The land was meant to be worked, to have horses. Cattle. It's wasted on some city dude who just wants to build himself a fancy house."*

According to the answering service, this new owner wanted work done on the stable. A stable meant horses. Gramps would be pleased…wherever he was.

She'd be pleased, too. On summer evenings, she and Gramma had sat on the porch swing, watching the horses in the meadow. The new foals would bounce and race across the green grass. In the far pastures, cattle would graze quietly. Those were treasured, peaceful evenings.

Halfway down the gravel road, she turned left into the driveway and studied the buildings with an eye to repairs.

Yes, the stable had been neglected. A new roof would be required, for sure, from shingles and possibly right down to the rafters. Door frame, possibly. If the roof leaked, the floored areas, like the tack room, might have rotted through.

She parked and headed for the small cabin. The log building was in poor shape, although the white and red rose bushes bracketing the decrepit porch added a note of brightness. Her first summer here, Dodger, the old cowhand who'd lived in the cabin, had given her riding lessons. The roses had been her return gift. He'd thought she was crazy…and she'd learned not everyone loved the same things. Rather than giving plants, she'd learned to bake him the cakes and cookies he loved.

Dodger had died while she'd been in college…and Gramps had

sold the property soon after.

Shaking off the bittersweet memories, she moved up the path.

The door to the cabin opened, and a man stepped out and came down the steps.

No. Oh no.

Her one-night stand.

Sawyer.

Seriously? She glanced up at the heavens. *Karma—seriously?* Surely she hadn't done anything bad enough to justify this humiliation. For Pete's sake, she was still raw from his rejection in the feed store two days ago.

She frowned as everything came together. Sawyer *Ware.*

Oh, hiss and spit, this was Atticus's brother who'd been a prisoner and was stabbed trying to prevent a prison escape and was later given an early release by the governor. She'd heard he'd stayed with Atticus after his release…which was why he'd been on the road the night Zoe was attacked. And why he had the scar on his side.

Note to self: Pay more attention to gossip.

She lifted her chin and walked up to the porch.

His brows drew together. "Mallory." His tone was unwelcoming, but at least he remembered her name.

At least, he'd been polite enough to *get* her name. She could be polite, too. "Sawyer Ware?" Maybe he wasn't the owner?

Unfortunately, he nodded.

"My answering service said you needed some construction work done."

His eyebrows lifted. His gaze flicked to her truck with the McCabe Construction logo, then to her attire—boots, jeans, work shirt. Her clipboard. He hadn't known McCabe Construction was her company.

Did he think she was visiting in hopes of turning a one-night stand into two?

She didn't let the insult change her expression.

After a second, he held out his hand. "I take it you're Mal McCabe."

"Correct." His hand was as callused and strong as she remembered. He was as careful with his strength as she remembered.

Having a good memory could really suck. "You want work done on the stable?"

"Right. And the cabin. Let me run down what I have in mind. For the bid, I'd like separate estimates for each building, breaking down the materials, labor, and time."

He was obviously a man who knew his own mind and what he wanted. Although it still hurt to remember how it had felt kissing him, being under him—being *with* him, she liked how he'd put his potent sexuality away.

If she got the job, it appeared he could keep things professional.

If he couldn't, she sure could.

AN HOUR LATER, as Sawyer waited for Mallory to finish examining the breaker box, he was still cursing the fates—and his own libido—which had set up this goat-fuck. Smart men didn't screw where they worked. Unfortunately, he had, and she was his only choice for a contractor. He already knew Larry Burns didn't want the job.

Well, Atticus had said both general contractors were good ones. Sawyer'd checked, and neither business had a history of disputes with clients or subcontractors.

Even better, Mallory—Mal—was obviously not interested in going for seconds. If anything, she downplayed her femininity. Work boots and jeans. A button-down shirt with her company logo—although, yeah, the blue somehow highlighted her green eyes. No makeup. Hair in a thick brown braid down her back. She wore a heavy tool belt. She wasn't trying to hide her figure, but the foremost impression was of strength and competence.

He liked her knowledge and attention to detail. She'd gotten right down in the dirt and then gone up in the rafters, checking for dry rot. In the cabin, she'd pointed out his idea of taking down a wall would mess with a load-bearing beam and had suggested alternatives.

Leaving the breaker box, Mallory walked over. "All right, I have enough information. Give me a day to play with the numbers, and I'll have an estimate for you."

"That works." He liked the way her attitude was all business…and couldn't help remembering when she was all sweetly submissive. *Not going there, Ware.*

At her pickup, he politely opened the door for her. "Do you have an idea when you'd be able to start?"

Her eyes narrowed, and she stared over his head as she thought. "My roofers can start right away, which is good, since it's not long until the fall rains and snows arrive. The rest of my crew is working on other sites. Offhand, it'll be a couple of weeks before everyone is here."

Reasonable. He wouldn't trust a contractor who had no work to do. "Good. I look forward to seeing your estimate."

She merely nodded.

Sawyer watched as the woman pulled left out of his drive and drove to the end of the road. After a right turn into her S-shaped drive, she headed uphill to her house on the south side of the mountain valley. Part of her wrap-around porch faced his land. The kitchen windows would look over the length of the valley toward the main road. He'd bet it had a nice view.

He studied the location for another minute. Toward the west, the rear of the house must overlook the tree-lined creek. Another nice view.

His cabin sat at the lowest part of the valley, close enough to the creek he could hear the musical babbling at night. And his windows looked out over the wealth of meadowland. All his.

Walking into his house, he glanced around. A couple of days earlier, his furniture had been delivered from the storage unit. He didn't have much, but over the years, he'd acquired a few pieces he liked. The black leather couch and two armchairs were damned comfortable and sturdy enough for his size. His heavy oak coffee table didn't groan when he put his feet up.

Although the king-size four-poster strained the limits of his bedroom, it accommodated his height…and his needs when he brought home a woman who enjoyed bondage.

His lips twitched as he glanced in the direction of his new neighbor. Having tasted her and heard the high sweet noises she made when she came, it'd been fucking difficult today to keep his behavior professional and...indifferent.

He had to appreciate how well she'd done the same. No innuendos. If she was dismayed at having to deal with a man she'd fucked, she hadn't let it show. He had to respect her for that.

With luck, it would work out. He'd do his part and keep his distance.

Chapter Eight

A WEEK LATER, Mallory climbed the ladder to the stable roof where her roofing team was working. The underlayment was in place. Russell was scooping trash into the dumpster, while Randy'd started on the shingles. "Looking good, guys."

They gave her mock salutes. The Booth twins were in their mid-twenties, city boys who'd fallen in love with the mountains. They weren't social enough to make good guides or work in the tourist service industries, but construction suited them to a T.

The other three in her crew were working on a remodel in town, and she'd stop by there later. She did a quick check of the stable interior and saw the electrician had updated the wiring. Excellent. A glance at her schedule showed she had a couple of hours free, so she headed into the cabin.

As she worked on the trim for the newly installed and enlarged kitchen window, she breathed in the scent of the pasture grasses. She should savor every minute of the last warm weather; winter was coming all too soon.

Through the window, she could see the Mastersons' horses grazing in their south pasture. Two geldings watched Ware repairing a broken slat in the fence.

Mallory shook her head. The man was far too watchable. When she'd arrived this morning, he'd been tearing down the dining room wall. His sweat-soaked tank top had clung to his pumped-up muscles...and her mouth had gone dry.

Foolish me.

Honestly, she didn't want to notice his sexy body. He'd hired her as a contractor. He was a client—nothing more, nothing less—and he'd get her best work, no matter their history. Firmly steering her thoughts back to construction, she walked out to her truck to get more nails.

Returning, she glanced around, trying to see what the place would look like when finished. The front of the cabin held the great room. The dining area and kitchen made up the back. In the very center, a staircase led to the bedroom loft.

She grinned. Talk about no privacy. With the bedroom overlooking the great room, this was definitely a one-person house.

The logs and chinking, as well as the roof beams, were exposed. Here and there, the rough plank floor was covered with heavy brown, black, and white area rugs in Native American designs. The heavy living room furniture looked solid and comfortable; however, there wasn't much else. No comfy pillows or throws. One lamp with a burled wood base sat on a lonely end table. Hooks beside the back door held a black felt cowboy hat and a jacket, and the kitchen was bare bones.

Then again, the man had just moved in…which made him a new neighbor.

Mallory grimaced. Gramma had been stringent about neighborly duties—like offering the bread and salt of welcome to newcomers. Under the silent weight of the ghostly decree, Mallory had baked last night. This morning, she'd left a loaf of rosemary bread, sea salt, and a container of her homemade soup in Sawyer's kitchen.

She needed to tell him it was there.

A couple of hours later, as she was cleaning her work area, Ware came in the back door and into the kitchen.

"Looks like the roofing is going well." His straw cowboy hat darkened his hard features and turned his blue eyes to indigo. Dirt and sweat streaked his face and muscular arms. Filling a glass of water, he drank it down, his Adam's apple moving up and down in his tanned neck.

She'd kissed that neck and nibbled along his jaw… *Don't go there.*

"Yes. It looks as if the rains will hold off long enough to finish."

Noticing the loaf of bread on the counter, he glanced at her. "I, ah, made bread and soup last night. I brought you some." As his face darkened, she added, "It's pretty good. I—"

His gaze filled with irritation, and his aura darkened. "Thanks, McCabe. But no." Without another word, he stalked out of the house.

Dismayed, she stared after him.

Well, his meaning was certainly clear. He was a client and nothing else. Drawing a line was his prerogative, but she'd assumed they could be friendly. He was her nearest neighbor, for heaven's sake.

Although Gramma's ghost would be appalled, there would be no more neighborly gestures. Because right now, it rather felt as if he'd kicked her.

BACK WORKING ON the fence, Sawyer saw Mallory drive down the road. Probably checking on her other job site in town.

He had to admit the woman worked hard and had no problem getting her hands dirty. This morning, she'd been up with the Booth brothers on the stable roof, then turned her hand to some excellent finish work on his new kitchen window.

He winced as he thought of his behavior a few minutes ago. He'd been damn rude. But, hell, she'd brought him homemade food—as a girlfriend would do.

She wasn't his fucking girlfriend.

Justified or not, he felt as if he'd kicked a puppy.

Dammit, he didn't want to be friends. She'd had her fun with him; now playtime was done and over. He sure didn't want her running over to his place every time she felt like scratching an itch.

Best to make his boundaries clear...especially since he'd liked fucking her so much he couldn't get her out of his head. He had to keep his damn distance.

His focus needed to be on his mission—patrolling Bear Flat at night, staking out the Aryan Hammers' house, and trailing the gang members. Midweek, he'd stopped a mugging, knocked the gangbanger unconscious, and left before the police arrived. In loose clothing and with a ball cap pulled down, he doubted the two elderly tourists could ID him—but they'd looked damned determined to make sure the skinhead went to jail.

One Hammer down.

Two nights ago, he'd caught four of the fuckers breaking into the feed store and, unfortunately, decided he couldn't take them all. He'd kicked over a garbage can, and the noise had sent them running. His jaw set. Next time, he'd take the risk and go after them.

Because one of these days, they'd go after Atticus again. Or they might hurt someone else. Women were fair game to those bastards, and the pretty contractor had job sites all over town. She worked late. Sometimes alone. If they went after her…

As the wood splintered around the screw, he realized what he was doing. Yeah, his mind wasn't on the work at all. He needed to break for lunch anyway.

As he walked back into the house, trying to remember if he had any food left in the fridge, his stomach let him know he was an idiot for turning down home-cooked food.

Growling at himself, he grabbed a frozen dinner out of the freezer, ripped the top off, and set it in the microwave. When he tossed the cardboard into the trashcan under the sink, he stared.

In the garbage, along with coffee grounds and trash, were a small loaf of bread and a plastic container of soup.

Yeah. He was an asshole.

Chapter Nine

AFTER WARE HAD drawn his line in the sand, Mallory did her best to stay out of his way, and another week passed with no altercations.

With luck, today would be no different. Mallory concentrated on finishing the installation of the new butcher-block countertop in the kitchen.

An early fall thunderstorm had forced Ware inside, and he was repairing the staircase railing. The man was good with his hands. No surprise. His aura indicated he'd endeavor to achieve competence with anything he attempted.

In an effort to keep her distance, she'd plugged her iPod into her portable speaker and turned the music up loud enough to discourage conversation. She didn't want to talk with him, since she might forget the discomfiting fact that he didn't like her.

At least, having made his opinion of neighborly gestures quite clear, he seemed willing to accept her as a fellow workman.

She had to remind herself his choices were his prerogative.

Hers were her own, too, and oddly enough, she still liked the man. Although he had the manners of a drenched cat when annoyed, he was otherwise polite. Her crew enjoyed his company. He didn't shy from work, kept his home tidy, and had paid his first invoice immediately.

In the fireplace, an early fire had died down to coals, leaving the room warm. Between the hammering of the rain and the haunting music of Celtic Woman, the cabin was a cozy place. Although Ware didn't talk, he wasn't on edge either, and they worked on their separate tasks in a pleasant silence.

The sound of a vehicle in the driveway drew her attention, and she moved to look out the great room window. "Not one of my guys."

Ware grunted and rose. As he stepped out the front door onto the decrepit porch—which Mallory planned to shore up, whether or not he asked—cool, moist air whipped into the house.

"Hey, bro," a man called. "Gin wanted to see how the renovations are coming. We brought you some lunch, too."

It was Atticus, Sawyer's brother, with his girlfriend, Gin.

As Atticus and Sawyer followed Gin into the house, Mallory saw how much the brothers resembled each other. Tall, well-built, brown hair, blue eyes—and yet, quite different. Sawyer's eyes were a pure dark blue. Atticus's held a tint of gray, and he was slightly taller and leaner, Sawyer more heavily muscled. Sawyer was clean-shaven with very short hair; Atticus had a mustache, trim beard, and collar-length hair.

Both were dangerously good-looking.

As Atticus set a box on the table, he spotted her in the kitchen, noted the tools Sawyer'd left all over the stairway, and grinned. "Hey, Mallory. Got him working for you now?"

"He came in to get out of the rain." She smiled back. "And then he couldn't stand watching someone else work while he sat around."

"Hi, Mallory." Short and redheaded, Gin opened the box and set out sandwiches. Her voice held a soft Southern accent as she motioned to the food. "We have more than enough food. Take a break and join us."

Mallory shook her head. Although she and Ware were getting along at the moment, she wouldn't rile him by forcing him to actually associate with her. "I'd love to join you"—which wasn't a lie, since Gin and Atticus were both nice—"but I have to check on my crew in town. We're almost finished with Sarah Larson's sunroom."

"Sarah showed me what you've done already, and it's gorgeous." Gin opened a Diet Coke. "I'm trying to talk Atticus into one."

Compliments on her work. Nothing could brighten a day faster. Mallory beamed. "Thank you. Sarah and I had fun designing the room—and in spite of the mess, she already considers it her afternoon refuge."

"I noticed." Gin smiled. "What's next on your slate?" Her interest in everyone and everything was just one reason the counselor was so popular in Bear Flat.

Even with no wish to change, Mallory did admire people who were so sociable. "Lisa Holder wants to expand her kitchen into a country style with room for a big table."

Gin nodded. "I can see why. Her kids are old enough to sit at a table, and a formal dining room is just not her, is it?"

"No." Mallory grinned. "She said it's so stuffy it makes her think of her mother-in-law every time they eat in there." Everyone knew how relieved Lisa had been when her fussy in-laws moved to Arizona. "I'll take down a wall and create one big kitchen/dining area, change the appliances around to make them more usable, put in glass-fronted cupboards, and bigger windows." Mallory smiled, envisioning the area as it would be. "It'll be cheerful and friendly and big enough for family meals."

"You really do love your work, don't you," Gin murmured.

"Absolutely."

Feeling Sawyer's gaze on her, Mallory finished packing her tools. Rising, she smiled at Gin and Atticus. "It was nice seeing you two." She nodded at Ware.

Out on the porch, she closed the door behind her and stopped. The rain had picked up, pounding down on the small covered porch, and her rain gear was in her truck. Bad planning on her part.

Under her feet, the sagging boards of the porch creaked—and whined.

Since when did wood whine? After another second, she heard the sound again.

She shook her head, opened the door…and hoped Ware had a heart under all his attitude. His aura said he did, after all. "Ware, you have a problem."

She'd forgotten there were two Wares inside. Both brothers

stepped out, crowding the tiny porch.

Sawyer frowned. "More dry rot?"

"Nothing so easy. Listen."

The men stilled. Listened.

Nothing.

Sawyer shook his head. "I don't—"

Whine.

He stiffened. "An animal?"

"Dog, I'd say. A coyote wouldn't make a sound." Mallory pointed down. "Under your porch." Unable to keep from grinning, she opened her toolbox and handed him a flashlight.

He jumped off the porch, glanced at the mud, and let out an exasperated grunt. To his credit, he didn't hesitate before kneeling in the pouring rain and shining the light under the porch. "Well, you're a fucking mess." He made a clicking noise. "C'mere, little guy. Let's get you warm and dry."

Mallory bit her lip as she listened to him…because his low crooning voice sounded the same as when they'd been in bed. To her everlasting annoyance, her insides went all melty.

SAWYER SHINED THE light over the dog again. Hell, it wasn't even a dog—it was a puppy. The dumbass had managed to wedge itself into a chink in the foundation. One more repair to schedule or other critters would end up under the cabin.

Gently, he shoved the pup back so he could ease its legs forward first. Reminded him of foaling and calving days back on the Idaho ranch. "There you go, pup. Easy now."

A squeak of pain ripped his heart right in two. A second later, he had it loose, and the mutt was trying to burrow into his stomach. "All right, we're out of here."

Holding the squirming, chilled body against his ribs, he edged backward until he was out from under the porch.

Staying dry under the overhang, his brother grinned. "Look at you. Seems like you spent most of your youth soaked and covered in mud."

"We both did, asshole." Despite Sawyer's token scowl, the

memories were sweet. Maybe some of his worst moments had happened on their ranch—but the best ones outweighed them. "Gotta say, being covered in mud was more fun when I was ten."

Gripping the pup around its bony ribs, he held it out for a good look. The dog had a sturdy build despite the lack of meat. Its fur was too dirty to determine the color, although seemed to be flecked white and gray. Its legs and cheeks were a lighter shade. Floppy black ears. Almost looked like a German shepherd, but shepherd pups were bigger. "Reminds me of the cattle dogs our neighbor used to raise."

Atticus nodded. "I'd say yeah."

"Aw," Gin said. "Even with the mud, he's awfully cute."

Here was a soft heart. Perfect. Sawyer smiled at her. "You like puppies, right?"

Att snorted. "Gin, we best get going, or we'll be late. Before you ask, bro, we already have a dog. Besides, you could use a mouser"— he eyed the pup—"when it gets bigger than a minute."

"You're a lot of help." It'd been a forlorn hope anyway. Sawyer tucked the pup back against his chest. "Thanks for the food, you two. It's appreciated."

"You're very welcome. Although a deli sandwich can't compare to the homemade housewarming gift Mallory brought over when I moved in with Atticus." Gin smiled at the contractor. "I've tried to make the rosemary-cheddar loaf and can't come close to yours."

A housewarming gift? Sawyer stiffened. Oh, *hell.* Talk about being hit with a stupid stick—he'd been completely wrong about Mallory's reasons for bringing him food.

Mallory smiled at Gin. "If you want, come over, and we can make some together."

"You're on." Gin followed Att off the porch, splashing through the puddles to the truck.

Mallory turned to Sawyer and held her hand out.

"All *right.*" Pleased, he started to hand her the pup.

She took a step back. "No, Ware. My flashlight—not the dog."

"You're female. Females always like puppies."

She snorted. "I do like puppies. My cat, however, says they're annoying."

"You have a cat?"

"Mmmhmm. Which is why this little guy is all yours."

Sawyer looked down. The puppy had snuggled down in the bend of his elbow, setting a tiny muzzle onto his forearm. One muddy picture of contentment. "Well, damn."

What the hell was he going to do with a dog? "I don't have any shit for dogs, and by the time I get him dry and—"

"I have a half-bag of puppy chow in my storage room. It'll hold you over until you can drive to town tomorrow."

Sawyer blew out a breath. "I'd appreciate it. Why does a cat owner have puppy food?"

"Because of strays like him. People see a pretty farmhouse or two and dump their unwanted pets...whereupon their pets end up as dinner for the coyotes, hawks, and foxes. Since some make it to my house, I keep food on hand." She turned away. "You two dry off, and I'll be back in a few minutes."

Before he could speak, she was trotting toward her pickup.

Mallory was one nice woman.

While she fetched supplies, Sawyer gave the pup a warm bath in the sink. It'd been a long while, but he knew the basics. Like mud was bad.

By the time he'd finished toweling the pup off, Mallory was back. After she had filled a small dish with water, another dish got wetted-down kibble. "I'd guess it"—a quick look had her revising—"*he* is a bit over eight weeks, so at least he's weaned."

"And starving." With an odd satisfaction, Sawyer watched the puppy dig into the food with tiny snuffling noises.

Now dry, the gray and white fur was fluffing out. Chest, legs, and cheeks were tan. Black nose. Black mask around his eyes. Its ear-tips flopped over. "Looks like an Australian cattle dog. Or mostly."

He rubbed the small head with one finger and got a tail wag. Friendly guy. Far too fucking trusting.

"He'll be a fine dog for this place," Mallory said.

"Or yours."

"Sorry, no. Besides, I don't have any stock for him to tend—and he'll want to work when he gets bigger." The woman smiled down at the mutt. Her brown hair was darkened to almost black from the rain, making her eyes even greener. Her wet shirt clung to her small breasts and revealed how her lean waist widened into a gorgeous round ass.

She was drenched and not saying a word of complaint. She'd brought him supplies—and hadn't let him push her into taking a puppy. Generous. Helpful. And not a wimp.

Dammit, he didn't want to like her.

And no matter how fucking awkward, he owed her an apology. "I'm sorry about the soup and bread."

Her eyes cooled. "Not a problem. My gramma was Slavic and deemed it an obligation to offer a new neighbor the traditional bread and salt. I hadn't considered how a gift might be construed."

"Funny what we absorb from our family." For one thing, his English teacher mother had taught him enough to realize the little carpenter had a hell of a vocabulary.

"Isn't it, though?" Hers had obviously left her with a talent of bowing out quickly. "I'm glad you have a pet, but remember—construction sites are deadly for animals. The crew will be here early tomorrow morning to finish up the roof."

"Understood."

She walked out the door, closing it firmly behind her.

"Well, mutt." Sawyer stroked two fingers down the bony back. "Looks like it's just you and me, kid."

Adoring eyes stared up at him.

Odd how something so little could change the entire atmosphere of a room.

Chapter Ten

WITH A FEW reusable grocery bags under his arm, Morgan Masterson crossed the street in Bear Flat. Damn Wyatt anyway. With his brother gone to some damn place in Africa, the guide work and household chores kept piling higher and deeper. Good thing the grocery store was open on Sundays.

Morgan scowled. It wasn't the workload that torqued his jaw. No, the house—what Pa had called the "clan" home—was too empty. Wyatt would be gone until late winter. Although Cousin Kallie still worked as a guide, she was married and living with her husband, Jake Hunt. Virgil'd brought Summer to live in the house, but they'd only been married a year and were still playing kissy-face. Made Morgan feel like a spinster aunt.

And lonely. He and Wyatt had been together more often than he'd realized.

As he stepped up onto the boardwalk, he nodded politely to a man leaving the grocery store with a plastic sack in one hand.

The guy stopped. "Morgan Masterson?"

"That would be me." Morgan looked the stranger over. A muscular six-two, an inch taller than Morgan. Close-cropped brown hair. Clean-shaven. The tan and sun lines said he spent time outside. A battered straw cowboy hat, dirt-stained jeans, ripped T-shirt, and work boots said he worked for a living. "What can I do for you?"

The guy stuck his hand out. "Sawyer Ware. I bought the property just down the mountain from yours."

The new neighbor, huh. Remembering the gossip, Morgan shook hands, not quite certain what he thought. Ware had tried to protect women during a prison break, but he'd been in prison in the first place for driving after drinking…with a fatality. Then again, Atticus had mentioned his bro had PTSD.

Be all that as it may, the man was Atticus's brother, and Atticus was a friend. "I saw you're fixing the place up. You've got a job on your hands."

"Yeah. I'm looking to bring in horses to lease out—or rent—for guide businesses that don't want the hassle of maintaining and training their own stock." He paused, obviously hoping for an expression of interest from Morgan.

"Sorry, the guy who makes those decisions for our business isn't around. And won't be around until late winter." Anger sparked in Morgan's gut. Their business was at a standstill…because Wyatt had taken his ass off to the other side of the world to find himself or whatever.

SUNDAYS COULD BE so satisfying. Mallory had cleaned her house, done laundry, and started a beef roast in the slow cooker. Ready to make a loaf of bread, she'd run into a problem—not enough flour.

Thus, this trip to Bear Flat.

After parking her pickup near the realty office, she strolled down Main Street toward the grocery store.

"Hi, Mallory!" a child called as he came up behind her and raced past toward a car and his mother, Lisa.

Mallory laughed and waved at Lisa, who had her other two children stowed safely in car seats.

Lisa waved back and motioned her last stray into the car.

Smiling, Mallory looked to see who else was in town…and froze.

Across the street, in front of the grocery, Sawyer Ware was talking with Morgan Masterson.

Darn it, she didn't want her day spoiled by Ware's attitude. Nevertheless, if she wanted to make bread, she had to buy flour.

Oh, get over yourself, Mallory.

Ware would greet her politely. She'd ask about the pup and be told it was fine, and that would be that. Just because her pulse increased every time she saw him, and her heart ached at his indifference, didn't mean she couldn't function. Her attraction to him was just…temporary. When she was old and gray, she probably wouldn't even remember his name.

She snorted. Plato said, *"The worst of all deceptions is self-deception."* So…*fine*. She'd probably never forget him, not in a million years.

It didn't mean she couldn't avoid him now.

In front of the bank, Mrs. Reed was sweeping around a half-barrel planter of orange and yellow nasturtiums. During the tourist season, the elderly woman and another shopkeeper kept the town's hanging planters and barrels filled with vibrant blooms. "Hello, Mallory. How is the lemon geranium doing for you?"

"Beautifully. I love the scent." Pleased with the diversion, Mallory leaned against a post. Maybe Ware would move on soon. "When I divide my sunset daylilies, would you like some?"

"I don't have anywhere to put them; however, Frances said she needed something bright for a sunny corner."

"Perfect." Frances ran a small bed-and-breakfast just off Main. "The daylilies will be happy there."

Another gardener who conversed with her plants, Mrs. Reed gave her an understanding nod. "They will, indeed. It's a cheerful place."

Mallory saw Morgan disappear into the grocery store. Maybe Sawyer would head away now. She turned back to Mrs. Reed. "I was wondering if—"

"Hey, old fart."

The sneering voice came from across the street, and Mallory turned.

In front of the hardware store, three gang members circled Verne like coyotes around weak prey. Over seventy years old, the skinny, half-bald logger was never sober, yet was a complete sweetheart.

"Oh, no." Mallory's hands closed into fists.

"Smells worse'n a skunk," one gangbanger yelled.

Another taunted, "What a fucking loser."

Swaying, Verne looked at the three men in confusion.

The biggest punk had a swastika tattoo on his shiny shaved scalp, which suggested the men were Aryan Hammers. One man was heavy with greasy black hair and a long beard. The third had a buzz cut and piercings everywhere—along his lower lip, curving around his ears, and studding his cheeks and eyebrows.

The bearded one shoved Verne from behind.

The old man staggered forward and hit the hardware store's display rack of tools. He'd barely managed to regain his balance when the man with piercings shoved him.

Mrs. Reed was close to tears. "We have to stop this."

"Yes. We do." Mallory started forward.

The yells had drawn Sawyer's attention, and after dropping his sack on a bench, he stalked toward the gangbangers. In the quiet afternoon, his smooth voice came clearly across the street. "Leave the old guy alone. He's not up to your weight class."

Mallory's heart skipped a beat. Many men would rescue women in trouble, like he had with her and Zoe. But to step in to save an old alcoholic?

Did the damn man have to keep proving he was a hero?

He was also way *outnumbered.*

She stared across the street, praying the gang would heed his advice.

Instead, the one with piercings made kissy noises at Sawyer. "Blow me, pussy."

"What the fuck? I know you, asshole." Moving toward Sawyer, the huge skinhead elbowed Verne out of his way.

The elderly logger hit the boardwalk and groaned in pain.

Uncaring, the skinhead stared at Sawyer. "You're the one in the papers—You fucking bastard, you and your brother killed Aryan Hammers." He grabbed a hatchet from the rack of tools outside the store.

"What the hell is going on?" Empty-handed, Morgan stomped out of the store.

Ware snapped, "Stay out of this, Masterson."

"Like hell." Morgan lined up beside Sawyer and scowled at the

Neo-Nazis. "Get the fuck out of here."

Jeering, the gang spread out. The enormous skinhead and the man with piercings headed straight for Sawyer.

"No, no, no." Mallory frantically punched 911 and pushed the phone into Mrs. Reed's hand. "Tell the dispatcher where to send the cops."

Taking the broom from the older woman, Mallory jumped off the boardwalk. Dodging a car, she ran to the other side of the street. Oh, sun and stars, how could she help?

Morgan had closed with the bearded hoodlum, hitting him as if he were a punching bag. Unable to defend himself against Morgan's big fists, the gangster staggered back.

A few feet away, Ware moved sideways to put the piercing-laden thug between him and the one with the hatchet. When the pierced gangbanger turned, Ware kicked him in the gut. The man folded in half. When Ware delivered an uppercut, the gangbanger was knocked backward, landing on the wooden planks near Verne. Knocked out cold.

The huge one with a hatchet made a growling sound and circled Sawyer, the hatchet blade held at ready. Then he lunged—and swung.

As Mallory stifled a scream of horror, Sawyer dodged the hatchet. Somehow, he managed to twist around fast enough to slam his fist into the gangster's kidney as he went past.

This was horrible. Stalled at the edge of the boardwalk, Mallory couldn't figure out how to help. The action was too fast.

With a furious roar, the huge gang member spun to face Sawyer again...and now his back was to Mallory.

A chance. Jaw set, she swung the broomstick as hard as she could. The handle thumped against the backs of his legs.

His knees buckled. As he started to fall, his arms went out for balance.

Sawyer punched him in the jaw so forcefully the gangbanger flew off the boardwalk and landed in the street.

Far too close to her.

A car skidded to a stop. Oncoming cars stopped on the other

side.

Shaking his bleeding knuckles, Sawyer glanced at her. "Thanks, babe."

"He-he had a hatchet."

"I noticed." A dimple appeared in his cheek. "You're sneakier than you look, little contractor."

"He could have *killed* you." Her heart was trying to pound out of her chest, and he was…*smiling?*

Groaning, the skinhead tried to sit up. A limp body landed right on top of him, knocking him flat again. It was the bearded man, out cold. Mallory backed up hastily.

"Back up some more, Mal." Grinning, Morgan grabbed the last unconscious hoodlum and heaved him on top of the pile.

"You getting into street fights now, bro?" The disgusted voice came from Virgil Masterson, who was striding down the boardwalk from the police station. The lieutenant was followed by a younger officer in his black uniform with weapons belt.

"Mallory." Virgil stopped beside her and appraised her quickly. His gaze rolled over the three Aryan Hammers and up to the boardwalk. After watching Sawyer help old Verne to his feet, he frowned at his brother. "Morgan, what the hell?"

"Hey, this is the most fun I've had since Wyatt left." After examining his bruised knuckles, Morgan grinned at Sawyer. "I can't believe you told me to stay out of it."

Virgil sighed and turned back to Mallory. "Can you tell me what happened?"

"Those three guys were harassing Verne, and they knocked him down. Sawyer told them to stop." She pointed at the skinhead. "This one grabbed a hatchet from the hardware display. Morgan knocked one guy out. Sawyer smashed another. And the third one with the hatchet"—she pointed to the huge skinhead—"I…uh…hit him with the broom, then Sawyer punched him."

"I saw. Very pretty swing you got, sweetheart." Virgil kicked the hatchet in the direction of his deputy and glanced at Ware. "I take it they're out for revenge against you as well as Atticus?"

Sawyer nodded, his face grim beneath the shadow of his hat.

Mallory remembered he'd killed an Aryan Hammer during the prison break.

Now the gang wanted revenge? The skinhead could have murdered him right here in front of her. Feeling as if ice had filled her insides, Mallory wrapped her arms around her waist.

Someone jostled her. Curious locals had gathered in the street, taking advantage of the stopped traffic.

"Now we've got fighting in the streets. All from the damned trash the prison brought in." Roger Simmons's New York accent thickened when he was upset. "Should toss all four of 'em in jail."

Four? Realizing his indictment included Sawyer, Mallory frowned. "Ware didn't start the fight."

"He's another damned convict, violent as all of them. Don't know why the hell he's still in our town."

Seriously? She shook her head. "Sawyer Ware isn't violent. Where do you get these ideas? You should get to know him before lumping him in with real criminals."

SAWYER HEARD THE gas station owner, Simmons, spouting off— nothing new—but Mallory had jumped to his defense.

Simmons grunted. "You're wrong, Mallory." He glared at Sawyer and stomped away.

Sawyer stared down at Mallory, feeling…odd. She'd told Simmons he wasn't violent. And, although her green eyes still sparkled with anger, she was pale. The fight had upset her.

Raising a trembling hand to push back her hair, Mallory asked Virgil, "Do you need me for anything?"

"Nah, little bit. You go on back to what you were doing. If I have questions, I know where to find you."

She nodded. With not even a glance at Sawyer, she walked away, still carrying her weapon. Quite the fighter, wading in with a fucking broom.

She crossed the street, handed the broom back to an older lady, and left. Not walking with her usual smooth glide.

Violence upset her.

She didn't like it.

She didn't think he was violent.

He felt as unsettled as when he'd parachuted at night into a choppy sea and been smacked around by every wave until he'd submerged.

How had he misread her so completely that night? She hadn't taken him to bed because he was an ex-con. She hadn't wanted some violent bastard. She'd wanted *him*.

The realization lifted a weight from his chest, one he hadn't realized was there. He pulled in a breath, deeper than the one before it. After a second, he realized Virgil was trying to get his attention.

"Yeah?"

"Come to the station and press charges. You, too, Morgan." Virgil snorted. "It'll serve you right to have to help fill out the damned paperwork."

Morgan laughed and slapped Sawyer on the back. "Let's go, buddy. My brother'll cry like a little girl if his paperwork isn't all pretty."

WITH THE PUPPY curled in a ball on his lap, Sawyer slouched in his leather chair and watched the sun climb over the eastern mountains. His eyes felt gritty, his stomach sour. It'd been a rough night. Not surprising. After any bloody confrontation, his nightmares returned.

But the guilt...now, that was new. He'd been wrong about Mallory. He'd been an asshole.

The night with her and what they'd shared had been different from what he'd believed. Odd how one realization changed everything.

No wonder he hadn't been able to get a handle on who she was.

Now he knew. She was exactly what she seemed—a fantastic woman with a big heart who kept extra food at home in case of strays, who took homemade food to new neighbors, whose construction crew adored her and worked to please her, and who had treated him professionally in spite of his behavior.

He'd treated her badly—and yeah, he felt like hell about it.

Now she'd seen him fighting for a second time, and she knew the gang was targeting him. And she didn't like violence. Would she bail out of his construction job at this point?

Sawyer scrubbed his hands over his face. Most of the stable repairs were done, and he could probably finish the rest if he had to, although *his* work would be a lot less professional.

In all reality, the repairs weren't what bothered him. It was the feeling he'd...lost something. Someone. Even when thinking she'd fucked him for a thrill, he'd liked her. Enjoyed her company.

If she walked away, he'd miss her, dammit.

The sound of her truck brought him to his feet. *Here it comes.* He could already imagine how she'd explain she had other obligations or how something had come up.

Holding the sleepy puppy against his chest, he opened the door.

"Good morning, Ware." Toolbox in hand, Mallory walked past him. In the drive behind her pickup, two more trucks pulled in. The roofing twins and another carpenter.

Not waiting for his response—because she'd undoubtedly learned not to expect a good morning from him—she set her toolbox on the counter as she normally did. "The roof should be done today. Then we'll start on the floors in the tack room and wash rack. The new sink will be installed today, too."

Sawyer stared at her. The puppy yawned with a high squeak.

Mallory laughed. "Does he have a name?"

She'd seen him punch two guys into oblivion. Wasn't the woman supposed to look nervous or something? "Achilles."

"Achilles." Beautifully curved brown brows drew together. "Like the Greek who fought Hector in the *Iliad*?"

"Very good." He grinned at her disbelieving stare. "My mother was an English teacher—hence Sawyer and Atticus. And our youngest brother..." He paused, waiting for the question.

She didn't fail him. "His name is...?"

Sawyer grinned. "Hector."

Fuck, he loved her laugh. Soprano voices were often shrill; hers was smooth and silken and full.

Suddenly, he needed a direct answer. "You know the Aryan

Hammers want revenge."

She blinked at his harsh tone. "Mmmhmm, I heard what Virgil said."

"Should I look for another contractor?"

Her disgusted expression made him blink. "No, Ware. We have a contract—that's why they call me a contractor. I finish what I start."

"I…" His throat clogged. Undoubtedly too much coffee. "Right."

The sound of the bickering Booth twins came from outside. "Russ, Priscilla thought *you* were an idiot. It was *me* she wanted."

"Dream on, dumbass. She asked me to get her a drink."

"Only so I could stay beside her. She liked me better…"

"Those two." With a huffed laugh, Mallory shook her head. "You're pretty good in a fight, Ware. Any chance you'd want to beat up the roofers today?"

Sawyer snorted and walked back to the bedroom to get changed.

And if he was grinning? Well, she couldn't see him, now could she?

Chapter Eleven

A WAYWARD STORM swept down out of Alaska on Thursday night to gift the mountains with a lovely blanket of snow—before changing to an afternoon rain. In celebration of making deadlines and returning to a five-day week, Mallory let her crew take off early on Friday. Herself included.

While cleaning up after her late lunch, she noticed the rain had stopped. If she walked down to get her mail right now, she could enjoy the last few remnants of snow.

After donning her red rain jacket—just in case—she strolled down the lane, taking deep breaths of the invigorating cold air. The lower forests were a dark green, and up higher, the slopes were still a pristine white. Down here in the valley, snow lingered in the curves of the meadow and the shadows of the trees.

Underfoot, the snow had turned to an unappealing, muddy—slick—slush. And slick. She skidded over a patch and barely caught her balance.

Halfway to the mailbox, a few sprinkles hit. Then a few more. *Murphy's Law, right? Go for a walk and the rain will begin again.* She pulled her hood up and laughed at the pattering sound. Rain or not, the world was beautiful.

She passed Ware's house and noted the dark windows and missing pickup. Not home.

Oh, honestly, had she just held her breath?

The roof on the stable looked good, and they'd finished just in time. Ware had been pleased…and had actually said so.

Wasn't it strange how his behavior had changed since the street fight last weekend? He still wasn't particularly friendly, didn't flirt or anything, but his edgy anger toward her had disappeared. Why he should have been mad to begin with, she'd never figured out—and she sure didn't know him well enough to ask.

She pursed her lips. Maybe he'd been adjusting to the outside world? What would it be like to be shoved into a concrete prison box to live? Regulated and restricted all the time. No wonder his aura had streaks of gray, and harsh lines bracketed his mouth.

Had prison turned him into such a good fighter? Despite her fear, she'd noticed how skillfully he fought—as if he'd been born to be a warrior.

No. Don't start that again.

It would be interesting to know where he'd picked up those skills, though. But she wouldn't ask others about his past. According to the Buddha, speech needed to be *"true, gentle, purposeful, and spoken with a mind of loving kindness,"* and hearsay all too often verged on the unkind.

If Ware wanted her to know more, he could tell her himself.

She grinned. His willingness to share would happen right about when Bear Flat turned into a palm-tree-filled tropical resort.

Besides, his past wasn't her business. He'd made it clear he had no interest in her as a woman.

Really, she shouldn't have made love with him that night. Maybe they'd have been able to be friends if she'd simply thanked him for seeing her home and gone inside alone.

She reached the end of her lane where it met the bigger road. Whiskey Creek Lane had three mailboxes in a row. Stepping over a pothole, she made a mental note to get the lane graded. Maybe graveled. At least the county had finally paved Kestrel Mountain Road.

Opening her box, she pulled out the single envelope—*"You have qualified for a credit card."*

Gah, junk mail—a total waste of trees. At least she could use it as fire starter. Even as she shoved it into her pocket and headed back down the lane, the rain picked up, turning into a steady patter with a few sprinkles of snow for seasoning. Mallory walked faster.

Despite the rain, a doe was browsing on the grass in the ditch. Two adorable fawns were cavorting nearby.

Mallory grinned, remembering Becca's first winter in Bear Flat when the city girl had left food out for the "poor, hungry deer" despite Logan's warnings. Becca had learned her lesson the following spring. Unlike grass-eating cattle, deer munched everything—like tulips and fruit trees and the rose bushes Becca had just planted.

Still... Mallory had understood her friend. Could anything be more irresistible than babies? As she walked, she watched the two fawns bounce after their mother. The first made a neat leap over the ditch. Then the other—

Mallory stepped into a rut and stumbled. Her foot came down on a slickened rock, slipped off, and with a burst of wrenching pain, her ankle twisted.

She went down. Hard.

SAWYER DROVE UP Kestrel Mountain Road, heading home. In his crate on the passenger seat, Achilles napped after his traumatic veterinary visit. Poking and prodding—and needles. Poor pup. Sawyer'd been in the hospital enough; he could sympathize.

He slowed the truck and turned onto Whiskey Creek Lane. Sleet smeared the windshield, and he flipped the wipers to a faster speed. Snow last night. Rain most of today. Now this mixture. Crazy uncertain weather. He grinned. In town, people had grumbled about the early storm; however, in prison, yard time outdoors was measured in minutes, and he'd acquired a whole new appreciation of everything nature had to offer.

Even a sky spitting snow, ice, and rain.

He passed Atticus's house. On the long stretch to his spread, with pastures on each side, a flash of bright red caught his eye. Something—no, someone—sat near the side of the gravel road.

Jesus, Mallory?

He jammed on the brakes, slammed the truck into park, and jumped out.

She had one ankle-high boot off and had removed her sock, leaving her left foot bare. Slowly, she was wrapping the removed sock around her right ankle over and above the boot in a clever kind of homemade strapping.

She looked up at him, her relief obvious. "Hey, Ware. Any chance I could catch a ride to my house?"

Hearing the pain underlying her casual words made his gut tighten. He squatted beside her. Under the dark green sock, her right ankle was swollen over the top of the boot. Sprained or busted. "Nope."

"But..."

"You're catching a ride to the medical clinic. Put your boot back on." Before she could give him some smart-ass response, he opened the passenger door, moved Achilles over, and returned.

She'd gotten her boot on, so he scooped her up and tried not to notice how well she fit in his arms. After putting her on the passenger seat, he set the small dog carrier on her lap. "Hang on to Achilles for me."

When he climbed in the other side, she frowned at him. "Take me home, please. My ankle just needs to be wrapped and—"

"You're going to see a doctor. Period." As he reached across her to fasten her seat belt, he caught her scent. Cool and clean as fresh cut grass. He could also feel her shivering. "How long were you sitting there?"

"Not too long. I have to admit, I wasted a couple of minutes in cursing." When a whine came from the crate, she gave the pup a finger to nibble on. "Easy, baby. Shhh."

Sawyer wasn't surprised when Achilles settled back down. This woman toted around serenity like other women carried purses.

After flipping the heat to high, he turned the pickup around and headed back to town. "Anything besides your ankle damaged?"

"Just my belief that I'd finally mastered the art of walking."

He grinned. From the tightness of her face, he'd guess her ankle hurt like hell, yet she wasn't crying or hysterical. Fuck, he liked her wry sense of humor.

In town, he parked in front of the clinic, moved the dog carrier to the driver's seat, and gave Achilles a chew bone to keep him busy. "Back soon, buddy."

Ignoring Mallory's protest, he carried her in. One damp, shivering, fragrant, soft armful. Remembering the feel of her naked body all too well, he had to concentrate on not cuddling her closer.

In front of the reception desk, he looked around the waiting room, noting the high-mounted motion detectors and the sensor to detect breaking glass. Good security as well as being located next to the police station had undoubtedly kept the place safe from the Aryan Hammers. One less business he had to worry about.

Mallory frowned at him. "You can put me down now."

Now, why would he do that when he was enjoying the feel of her in his arms? "I'm good."

"Mal!" A pretty blonde dressed in blue scrubs rushed out from the exam rooms. "What happened?"

"Hey, Sunny. I twisted my ankle. Nothing major." Mallory scowled up at Sawyer. "He's being overly macho."

Catching Sawyer's grin, the nurse snorted. "I see. In that case, Mr. Macho, can you bring her to the back?" She led the way to an exam room.

After setting his delightfully tough little neighbor on the table, he stepped back.

"Sawyer, I know you met Virgil Masterson last week." Mallory motioned toward the nurse. "This is his wife, Summer, aka Sunny to some of us."

"Pleasure." After nodding at Summer, Sawyer gently tugged Mallory's wet coat off.

As the nurse unwrapped the improvised sock "strapping", Mallory's voice tightened with pain. "This is my neighbor, Sawyer Ware, Atticus's brother."

Summer smiled at him. "Atticus has talked about you. It's nice to meet you."

After dropping Mallory's coat on a chair, Sawyer frowned. Despite the warm room and her heavy green sweater, she still shivered.

Dammit, she was probably hypothermic. "Got any warm blankets, Summer? She got pretty chilled before I arrived."

"In the cabinet in the hall." Summer eased Mallory's boot off and shook her head. "This is pretty swollen, Mal. I'm going to cut your sock off."

A couple of minutes later, Sawyer wrapped a heated blanket around Mallory. Her sigh of pleasure eased the knot in his gut and made him smile.

The exam room door opened.

"Mallory. Looks like you took a spill." The doctor was lean with receding gray hair, glasses, and a standard white lab coat. He glanced at Sawyer. "I'm Dr. Vickers. Are you a relative of Mallory's?"

"Neighbor. Sawyer Ware."

"Good to meet you. If you'll wait in the reception area, then—"

"I'll stay." Sawyer crossed his arms over his chest. "She's a mite on the stubborn side. I'd rather hear what's wrong and what needs to be done from you instead of her telling me everything's fine, and she doesn't need a thing."

Summer snickered. "He knows Mal pretty well, doesn't he?"

After giving the nurse a scowl, Mallory turned her gaze on Sawyer. She apparently understood his obstinate expression since she only sighed and didn't protest.

Her disgruntled pout was damned cute.

Lips twitching, the doctor set to palpating the bones on each side of her ankle and foot.

Sawyer frowned. Her swollen ankle had doubled in size with reddish bruising on both sides. Looked fucking painful.

As the doc poked and prodded, Mallory didn't let out a sound, although her fingers curled around the exam table edges so hard her knuckles went white.

Unfortunately, they weren't good enough friends for him to hold her hand. The contractor was damn tough—and was breaking his heart.

"Does she need x-rays?" he asked as the doc helped her take a few steps.

"Not according to the Ottawa protocol." The doctor smiled at

Mallory. "It appears you escaped broken bones, but you have a nice healthy sprain."

"Strap it up and put ice on it, right?" she guessed.

"Exactly right." The doc smiled at her. "Elevate your ankle. No aspirin. I want you to use crutches for two days. You can touch your toe for balance as long as you keep most of your weight off your foot."

"Crutches?" She frowned at him.

"Yes, crutches." He glanced at Sawyer. "Are you taking her home?"

"Yep. I'll keep an eye on her."

"You'll have your work cut out for you." The doctor started his work on the ankle.

Mallory turned to stare at Sawyer as if he'd grown a second head. *Too bad.*

BY THE TIME Sawyer got Mallory home, the sun was close to setting, and the rain had slowed to a drizzle. As he walked around his pickup, he studied her house in the remaining daylight. It was a two-story, white clapboard with a steel gray roof and dark red shutters. The wraparound covered porch held a wide porch swing, chairs, and tables. Planter boxes studded the dark red railings.

Carved lions curled around the posts. *Interesting.*

As Mallory tried to maneuver herself out of the truck with the crutches, Sawyer snorted, reached in, and picked her up.

"I can walk."

"Sure you can. Do it tomorrow." As if he'd let her try to manage crutches in the twilight and rain.

Once inside, he carried her through the small foyer and past the kitchen on the right. A bathroom was on the left, and Sawyer paused at the reminder.

Females. "Bet you could use a bathroom break, right?"

"Yes, please." When he looked down, her face had turned red with embarrassment. Damn, she was cute.

Remembering the way all too well, he took her to her master bedroom and into the large, spotless bathroom. With blue and white floral wallpaper, blue hand towels, and a fanciful old-fashioned mirror over the sink, it seemed very feminine. He set her down, held her steady until she had a good grip on the washstand, and removed her coat. "Stand there a second."

He rummaged in her dresser drawers, digging out sweatpants, a T-shirt, and a loose sweatshirt. A drawer filled with bright undergarments made him step back. Uh-uh, not going there.

Great. Now he was wondering if she'd worn something so sexy under her clothes.

"Here's dry clothing." He set the pile of clothes on the counter next to the toilet. "I'm going to fetch your crutches, and I'll set them right outside the door here."

"Got it." Her voice softened. "Thank you, Sawyer. For everything." Her jade sweater made her big green eyes simply stunning.

He smiled down at her. She thought he was leaving? *Wrong, pet.* Not worth the bother to correct her now. He'd been around enough women to know their thinking went to hell if the need to piss was urgent.

After leaving the crutches by the door, Sawyer went outside to give Achilles a run in the front yard.

Once done, he carried the pup and crate in, then prowled through the downstairs level of the house. The house was maybe forty years old and in excellent shape. Staircase in the center. Master bedroom on the left—and he had fond memories of that room. The right half of the house was an open arrangement with the kitchen and dining area in the front. In the back, a large great room opened to a sunroom.

With high ceilings and huge arched windows, the rooms were as filled with light as an oceanside cottage. In the great room, a pale blue and white Oriental carpet lay over a gleaming golden hardwood floor. The colorful pillows piled on the white slipcovered furniture looked like vivid blooms. Lush plants spilled over wrought-iron stands in the corners and hung from macramé hangers in front of the windows.

He could feel his tension seep away. Could a room radiate peace?

Hearing Mallory exit the bathroom, Sawyer tucked Atticus in his carrier and headed back to perform escort service.

Her eyes widened when he appeared. "You're still here."

"Yep." Standing close enough to catch her, he let her use the crutches to walk to the great room. As she sat and leaned back against the couch's armrest, he lifted her legs, propped the injured one up on pillows, and tucked a fluffy knitted blanket around her. "Want some coffee or something to eat?"

"Who are you, and what have you done with Ware?" When he laughed, her eyes widened more.

Well, hell, she was right to question him. Too bad he lacked any answers for her. Damned if he knew what he was doing, either. Nonetheless, he couldn't leave her here, hurt and alone. "Coffee? Food?"

She eyed him warily. "All right. I'd like some tea, if you know how to make it."

"I spent time overseas. I learned."

He got a kick out of her old-fashioned whistling kettle. As the water heated, Sawyer rummaged through the cupboards to determine if he should fetch food from his cabin.

Nope. She had plenty of food, both fresh and canned goods. Looked like she was well prepared for the apocalypse…or being snowed in.

She sure as fuck had enough tea. What kind of a person owned a dozen different kinds?

He shook his head. The little contractor might downplay her gender on the job, but her home was all woman. Tiny herb plants lined the large kitchen window, which looked out on the front porch. The white cupboards were glass-fronted, the islands and countertops a white marble. A vase of yellow and white mums stood on the counter next to a bowl of apples. The carved paper towel holder was an elongated cat.

He found a china teapot sitting on the island, chose a chamomile-peppermint tea mix, and poured in boiling water. A carved tray—another feline—held the teapot and two cups. Noticing a hand painted stoneware jar, he checked it and scored big.

Real oatmeal-raisin cookies. Home-fucking-made.

He ate two on the spot and was reaching for a third before he caught himself. *Focus, Ware.*

But he added ample cookies to the plate on the tray.

After setting the tray on the sturdy oval coffee table, Sawyer squatted next to her and handed her a filled cup. "Here. Drink some tea, and we'll get you warm from the inside."

She looked at him—and flushed.

Yeah, there were other ways to warm a woman up from the inside, but it wasn't what he'd meant. Instead of teasing her, he gave her a level look, which made her drop her gaze.

She took the cup. "Thank you. And...I didn't mean to be rude earlier. About you being helpful."

"Not a problem. In fact, I'll give you another chance to show your mean side—I'm staying the night."

"What?" Her jerk almost spilled the tea, and he closed his hand around the cup and over hers. Her fingers were chilly.

"New crutch users shouldn't be left alone. Backup is needed. By tomorrow, your ankle will be sturdier—and won't give out if you need it when you're on the crutches. Today, you're still learning. Hell, I've seen even SEALs go down their first time using the damn things."

"SEALS?" WAS THE man delusional? Mallory sputtered. "Seals don't even have legs."

He turned those blue eyes on her, and a genuine smile transformed his face. A stern jaw, a hard face, cold eyes. And...his smile would melt an ice queen. It was good he didn't want her, or she'd be lost.

"Not the furry kind. U.S. Navy SEALs." He sat on the coffee table, his legs so long his knees brushed her hip. "I was in the service."

"Oh. Right." She dared a question. "Did you want to leave the Navy, or did you get hurt?"

"Got a medical discharge. Took some shrapnel. And my head got fucked up." He looked away. "I'd planned to stay in for my twenty."

She studied him, seeing the way his aura had darkened with...grief? "Does *fucked up* mean you had a PTSD kind of thing?" His nod confirmed her guess. "You should know who you invited into your house."

She waited. This was apparently something he had to say.

"I wasn't sleeping because of nightmares. Then I had a couple of drinks with a buddy who got wasted, so I had to drive." On his knee, his hand tightened into a fist. "I fell asleep at the wheel, and the car drifted into the other lane."

She'd known the outcome—but not what had led up to it. She laid her hand over his. "There was a wreck..."

"Yeah. Oncoming headlights woke me. I yanked the wheel to avoid a collision and skidded right off the road—down the side of a mountain. The family in the other car was all right. I wasn't hurt too bad." He took a slow breath. "My friend died."

"Sawyer, I'm sorry." He had so many reasons for the darkness in his aura—war, death, grief, guilt. Tears burned her eyes, one trailing down her face.

He used his fingertips to wipe her cheek and shook his head as if he felt nothing, yet she could see the wounds slicing deep into his soul. "My time in service and having PTSD meant my sentence was lowered to a misdemeanor DUI manslaughter charge, but the judge gave me a couple years in prison. I deserved it." The stark look in his eyes said he thought he'd deserved more.

His friend had died. By the sun and stars, how such a loss would hurt...

"Shit happened, and I got released early."

The "shit" being how he'd risked his life during the prison breakout.

He ran his hand through his short hair. "Figured you should know the facts. I thought you already knew when—"

"When I took the job?" Trying to seem unaffected, she sipped her tea.

A corner of his mouth tipped up. "When you said you knew exactly what I was and went to bed with me. Some women find felons and violence exciting."

She choked. "*What?*"

Amusement lit his eyes.

"You're serious. Women actually…"

His smile faded. "Yeah, they do. Or they cross the street to avoid being anywhere near an ex-con."

Oh. "You weren't sure what I knew, so that's why you told me all this today?"

He nodded. "And why I'll let you call someone to stay with you if you're worried about me sleeping on your couch tonight."

"You'll let me, huh?"

He snorted. "I don't scare you, do I?"

"Scare, no. Irritate, yes. You've sure been rude a time or two." *Don't ever give the man soup or smile at him in stores.* Her brows drew together. "When I saw you in the feed store. You were rude because you thought I'd only"—*wanted you? Made love to you?*—"f-fucked you because of your convict status?"

He winced.

Oh, that was so it. She'd thought he was wonderful, had fallen for him, and he'd thought she was… "If you thought I was such a sleazy person, why in the world did you… Why didn't you just slam-bang and leave?" Her cheeks heated as she thought of how he'd concentrated on her pleasure.

He shrugged. "A gentleman sees to the lady, even if she is just looking to score on a SEAL or a convict."

"Ah." His words, *just looking to score*, sounded somewhat bitter. She'd thought men liked sex, no matter how shallow. *Males. Sex.* The words went together like peanut butter and jelly. It seemed Sawyer was different. "I guess a guy eventually starts feeling as if he's being used, huh?"

"Got that right." His face softened, and he ran a slow finger down her cheek. "Although it bothered me to think you got off on violent men, I enjoyed our night." The gentle look in his eyes said he was telling the truth.

The hard knot of pain wrapped around her memories slowly unraveled.

"So." He straightened. "Can you trust me to be a gentleman and care for you tonight? Or do you want a phone so you can call someone?"

"Listen, I don't need babysitting. I can—"

"I gave you an either/or question." His expression was firm. She'd bet he'd been an officer in the military.

"Stay."

His expression eased enough she could see he was pleased. "Good. Let me get a fire started, then."

As he rose, she settled back, feeling as if she'd strayed into unfamiliar territory. Sawyer Ware would spend the night. Here. And they weren't friends. Not really. Having touched her, seen her naked, kissed her intimately, and been inside her, he knew her body. He knew her mind not at all.

Yet he'd carried her, taken her to the doctor, told her about his past. They'd spent quiet hours together in his cabin during the remodeling. She smiled. Maybe they knew each other better than she thought.

After the fire began to blaze, he closed the glass door on the fireplace insert and returned to sit beside her. A whine made him glance at the puppy in the carrier. Achilles had woken up. "You mind if I let Achilles run around inside? I'll take him out often, but if he's loose, there's a chance he might piss on your floor."

She laughed. "It wouldn't be the first time. I've hosted strays until I could find them homes. Aslan is good with other animals."

"Seems to me, you said different when I tried to get you to take Achilles. Your cat finds puppies annoying."

"He does…at times. Other times, he thinks they're interesting."

He gave her a hard stare. "You wanted me to have a damn puppy."

She tried not to smirk.

"I'm going to remember how sneaky you can be."

"I'm not…"

With a disbelieving snort, he rose. "Ready for a sandwich when the pup and I get back?"

She struggled to sit up. "I can make it."

"You can lie still."

The firm order made her bones turn fluid and her insides go all gooey. She couldn't keep from staring at him, and when her eyes met his, the couch seemed to drop.

He smiled and touched her cheek with his fingers. "Those big eyes of yours are something."

The flutters in her stomach increased until he released her gaze. "Take a rest, Mallory. We'll be back in a bit."

As he and the puppy headed out the front door, Mallory snuggled lower into the nest of pillows. The fire crackled busily, and she could hear Sawyer's low voice outside, talking with the puppy.

She wasn't alone. The comforting knowledge was unexpected—and wonderful.

Chapter Twelve

S ANDWICHES FOR SUPPER was within his cooking abilities, thank fuck. Once the food was ready, Sawyer carried the tray into the great room, stopped, and simply...looked.

By the light of the fire, he could see Mallory was sound asleep. Freed from the usual braid, her rich brown hair fell over her breasts, and the firelight brought out chestnut and copper strands. Curling slightly, her thick eyelashes were the same color. Her lightly tanned skin was flushed, probably from the huge orange-and-white cat sprawled across her chest.

Mallory owned one fucking big cat.

Had she said the beast—*Aslan*—got along with other animals? Sawyer glanced down at the pup at his heels. "You'd better hope that monster is friendly, Achilles. Looks as if it could eat you in one bite."

A tiny tail wagged back and forth.

Sawyer set the tray on the coffee table and exchanged stares with the feline guard. Shove it away? Not happening. He cleared his throat. "Mallory. Hey, sleeping beauty, time to wake up."

She didn't move.

One part of him was appalled she could sleep so heavily an intruder could approach. The other part felt envy.

When it came down to it, one of the reasons he'd served in the military was so a woman like this could sleep without worries. He leaned forward and caressed her cheek. Silky soft and warm.

Dammit, he needed to keep his hands off. He had a job to do

here in Bear Flat, and if he survived, well, he still wasn't a good bet for any woman.

He ran a finger over her lips and felt the attraction, the sheer need to kiss her. With an effort, he pulled his hand away and cleared his throat. "Suppertime, baby."

Blinking, she looked up with an unfocused gaze. "You have pretty eyes," she whispered.

So did she. The pale green of new leaves in spring and clear enough to read every emotion in her heart.

Dumbass, she's not for you. With a frown, he moved back.

She stared at him, waking slowly. Ah, hell, now he wanted to spend the night in her bed, to see her all mussed up in the morning. To take advantage of such adorable grogginess and enjoy himself as a man would.

Behave, Ware. He had a mission. Getting involved with Mallory wasn't in the battle plan. Jesus, all this jumping back and forth between staying unattached and wanting her was going to give him whiplash.

Ignoring the way his jeans had grown tight, he cleared his throat. "I have supper for you; however, you'll have to move the beast first."

"Beast?" She followed his gaze. The massive cat had retreated a foot and now sat on her thighs, watching Achilles. "Oh. Off, please, Aslan."

His long golden tail flicked.

She grinned and wiggled her legs. "Be nice, oh lion. I'm hungry."

After waiting long enough to establish that moving was his own idea, the cat stalked down the couch to settle on the armrest and monitor the small four-legged intruder.

Achilles planted his butt on the floor and stared back, tail wagging hopefully. *Want to play?*

Sawyer shook his head. "Good luck, pup."

As Mallory struggled to sit up, Sawyer gripped under her arms and lifted her. He could feel her muscles—the woman did manual labor for a living after all—but she also had the soft, soft feminine padding that could turn a man's mind to mush. He got her positioned so her back leaned against the armrest, but his hands didn't want to let go.

Her gaze lifted, her lips slightly open, her eyes wide. Too fucking appealing.

He brushed a kiss against her lips. Lingered. Took a little more, because, damn, her lips were soft.

Ordering his hands to let her go, he straightened and turned away. "Got soup here. I figured if you had it in the freezer, you must like it."

He set the tray on her lap. A glass of milk. Tomato soup—which he'd bet was homemade. A deli meat sandwich. He'd had to slice the bread to make it. From the big jar of yeast he'd seen in the refrigerator, he figured she made her own bread. Had he ever met anyone who baked her own bread?

"This looks great. I hope you made yourself some, too." When she smiled up at him, her green eyes were warm.

"I did. And Achilles is acting hungry. Do you still have puppy chow?" He'd returned the bag she'd brought him after picking up some at the grocery.

"It's in the pantry on the floor on the left."

In between bites of his own sandwich, Sawyer got Achilles started on water-softened chow.

As the puppy buried his nose in the dish, making snorting sounds, Aslan stalked over for a sniff. Achilles was too hungry to care, although he looked up long enough to offer a tail wag before returning to the more important matter of a meal.

The cat sat and watched the puppy like a mouser at a rat hole. Obviously, the feline knew which animal would win any encounter.

Sawyer knew, too. He finished off his sandwich and asked, "What kind of a cat is he?"

"Part Maine Coon. Apparently, Kallie Masterson's cat sowed a few wild oats around the area before being neutered. Near winter, Aslan showed up here, starving and nearly feral." Mallory drank her milk and set the empty glass down.

Pleased she'd finished everything he'd given her, Sawyer set the tray on the coffee table and returned to watching the animals.

The cat sure wasn't starving now. His golden fur gleamed with health. The long tufts on his ears made him look like a bobcat. "Aslan sounds familiar."

"Aslan is the talking lion—the king—in the Narnia series. Mom used to read it to me when I was little."

"Ah." The white ruff did give the cat a lion-like appearance.

"I'm babbling. Sorry." Color rose in her cheeks.

She thought she was babbling? Two sentences? Sawyer suppressed a smile. Actually, for the quiet young woman, more than one sentence *was* babbling. Felt like a gift, though. "Does your mom have anything to do with why the porch posts have carved lions?"

"Good guess. When she was around ten, Gramps gave her a carving set."

"Does she live here in Bear Flat?"

Sorrow filled her eyes. "No. Mom died when I was sixteen—complications from hepatitis." Her lips curled in a wry smile. "She was a sculptor, and a Wiccan New Ager, and a single parent, and what Gramps considered a terrible role model. When she got pregnant at seventeen, she and Gramps had a big fight—and she ran away to a commune. They finally made up when I was eleven."

The mother had definitely influenced her daughter. Sawyer glanced around, feeling the quiet peace of the house, seeing the plants and candles everywhere. The house—and Mallory—felt in tune with the earth. In his travels, he'd come to recognize and honor the gift. "Your grandparents are gone now, too?"

"Yes. Gramma a few years ago, and Gramps last year. The construction company was his, although I took over years ago." She sighed. "I'm alone now."

He understood all too well. Although he still had Att and Hector, the loss of the military and SEAL teams had almost gutted him. He ran his hand over her hair, wanting to erase her sadness. "I'm sorry, Mallory."

"Thanks. Anyway, Mom started the cat trend—and I continued it." Mallory gestured toward a corner where a gleaming black panther twined around a pot of trailing vines.

He rather liked the wicked look in the feline's eyes. "Sure beats fat pigs and cows. Have you noticed how farm animals are always grinning? I figure after dark they'll creep into the bedrooms and tear throats out."

"Like Chucky?" She broke into giggles. "We need to improve your movie viewing choices."

That ridiculously sexy *laugh*. As his willpower crumbled, he took her hand. "Do we?"

Dammit, he wasn't going to be able to hold out against her appeal. Yet, he couldn't risk this sweetheart getting hurt.

Still, she was a strong, independent woman. Maybe she'd be willing to play without involvement.

WHEN SAWYER PICKED up Mallory's hand and kissed her fingers, she felt the zing straight to her toes.

His blue eyes trapped hers as he asked in his whiskey-smooth voice, "So, no horror. You want to watch something sexy, maybe?"

Her mouth went dry. "Uuuh…"

The corners of his mouth quirked up. "Baby, now I know you're not into convict-fucking or put off by an ex-con, all bets are off."

All bets are off? Did he mean what she thought he did? She swallowed, knowing she should say no. This man could break her heart.

The word didn't rise to her lips.

"Let's get you changed for bed, hmm?" He scooped her up before she could speak.

In the master bathroom, he carefully set her on her feet and handed her the nightgown that'd been lying across the bed. "Call me when you're done."

Before she could demand her crutches, he left and shut the door behind him.

Men.

Balancing on one foot, she frowned at herself in the mirror. Her hair was a tangled mess. Although she'd washed off the mud earlier, her face was reddened from the wind, with a scrape on one cheek where she'd fallen into the brush. No makeup. She rarely wore any, but face it, when he looked at her as he had, she wanted to be everything that was female.

Don't be silly. He knew her now—well, sort of—and knew she wasn't a makeup kind of woman. The heat in his gaze said he liked how she looked anyway.

Fair enough. She liked how he looked.

She washed up and did her evening routine as if she didn't feel her heart pounding, as if her skin didn't feel so much more sensitive. Finished, she donned the nightgown. Pushing the door open, she balanced in the doorway. "All done."

Crouched, he was perusing the under-the-window bookcase, and she almost squeaked a protest. Oh, bloody *claws.* She kept her romances—including her new BDSM books—in the bedroom where visitors wouldn't see them.

She hadn't exactly thought about an overnight guest.

He rose, tossed a book on the nightstand, and walked over, giving her a slow, appreciative smile. "I like nightgowns."

"I don't think it's your size, Ware."

His grin flashed. "Well, I should check, don't you think?" He pulled her against him, holding her steady so she didn't need to put her sore foot down. His hands wandered over her ass and up her back.

The wave of heat rushing through her was amazing. "I-I don't think you can measure a nightgown by feel."

"No? Should I look for the tag?" Even as his right hand brushed her hair back from her neck, his left closed on her breast. When she gasped, he chuckled, his lips moving over her neck. And his hand...his hand...

He held the weight of her breast in his palm, caressing gently, fingers teasing the nipple to a peak. Just...playing.

"Sawyer," she whispered, unsure if she was objecting or urging him on.

His other palm cupped her jaw as he drew back to look into her eyes. And his lips curved. Apparently, *he* had no trouble reading her. He swept her up in his arms, carried her to the bed, and sat her on the mattress. He'd already pulled the white ruffled bedspread and covers down.

When he dimmed the glass-and-brass chandelier, she realized

he'd lit the candles on the dresser. The warm glow flickered on the walls. The soundtrack from *The Lord of the Rings* drifted softly from the speakers.

And here was her very own horse lord.

Becca had said he'd have rope...and a big sword. She choked back a laugh.

"All right, pet. I have a couple of questions for you." He sat next to her on the bed, all muscles and hard body. "In fact, let's play multiple choice. Did I mention my mother was a teacher?"

Her laugh eased the tight muscles in her chest, at least until he traced his finger over her lips.

"One: I sack out on the couch with the cat. Two: I stay in here with you, and you get some normal, everyday exercise."

"Exercise?" she said faintly. "Is that what it's called?"

Although he grinned, his hand curled under her chin firmly. "I mean, if you choose option two, I will fuck you until you can't remember your own name."

"Well..." She'd already made up her mind.

"No, wait. There are strings to this. Fucking doesn't create a re-lationship—not to me. We're neighbors, but it doesn't go further. I can't afford..." His jaw tightened. "I'm not looking for a girlfriend. Can you accept that?" His eyes held hers, steady, determined...and filled with a haunting desire.

She studied him in return. His aura was so beautiful, the dark-ness smaller than it had been. He wanted her...so much...and he desperately needed more than sex. Why was he so blind?

But he was.

Each person, including this man, had the right to choose his own path, even if ignoring his own needs. After all, Sawyer had been bluntly honest in laying everything out and leaving her free to choose.

The decision wasn't easy. He could damage her. Not her body, but her heart. Her emotions were already engaged, and if he pulled away—again—it would hurt badly. Yet, if she said no, she'd regret it. Forever.

Leap and the net will appear. "Yes."

When she reached for him, he shook his head. "Not so fast, pet. Option three: you find a scene from this book and we...act it out." He picked up the book from the nightstand.

Holy cats, it was Becca's book. The cover showed a woman in bondage.

Mallory's face heated. "Listen, just because I have a book..."

His gaze was level, and he wasn't embarrassed at all. "Baby, BDSM is a common fantasy for men and women. Some people prefer to read or dream about it. Some want more. What about you?"

"I don't...know."

Thoughtfully, he brushed her cheek with his knuckles. "Never tried anything?"

"No." Her nipples had bunched so tightly they ached—and she was far too aware her silky nightgown didn't conceal a thing.

"You liked being held down last time."

Could her face get any hotter? Womaning up, she nodded. Because she *had* liked it.

"Yeah. We'll go slow, pet." He handed her the book. "What's your favorite scene?"

Her breathing had little hitches as she silently found the page and handed the book back.

He read the page and the next. "No flogging or spanking here. This is all about bondage." His unwavering gaze met hers. "Did you learn about safe words in your reading?"

"A word to call everything off? Yes."

"Good. If you need everything to stop, use *red*." He shook his head. "Actually, baby, this isn't good. You don't know me well, and we're not in a public place. Do you know any women in this area who are into BDSM?"

"Ah, yes. I have a friend who is."

"Good." He handed her the phone from the bedside stand. "Tell her you're doing a scene with me at your house. Have her call if you don't touch base in a couple of hours—and notify the police if she can't reach you."

"Seriously?"

"Very." His face was stern. "This is your safety we're talking about. You should be a hell of a lot more careful."

It took an effort not to smile at him. Not to tell him he had a trustworthy aura. He not only wouldn't believe her, he'd probably think she was crazy.

When his brows lowered with impatience, she dutifully called Becca. In another moment, Sawyer'd probably lecture her on how she shouldn't have been with him the first time, either.

"Hey, Becca, can I ask you for a favor?"

"Always."

Her friends were amazing. Mallory smiled, then blew out a breath. "This is kind of embarrassing. I'm doing a…a scene…with Sawyer Ware at my house. And I'm supposed to check in with you in a couple of hours, and you're supposed to…"

"Rescue you if you don't check in. Absolutely." Becca hesitated. "Do you know him well enough?"

"Yes. I do. I, uh…*see*…him clearly, and I trust him."

Becca caught her meaning. "Well, all right. I'm glad you called and are being careful."

As Mallory clicked OFF, she shook her head. How come those BDSM books hadn't included this step?

"I've seen you wear bandanas at work," Sawyer stood beside her dresser. "What drawer?"

"First on the right."

He pulled a couple of bandanas out, opened her closet, and took a belt off the hook.

Watching him, she felt her heart pick up speed. Despite over-indulging in alcohol last time, she wondered if drinking another half bottle of scotch wouldn't be a fine idea right now.

As he walked back to the bed, he grinned. "Look at those wide eyes." Leaning down, he kissed her, hummed, and deepened the kiss. His lips were firm as he gripped her hair and tugged, tilting her head back as he possessed her mouth completely.

The room grew warmer.

He straightened and released her. From his pocket, he pulled a multi-tool, extracted the scissors, and laid it on the bedside table.

"Hold your hands up, palms facing each other, and a few inches apart."

Still sitting on the edge of the bed, she frowned. How could he tie her up in this position? But she complied.

After twisting the blue bandana into a rope-like strand, he tied the ends together and placed it around the outside of her wrists. Were they going to play cats-cradle? He wound the red bandanna around both ropes of the blue one between her wrists until it resembled a hangman's noose with two ends—which were around her wrists. "Pull on it," he said softly.

She did. The bandannas were tight enough she couldn't pull her hands out of the "nooses." Her breathing faltered until she looked up into his calm blue eyes.

He was watching her, his pleasure as obvious as the bulging erection in his jeans.

She swallowed. "You enjoy this?"

"Yeah, I do. If a woman is onboard with the plan, I like taking away all her choices of how and when she gets pleasure…and driving her past what she thought she could take."

Her mouth went dry even as the bones melted right out of her spine. Her arms dropped.

"Lie back, little contractor." With big hands, he flattened her onto her back. Her gown was still on, and the slight covering…helped…as she stared up at him. He looped the leather belt through the spindles of her metal scrollwork headboard and through the bandana rope between her wrists—then fastened the buckle. When he pulled her down in the bed, her arms were pulled up above her head.

"You d-did that bondage thing awfully easily," she whispered. "Like you've done this before."

Smiling at her, he took a couple of condoms from his wallet and tossed them on the bedside table. "I already knew I preferred being in charge in the bedroom, and when Atticus took me to a BDSM club for my college graduation present, I felt as if I'd found a home."

He'd probably graduated around twenty-two, and she'd guess he was in his low- to mid-thirties. "You've been a Dom well over a decade?"

"Yep." He took off his heavy flannel shirt and dropped it onto a chair. The light in the room was brighter this time, giving her a fine view of his muscular chest. A dusting of curly chest hair over his pectorals tapered into a narrow line down his abdomen to his jeans. The scar below his left ribs had lightened to pale pink. Older scars decorated his torso: small marks formed a scatter pattern, a long thin scar sliced up his right side. The evidence showed he'd had a rough life—but he'd survived.

The silvery chain around his neck held military dog tags.

"You weren't wearing dog tags before, were you?" she asked.

"Nah. I don't usually." He gave her a rueful smile as he pulled the chain off and tossed it on his shirt. "But if I'm missing the Teams, I sometimes wear them for a day."

Despite his light tone, she could hear the thread of grief. He had the kind of heart that cared deeply. "Memories can be comforting. When I miss Gramma, I'll bake her favorite recipes—even though they're so high fat and sugar that one bite invites a heart attack."

Sawyer's smile turned real. "Let me know when you're baking. I'll throw myself in front of you and take the hit."

She snorted. "You're a brave man, Ware."

"Yep, that's me." When he unbuttoned his jeans button, anticipation flooded through her like the waters of a rushing creek.

But then he sat back down on the bed.

She frowned. "Your jeans?"

"Later." His smile was slow, the blue in his eyes darkening. "I want you bare for me." Gradually, he drew up the hem of her nightgown to reveal her legs. Her pussy. Her breasts. He stopped, leaving the material bunched at the base of her throat.

Exposing all of her body.

She could feel every slight breeze across her overly heated skin. Her nipples were achingly tight, and she was damp between her legs. She realized she was pulling on the restraints around her wrists.

Sawyer simply watched with a faint smile.

OH, YEAH. SAWYER'S cock was straining forward so hard, his jeans zipper would probably leave an imprint.

"You're as beautiful as I remembered." Slowly, he stroked his fingertips down her restrained left arm, across her collarbone, and down. Down to where the golden tan on her shoulders and arms faded to a luscious creamy white over her breasts.

Those perky breasts. Her pectoral muscles, built up from construction work, made her breasts sit high on her chest. The nipples were small and as tight as raspberries. He stroked down her side, feeling the ribs under the female padding, and flattened his hand over her slightly softer abdomen. "Breathe, pet."

Her eyes seemed even greener as she watched him, and a small crease between her brows proclaimed her worry. Flushed cheeks, parted lips, jutting nipples. She was nicely aroused.

"Sawyer." She swallowed. "What are you doing?"

As in…why wasn't he getting down to business? He had to remember she hadn't been with a Dom before.

"I will do whatever I want, Mallory." He cupped one breast, felt her jolt, and reminded her, "Because there isn't anything you can do to stop me."

She instinctively yanked at her wrist restraints, and even in the dim light, he could see her pupils dilate.

Was there anything more fun than seasoning a stew of arousal with a sprinkle of anxiety? Maybe he wasn't a master of the kitchen, but with little subbies, he knew his way around. He moved toward the foot of the bed. "Spread your legs for me, pet."

Even when a woman was excited and wanting more, something instinctual must keep her from wanting to part her legs.

Mallory's legs separated slowly, and he knelt between them, running his hands over her shapely thighs. Leaning forward, he rubbed his stubbled chin over her peaked nipples.

She gasped, and he heard the scrape of the belt on the headboard as she pulled on the restraints.

Hmm. Did the tugging mean she liked abrasion or hated it? He had the time and opportunity right now to find out. He slid his tongue around one nipple and the other.

Another gasp. Another quiet scrape as she tried to lower her arms.

That sounded positive. Testing further, Sawyer licked and sucked, teasing slowly, occasionally scraping with his day's growth of stubble. Fuck, he liked her breasts; he could play like this forever. Although his throbbing cock was getting painful.

Her breathing sped up, and her hips were giving tiny twitches of excitement. He'd call her response a green light. What about pain? Carefully, he sucked lightly on one nipple and then used his teeth.

A light bite got a gasp and wiggle. *Green.*

But when he continued, biting enough to cause more pain, her entire body went rigid, and she made a soft sound of protest.

There was his answer. He stopped and laved the tormented little nub in apology. Now he knew she wasn't a masochist. She didn't mind a tiny edge of pain; however, he'd have to keep it light. He could work with this—would enjoy it, in fact. Hurting a woman, no matter how much the submissive wanted pain, brought uncomfortable memories of the abuse his mother had endured.

Slowly, he teased Mallory's other breast, feeling it swell as he licked, sucked, and used his teeth very, very lightly. Just enough to have her arching for more. Moving down her torso, he nibbled her belly, nipped and nuzzled each crease between hip and thigh.

A slow inhalation brought him her light musky scent.

Her breathing was fast and shallow. Perfect. Under his cheek, her inner thigh was toasty warm. When he looked up, her eyes were closed, and her face was nicely flushed.

Forming his tongue into a small point, he flicked in a circle around her clit, tapping and rubbing everywhere except on top.

Her low moan was its own reward.

For a moment, he used his teeth on her inner labia, pulling and running his tongue over the pinned hot flesh.

She tried to raise her hips.

Balancing on his left elbow, he slid his right middle finger inside her entrance. She moaned again as her cunt clamped down on him. As he slid his finger in farther, his cock jerked as if to remind him it was designed for that little chore.

No, he wanted her in a fever of anticipation first. In fact, he wanted to watch her come. Unable to resist, he bent and swirled his tongue around the little pearl standing out so nicely and then sat back on his knees. After increasing to two fingers in her cunt, he parted her labia, pulling everything back to expose her clitoris.

Pink and swollen and glistening.

After slicking his fingers in her wetness, he rubbed one side of her clit and the other, studying her responses. Just...enjoying himself.

The hood above the clit was extremely responsive. Rubbing the sides made the nub engorge even more. Slow vaginal penetration tightened everything. *Oh yeah.*

Her breathing became shallower. Her legs quivered. Her core tightened around his fingers.

Not yet, baby. He slowed and lightened his touch.

ARGH, HE WAS going to kill her. She was so close to coming that every penetration of his fingers spiraled everything higher and higher. But he was moving so *slow*. His fingers would press inside and gradually withdraw. With his other hand, he drew one fingertip in leisurely circles around her clit, and the rigid nub ached with need.

She rolled her head back and forth, straining her hips upward.

He made an amused sound.

With an effort, she opened her eyes to see him comfortably kneeling between her legs and...playing. He alternated between watching her pussy and studying her face. As he met her gaze, his dark blue eyes were alight with pleasure. Rather than hurrying to get her off so he could take his turn, this...Dom...was deliberately teasing her.

She tried to reach down and do *something*, but she couldn't move, and the realization he could continue, could do whatever he wanted, sent an urgent ripple through her.

When his finger touched right on top of her clit, the feeling was so exquisite her eyes closed.

He chuckled.

A second later, she felt him move and his tongue, his incredibly hot, wet tongue slid in circles around her clit, rubbing expertly.

Oh, mother of cats.

When his impaling fingers began to thrust faster, her core clenched around him, and she coiled, spring-tight, teetering at the edge.

"That's it, baby," he murmured. As he held her firmly open, his lips closed around her clit, and his tongue ruthlessly rubbed right on the top.

Her center squeezed his fingers as the pressure grew and grew to a glorious peak—then the landslide broke free, sending heart-stopping pleasure roaring through her, increasing with each rippling spasm until the unstoppable waves of pure sensation and the roar of her pulse drowned out all else.

His tongue moved over her, bringing her down gently, drawing the climax out. Just as she began to relax, he suddenly sucked on her clit, hard and fierce, and with a helpless moan, she went over again.

Laughing, he moved off the bed.

With her heart still hammering like a nail gun, she managed to turn her head and watch him finish stripping and don a condom.

Then he was between her legs again. She felt his forearm beside her head, his legs between hers, his cock at her entrance. Closing her eyes, she waited for the wonderful feel of him.

"Look at me, Mallory," he said in a smoky-smooth voice.

Her eyelids lifted, and she tilted her head to look at him.

"Your hands are still tied to the headboard, pet." His lips curved up slightly. "Seems like all you can do is take me. Feel me as I fill you with my cock." His clear blue eyes met hers, pierced her as his shaft entered her, slowly, ruthlessly stretching her as he slid deeper and deeper. His gaze kept her trapped, enforcing the knowledge of her helplessness.

When he was completely in, he held there, and all she could do was stare up at him as her insides throbbed around his heavy cock.

"Yeah, there's the look I wanted," he said softly. With his hard hand under her chin, he tilted her head farther so he could take her lips.

She'd never felt so defenseless in her life. Never felt so possessed.

Even without him moving, with just the knowledge of his control over everything, her arousal ignited again until she shuddered with need.

He knew. When he lifted his head, he was smiling slightly. Slowly, he began to push in, pulling out slowly, pressing in faster, and rotating his hips to ensure his cock rubbed against every part of her. With each stroke, his pelvis rubbed over her exquisitely sensitive clit, sending more heat lancing through her system.

AS SAWYER WITHDREW, the soft lips of Mallory's pussy tried to hold onto his dick. Fuck, she felt good. He pressed back in, feeling the hot satin close around him, slick and tight as she grew closer to coming. This time, he'd be inside her when she came.

Buckle down, Ware. Maintaining his control, he felt the pressure build up at the base of his spine until he could swear he would explode.

Worth it, though.

Mallory was giving tiny sexy moans with each stroke, and her hard little nipples were delightful where they rubbed over his chest. If her hands were free, she'd be digging ruts into his shoulders.

Smiling, he levered himself up far enough to slide his fingers over her clit.

With a high, clear tone, she climaxed, her cunt clamping down on him like a convulsing fist.

Fuck, yeah. As he lost the reins and hammered into her, heat shot from his balls to his shaft and out in ferocious, mind-blowing spasms. The pleasure was so intense, he groaned as he slid a hand under her ass to pull her even closer.

Even as her core squeezed him dry, she rubbed her cheek against his shoulder. Incredibly sexy and staggeringly sweet.

Pulling in hard breaths, he lowered his head to kiss her silky hair and nuzzle her temple.

Eventually, when he could move again, he eased out, feeling a regret at losing the warmth of her body. Of her.

After disposing of the condom, he sat beside her on the bed and undid the wrist restraints.

As he rubbed the dents out of her wrists, she laughed and showed him where her fingernails had dug into her palms. "It's just as well you had my hands out of the way, or I might have scratched you."

His dick gave a throb of anticipation. "Huh. Next time, I'll leave your hands free—and tie your legs apart."

The wide-eyed look she gave him was enchanting.

Laughing, he reached out and snagged the phone. "Call your friend and tell her you survived."

"Survived? That would be a lie—I'm a *wreck*." With a huffed laugh, she took the phone.

Grinning, he headed out to the kitchen to get ice for her ankle.

THE NEXT MORNING, while Mallory showered, Sawyer tossed the dog carrier in his pickup and set Achilles down in the grass.

Achilles did his duty, squatting the minute he'd been put down.

"Good job, buddy."

Sawyer jammed his hands in his pockets and looked away from the house, trying not to think of Mallory naked and in the shower. He frowned. Everything about her was too damned tempting. Waking up with her in his arms had felt right. Comfortable.

And dammit, he couldn't afford to get comfortable with her. Thank fuck he'd made it clear before they started that this was a no-relationship deal.

Too unsettled to go back in, Sawyer walked with Achilles around the house. In front of the porch, a rose bush provided a green backdrop to bright yellow chrysanthemums. A small lawn led to a sandy area where chairs surrounded a fire pit.

Continuing, Sawyer followed Achilles down a small path to a clearing concealed by the tall shrubs. The grass there was clipped as short as a putting green without any holes. Not for golf, apparently. A garden pond curved around one side of the perfect circle. Near the water, purple sage grew at the base of a female statue. Breathing in, Sawyer could feel the tranquility.

Much like the peace he felt in Mallory's presence.

Yeah, well, don't think that way. Peace wasn't in his future. Not anytime soon. He had to keep his focus, to be free to move at a moment's notice. He damn well had to keep civilians out of the fire zone.

Trouble was, considering what he'd just spent the entire night doing, he had no self-control when around Mallory. He needed to stay away from her. Far fucking away.

With a scowl, Sawyer turned around. "Let's see what's in the back, pup."

The south side of the house faced away from the road and held a huge garden surrounded by two four-foot fences. Some sort of cover crop—winter rye, maybe—was sprouting in several of the raised beds. A few plants were frost-burned from the early freeze. Hoops covered one bed, and he could see lettuces and spinach through the clear plastic.

Nostalgia hit with a swift ache. Mom had tended a garden very like this one.

"C'mon, Achilles."

The sunroom was in the back and, as he'd thought, had a hell of a view of the gurgling creek. As he and Achilles reached the north slope facing the road, a car climbed the drive. Picking up the pup, Sawyer went to see who'd arrived.

A petite woman with short black hair stepped out of the SUV and headed toward the house.

Mallory opened the front door and maneuvered out onto the porch. She was doing better with the crutches. "Hey, Kallie." She shook her head. "In the clinic, Sunny warned me she was going to call you and Becca."

"She did. Nice crutches." Kallie frowned. "How busted up are you?"

"Not busted." Mallory leaned on a post as her friend trotted up the steps. "I tripped on my own two feet and twisted my ankle."

Kallie gave the little contractor a hug. "Sunny'd planned to swing by, but Doc called her in early. She was worried you'd be here alone and need something."

Mallory pointed to Sawyer's truck. "I had help. Sawyer's around somewhere with his huge dog."

Taking the cue, Sawyer came around the porch to the steps. "Morning."

Seeing the pup in his arm, Kallie grinned. "*Huge* dog?"

"Well, he has a huge name," Mallory said. "Meet Achilles and his owner, Sawyer Ware."

When the brunette noticed Sawyer's half-buttoned flannel shirt, her grin faded. "Good morning."

"Sawyer, this is Kallie Masterson Hunt. She and her cousins own the Wilderness Guides over there." Mallory waved at the oversized house across the valley. "She's married to Jake Hunt who runs Serenity Lodge with his brother."

He nodded. "Good to meet you."

Kallie Hunt's black gaze held a fair amount of suspicion. Undoubtedly, his reputation had preceded him...and here he was, having obviously spent the night.

Of course, she might simply be pissed off he'd sucked her cousin into participating in a street fight.

After giving Kallie a quizzical look, Mallory turned to Sawyer. Her smile was warm. Sweet. "I made you some coffee. If you're ready, I can—"

"No. Thank you." He kept his voice level. Reasonable. Firm. And detached. "Since you've got help here, I need to get back to work."

Dammit, he hated the way her smile disappeared. Nonetheless, he'd warned her last night of the rules of engagement. "Next time, *drive* to the mailbox. Don't walk. I won't always be around to pick you up."

"I understand." Her words—and her expression—held an acceptance he didn't deserve.

It would've been easier on him if she'd yelled at him. Instead, his chest felt like he'd caught a .45 slug.

As SAWYER DROVE away with Achilles on his lap, Mallory stared after him.

Gone.

She'd been discarded again, only this time was worse. And she couldn't be angry. He'd been clear he didn't want any relationship or involvement. She just hadn't realized he'd return to being cold. His distance...hurt.

Kallie set a hand on her shoulder. "You okay?"

No. Really not. "My ankle's a bit sore." Pulling her gaze from the lane, she sucked in a stabilizing breath. Anchoring herself in the bright morning, she let the heartache move through her and away, like a bobbing twig in a swift-flowing stream. "Want some breakfast?"

"Actually, I brought you some. Becca sent cinnamon rolls with orders for you to indulge in some sugar and white flour."

Mallory laughed. "The boss has spoken." She took a hand from her crutch and waved toward the door. "Let's eat."

Kallie shook her head. "Can't. I have a corporate group to guide up to the lakes for team-building exercises. I just ran over to make sure you were all right and to bring the rolls." She held up the bag. "Let me put these on your table."

Mallory nodded and watched her friend disappear inside.

When Kallie returned, she hesitated. "Shut me down if I'm out of line, but did you know Sawyer spent time in the prison here?"

"I knew."

"He seemed awfully at home."

Like he'd spent the night in her bed? Mallory felt her cheeks heat. "He went out of his way to get me to the doctor and spent the night to be sure I was safe. He was being a good neighbor." Which was all he wanted to be.

The...the *dumbass.*

"Oh. Well." Unlike Becca, Kallie wasn't the type to push for more. She put her arm around Mallory. "I'm sorry. I know he's Atticus's brother and probably a nice guy, and you're an adult. I'm just in a grumpy mood, I guess."

Mallory narrowed her eyes. Although Kallie's aura was difficult to see in the bright morning light, an unhappy darkness tinted the edges. "What happened?" Mallory asked softly.

"Oh, Mal. Someone broke into Pottery and Pages last night and destroyed a bunch of Mrs. Reed's glassware. Probably because there wasn't any money in the cash register."

Mallory swayed, feeling as if a rafter had fallen on her. "Oh, no."

"I'm so angry—and wishing all the creeps had left when the prison closed. I didn't mean to be judgmental about your guy."

Not my guy. The knowledge hurt.

Kallie's gaze went across the valley. "This was such a safe place to grow up. People trusted each other. And now…"

Now there were drugs, graffiti, assaults, and robberies. "I know. I miss what we had, too." Mallory's memories went back almost as far as Kallie's. At eleven, she'd started spending summers in Bear Flat and had gone to school here for her high school junior and senior years. "But Sawyer truly is an honorable man."

"Don't tell me—he's got a pretty aura?"

"He does. The colors show he's strong, loyal, and brave. He's not as sociable as your Jake—no orange—but otherwise, their auras are much alike." She wouldn't mention Sawyer's black streaks of pain.

Kallie snorted. "You know I don't hold with new-agey stuff."

Mallory just smiled.

"Okay, so I've never seen you wrong about a person. He might be the first, you know."

"You're as stubborn as Wyatt. Maybe even Morgan."

Kallie laughed. "Now you're just being mean. Fine, Sawyer's a nice guy—and I won't be grumpy anymore." Back to her usual even temper, she gave Mallory a hug and trotted down the steps to her SUV.

As Mallory watched Kallie drive away, she sighed and turned to go into her quiet, lonely house.

Chapter Thirteen

H AVING LEFT HIS pickup in the ClaimJumper Tavern's parking lot, Sawyer had dressed in stylish prowling colors—black on black—and patrolled the town's back alleys.

It was quiet, which wasn't surprising for a chilly Wednesday night near the end of October. Tourist season was over, although the town celebrated Halloween as if still inundated with visitors. Along the boardwalk were dangling skeletons and ghosts, spider webs and ravens, all illuminated by orange lights along the roof. Despite the recent break-in, Pottery and Pages had hosted a pumpkin-carving contest with the winning entries displayed in store windows.

The weekly newspaper had listed their choices for best-decorated houses, from "Seriously Scary" down to "Safe for pre-schoolers." Unable to resist, Sawyer had driven by the "Seriously Scary" choices on his way in tonight. *Good shit.*

Bear Flat was a hell of a little town.

As Sawyer patrolled the south alley, which ran parallel to Main Street, he checked each business. Robbers typically used back doors and were rarely as quiet as they'd hoped. He slowed to listen. A lone car drove down Main. A woman's laughter came from an apartment over a business.

Country-western music drifted from the ClaimJumper as he went past.

Once he reached the end of this alley, he'd check the cross-alley and return to the tavern for his vehicle. Almost done, thank fuck.

His boots felt as if they were loaded with lead and dragging in the dirt. He'd been up late every night, either observing the Aryan Hammers' house or patrolling the town. By himself.

In the SEALs, someone had always had his six. In Bear Flat, he was on his own. If shit hit the fan, Atticus would try to help. Unfortunately, his brother was the law, and Sawyer's tactics weren't exactly legal. Might even be called something insulting like *vigilantism*.

But he wasn't out for revenge or justice after the fact. He wanted to catch the bad guys in the act and leave them for the law—like a citizen's arrest. If a few heads or bones got busted during said citizen's arrest, well...*oops*.

Unfortunately, his plan had a few flaws—like he couldn't stay awake every night. He had work to do on his property and a four-legged ball of energy to care for.

Yeah, he was tired.

And irritable, too. His night with Mallory over a week ago had created a craving for...for what?

He shook his head and checked another door.

For more than sex. Finding someone to fuck wasn't difficult, but he wanted more than just sex. With Mallory, he'd found it—warmth, concern, friendship, affection.

Yeah, she was someone special. Last week, he'd hiked up to a remote mountain lake. The only sounds had been the slough of the wind in the pines. Lying on the sunny bank, he'd breathed in the clean air...and the peace.

Being in Mallory's presence, he felt that same sense of tranquility.

Last week for the final days of remodeling, he'd kept their interactions short and impersonal. Staying businesslike hadn't been easy when all he wanted to do was pull her up to his loft bedroom and take her. Slowly and thoroughly. And then sleep with her in his arms.

On Friday, he'd given her the final construction payment with his thanks.

Dammit, he missed her. Missed listening to her banter with her crew, teach the Booth brothers fine carpentry—something the young men could do during the winters—and play with Achilles.

It was good she was gone and the temptation was removed.

Speaking of temptation, get your head in the game, Ware.

Silently, Sawyer approached the T-intersection where this alley ran into another. From the shadows, he checked around the corner. Nothing in sight to the left or right. Straight ahead was the rear of the professional building that housed the local law and CPA firms, counseling offices, and realty office. He crossed to give the doors a quick check. All good.

A change in the light caught his attention.

Backlit by the streetlight on Main, two men moved into the alley.

Well, well, well.

All his muscles tensed. Knowing the men's eyes required a few seconds to adjust to the lack of light, Sawyer crouched in the shadows behind a small dumpster.

One man was Sawyer's height and moved like an athlete. Light glinted off his shaved scalp. The other was average height and weight with short, light-colored hair. They might be locals simply taking a short cut, but their wary bearing was suspicious.

Considering their coloring and build, he doubted they were in the Mexican Mafia's offshoot gang. With luck, he had a couple of Aryan Hammers.

As Average Man watched the alley with a black box in his hand, Skinhead was messing with the back door to the veterinary office— the same office where Achilles had received his shots not quite two weeks before.

Veterinarians performed surgery and would have narcotics on the premises. Sawyer frowned. He'd bet the black box was a wireless jammer. Although the medical clinic had an excellent security system, a veterinarian might not be as careful.

When Skinhead succeeded in opening the door, no alarm went off.

Sawyer sighed. Yep, it was a crap security system. Idiot veterinarian. The guy probably didn't have a heavy-duty lockup for controlled substances, either.

The two burglars disappeared into the building without leaving a guard on the exit. Tension crept into Sawyer's body. Here was a chance to get rid of a couple more Hammers.

And, as any operator knew, action always held the possibility things would go wrong. Someone might be killed. Adrenaline flowed into his veins, drying his mouth and increasing his heart rate.

After yanking on a black ski mask and black latex gloves, Sawyer stole down the alleyway and waited outside the back door. He wasn't about to enter a building where a burglary was taking place. One prison tour was enough.

A while later—felt like the slow bastards had taken forever—the men walked out and past him before looking around. Definitely incompetent.

Sawyer reached out and slammed their heads together, clocked one in the face then the other. While they were still stunned, he got them zip tied, wrists and ankles, like rodeo calves. In the process, he thumped one asshole against the blacktop for moving too much and the other for cursing too loudly.

Now silent, they glared at him. What with his oversized hoodie and balaclava, he figured they wouldn't see much. Without speaking, he tossed one gangbanger into the building, and heaved in the other.

Using one of his throwaway cell phones, he dialed the Bear Flat police station and secured his vocal changer's padded cup over the phone mic. When the station answered, he spoke into the voice changer box. "Two men broke into the veterinary office on Gold Dust Avenue. They're still inside. Better hurry."

After removing the cup, he smashed the phone under his boot and tossed the pieces into the dumpster.

Catching a movement to the right, he spun.

A man stood in the entrance to the alley. He was about six-four and bulky with muscle. With the backlighting, Sawyer couldn't make out his features. His scalp was shiny. Shaved. Probably the getaway driver wanted to see what was taking the others so long.

From the man's size, Sawyer wondered if this was Animal, cousin of the convict Atticus had killed. He was one of the bastards who'd tried to kill Att with a tire iron.

Eyeing the distance to the Aryan Hammer's head honcho, Sawyer gave a frustrated growl. He couldn't catch the bastard before the cops arrived, and even if he could, the asshole hadn't—technically—done anything.

The first notes of a police siren sounded out on Main.

The gangster jolted, backed out onto Main Street—and bumped into an elderly woman. Without a second thought, the bastard backhanded her and knocked her hard into the wall.

With a pained cry, she crumpled.

The Hammer took off running.

Goddamn bastard. Jesus, how bad was the old lady hurt?

Seething, Sawyer ran toward her—and skidded to a stop when a police car pulled up at the alley entrance.

As the cops jumped out, Sawyer dodged back into the alley behind the ClaimJumper. After ripping off his ski mask, gloves, and black sweatshirt, he bundled everything into a thin waterproof bag. At the bushes surrounding the ClaimJumper parking lot, he dropped the bag into the hole he'd dug there weeks ago. A swipe shoved the bark mulch in place.

In a white Guns N' Roses T-shirt and jeans, he crossed the parking lot. Sticking to the shadows near the taller vehicles, he reached his pickup without being seen. He could feel his hands shake with his anger. Animal had hit the woman as if she were an annoying fly. Not giving a damn. Not caring she was a fragile, elderly lady.

Sawyer leaned on the hood of his truck and slowed his breathing. The cops would take care of the woman. There was nothing he could have done.

Guilt tangled up inside him anyway.

But dammit, he was doing everything he could to drive the Aryan Hammers out of Bear Flat, and his actions were having an effect. If the cops arrested the two Hammers tonight, the gang would be reduced to about four members. Surely they'd consider Bear Flat a losing proposition and return to Los Angeles. His mission was almost accomplished.

He shook his head, thinking of the old woman. *God, don't let anyone else get hurt.*

After a minute, he realized he was swaying in time with the country music coming from the old brick tavern. With adrenaline still zinging through his veins, the happy hum of conversation and laughter drew him like iron to a magnet. Whether anyone would talk with an ex-con or not, at least he'd be around people.

He headed for the front door.

Inside, the noise and heat of the crowded room reminded him of the prison yard in deep summer. Seemed pretty appropriate to hear Johnny Cash singing "Folsom Prison Blues".

Yeah, Johnny, I'd like to keep from being locked up again, too.

Even on a Wednesday night, the place was two-thirds full with loggers, ranchers, locals, and a scattering of tourists. As usual, as he crossed the room, he collected several unwelcoming stares.

Behind the bar, Gustaf saw him and picked up a glass. His bushy gray eyebrows lifted in inquiry as he touched the Budweiser tap.

Although the old Swede's obsession with Johnny Cash was exasperating, he apparently also had a hell of memory.

"Thanks, no." Alcohol and exhaustion—Sawyer fucking knew better. "How about a Coke?"

After paying for the soft drink, he turned to survey the room. Through the front window, colored strobe lights reflected off the stores across the street. The rest of the cavalry had arrived in the alley.

He hoped the police appreciated their zip-tied presents…and never figured out where they came from. His shoulders tensed. Att would be pissed off if he knew Sawyer was involved.

Too bad. Sawyer'd be pissed off if his brother got killed by the bastards.

Hell, they'd already busted Att's ribs.

Damn, the Ware brothers were a mess. What with their asshole stepfather, rodeo events, and the military, he and Att'd accumulated enough damage to look like they'd rolled in barbed wire. Hector didn't lag far behind.

Sawyer shook his head. It was a wonder Mallory hadn't fled when she'd seen his scarred-up body. Nonetheless, although she didn't like violence, she didn't flee from it either. He smiled, thinking of how she'd wielded the broom without flinching.

In battles and at the construction site, the woman simply took on what was set in front of her—honestly, efficiently, and competently. Yet, she was so fucking serene. Her hands created beauty, not death. She filled her home with flowers, grew vegetables, and had puppy chow in case of strays.

In the sandbox, some soldiers frantically lived as if any second might be their last. Mallory also lived in the moment, but peacefully and with joy. He'd watched the delighted way she greeted...everything...from wayward puppies to an incoming storm. He'd never met anyone more present.

More loving.

Nonetheless, his feelings didn't matter. Nothing had changed. He needed to stay away from her.

With a sigh, he drank his Coke, watched the patrol car lights' reflections, and listened to the country-western music.

As exhaustion slowly replaced adrenaline, he knew he was done for the night. Achilles would be up early, raring to go.

Dammit, he couldn't patrol the town every night, hoping to catch an Aryan Hammer up to no good. They were smart enough to vary their routines—or even stay in for a night.

Time to invest in some technology. He huffed a laugh, thinking of Bart Holder. The hardware store owner probably didn't carry tracking devices.

It seemed like a trip to San Francisco would be in his near future. He smiled. Not a bad idea, actually. Achilles'd love a road trip, and the city would widen the pup's horizons. Maybe Mallory would like to join them?

Dumbass. No, Ware.

A man entered the bar, looked around, and headed straight toward Sawyer.

Morgan Masterson. Not as massive as his cop brother, the leanly muscled wilderness guide was closer to Sawyer's size, although cowboy boots and a black Stetson added inches. He had gray eyes in a weather-roughened face, and a full mustache down the sides of his mouth to his jawline. Might be in his early thirties. Age was tough to judge with outdoorsmen.

Masterson held out his hand. "Ware. I hoped you'd be here.

Even swung by your spread on the way here."

"Is there a problem? Fencing down somewhere?" The north fence ran between his property and Masterson's—and was the one fence on his place in fair shape.

"Nah." Handshaking over, Morgan grinned. "I saw the *attack* pup you got. Nice breed. You planning to run some cattle to keep him busy?"

"Maybe a few. Gotta say, getting a dog wasn't in my plans. I found him under the porch."

Morgan's face darkened. "Puppies usually get eaten after getting dumped."

"So Mallory said." And it'd bothered Sawyer. Now…knowing Achilles…the thought fucking stabbed into his chest. "Only an asshole would abandon a puppy."

"Watch it, Ware. Getting all soft will screw with your dangerous convict rep."

Sawyer scowled at Morgan's grin. "Did you have a reason to see me—or are you just here for general harassment?"

"I had a reason, even aside from thanking you for the street fight. Hell of a lot of fun." Morgan leaned against the bar. "I'm looking for help. Your brother says you're better with horses than he is—and he's damn good."

Sawyer considered. "I'd call it about even. Our kid brother is the best of us."

"So I hear." Obviously deliberating, Morgan stroked his mustache with his thumb and forefinger. "I've got a problem. I'm taking some fishermen into the backcountry for a week, starting Monday. My brother's off volunteering his ass in Africa. Kallie's going on vacation with her husband. Normally, Virgil would pitch in to tend the stock, but the police department is bogged down with the crap going on in town."

Att was overworked as well. If Sawyer could reduce the Aryan Hammer population, the cops might catch a break. "And?"

Gustaf shoved a glass of beer across the bar to Morgan, who nodded his thanks before looking back at Sawyer. "Any chance I could hire you to look after the horses and keep an eye on the cattle?"

Sawyer blinked. Despite the build-up, he hadn't seen the request coming. The answer was easy. Helping out was what neighbors did. "Sure."

Morgan gave a satisfied nod. "We usually pay—"

"Nah. I figure, if anything, I owe you for the work you've done on our shared fencing. Have you seen the other three sides of my fences?"

Morgan winced. "Yeah, I noticed."

"You know, when I was little, mending fence annoyed the hell out of me." Sawyer shifted his weight and confronted the elephant in the room. "After a year in prison, fixing fences feels like the sweetest work I've ever tackled."

After a second, Morgan chuckled. "Bet it does."

"When can I meet the stock and get a rundown of problems?"

"How about tomorrow morning?"

"Around eight?"

Morgan nodded. "I'll be in the barn."

As Masterson turned to pick up his beer, Sawyer shook his head. Bonding during a street fight. Who knew?

ABOUT THE ONLY time Mallory regretted living so far in the country was near Samhain. When she and her mother had lived in San Francisco, they'd elaborately decorate their tiny house for the numerous Halloween trick-or-treaters. Here, no one would see the decorations.

Still, she had her own rituals and decorations to mark the changing of the seasons, even if she was the only one to enjoy them.

After she finished attaching her straw man to the garden fence, she set a garland of rosemary on its head. Made of straw and withered plants, the King of Winter would rule over her garden until Beltane.

At the sound of a vehicle coming up the drive, Mallory rose to her feet.

A minute later, Becca parked and slid out of her car.

"Becca!" Mallory waved her friend over to the garden. "You came to visit without bringing Ansel?"

"He and his daddy are painting one of the cabins."

Wouldn't that be a sight? Mallory snickered. "I'm sure Ansel will be a wonderful helper. Poor Logan." Ansel was a little over a year old and born bossy. And adorable. His daddy was so terrifying even loggers gave him a wide berth—but Logan was pure putty in his little son's hands.

Clad in jeans, a chemise, and a half-buttoned flannel shirt, Becca let herself through one garden gate and the other. As Aslan left his small patch of sun to inspect the visitor, she bent to stroke his golden fur. "You know, I've never asked why you have two fences around your garden."

"For the deer." Mallory knelt beside the folded-up plastic of the hoop row cover. Despite the freezing nights, her salad greens looked perky. "To keep deer out, it takes either a nine-foot fence or two shorter fences. They can't judge distance well and won't jump if they might get caught in the middle."

"Huh. Very sneaky...and good to know if I ever want to try growing roses again." Becca settled on the old wooden bench, leaned against the fence, and tilted her face up to the blue sky. "It's nice to have sun."

After a moment of fraught consideration, Aslan condescended to settle in her lap where petting could proceed.

"The sun feels good." Mallory harvested romaine and spinach for her evening salad, picked up her basket, and moved down the raised bed. "Want some Brussels sprouts?"

"Sure, I'll take a handful, but not more. Logan considers them disgusting mini-cabbages."

Mallory snapped off a tiny green ball and laughed. "What a perfect description."

"Don't encourage him, Mal. He'd happily ban all vegetables from the kitchen." Smile fading, Becca gave her a careful look. "Are you ready to talk about the scene you did with Sawyer Ware? Kallie said she saw him here the next morning, and he..."

Ah, friends. Mallory'd known this time would come. With Serena and Missy gone to San Francisco, Kallie, Sunny, Gin, and Becca were gradually becoming good friends. And good friends shared. "I'm sorry. I should have called you last week, but I wasn't sure what to say. Wasn't ready to talk about it."

Becca's face darkened. "Was it a bad scene?"

"It was wonderful." Mallory picked more sprouts. "*He* was wonderful, Becca. And that's the problem." She sighed, thinking of his resonant voice, his powerful hands, and his generosity in bed. "He told me quite honestly—beforehand—he doesn't want a relationship. However, during sex? He was amazing."

"Oh." Becca slumped back against the post. "Well, there's a complication. You know, it would be easier if I could hate the man."

Mallory grinned. Her friend was quite as protective as her husband. "I know. Having him as a neighbor is awkward." She had to drive past his place every day. If she was up late, she'd hear him leaving and couldn't help wondering who the lucky woman was. If she sat on her front porch, she saw him working on his fences or playing with Achilles. She couldn't keep from looking, and her heart would lift…then ache.

Becca scowled. "Want Logan to beat him up anyway?"

Mallory said gently, "A person has the right to decide what he wants—or doesn't want—from a relationship. He was honest and upfront. I'm sad he doesn't want more, but I can't fault his character."

"Fine." Pouting slightly, Becca took a minute to stroke Aslan into low purrs. "I guess the next question is if you enjoyed the BDSM portion of your evening. Since you needed a check-in, I'm assuming bondage and maybe some pain? Or did you like only the Sawyer and sex part?"

"You know, it's scary to understand what you're asking." Feeling her cheeks heat, Mallory moved to the end of the garden bed to pull a few beets. "Your guess is right, and I did enjoy it all. I trusted him to take care of me, and he did. The BDSM part fulfilled a part of me I hadn't realized was needing something. I don't know if that makes sense."

"Oh, it totally does." Becca smiled. "I always thought sex was overrated until I met Logan, and he went all Dom in bed."

All Dom. Like the way Sawyer's voice had taken on an edge of steely authority. Mallory sighed.

"All right, then." Becca's gaze met Mallory's. "Wasn't this the weekend you're going to San Francisco to see your friends?"

Mallory nodded.

"While you're there, do you want to visit a BDSM club? Logan and I can get you a guest pass into Dark Haven."

Pulse quickening, Mallory considered. She'd heard of Dark Haven. Had even met a couple of the members who'd attended the Mastersons' Fourth of July parties. "Going by myself sounds a little dangerous."

"I wouldn't recommend it normally, but we'll ask Xavier to watch out for you."

"I wouldn't have to…do…anything?"

"No." Becca smiled slightly. "It's good to see the various kinks and power dynamics. Since they're having a Halloween theme night, your costume should be easy. And you'll get an idea of whether it's Sawyer who attracts you or merely the fact he's a Dom."

Go to a BDSM club. Serena would think she was crazy.

Mallory huffed a laugh. Serena would be *right*. "Sure. I'd love to see the place."

FRIDAY AFTERNOON, SAWYER wandered around the reception room of Demakis International Security. The receptionist, an older woman, didn't seem concerned with his restlessness. Come to think of it, a security and bodyguard business probably had plenty of uneasy clients.

While driving to San Francisco, Sawyer had recalled that Atticus had helped rescue the girlfriend of a Demakis International agent named deVries.

It was a good bet deVries would know where to find reliable, easily concealed equipment.

A shame there wasn't equipment to stop a crime before anyone got hurt. Sawyer shook his head. At least the elderly woman who'd been hurt last night was going to be all right.

At a concerned look from the receptionist, Sawyer realized his hands had closed into fists. He gave her a reassuring smile and saw her relax.

"Mr. Ware?" Two men entered the reception room. With the lethal grace of a martial artist, the one who'd spoken was a muscular six feet. In his mid-forties with black eyes and silvering black hair, he studied Sawyer for a moment before extending his hand. "I'm Simon Demakis."

The owner? *Jesus.* Sawyer shook his hand, noting the scarred knuckles of a fighter. "Good to meet you."

"DeVries," the other man said in a sandpaper-rough voice before shaking Sawyer's hand. DeVries was a couple of inches taller than Demakis, hair cut military short—like Sawyer's—and possessed a fit build and military posture.

"Atticus's brother, right?" deVries said. "You got shanked trying to keep the assholes from taking Gin?"

"Yeah. They got her anyway." He'd failed...and the prisoners had captured both women.

"You're not God, man," Demakis said. "It was six to one, and you took out two of them."

"Bad odds," deVries agreed. "You wanted to see me about getting equipment?"

"Ah, yeah." Sawyer hesitated. Talking to deVries about operations against the Aryan Hammers was one thing, discussing illegal tactics in front of the company's owner was entirely different.

From the glint in Demakis's eyes, he knew. "Let's talk in here." He led the way to...hell, his office. It was a comfortable room. The cream walls and carpet were balanced by a mahogany desk and dark leather furniture. Richly colored abstract paintings depicted the Golden Gate Bridge and San Francisco's skyline at sunset.

Rather than establishing a distance behind his desk, Demakis took a chair in a sitting area off to one side.

Mrs. Martinez entered with a coffee pot and accessories, asked

Sawyer's preferences, and served everyone before disappearing quietly.

Talk about being spoiled. Sawyer shook his head...and realized from Demakis's raised eyebrows he'd seen. "Sorry. I was thinking you're well served, Demakis."

DeVries laughed. "He's fucking spoiled, you mean. You're right."

The owner's grin showed he'd taken no offense. The laughter faded from his face. "Last time I talked with Atticus, he was pleased you were setting up as an outfitter for local guide businesses. Did your plans change?"

"Ah, no, I'm working toward that goal."

"This got anything to do with Atticus getting attacked?" deVries asked.

Didn't it just figure deVries would catch on?

When Sawyer hesitated, deVries frowned at Demakis. "You know, boss, having you here is putting a choke hold on the information."

Demakis's gaze on Sawyer was uncomfortably perceptive. "Ware, let's put the cards on the table. I'm not a cop. My company doesn't break the law. Nonetheless, if you need equipment to keep Atticus from being hurt again, I'd like to assist. If this is for revenge, I'm out."

Sawyer considered. After dealing with prisoners, submissives, and insurgents, he had a well-developed lie detector. These two were as straightforward as they came, and they could help.

"All right, it's like this..." Piece by piece, he laid it out for them. A violent gang bent on revenge. A town overwhelmed by violence. A brother and civilians in harm's way. An ex-con who couldn't act openly, but who had a shitload of experience in covert operations.

"Sounds clear enough." DeVries smiled slowly. "I wouldn't mind visiting and lending a hand. It's been a while since I had a good fight."

Sawyer gave him a hard stare. "Atticus met you because your lady had been kidnapped. She's had enough trauma in her life."

DeVries scowled.

"He has a point, Zander." Grinning, Demakis turned to Sawyer. "However, my equipment comes with a stipulation—you will call us if you get in a bind. I have friends in Bear Flat, and I don't like knowing they're at risk. Deal?"

Sawyer couldn't speak for a moment. He'd left the Teams, had no backup. These were men he could work with, could trust to have his six. "Deal."

"Good." Demakis leaned back, coffee in hand. "On another subject, Atticus also mentioned you're a Dominant in the lifestyle."

Sawyer set his jaw. His BDSM practice wasn't something he shared with others. "When did my brother turn into a gossip?"

Demakis's grin flashed. "When I asked him. I got the impression you two shared most of your hobbies." He set his cup down. "Zander and I belong to a local club and will be there tonight. Would you like a guest pass?"

The question was...unexpected. More than the offer of a backup, this was an offer of friendship. "Yeah. I would."

Chapter Fourteen

SERENA HAD THROWN a hissy fit when Mallory'd revealed her plans for the evening. *"A BDSM club? By yourself? Those people are into whips and…and whips. Have you gone stark raving bonkers?"*

But once assured that Mallory would have someone watching over her, Serena had been a wonderful help in figuring out a costume.

Dressed appropriately—she hoped—Mallory stepped out of the taxi she'd taken from Serena's place. No flashing signs. No floggers lying in the gutter. Just a huge brick building. Was this the infamous BDSM club? Only a small gold plate served to identify the place. *Dark Haven.* Looking up at the ominous black door leading into the club, she felt as if she'd shrunk to hobbit size. *"I think we might have made a mistake leaving the Shire, Pippin."*

Still, Becca and Logan had gone to some effort to get her in. *"Courage, Merry."*

She swallowed, pulled the door open, and saw only a normal-appearing reception room. *Whew.*

Behind the wide desk, a young man attired in what she'd call *faun-in-bondage* gave her a blinding smile. "Welcome to Dark Haven. Can I have your card?"

She shook her head at his extended hand. "I'm not a member."

"Oh, sweetcheeks." He looked at her woodland nymph attire. "I love your costume. It's perfect for our mythical creatures theme, but the club is a private one now. You have to join before you can come in."

Last chance to escape. Unfortunately perhaps, Becca's friend was expecting her. It would be rude to be a no-show. "Actually, someone named Xavier was to vouch for me. My name is Mallory."

"Really?" He consulted a paper on the desk. "Awesomesauce. You're cleared, but the note says you're to wait so he can take you around." He waved at the far wall. "I'll have someone let him know you're here. I'm Dixon, if you need me."

"Thank you." Relocating to the wall, Mallory stood for a minute. Having an escort was wise, yet being accompanied could be awkward. The members inside would probably be doing...intimate...things and there she'd be, attempting to converse with a stranger while her face got redder and redder.

All she wanted to do was look around; surely, she didn't need a guide for that.

A glance showed Dixon was occupied with a noisy crowd of elf lords and maidens. *Okay, then.* When a black-clad, dragon Domme walked past to enter the main clubroom, Mallory followed.

And came to a sudden halt just inside the door.

Holy cats. After sidling along the wall a couple of feet from the door, she simply stood and gawked. The huge room was decorated to look like a dark forest, with walls and pillars of green trees and a silvery moon overhead providing light. The costumes ranged from cute pixies to terrifying monsters, and the amount of clothing sure varied.

Two female fairies wore nothing more than flowery tattoos.

A Sasquatch in a full-body fur suit stomped by and, unlike the Big Foot figurines in tourist traps, this one was...ahem...anatomically correct.

The back of the room held a flower-and-leaf-wreathed bar. Spotlights lit raised wooden stages on the right and left walls. On one stage, a horned demon in black robes was flogging a young, furry-legged, shaggy-haired Pan.

Shouting drew her attention.

"I don't see what the problem is, dammit! Let me go!" A rotund drunk was purple with anger as two tall men pulled him past Mallory and out the door.

A minute later, the two escorts reappeared and stopped inside the door.

The taller man's aura was a dark, dark red, and his black eyes snapped with anger. Clad in an impeccably tailored, 1800's black suit, he wore his black hair in a long braid down his back. "He was actually going to use a whip. In his condition." His deep voice held a slight European accent.

In a modern black suit, the other man shook his head. "They know if they drink here, they can't play, so some will have a few first. You can't stop them, not unless you demand a Breathalyzer on entry and a drug test as well."

"You have no idea how tempting that is. Liars anger me."

Oh, that was the understatement of the year. She could feel fury radiating from him.

He noticed her watching, and his black gaze met hers with a punch of power. His dark brows drew together, and his face hardened as all that anger came to bear on her.

Uh-oh. She took a step away from them.

He advanced. "You're not a member. How did you get in here?"

Under his scowl, she had an overwhelming urge to scurry into a dark corner and hide. "I was—"

"Back off, Leduc. You're scaring her." To her surprise, Sawyer appeared. He put an arm around her waist and turned to get between her and the angry man.

"S-Sawyer?"

He squeezed her waist. "I know you wouldn't break the rules, pet. Can you tell Leduc how you got in?"

"One of the members, someone named Xavier, cleared me to visit." Mallory hated the way her voice shook.

"I didn't—" Leduc's gaze ran over her again more slowly. "Might you be Logan's Mallory?"

"Logan's?" Sawyer turned to look at her.

"Becca and Logan arranged for me to be allowed in here, yes."

The other man let out a laugh and slapped Leduc's shoulder. "Memory—it's the first thing to go." He turned to her. "I'm Simon, and this is Xavier, who owns Dark Haven."

The owner? *Nice, Becca. You might have mentioned that.*

Xavier was still frowning, although his aura had lightened. "Did Dixon not ask you to wait for me in the reception area?"

Uh-oh. "Yes. But…I didn't want to impose on your time." Or to be forced to talk with a stranger here.

"Independent submissives, the bane of our existence," Simon murmured.

"Isn't that the truth?" Xavier held out his hand. "In that case, welcome to Dark Haven, Mallory." Xavier's smile revealed sharp fangs, his only apparent concession to a costume. On him, the fangs were intimidating rather than looking foolish. This man could make her believe in a thousand-year-old vampire aristocracy. When she took his hand, he held it for a moment. "Unfortunately, imposition or not, I can't let a novice wander around Dark Haven without an escort."

"But there are options as to who serves as your escort." The corners of Simon's dark eyes crinkled. "I'm willing to help. Or…Sawyer, you're an experienced Dom and had the grand tour earlier. Would you care to show Mallory around?"

Arm still around her waist, Sawyer looked down at her. Today, his gaze wasn't indifferent. Today, his gaze held…affection. Amusement. And enough hunger to send heat through her, starting at her toes right up to her hair. "Little contractor, who do you want for an escort?"

She swallowed. Hadn't she told herself she would stay away from him? Not leave herself open to any more damage? And yet…and yet…she couldn't deny her own desire to be with him.

This wasn't all lust—her feelings went deep. A newly-planted sapling didn't expend energy on showy leaf growth but would extend its roots down and down to anchor itself deep in the earth.

Lust held no roots. Love…did. Oh, this wasn't good.

As Sawyer bent over her, their auras mingled in a beautiful swirl of colors. "Mallory?"

"You. If you don't mind?"

His smile was slow and unexpected. "We'll take all the time you need." He glanced at Xavier. "You good with this?"

"Yes and no." Xavier's gaze was reserved. "Return her to me when you're finished with the tour. If you decide to play, one of our staff will be nearby to monitor." A smile curved his lips slightly. "I'd prefer Logan not feel that I let him down."

"Sounds fair." Sawyer took her hand in his big warm one.

Mallory hesitated and tilted her head toward Simon. "Might I ask what mythical creature you are?"

Xavier actually laughed.

"Of course, pet." Simon had a delightful smile. "Xavier bet me that I couldn't outclass him."

Mallory frowned. Simon's contemporary black suit was lovely, however, not nearly as marvelous as Xavier's nineteenth-century attire. "And...?"

"I'm God."

JUST LISTEN TO her, Sawyer thought. Mallory's clear, melodic laughter was open and honest and fucking beautiful, and both of the Dark Haven Doms smiled in appreciation.

Dammit, he'd missed hearing her laugh—and he shouldn't have his arm around her. Regrettably, the surprise of seeing her and realizing she was frightened had drawn him right across the room. Despite his plan to stay away from her, here he was.

Here, he wanted to stay.

"Enjoy yourself, Mallory," Xavier said. "When Sawyer brings you back, I'll introduce you to my Abby."

As the two Doms walked away, Mallory whispered, "Is his Abby a church or a person?"

"His wife—a college professor. Simon is married to Rona, a hospital administrator. Both will be here later." Needing to touch her, he caressed the sweet curve of her cheek, then guided her out into the room. "I had dinner with them earlier. I think you'll like them."

As he led her past the left stage, she gasped and stopped.

To one side was a rack of edged weapons and tools, ranging from a fillet knife to a field scythe. The Top was drawing the edge of a butcher knife down a woman's bared back, creating a thin red line. Similar lines covered her skin from shoulders to ass. Edge play with an edge.

Sawyer smiled. From Mallory's appalled expression, this would never be her kink.

With an obvious effort, she pulled her gaze away. "You're a member of Dark Haven?"

"Just visiting since I'm in town." She didn't need to know what had brought him to San Francisco. "Atticus knows Simon, so Simon invited me."

"Oh. Is this place like other...uh...BDSM clubs?"

Fuck, those wide eyes were delightful. He tilted her chin up to give her a hard kiss and inhaled her clean fragrance. Could a person miss a *scent*? Face it, he'd missed everything about her. "Bigger than a lot of them. Nice layout, too."

The top floor had the two stages with seating in the center to watch the action. The far wall held a bar, which had rules about no playing after drinking.

Next to the bar was a crowded dance floor. Sawyer watched a row of unicorns doing an improvised line dance. Pony play, mythological style.

"Hmm." Mallory motioned to the tables and chairs scattered between the stages. "Can we sit so I can regroup? Right now, I feel like a prey animal."

He grinned as he realized what she meant. On a normal night, a pretty woman in a BDSM club might well feel targeted by single Doms. Tonight, though, the submissives had come as cute mythological creatures—pixies, fairies, and elves. In contrast, the Dominants were predatory monsters—goblins, werewolves, and vampires. The difference lent an edgy, ominous feel to the club atmosphere.

"Sitting sounds fine, pet."

As he seated her, she tilted her head. "You're wearing an interesting costume."

"Simon and deVries—another of Att's friends—rounded up the outfit." He was shirtless and wearing his own black boots. The dark brown, fur-covered pants—complete with a long tail—were courtesy of Simon. Thank fuck the tail wasn't so long he was tripping on it. His ears were pointy, and he had large horns spiraling back. Since he always had a dark five o'clock shadow, by shaving his upper lip, he'd achieved a nicely animalistic appearance.

"A satyr, right?" She laughed. "A lusty Greek god?"

"You did your homework, didn't you?" And she'd come as a…a what?

She was barefoot. Her just-past-butt-length green dress was loose and nearly transparent. Makeup made her big eyes even larger, and leafy vine tattoos ran up her cheeks and over her forehead. The sides of her rich chocolate brown hair were pulled up and braided with leaves and flowers. The rest of her hair was loose, hanging freely to mid-back. "Elf?"

"Close. Woodland nymph."

"That fits." Clever girl to pick a costume that matched her quiet, woodsy personality. Loud and gaudy wouldn't have suited her.

Leaning back, he extended his legs and studied her. The more he knew her, the more she drew him in. She had a service submissive's need to give, yet was strong enough that her personality wouldn't disappear under a Dominant's. She'd expect balance in a relationship. If upset, she'd probably walk away until her anger was under control—and then expect to talk over the problem.

They hadn't talked.

Her gaze was on him, rather than the surroundings. "What's wrong, Sawyer?"

She was damn perceptive, wasn't she? He gave her the unpalatable truth. "Twice now, I've planned to stay away from you, and here I am. Again."

"It's a pattern, all right." She blew out a breath. "You said you don't do relationships. Can you share with me why?" Leaning forward, she covered his hands with hers.

Her ability to touch people, not in a sexual way, but human to human, simply awed him.

How much could he tell her? Unable to help himself, he gathered her hands in his. Although she had small, delicate fingers, her palms had the calluses of a hard-working person. Why did he have to like that so much? "I've been in prison, pet. Been in the military."

"I know. Do you think your past matters to me?"

"Actually"—he squeezed her hands—"I know it doesn't. However, my present is the problem. I've been—" He shut his mouth, realizing he'd almost blurted out everything. Jesus, he hadn't even told Atticus of his night patrols. Nonetheless, under her clear, green gaze, he wanted to unload. Wanted to talk about his worries, his fears, get her opinion.

Don't do it, Ware.

"I'm involved in things that aren't exactly...peaceful." Yes, peaceful was a good word.

Frowning, she looked down and pulled his hand closer.

Hell. He still had bruises from punching the assholes at the veterinary clinic.

Alarm filled her eyes. "Did those gangsters who hate you come after you?"

"More the reverse." Dammit, his mouth needed a lock on it.

"Reverse as in...you went after them?" Her eyes narrowed. "Why?"

"Why n—"

"Don't you blow this off as if it's funny." Her glare held a sting.

"You're right. It's not funny." He wanted to share so badly, he had to edit his words more carefully than normal. "Mallory, if I see someone doing something illegal"—*like breaking and entering or stealing or dealing*—"I can't stand by and do nothing."

Her face softened. "But why would you stay away from me because you're helping people?"

"You don't like violence, nymph. It bothers you."

"Yes. But violence is part of our world. I honor you for defending those weaker than you." The look in her eyes said she liked who he was—and seeing her admiration shook him to the depths.

When she held his battered, war-scarred hand against her silken cheek, he had no words. The room faded in the warmth of her presence, like the glow of moonlight on a night sea.

Maybe...maybe he didn't have to stay away from her. The gang was down to its last few men. There was no way the Hammers could remain in Bear Flat, not when their members kept getting arrested. It was almost over.

He could have a life. Could have her. Hope rose inside him, filling him as he stared at her.

A tenor voice broke into their conversation. "Sweetcheeks, you disappeared on me."

Mallory looked around and smiled. "Dixon. Are you off duty now?"

The young man from the reception desk frowned at Mallory. "You were supposed to wait for My Liege."

"Who?"

Sawyer provided, "My Liege is what the submissives call Xavier."

"Oh." Mallory smiled. "Don't worry, Dixon. I found him."

"Is *that* what happened?" Sawyer asked with a grin.

She kicked him under the table, making him laugh.

A goblin clapped a hand on Dixon's shoulder, and the young submissive looked at the man with a rueful grin. "Sorry, Sir."

"You will be, boy. You will be." The goblin's Texas accent held a distinct threat.

Sawyer stiffened, then relaxed at the amusement and affection in the Dom's eyes. Dixon wasn't in trouble.

Dixon's Dom held out his hand to Sawyer. "Stan."

"Sawyer." The handshake he received was firm and carefully controlled. Yeah, the boy would be fine.

"You know, guys, I don't understand the huge need to have an escort." Mallory waved her hand airily. "There's nothing frightening here. I've seen more skin at a Chippendale's show."

When Dixon and Stan stared at her in disbelief, Sawyer broke out laughing. "I haven't taken her downstairs yet."

"Oooh." Dixon snickered. "You're so going to eat your words, girlfriend. Come and find me after you've had the *whole* tour." He turned to Stan. "I'm ready, Master."

"Good enough." With a smile, Stan said to Sawyer, "Sorry for the interruption. Dixon is difficult to stop when he gets a burr under his saddle."

Under his breath, Dixon made a "*pffff*" sound.

Gripping Dixon's nape hard enough the impertinent pup squeaked, Stan removed a cane from the clip on his belt and pulled the young man away.

As the two headed toward the stairs to the dungeon, Sawyer nodded. Someone was going to get the walloping he quite obviously wanted.

Taking Mallory's hand, Sawyer rose. "Time to show you the rest of Dark Haven."

A glimmer of worry appeared in her eyes as she let him pull her to her feet. "All right. I'm game."

That she was. It was intriguing she'd come to a BDSM club on her own. He knew she'd liked their night together, but to show up here? She wanted more.

Fuck, he wanted to give her more.

As they went down the stairs, the music changed from sexy dance music to the flogging-inducing beat of Joachim Witt. Undoubtedly, European-educated Xavier enjoyed the German lyrics.

The dimly lit dungeon filled the entire downstairs. Several scene areas were spotlighted, others left in the murk. *Nice.* Depending on their taste and their plans, some Tops preferred a dark atmosphere, and some wanted to see the blood they spilled. To each his own.

The nymph came to a halt, and Sawyer grinned. "There's a tad more skin exposed down here, isn't there?"

Her eyes were wide. "I thought I knew what I'd see; I had no idea."

Taking her hand, Sawyer pulled her close and let her look. Even small dungeons were overwhelming the first time, and Dark Haven had a huge room with ample equipment. All the X-shaped St. Andrew's crosses were being used. Submissives of all sexes were strapped to the various spanking benches and bent over in stocks. The far end was roped off for single-tails and longer floggers. "Let's walk around. Stop me if you see something you like."

He might know before she did, since he intended to keep a very close eye on her. Smiling, he guided her toward the rear, past the long line of scenes. They passed a woman on a cross who was crying, begging, and trying to escape the Top's flogger.

Turning, Mallory buried her face against Sawyer's shoulder.

"Easy, pet." He glanced at the scene and had to conceal his own flinch. "Remember the submissive has a safe word."

Mallory looked up at him, worry in her eyes. "Do you honestly like this stuff?"

"Ah, baby. *This stuff* has a wide range of options." He considered, then sighed. Honesty was required between a Dom and sub—or even between a casual Top and bottom. "Because my stepfather abused my mother, I tend to be uncomfortable with heavy impact play."

"Impact?"

"Just what it sounds like. Spanking, slapping, punching, flogging, whipping, caning..."

She shuddered. "I think we can agree to avoid impact play."

Probably. Even so, there was a wide range between light and heavy. He'd have to give her a taste, since newbies had rarely experienced the effect a little pain could have on pleasure.

He smiled when she stopped at a scene where a woman was strapped down on a bondage table. The Mistress was still restraining her submissive, so the bondage was what had caught Mallory's attention.

As they wandered the room, every bondage scene got a long look. Wax play was a maybe. Oddly enough, the one suspension scene didn't appeal to her. Or the cages. She sped up to pass the impact play scenes. Sensual play got second glances. Gags...hmm.

He motioned toward a female submissive wearing a basic ball-gag. "Should I use a gag on you?"

Mallory took a step back...and flushed. In a husky voice, she protested, "I...I don't think so." Aroused, but scared.

Hmm. Not tonight. Hopefully, there would be other nights. He smiled at her.

WHEN SAWYER SMILED with such absorbed calculation in his dark blue eyes, Mallory's heart turned over inside her chest, and her insides went molten. Oh, what he could do to her with just a look.

"Why are you smiling at me like that?"

His fingers brushed down her cheek. "Don't worry, little subbie. We won't play with gags this time."

This time. He hadn't put any emphasis on the words.

He didn't have to.

She tried to feel relieved he wasn't planning anything scary tonight.

He wasn't, was he?

"Sawyer, I believe?" The man who approached was probably around forty. Tall, leanly muscular, with aristocratic features. His wavy brown hair was swept back, his brown mustache neatly trimmed. And he was dressed as...hmm, Thor? Weren't all the Doms supposed to be bad guys? So was this man submissive in spite of the authority he carried?

Almost matching his eyes, the predominant color in his aura was an unusual turquoise indicating he was an organized person, dynamic and influential. But the muddy brown and gray showed he'd suffered in the past and hadn't worked through the issue.

"I'm Sawyer." Sawyer pulled her closer and gave the man a once-over. "You're dressed as Thor?"

"Actually, his evil brother, Loki." The man gave a slight bow. "Or Ethan works."

After the men shook hands, Ethan held up a leather bag. "Simon and Xavier were asked to assist with a scene and drafted me to find you. You have Xavier's permission to play if you wish. Simon had a toy bag filled for you."

"Simon read me well, didn't he?" Sawyer looked down. "Mallory? Want to participate rather than observe?"

"I...don't know." *Play?* Mallory glanced at the scene to the left where a woman—a Mistress?—was flogging a burly older man so hard that tiny drops of blood had appeared. Anxiety shivered through her. That wasn't what she considered fun.

He glanced at the nearby scene, and his gaze softened. "Nymph, I wouldn't do that, even if you wanted me to."

"Oh." Her shoulder muscles started to unknot. "But we'd...play...in front of people?"

"Yes, in public, although we can find a quieter corner." A corner of his mouth turned up. "If we're here, you won't have to call your friend to check in. Being in public means not worrying about the Dom turning into a serial killer."

Ethan chuckled. "Or, more likely, disregarding your limits."

His aura really was beautiful. Unthinking, she started, "I like your"—*um*—"accent."

"Thank you, poppet." He smiled and added, "It always reappears when I return to England, then fades in a month or so. Be that as it may, I think you're stalling…" He glanced at Sawyer.

"Yes, she's evading an answer." Sawyer tilted her chin up with two fingers. "We don't have to play, pet. However, in a public place, I can take you further than I did last time. Because it would be safer for you."

Under the intense blue of his eyes, she couldn't find a reason why not. In fact, her body yearned for his touch. For him. Her gaze caught on the slight curve of his firm lips…and the crease to the right of his mouth slowly deepened.

Oh. She was staring at him like a star-struck girl. *Think, woman.* Did she want to do a scene with him out where people could watch? "I'll try."

"The club safe word is *red*, Mallory," Ethan said before asking Sawyer, "What kind of scene do you have in mind?"

"Bondage, definitely. I'd like to see how she does on a spanking bench, although we won't employ it in that way. I'm thinking mostly sensual play. She's new." Sawyer looked at her. "I want to try a few things and see what you like, pet."

She nodded. Trying stuff out was…well, what she was here for, although she'd thought merely to watch.

"Very good." Ethan's gaze traveled around the room. "Ah, I know just the device. The bench has a quite useful attachment. Follow me, please."

Ethan wove through the room easily, collecting quiet greetings from various Doms and bowed heads from the submissives. A few looked as if they wanted to fling themselves in front of him to be noticed. Well, she could understand that—the Englishman was truly

gorgeous, and the refined authority he exuded was compelling.
And yet, Sawyer's rock-solid power was even more exciting.
Ethan evoked an impulse to bow. With Sawyer, she wanted to
salute…or kneel.

In a corner, Ethan stopped beside an odd device that vaguely
resembled the other long, padded sawhorses in the room. Or maybe
she should call them super narrow picnic tables. The submissive lay
on the top, and her forearms and knees were strapped to the planks
on either side, putting her into a doggy posture. This table was wood
with black padding, but the top was shorter than the lower boards.
And she saw various attachment-like things under the table.

After a slow look, Sawyer grinned. "Perfect. And in a corner, no
less."

"I'm glad you approve." Ethan added, "If you like, I'll stay long
enough to show you how the attachments work."

"I'd appreciate it." Sawyer pulled her closer. "I want you to strip
while I check the toys Simon lent me." Lowering his head, he kissed
her lightly, teasingly, then deeper. Wetter. He gripped her loose hair,
pulling her head back as his tongue stroked hers and explored. His
other hand cupped her ass, pulling her against his hard erection, as
he claimed her lips.

The room dissolved until all she felt was *him*—his mouth, his
hands, his muscular body.

Straightening, he held her until her head stopped spinning,
kissed her forehead, and…waited.

She stared at him for a second. *Oh. Strip.* Biting her lip, she
glanced around. In the corner, the bench faced a wall, and a few
chairs formed a boundary between this "area" and the center scenes.
Farther down the wall was a scene with an X-shaped cross. Sawyer
was right. The corner was quieter. Unfortunately, people still
wandered past. They'd see her.

Mallory tried to slow her breathing. She'd gone skinny-dipping,
and in many Peace Corps countries, nudity was common. But she'd
never been publicly naked in a…sexual…type situation.

Sawyer leaned patiently against the wall with arms folded over
his chest. His expectations were clear.

She didn't want to disappoint him.

Well, she didn't have much to remove, at least. Because of the sheer dress fabric, she hadn't worn underwear. Casting her inhibitions away, Mallory pulled her dress over her head and stood there. Naked.

Sawyer's gaze warmed. "Good girl." He glanced past her. "Lovely, isn't she?"

"Quite."

Mallory felt the heat of a blush in her face. *Spit and hiss*, she'd forgotten all about Ethan.

When Sawyer smiled, she realized his gaze had never left her face; he was reading her expressions the way she did auras. He pointed to the floor beside the bench. "If you'll kneel there, I'll check what Simon lent me."

The floor was hard against her knees. Cold. Her breasts wobbled, making her all too aware of her nakedness in a room of strangers. She felt appallingly exposed—and excited.

Sawyer had set the toy bag on a wooden rolling table in the corner, and as he pulled out various things, the knowledge that he'd use whatever he found on *her* sent goose bumps parading up her skin.

He took out a paddle and a cane, and to her relief, returned both to the bag.

A mushroom-headed thing stayed out. Sawyer glanced at Ethan. "Electric socket?"

"Beneath the bench."

Sawyer caught her staring. He squatted on his haunches, putting his hands on each side of her face as he looked into her eyes. "You're doing very well, Mallory," he murmured in his smooth voice. "Now, go one step further. Submissives in the kneeling position keep their backs straight—and their eyes down. Look at the floor."

She searched within herself for her instinctive need to refuse such orders...and found only pleased acceptance instead.

When her resigned sigh escaped, his lips quirked up. He pressed a light kiss to her lips before he rose.

While looking down, she couldn't see what he was pulling from the bag. Her anxiety rose a few degrees, which was probably the entire point, wasn't it?

"This should be a good start," he said finally. "Ethan, let's get her onto the bench."

"Permission to touch?"

"Granted."

Sawyer bent, took her hands, and pulled her to her feet. *What did 'permission to touch' mean?*

She found out seconds later after Sawyer guided her to the end of the padded stomach-height table.

"Face-down position, pet."

She put a knee on one low plank and swung her other leg over. The long, narrow length of the top supported her torso. Sawyer positioned her right knee on the lower padded board. On the other side, Ethan did the same. Although Sawyer stroked her leg as he drew a strap over her ankle and secured it, Ethan's hands were firm and impersonal. They moved up and strapped her forearms down in the same way.

When they finished, she was restrained on her forearms and knees with a long bench under her torso. The lower benches were far enough apart to force her thighs open into a wide V.

She lifted her head and looked around. It was humiliating to have her nether side facing the room. Otherwise... "I guess this isn't so bad," she said, half to herself.

Ethan's clear blue eyes met hers—and she saw his amusement before he reached under the table beside her waist, pulled out a strap, and waited.

At the bottom end of the table, Sawyer gripped her hips and pulled her toward him until the table edge was under her pelvis. And her ass stuck way far out. Too far.

Even knowing her behavior wasn't obedient, she attempted to wiggle back up the table.

The reason for the strap—and Ethan's amusement—was clear when he handed it over the table to Sawyer, and Sawyer pulled it snugly over her waist and secured it.

Her next attempt to move up on the bench failed completely.

Her ass was going to remain stuck out in the air.

Sawyer was watching her face, and laughter danced in his eyes. He glanced at Ethan. "I love bondage." With an intimate smile for her, he reached under her chest and moved her half-squished right breast out to the side, then nodded at Ethan—and the other Dom did the same.

It felt…weird…to have a stranger touch her. Yet, Sawyer's gaze was on Ethan, monitoring everything. The feeling of being protected was lovely.

Sawyer pulled the equipment table closer, removed something she couldn't see, and both Doms crouched under the bench, messing with the equipment. Absentmindedly, Sawyer was stroking her thigh, and his warm touch was incredibly reassuring.

"When you're ready," Ethan was saying, "simply turn it on and lift up. It takes a firm grip to move it side to side. This is the release lever when you're ready to lower it."

"Got it." Sawyer chuckled. "That's a nice design."

"It is indeed quite useful." Ethan rose and looked at her. "Again, poppet, the club safe word is *red*. Will you remember that?"

She nodded.

With a slight smile, he touched her cheek. His gaze lifted to Sawyer. "If you have everything in hand, I'll check on a couple of other scenes. However, I'll be in the area and will return off and on to monitor. Don't hesitate to ask someone to find me if you need anything."

"Will do. Thank you, Ethan."

As the Dom strolled away, Sawyer ran his hands down her back. His callused palms were hard—and ever so gentle, despite his strength. "Relax, Mallory."

She closed her eyes, hearing the sounds of the dungeon around her, the snapping of some sort of whip, moans, low-voiced directions. Under it all was the low thrumming music of Mechanical Moth. "Black Queen Style". Her heart took a rhythm in time with the beat.

As Sawyer's strong fingers massaged the tightness from her shoulders and the muscles down her back, she felt as if she were melting into the table.

Bending, he kissed her nape and down her spine.

Her toes curled with delight.

"Such a beautiful ass," Sawyer murmured. He kneaded her cheeks, edging ever closer to her exposed…wet…pussy.

When he finally slid his fingers over her folds, a shuddering heat coursed through her.

Oh, sun and stars. With a low moan, she wiggled, wanting…needing more.

"Easy, baby. We're not in any hurry tonight." He drew his finger slickly around her clit.

He might not be in a hurry; she *was.*

Slowly, his finger slid inside her, thrusting in and out, raising her arousal even higher. His other hand caressed her bottom—and then he slapped her ass lightly.

And again, harder.

The sting shocked through her. "What are you *doing?*" She tried to lift up and couldn't move. "That *hurt.*"

"Easy, Mallory." He chuckled, totally at ease. "Some women like an edge of pain. For many, it enhances the experience, and you don't know if you don't try. In addition, there are many kinds of pain. You might like one and not others. Try a few more swats on your ass, nymph, and we won't go further."

He paused. Giving her the chance to say no.

Gritting her teeth, she tried to relax. But, hiss and spit, her bottom *stung.*

After a minute, he slid his palm over her butt cheeks, keeping his other hand pressed against her pussy. He delivered two more quick smacks and stroked again. Another.

Ouch.

"I'm not seeing any indication you like this, pet." She felt his lips touch where he'd struck her. A gentle kiss. Running one hand over her back, he moved to the head of the bench.

Unsure if she wanted to be here any longer, she pulled at the restraints on her wrists. Her chest was hollow with disappointment.

Crouching, he caressed her cheek and looked into her eyes.

"Mallory?"

"You shouldn't—" At the concern in his eyes, she bit back the rest of her words. "I don't like getting hit." On the other hand, he hadn't hit her that hard, had he? Really, the swats hadn't been harder than ones she'd received from friends. She breathed out slowly and admitted, "You scared me."

"I see that. I should have explained better what trying things out might mean." His hand was warm on her cheek. "I plan to try a variety of common techniques. A few you might find mildly painful. You might find the pain transforms into pleasure, into excitement. Nothing I do will result in more than briefly red skin."

Mildly painful she could take. She wrinkled her nose. "I didn't find getting spanked exciting."

His lips curved slightly. "I noticed. I'll always stop and talk if you need that, pet. If you truly get frightened, use your safe word."

She frowned. "I'm not sure I understand the difference between wanting to talk and using a safe word."

"Ah." He considered. "If you want to talk or look uncomforta-ble—or even say no—a Dom's first response will be to stop what he's doing and check in, see what's wrong, maybe talk you through it or change the technique. If you safeword, the Dom will immediately start releasing restraints to get you free. The scene is done right then."

"Like a panic button."

"Exactly. Some people use *yellow* to say they need something changed without stopping the scene. *Green* means you're enjoying it, keep going."

"I can remember those."

"Good. But, Mallory, you're new. Even if you forget the colors, it's all right. I'm going to be right with you, figuring out what you're saying. What you need." His eyes were steady on hers. He was totally in control of himself—and her.

Hearing he wouldn't go faster than she was ready for and would listen to her concerns eased the edgy worry in her stomach. "Okay."

"Ready to continue?" His finger stroked over her lips, and the heat in his gaze spiraled her own up higher.

"Yes. Um, yes, Sir?"

His grin was fast. "Having been a captain, I always like hearing a ready *yes, sir,* or *aye, aye, sir.*"

Hadn't she just known he'd been an officer? She snorted and got a quick kiss.

As he rose, she noticed the healthy bulge in his furry pants—and the height of the table put that bulge level with her mouth. Clever people, these Doms.

To her surprise, he didn't move back to her pussy. She felt his warm hand cup her dangling breast.

Ooooh.

His chuckle said her tiny wiggle didn't go unnoticed. He played gently, then harder, rolling the nipple between his fingers as the fire inside her blazed hotter and hotter. His powerful fingers pinched the peak right to the very boundary of pain, sending zings of electricity straight to her pussy.

His free hand gripped her hair and pulled her head up. His determined eyes held hers, reading her right to her soul as he pinched her nipple again.

Every bone in her body melted into the bench, leaving her limp. And wet.

Very, very wet.

His firm lips relaxed into a smile. "There's a pain that agrees with you, pet."

If she could catch her breath, she might agree. As he gently let her head down and stroked her hair, a tremble ran down her spine. From the quirk of his mouth, he'd also seen how having her hair pulled affected her.

He picked up something from the table. Running his hand over her back, he rounded the table to the other side and leaned over to kiss her nape and shoulders. She felt his hand close on her left breast. Again, he pinched the nipple, and the throbbing increased there—and in her clit—until it, too, felt massively swollen.

"Yeah, you like that edge," he murmured. Hand cupping her breast, he kissed her tenderly, lingering sweetly on her lips. Moving down, he kissed the curve between her neck and shoulder, and lightly bit here there. As his fingers worked her nipple, his other hand closed on her shoulder, holding her down as he bit her nape.

Heat swamped her, as if she'd been lowered into an erotic fire. The moan that came from her was one she'd never heard before.

He continued with firm nips up the back of her neck.

Goosebumps rose all over her body, sensitizing every inch of her skin. She wasn't sure—her eyes might have rolled back in her head.

He straightened and then both his hands were on her left breast. Something cold pinched the nipple…and tightened.

Ow. She tried to pull away, but the waist strap was too tight. She couldn't move. Slowly, the pain transmuted to a low, urgent throbbing, and she realized she was panting.

His hand was on her shoulder, his gaze on her face as he studied her. "Nice. Let's put a clamp on the other breast so you don't feel unbalanced."

"But…" Her protest died under his perceptive gaze. It hurt…*wonderfully*…and he knew it.

This wasn't who she thought she was.

But a woman should know herself, accept herself. "Yes, Sir," she murmured and won herself an approving kiss.

When he did her right breast, both her nipples throbbed in time with her heartbeat.

His fingernails ran down her back, and the feeling was amazing. With one hand, he stroked her back with something fluffy and kitten-soft. His other hand wore a glove—one with tiny sharp spikes that he ran over her increasingly sensitive skin.

When the fluffy fur and the sharp spikes moved across her still burning, spanked ass, she felt as if her bench was rocking. As if her thoughts were drifting up and out of reach.

Her nipples pulsed with a low ache, her skin glowed with heat—and her center was a volcano filling with fiery need.

AH, JUST LOOK AT HER. The nymph's face was flushed, her lips parted, and she was giving soft little moans. Fuck, she was lovely.

She'd completely forgotten she was in a public place.

Well, this might remind her, at least for a moment or two. After pulling a condom over a slender anal plug, he lubed it and moved between her parted thighs. "You might not like this, Mallory, but let's try it and talk about your feelings later."

A frown appeared between her brows as he stroked her clit gently, rousing her more. She was already soaking wet. He massaged her ass cheeks and parted them. Using the slick plug, he rimmed her anus.

She gasped—and the ring of muscles clamped shut.

Sawyer grinned. Simon was a prudent host—the anal toy was the smallest size. Not big enough for her to need stretching. So Sawyer simply, mercilessly, pushed the plug in.

She squeaked like Achilles when the pup had fallen off a footstool.

Smothering a laugh, Sawyer stroked her back, letting her adjust. "This is called an anal plug. Your ass has lots of nerves—and this wakes them up.

She squirmed unhappily. "Those nerves were perfectly happy being asleep, thank you."

His laugh broke free. Fuck, she was something.

From the corner of his eye, he noticed Ethan and Simon. Both were grinning as they strolled on to the next scene.

Face turned toward the wall, Mallory hadn't noticed.

Giving her a reprieve, he rounded the table, took himself a kiss—which she still gave generously—and used the vampire glove and rabbit fur on her back until she relaxed again.

That wouldn't last long.

He picked up the silicone dildo. Slender and long, it had thin straps at the base that would secure it inside her. After sheathing it with a condom, he pushed the shaft into her wet cunt—and heard her breathing stop.

Ah. She probably wasn't accustomed to both her ass and cunt being filled.

The color in her face increased to a heady pink, and every breath brought him the scent of her lightly musky arousal.

Slowly, firmly, he stroked the dildo in and out a few times—just for fun. He secured it in place, attaching the rear straps to the waist strap over her back. The anterior straps snapped to the table beneath her. He patted her squirming ass in approval.

Was that a curse word she just used?

Picking up a feather from the table, he smiled. He'd tease the upper half and let the lower part simmer for a bit. Torturing a little subbie—was there anything more fun?

After another slow round of sensation play, she was breathing fast, obviously getting desperate for more.

Yeah, she was going to get so fucking much more.

He went down on one knee to where he and Ethan had set up the condom-covered Hitachi wand in the clamps beneath the bench. He ratcheted the metal arm upward until it barely brushed Mallory's clit. Locking it in place, he turned the overpowered vibrator on the lowest setting.

"Aaaah!" She tried to raise her bottom, to lower, to squirm.

With the remote in his hand, Sawyer walked back to the head of the table. "That should keep you from feeling neglected...while I take a turn."

Such beautiful green eyes, although they were a bit dazed looking right now. "What?"

He unfastened his pants and released his cock. "I want your mouth, pet."

Her lips formed an O, and to his delight, the heat increased in her eyes. "Yes, Sir."

Here was a woman who liked giving blowjobs. Could she be any more perfect? When her mouth opened, he fed her his cock, feeling a rush at the engulfing heat. He only gave her a couple of inches so he could revel in the feeling of her wet tongue circling the head. Her lips closed firmly just below the helmet.

She made a low, "Mmmm."

Slowly, he advanced—and she relaxed her throat and took him right to the hilt. Jesus, she felt amazing.

As she swallowed, her throat constricted around the head. She was deliberately giving him even more pleasure.

His eyes almost rolled back in his head. *Cannot. Come. Now.* He sucked air slowly and withdrew to get himself under control. "You're good at this, baby."

Pleasure lit her eyes. "All that reading pays off, I guess."

Remembering the shelf of BDSM books, he laughed. Yeah, he could see her doing research on how to please a man. "I love bookworms." Being restrained, she couldn't move much…which was the point…so he slowly pushed back in. Rocking his hips, he face-fucked her gently and watched her response.

From the wiggling of her hips, the vibrator obviously had her close to coming, yet she was enthusiastically sucking and licking his cock when he permitted. Her delight in giving head was obvious. *All right, then.* He wrapped her hair around his fist, immobilizing her head completely, and increased his thrusts.

SHE COULDN'T DO *anything.* The sensations swept over her—the hand fisted in her hair, trapping her. The cock filling her mouth. Her clamped nipples throbbing. The waist strap holding her down.

Being so helpless was devastating. And wonderful. The entire world, even the air, sparkled with excitement.

As the huge vibrator hummed against her clit, her pussy and anus tightened around the impaling toys. Her whole body was turning into one giant, quivering nerve.

And his cock was so hot, so thick. She traced the veins with her tongue, sucking gently, and breathed in his masculine scent.

To her disappointment, he pulled back and released her hair.

His gaze captured hers, such an intense blue. "I'm going to finish inside you, pet—and I'm going to take you hard. With the plug still in your ass."

A wave of heat rushed through her, and the noise that escaped her sounded…greedy.

He chuckled and kissed her lightly before walking down the side of the bench, pausing to jiggle the nipple clamp and increase the aching throb in her breast.

She heard the sound of a condom wrapper, before, ever so slowly, he withdrew the dildo from her pussy. There was a pressure at her entrance, and he pushed barely inside.

Oh, his cock felt so different from the dildo. Thicker. Hotter.

Like living iron.

Then with one unhurried, ruthless penetration, he entered her.

Mother of cats. With his thick cock and that anal plug inside her, everything was far too full. She froze, afraid even to move as her lower half pulsed around the intrusions.

His chest was against her back and he reached down to play with the nipple clamps. The pressure on the left one disappeared. He'd removed it, she realized, a second before blood surged back into the abused tissue.

"Aaaah!" It hurt...yet didn't quite. The sensation was as hot as fire, yet sweet, a liquid rain of sensation. She sucked in air, and after a minute the pain eased.

"There's a good girl," he murmured, kissed her shoulder...and removed the right clamp.

Hiss and spit. Pain. Not pain. Disconcertingly, as her nipples pulsed with the glorious hurting, so did her clit. Under his weight, she squirmed as every nerve in her body sizzled with heat.

Suddenly the vibrator on her pussy sped up, thrumming hard against her swollen clit.

Her muscles tensed; her insides clamped down. "Ah, ah, *ahhhh.*"

He drove in hard once, twice.

Everything inside her contracted and exploded. Sensation seared through her, boiling through her veins, singing across her nerves. She spasmed around his thick invading shaft, and even more waves of pleasure shook her.

As he turned off the vibrator, her body simply went limp.

He was laughing, she realized...eventually...but he hadn't come, and his cock was still heavy and hard inside her, moving gently as she eased down.

But, oh, he felt good.

Gradually, he increased his speed. His hands gripped her hips, holding her firmly. She could feel his thighs rubbing against the inside of hers, hear the wet sound of his cock entering her. So erotic.

So controlled and firm.

"Jesus, nymph, you feel amazing." He rolled his hips, hitting every nerve inside her. "I like seeing your nipples bright red from the clamps. My bite marks on your neck."

Everything he mentioned woke those areas again.

"I like you with a plug up your ass and feeling how tight you are around my dick."

And she could feel him inside her, so very hot and steely hard.

"I like tying you down and positioning your cunt so you're easy to take. I like knowing you can't move from where I put you."

Somehow, the straps over her forearms and ankles seemed to tighten. The waist restraint trapped her, forcing her to take whatever he gave. She couldn't help wiggling against it. Pulling at the straps.

Pinned. Helpless.

The table seemed to drop a foot.

"I like knowing I can make you come again, whether you want to or not." Before she could react, the vibrator on her clit resumed, harder and faster.

His cock pressed in again, relentlessly taking her. "And I fucking love being inside you."

Her core clenched with the exquisite torment as the molten pressure built inside her again.

Suddenly, the anal plug moved, and she jerked in shock.

Pulling and twisting the plug, he was forcing those nerves into a sizzling awareness. As he played with the plug, slowly, he withdrew his cock.

As the vibrator hummed loudly, her clit tightened and tingled. The entire area from her ass to pussy was throbbing and so sensitive every movement of the plug pushed her closer.

Her breathing paused, every muscle taut with anticipation, as she hovered on the edge.

Then he rammed his enormous cock in.

Her whole center clamped down around it, convulsing with pleasure...and the rushing of sensation through her veins was like the flooding of the creeks in the springtime, an incredible roar of pleasure that didn't stop.

His hands tightened on her hips, and he forged deep, climaxing with her, and each jerk of his cock made her contract around him harder.

Somewhere in space, she could feel his hands moving over her, but the spring floods had torn her loose, and she was floating, riding the rippling water downstream to where it flowed into an endless ocean.

AFTER CLEANING HIS groggy little subbie, himself, and the equipment, Sawyer slung the toy bag over his shoulder and picked Mallory up. Crossing the dungeon area, he headed for the quiet aftercare corner with its dimmer lights and more comfortable chairs. He sat down, settled Mallory on his lap, and re-wrapped the blanket around her.

Blinking, she looked around. "Where are we?"

"In a quiet spot to recover." He brushed damp tendrils of hair away from her face and pulled dangling leaves from her hair. "You look like a thoroughly debauched nymph."

"Mmm. You did a most thorough job of debauching."

Drinking in her smile, he caressed her cheek. "What did you think of the scene?"

She flushed. "I…um…came. Like a lot. Couldn't you tell?"

"Sure." He ran a finger from her high cheekbone to the corner of her mouth. So fucking smooth. The crease beside her mouth was a laugh line. Yeah, she did far more laughing than scowling.

After a second, he realized he needed to explain more fully. "Getting a woman off isn't difficult, nymph. A BDSM scene is more than just sex—doesn't even have to *have* sex, for that matter. A scene should push some boundaries, increase trust, reveal a little more about both Dom and sub. Shake up the world a little."

"Oh." Her green eyes were still slightly glazed. "I think you managed it all. You taught me more about what I like than I'd learned in thirty years."

"Good to know."

She pushed the blanket back enough to press her palm against his cheek. "You have more patience than I'd expected and more determination. You didn't stampede me, yet…you didn't let me back away, either. Even so, I knew you'd honor my safe word if I used it."

She gave him a hesitant look. "Was there anything else I could have done...for you?"

Someone who wanted to give more than receive. A service submissive. Damn, she pulled at his heart. He lifted her hand and kissed her palm. "I was completely satisfied, baby."

No, that wasn't enough. She deserved the kind of answer he'd demand from her. "I loved being with you—your responses were honest and beautiful. And for my own pleasure? You have a great mouth, and I look forward to enjoying it again." He ran his finger over her lips. "I already knew I liked being inside you. One of my kinks is how much I like taking a woman who's bound—especially when she gets off on being restrained as much as you do."

The color rose in her face.

He ran his finger over her cheek to see if the temperature of her skin also rose. And grinned because it did. "Finding out what you like and testing your responses was just plain fun. Pushing you to take a bit more...that fulfills the Dom in me." The next wasn't as easy; nonetheless, he dredged up the guts to lay it out. "You know my past—and that I'm still involved in violence."

Her eyes were so open and clear.

"To have you trust me anyway means fucking everything."

"Oh, Sawyer." She twisted to put her arms around his shoulders. "You aren't fighting because you enjoy it, but to save others." Pulling his head down, she lifted her lips for his kiss.

Her lips were soft. Giving. Minutes ago, when he'd carried her across the room, she'd closed her eyes and cuddled closer. Trusted him.

Jesus, she was destroying him.

She whispered against his lips, "You're my hero, Sawyer Ware. And I love you."

The words breached his defenses and slid into his soul like the sharpest of knives. "You can't. No." What the fuck had he done? "I'm not... You don't know me. Don't, Mallory, don't do this to yourself."

He pulled in a shuddering breath. "Baby, feeling...affection...for a Dom is all too common after a scene. You don't really care for me that way."

"You idiot, I loved you before today. All the scene did is loosen my tongue so I blurted it out."

She tilted her head, looking into his face, and her lips actually curved. "Oh, Sawyer, love is simply a *feeling*, not a Yuletide gift exchange. Like warmth from the sun, it simply exists and won't disappear...even if the recipient protests."

He stared at her.

She *loved* him.

Her revelation tore loose knowledge he didn't want...the realization that he loved her.

Oh, fuck. He did. Yet the words wouldn't come. They bubbled deep in his chest, blocked by years of war and the thick door on his concrete cell. "Mallory..."

When she tilted her head and looked at him with those wise, clear eyes, he didn't see a young woman, but one eons old, possessing the unyielding strength of a mountain, the patience of the stars.

"Are you going to pull away again, Ware?"

"Fuck, no." The words came from his depths. He tightened his arms around her, holding her as if he could meld her into his body.

Eventually, he heard her gasping for breath—and giggling.

"Sorry, nymph." After easing his embrace and sitting back, he smiled. Her blanket had fallen away, baring her to the waist. Her nipples were still red from the clamps, her breasts high and swollen. What man could resist enjoying the sweet sight?

When her gaze followed his, he had the pleasure of watching pink roll from her breasts upward. She pulled the blanket up with a reproving expression that would have been appropriate on a nine-teenth-century schoolmarm.

"For someone who—" He broke off at the sight of Xavier, Abby, and Ethan. Unable to stand, Sawyer smiled to show they weren't interrupting a heavy aftercare session. "Mallory, this is Abby, Xavier's wife and submissive, and a college sociology professor. Abby, meet Mallory, a general contractor in Bear Flat. This is her first time in a dungeon."

Medium height and weight, the professor had pale, flawless skin, short, fluffy blonde hair, and gray eyes. Next to Xavier's dark Native American coloring and size, she looked like a fragile porcelain doll. "Welcome to Dark Haven, Mallory. I hope you're enjoying your visit."

Mallory smiled. "I am—although I'm still a bit overwhelmed."

"Oh, I understand." With a grin, Abby added, "My first night here, I was introduced to Xavier. A minute later, he tells me, '*I need your breasts for a few minutes.*' I almost ran out of the place right then."

The sound Mallory made was somewhere between a snort and a giggle as she glanced at Xavier and told Abby, "Would you believe, I had about the same reaction when I met him?"

Xavier's lips twitched.

Sawyer waved at the nearby chairs. "Would you care to join us?"

"We would be delighted." Xavier took a chair and pulled Abby onto his lap.

"Thank you, no," Ethan said. "I came to see if you had any questions or concerns. Simon has left and said to tell you he'd be in touch."

Sawyer motioned to the bag. "Please let him know I appreciated the loaner. All the toys were condom-covered during use and wiped down after."

"I'll let him know."

A pretty brunette submissive trotted up to the aftercare area and stopped.

When Ethan lifted his eyebrows at her, she blurted out, "Sir Ethan, my Dom has the wax play stuff set up. Can you come and help?"

"Of course, poppet." He picked up the toy bag and nodded to Sawyer. "You two look good together. It's been a pleasure."

As he walked away, Mallory frowned. "Is he all right? His aur—ah, he looked sad."

Xavier tilted his head. "You're very perceptive. He had a reminder of someone he...lost." His unreadable expression gave no further clues.

Loss. Nuzzling Mallory's hair, Sawyer felt a sharp stab of pity for the other Dom.

Damn, but he tended to forget how lucky he was. He had brothers who'd be loyal to death. New friends—including one who jumped into street fights with him and others who dragged him to BDSM clubs. And he had this strong, amazing woman who said she loved him.

As if she could see his thoughts, Mallory hugged him before asking the other two, "I've read submissives often call their Doms *Sir.* Is using it as a title normal? *Sir* Ethan."

Abby laughed. "In his case, it's a real title. One of his submissives discovered he's a baronet—and in England, he's called Sir Ethan. She began calling him Sir Ethan—and now everyone does." Abby grinned up at Xavier. "I rather enjoy calling you *My Liege.*"

At Xavier's exasperated sound, Sawyer grinned. "Makes me grateful I don't belong to a club. No damn titles for me."

But when he glanced down at Mallory, mischief gleamed in her eyes before she whispered, "I love you...my captain."

The first part of her statement filled him with warmth. With pleasure and unspeakable gratitude. He didn't deserve her love, but, damn, he wanted it.

After a second, he considered her last two words. *My captain* after he'd said he didn't like titles? It was beginning to appear that he had a brat on his hands.

When it came right down to it, he liked brats. Cute ones. Like the one he held in his arms. He whispered back, "My nymph, I didn't think you liked being spanked. Or did you..."

She only giggled at his threat.

I'm so screwed.

Chapter Fifteen

TUESDAY AFTERNOON, SAWYER worked on replacing the stalls in his stable. It was November first, and autumn had flown by.

With a patter of paws, Achilles raced through the open door of the stable and dropped a stick at Sawyer's feet.

"Naptime is over, huh?"

Yesterday and today at Masterson's spread, the pup had worked his fuzzy butt off trying to herd his person, the cattle, and the horses, while Sawyer tended the stock. It was good the dog wanted to help. Nonetheless, all that enthusiasm was exhausting to watch.

Grinning, Sawyer threw the stick back out the open door.

Achilles raced after it, not quite tripping. The pup was growing fast—and experiencing all the clumsiness that came with having paws too big for his legs.

Sawyer knew the feeling. As a kid, he'd stumbled over his own boots often enough that his stepfather, Reuben, had labeled him *clumsy* as well as *worthless*. At least Sawyer's reputation for being uncoordinated meant Reuben never realized how often Sawyer knocked over shit to divert punishment from Hector.

A drunken asshole, Reuben hadn't been the brightest bulb in the chandelier. He'd hated—and respected—sociable, athletic Atticus. He'd sure never understood Sawyer's liking for solitude and horses.

Made for an interesting childhood. After experiencing Reuben's fists as a kid, he'd found the SEAL's SERE—survival, evasion, resistance, and escape—training less of a challenge than he'd anticipated.

Achilles trotted back with the stick, tail raised proudly. Sawyer threw it again, and another chase ensued.

Needing a break, Sawyer headed for his cabin. Time for more coffee. Last night, after leaving Mallory warm and sated in her bed, he'd spent an hour sliding under each Aryan Hammer vehicle to attach the GPS tracking devices he'd gotten from Simon. If the gang used their cars, he'd know when they left at night.

All data was sent to his phone, which would sound an alarm when a notification came in. With the monitoring in place, maybe he could catch up on sleep…and have more time with Mallory. In bed. Jesus, the little sounds she made right before she climaxed were enough to drive him crazy. When finished, he wanted to start right back up again.

This morning, he'd wakened first and watched her sleep. Watched her slowly rouse. When she saw him, her eyes had warmed, and she'd smiled. Yeah, his heart had fucking turned over in his chest. She really did love him.

She deserved someone better than him.

But…she wanted *him*, and he'd given up on talking her out of her foolish choice, because, fuck, he wanted her just as much. Being with her was like finding summer after an eternity of winter storms.

Hell, just thinking about her made him hard. He stopped in the middle of the yard and arranged himself.

Although his mission wasn't over and he shouldn't allow himself to be distracted, the endgame was approaching. Not many Hammers remained in Bear Flat. When their decreasing numbers reached a certain point, they couldn't afford to stay.

Once the gang left town, Sawyer could live a normal life. Run his outfitting service. Raise and train horses. Help Mallory with her garden. Teach Achilles to be a good cattle dog. He could be a part of this town, and with Mallory beside him and Att at his back, there was nothing he wouldn't take on.

Yeah.

His cell rang, and he yanked it out. "Hey, Hector. What's up?"

"Bought my land, bro. I got the place I wanted at the price I wanted."

"The one at the foot of the mountains?" Sawyer visualized the spread he and Hector had looked at. A partially wooded perimeter surrounded wide pastures. Solid outbuildings—a barn and two stables. Two-story farmhouse.

There was enough land Sawyer could pasture his stock there in the winter, and during the driest summer months, Hector could bring his horses here, where there would still be grass.

"Put a hell of a dent in my share of the ranch proceeds," Hector said. "That hurt some."

"I know the feeling." Sawyer grinned. As co-owners of the Idaho ranch, the three of them split the profit, although Hector received an additional ranch manager salary. The sale had netted them a good chunk, and since Sawyer had always lived on base, he'd already had a fair amount of savings.

But what with buying land and needing to purchase trail stock, brood mares, yearlings, and tack for the business, he sure wouldn't be rich—although he had enough to survive on until the outfitting business turned a profit. "Once the snows set in here, I'll come down and help you get your place set up."

"Sounds good. I've missed having you and Att close."

"Yeah, me, too." He looked forward to introducing Mallory to Hector. "What'll you do now?"

"I'll be in Idaho until the stock I'm keeping is moved. Once that's done, I'm taking the first vacation I've had in years. Someplace tropical. I'll learn to scuba dive. And get to stare at mostly naked women."

Sawyer grinned. Sometimes he forgot his little brother was a full-grown man. Jesus, Hector was over thirty. "Knock yourself out, bro."

Meantime, he had a stable to fix, Masterson stock to tend, a wonderful woman to pamper, and a gang to run out of town.

Chapter Sixteen

"**B**ACK IN THE day, my grandparents and I would come to the Mother Lode all the time for steak dinners." Mallory surveyed the remnants of the girls'-night-out feast and shook her head. "Gramma would have been appalled at this travesty of a meal."

Sitting between Kallie and Becca, Sunny grinned. "Appetizers and desserts are the best part of any meal. Why waste time on a main course?"

"This was brilliant." Beside Mallory, Gin scooped up a bite of her crème brûlée and mmmm'd in delight. "Usually, after a regular meal, I never have room for dessert."

"Exactly." Having been the one to suggest the idea, Kallie looked smug.

With a sigh of repletion, Mallory leaned back in her chair and gazed around. The rustic restaurant hadn't changed since the first time her grandparents had brought her and Mom here. On the rough plank walls, antique mining tools—picks, shovels, gold pans—vied with vintage black-and-white photos. Glass-topped wagon wheels made round tables. A gleaming wood bar along one side provided the fancy drinks Gin loved.

"All right, Miss Mallory," Becca said.

Mallory raised her eyebrows. "What?"

Becca turned to the other women. "I've been patient, right?"

Gin looked at her blankly. "You? Patient?"

When Becca glowered, Sunny jumped in. "You are a miracle of

patience, Becca. We live in awe of your long-suffering nature."

"Much better. However, my miraculous patience is exhausted." Becca pointed at Mallory. "First, in case you didn't know, everyone here has visited Dark Haven—and all of our men are Doms. Your text that you'd had an *okay* time in the club was totally inadequate. I want a full report."

Sunny's spoon dropped to the table. "Mal? Tell me Becca's joking."

"You sent her to Dark Haven?" Gin frowned at Becca. "Seriously? Did she have any idea of what she was getting into?"

Mallory rolled her eyes. Talk about being surrounded by mother-hen personalities.

At the same time, she had to smile at Becca, who hadn't shared with the gang until now. Truly, that did show amazing—and unusual—discretion.

Kallie waved her fork at Mallory. "Spill the details, girl."

"I did have fun." What an understatement. Stalling, she took a bite of apple cobbler.

"Mallory…" Becca warned.

She took another bite. For the love of cats, what could she say? In many ways, her entire world had changed. Sawyer was in her life now. She'd admitted she loved him. Maybe he hadn't said it back, yet the affection he showed her, the caring, wasn't just in bed but all the time. He'd spent every evening with her, every night in her bed, had breakfast with her in the mornings. Texted her during the day.

Apparently, his objection to being in a relationship was over and done. In fact, since she already had an IUD, they'd gone to the clinic Monday morning to get tested so they could dispense with the condoms. She smiled, thinking of how nice it would be to lose that barrier.

She realized Kallie was frowning with impatience for the report.

"Dark Haven, right. Well, I guess I'm kinkier than I thought." Mallory couldn't think of what else to add. "It was Halloween, so everyone was in costume, and those were amazing. The unicorns had shoes that looked like hooves."

"Pony play with a twist." Sunny laughed. "Did you meet My

Liege and Simon and the Enforcer?"

"Xavier, yes. He's a bit intimidating." Mallory got snorts for her understatement from the others. "Simon was very nice. Who is the Enforcer?"

"That's deVries. Big, military-looking guy. Short hair." Gin narrowed her eyes. "Actually, he reminds me of Sawyer. They give off the same *'I'm a predator at the top of the food chain'* vibe."

Mallory grinned at the description. "I must have missed seeing deVries." Because she'd been concentrating on her own military-looking guy. And what he'd been doing to her.

He'd done even more since. In fact, he'd said he appreciated her bed's fancy scroll design, then had shown her what he meant. Who knew a person could be tied up in so many ways?

She should never have let him see her doing yoga. He'd certainly taken full advantage of her flexibility.

Feeling her temperature rise, she turned to Becca. "So, are you going to close down Serenity and vacation somewhere warm this winter? Now that Ansel is older?"

"Changing the subject, hmm?" Becca laughed. "All right. As long as I know you had fun, I won't push further."

"You're a good woman," Mallory told her.

The waitress arrived to take orders for more drinks or coffee, and Mallory settled back.

If she and Sawyer continued to see each other, she'd let Kallie and Becca know. Although Sunny'd seen them together at the clinic on Monday, the nurse was very discreet.

And right now, Mallory wasn't ready to share. Because…well, he'd already backed away from her twice.

Yes, she loved him. Unfortunately, love wasn't always enough to hold a relationship together. He had his own goals, and after his exciting life, he might find being settled wasn't what he wanted. Or his dream of a future might not include a quiet home life.

She needed to live in the moment and enjoy what they had without trying to build it into something more.

Not an easy assignment for a person who built dreams for other people every day.

▲

CRAVING EASY-TO-PREPARE FOOD, Sawyer drove into town and grabbed a big lasagna from the grocery's frozen food section. At least he'd made it before the store closed.

Since Mallory had joined her girlfriends for some female thing, he was on his own. He smiled. He couldn't complain; he'd been with her every evening and night since Dark Haven.

To his relief, the Aryan Hammers had been quiet. He wasn't sure how Mallory would react if and when the GPS tracker alarm had him hauling his ass out of bed to intervene in a burglary. Dammit, he didn't want her to worry.

Or to know he was tight-roping on the edge of breaking the law.

As he walked out of the store, the street was lit only by the Victorian style streetlights. The Mother Lode restaurant, and the pharmacy, grocery, and tavern were still open with customers coming and going.

With the seasonal decrease in tourists, the gang members were easy to spot. Three members of some offshoot of the Mexican Mafia sauntered down the boardwalk. Across the street, a neo-Nazi was leaning against the railing in front of the shoe store. Interesting. The Aryan Hammers were rarely alone.

Two clusters of high school kids were also wandering the street. Most wore plain jeans, T-shirts, and various sweatshirts. Two were in hoodies and hovering close to the gangbanger.

As Sawyer tossed the grocery sack into his pickup, he noticed the two kids had moved in and were talking to the lone gangbanger.

Damn. He'd give odds a drug deal was being set up—and the Aryan Hammers were into crystal meth, about the most addictive substance known to man.

Sawyer growled under his breath. There was no way he could intervene and stay anonymous. But, dammit—no matter what those teens thought, they were just kids. He had to step in.

He pulled out his phone and texted Att: *You got a dealer setting up a buy with kids near the shoe store. See you there.*

There. He'd notified the cops, all virtuous and shit. If things went sour, for whatever reason, the cops would be there for backup. The teens would have help.

Slamming the door of the pickup, he headed down the boardwalk. The kids and skinhead were moving casually toward the alley that ran between the shoe store and the post office.

He didn't recognize the dealer. With luck, the non-recognition would be mutual.

Didn't matter. The teens, no matter how foolish, were part of his new town. He hadn't fought his ass off overseas to come home and watch kids being targeted. Addicted.

His best bet would be to act like a clueless local who'd blundered onto the scene.

A couple of minutes after the trio disappeared into the dark alley, he edged just far enough to snap three quick pictures. *There.* If the kids got away, Att could probably enhance the poorly-lit photos and find them.

Sawyer pulled his hat brim lower. He'd concentrate on the dealer…who'd just looked around. What with the streetlights behind Sawyer, probably all the asshole could see would be a dark shape.

Reminded him of a movie…the one where some idiot, trying to be a hero, had been shot dead.

Yeah, it could happen. Muscles tensed and ready for action, Sawyer sauntered into the alley and said loudly, "What's going on back here?"

"Beat it, motherfucker," the dealer said.

"Hey, you're one of those *skinhead* types." Sawyer took another step in. "Are you selling *drugs?*"

The teens shied back. The tall, brown-haired one pocketed a baggie as the dealer shoved bills into his jacket. The buy was complete. That should make Att happy.

"Drugs are a bad idea, boys," Sawyer told them. "If you keep this up, you'll end up in front of a judge, and prison sucks." No truer words had ever been spoken.

The two exchanged looks and started edging away from Sawyer and the skinhead.

The skinhead made an annoyed sound. Well over six feet, he was emaciated as hell, showing the dumbass used his own product. He *snicked* open a switchblade. "You don't know who you're messing with, you fucker."

Sawyer took a step back and let his voice go higher. "That's a *knife*." *Dammit.* His gut tensed. It'd hurt like hell when Slash had knifed him last summer.

He needed that blade farther away from the kids. He raised his voice. "Only pussies carry knives. Guess that makes you a pussy."

"Fucker, you're *dead*." With an enraged growl, the dealer charged.

Sawyer faked a dodge to the right, spun left, and slammed the man's knife arm into the post office's brick wall.

Bones snapped, and Sawyer's gut turned over. *Seriously?* He hadn't used that much force.

Screeching high and loud, the dealer dropped the knife.

Sawyer spoke past the thickness in his throat. "Boy, you need to take more calcium." He kicked the dealer's knee, and the gangbanger landed on the ground, crying and begging.

When the darkness of the alley suddenly increased, Sawyer crouched, checked his six—and relaxed.

Virgil and Att stood in the opening to the alley, their bodies cutting off the light from Main Street.

A patrol car pulled into the alley from the other end—and the two kids who'd fled in that direction skidded to a stop. The car advanced, herding the boys back and illuminating the alley.

"Got a problem here?" Virgil asked Sawyer mildly, his gaze on the two teens.

"The tall boy bought something and stuffed the baggie in his front right pocket. The money is in this guy's"—Sawyer nudged the dealer with his toe—"inside jacket pocket. When I asked what was going on, the dumbass tried to knife me."

"Nothin' happened here," the brown-haired teen yelled, suddenly finding his courage.

The other kid's face was almost as pale as his hair. He shoved his friend. "Are you crazy? That dealer tried to *stab* him."

Ignoring his shorter friend, the brown-haired boy glared at Sawyer. "It's your word against ours."

"Well, my word along with the pictures I took," Sawyer said.

The boy groaned.

"Oh, fuck." The blond collapsed onto the blacktop. "Dad's gonna kill me."

Att snorted. "Better your parents yell than you end up rotting in the ground."

A crowd of people was gathering around the alleyway.

Virgil rolled the dealer over, realized his arm was busted. "Guess I don't need to handcuff you, do I?" He sent Sawyer an unreadable look before saying, "Can you call for an ambulance, Atticus?"

"Can do."

Sawyer started moving out of the alley, when he heard Virgil add, "I'm glad you saw the deal going down, Sawyer. Thanks for intervening and keeping drugs away from our kids."

When the people in the small crowd echoed Masterson's thanks, Sawyer didn't know what to say.

But it felt good.

"Way to go, bro." Slapping Sawyer's shoulder, Att pocketed his phone and headed for the kids. "See you at the station for your report."

Paperwork. Great. At this rate, he might as well be working for the force.

Chapter Seventeen

A FTER FEEDING, WATERING, and medicating Masterson's horses, Sawyer had turned them out into the smallest pasture to enjoy the grass.

As he mucked out the stalls, his muscles warmed to the exercise. It was good to be healthy again. And eating well. Mallory could make even vegetables in an omelet taste fantastic. And her bread with homemade strawberry jam? Hell, he might move past healthy right to a potbelly.

He tossed new bedding into the cleaned stall, breathing in the fragrance of clean straw. Damn, he'd missed having horses—even missed the chores. Contentment was a low hum in his blood.

It was shaping up to be a fine Friday.

When he'd wakened with Mallory in his arms, he'd simply held her and watched the dawn light brighten the room. Her slow breathing had been warm puffs on his bare chest. A rumbling purr had come from her massive cat at the foot of the bed.

Eventually, he'd rolled and pinned her under his body, then listened to her little sighs as he heated her up. When she took him inside her and wrapped her arms and legs around him, it felt like coming home.

And when they'd finally rolled out of bed… Sawyer grinned. Was there anything more delightful than a grumpy Mallory in the morning?

Racking the hayfork, he headed out of the barn with the wheelbarrow of manure. Achilles roused and ran in circles, giving high yaps at the menacing cart, which could obviously eat small puppies.

Returning from the compost pile, Sawyer spotted Virgil Masterson leaning against the corral fence. Arms folded over his chest, the police lieutenant was wearing a black uniform shirt.

A uniform. Sawyer's muscles tensed—and Achilles stopped dead, looking up with dark, worried eyes. Sawyer forced himself to relax. He wasn't incarcerated. He hadn't done anything wrong... Okay, that was debatable. Nonetheless, he hadn't been *caught* doing anything illegal.

"S'okay, pup. Go say hi." As Achilles ran forward, Sawyer nodded politely. "Masterson."

"Ware." Virgil bent down to greet the tail-wagging puppy. "You've done a great job with the horses. I saw you brushing Dodger yesterday—without being bit or kicked. That damn Thoroughbred hates being curried."

Sawyer shrugged. "The breed can have sensitive skin. I bought him a soft rubber currycomb and softer finishing brush. He's mellowing out."

"Fuck, who would have thought? He's our only Thoroughbred."

Admittedly, the way Dodger pinned his ears back and showed teeth, he looked belligerent—not like a sensitive sort of guy.

People often misinterpreted surly behavior in horses...and in humans.

Sawyer leaned the wheelbarrow up against the barn. Stalls were done, horses watered and out. The rest of the day was his until he tucked the stock in for the night. Maybe he'd reward himself with a ride later. "Are you taking the day off, or did you stop by to compliment me on my babysitting techniques?"

"Neither." Masterson eyed him. Like a law officer. "There've been a couple of incidents that lead me to think we have a vigilante in town."

Sawyer's gut tightened, and he bent to ruffle Achilles's ears. Att, Morgan, and Mallory all considered Virgil to be an honorable cop who truly believed in protecting and serving the public. And obviously, he was damn smart.

Straightening, Sawyer gave the cop a level look. "Vigilante type actions aren't unheard-of when a gang moves into a neighborhood."

"This is true." Masterson's tone got exceedingly dry. "Seems like this one is pretty fucking competent."

Sawyer might've been pleased with the indirect compliment if fear of prison hadn't been congealing his guts. "You got a point, Masterson?"

Masterson rubbed his face. "I like you, Ware, but we don't need any vigilante shit here. If it's you,"—his gaze hardened—"stop now. Even if I sympathize with why, I'll put you away."

The thought iced Sawyer's veins. He wasn't sure he'd survive another year of prison.

Didn't matter. Att wouldn't be safe as long as there were Aryan Hammers in town. "I'd expect no less, Lieutenant."

Virgil tilted his head and moved toward his car.

"Masterson, one thing."

Virgil turned.

"The Hammers are out for revenge. As a detective, Atticus doesn't patrol, but he's still at risk. Can you—"

"We can. He's one of ours. Now that we know the danger, we're keeping an eye out." Masterson moved his shoulders. "Even when he gets pissy about it."

"Good enough. Thanks."

"Yeah." Masterson nodded. "I think we understand each other then."

As the cop walked away, firmly on his side of the law, Sawyer pushed his hat brim up and watched. Yep, understanding had been achieved.

Change in his plans?

Yep. He'd be more careful about covering his tracks.

Chapter Eighteen

O N SATURDAY MORNING, Mallory walked out of the bedroom, tying the belt of her robe around her. She smiled at the sight in the great room.

Having started a crackling fire, Sawyer was sprawled in a chair with Aslan on his lap and Achilles in a small ball at his feet.

Aslan, having excellent ears, turned his head and gave her a contented smirk. *Good choice in males, Mallory. He has excellent hands.*

Mallory smiled back. *Yes, he really does.* He also looked quite fine in just a pair of jeans. The man truly had a drool-worthy chest. "Good morning, Mr. Ware."

Opening his eyes, Sawyer studied her with a lazy smile. "Now, don't you just look bright and awake."

"You..." She half laughed. "You are an *evil* man." She'd been sound asleep, curled up with him at her back. Even before she'd fully wakened, he'd stroked her clit, and by the time she realized what was happening, she was feverishly aroused. Tightening one arm around her, he had held her in place, slid inside her, and taken her quite...vigorously...from behind.

She'd come twice. Needless to say, after that, she'd been wide awake.

Didn't the man understand the joys of waking slowly? Then again, he was male and came equipped with his own alarm *c'ock*, right?

"Does this mean you won't make me breakfast?" Oh, his blue

eyes could steal a woman's heart.

"Did that *pitiful me* expression succeed with your mama?"

"Like a charm." Although he grinned, his aura darkened slightly with grief. And…bitterness?

She hesitated, but now wasn't the time to discuss past hurts.

"Actually, it's your turn to make breakfast." She almost snickered at the way his face fell. However, having tasted his cooking, she wasn't about to insist he prepare a meal. "I'll make a deal with you, though. Any morning you meditate with me, I'll make you breakfast."

His coffee stopped on the way to his mouth, and alarm filled his face. "You want *me* to meditate? Seriously?"

"Yes, Sawyer, you." She smiled at him. "I think you'll find you like it more than you think."

His indignant huff sounded like Aslan's when the cat was pushed off a lap. "You drive a hard bargain, nymph. Would this be considered a dubious consent meditation? Do I get a safe word?"

She snorted.

Sawyer rose. "I'll give it a shot. Let me put Achilles in his crate."

After the puppy was tucked away with a chew toy, Mallory led Sawyer into the sunroom. Although morning sunshine streamed through the tall windows, the room was still slightly chilly. After a second of consideration, she pointed to a chair. "Why don't you sit there? Keep your spine straight and relaxed."

While he settled in, she took her usual cushion and sat cross-legged on the floor. As usual, Aslan sprawled nearby to supervise. The sun glinted off his white ear tufts.

"Now what?" Sawyer asked. His lips twitched. Amused, was he?

"Now you sit quietly, and let your mind go empty." Because he was a competitive soul, she added, "Count each breath."

"Until I get to a certain number?"

"No, just keep counting in your head until I tell you the time is up. However, every time a thought drifts through your empty mind, you restart your count at one."

Such a look he gave her. Without a doubt, the thought currently drifting through his mind was that she was certifiably insane. She held back her smile.

He waited a second, as if he thought she was joking. "Right." With a sigh, he frowned and closed his eyes.

Closing her own eyes, she reminded herself to return after twenty minutes—no, better make it ten minutes—and let herself fall into the universe.

Time passed.

After ten minutes, she sped up her breathing, pulled herself into the now, and opened her eyes.

Sawyer still sat in the chair, back straight, his breathing long and slow. His aura was slightly clearer, and the darkness had diminished, even with that brief a time. Yes, meditation would be good for him. As she watched, she saw him frown before relaxing again.

"Sawyer, time to start the day," she said quietly.

He opened his eyes and started to move.

"Take a minute to return to normal."

He settled back. "You do this every day?"

"Mmmhmm." When she saw he'd transitioned nicely, she rose, put the cushion away, and pulled him to his feet. "What was the highest number of breaths you reached before starting at one?"

Walking into the kitchen behind her, he made a disgusted sound. "Three." He took a seat at the island, as she pulled out the makings for omelets. "Sometimes two. I thought I had a fairly peaceful mind." He looked adorably irritated with himself.

"Practice will help." Leaning over the island, she pressed a kiss to his firm, annoyed lips, and handed him a fresh cup of coffee. "It was nice to have company today."

His expression softened, then his eyes narrowed as he looked around her home. "Do people give you grief about your lifestyle? Meditating and"—he waved his hand in the general direction of candles, cat carvings, and plants—"all this?"

"I get teased occasionally, especially if I talk about auras."

He set his coffee down and gave her a disbelieving stare. "Auras. That's like a glow around people or something?"

"Exactly so." She shook her head. "Apparently the talent appears in my family off and on. Mom said her grandmother had the ability."

"What exactly do you see?"

"It's like a halo effect around the whole body. Colors give me an idea of personality traits. Darkness indicates problems of various kinds."

"Interesting." Despite the skepticism in his gaze, he hadn't completely dismissed the idea.

"Ready for breakfast?" When he nodded, she started sautéing mushrooms, onions, and green peppers. Realizing he still stared at her, she shook her head. "Seeing auras isn't that useful a talent, and I only mention it to close friends."

"So people in town don't gossip about you?"

She snorted. "Not really. I'm sure you collect more."

When his gaze hardened, she winced. That had come out wrong. He didn't like being seen only as a convict.

She walked around the island to push between his legs and give him a warm hug. He rarely initiated hugs, but if she offered one, he totally returned it. Sawyer gave fine hugs. "They're probably wondering what a hunk like you is doing with a quiet gardener homebody. Compared to your life, mine has been pretty boring."

"The locals think you're boring?" He lifted her chin. "Do you have no idea of how strong you are? How balanced? How peace follows you"—his lips twitched—"even in all the noise of a construction site?"

Her mouth went dry at the look in his eyes.

"It's odd. I thought you were appealing when I met you. Now"—he frowned—"now I think you're one of the most beautiful women I've ever known." Before she could process his words, he kissed her. Slow and gentle and devastatingly thorough. His hand on her ass pressed her against an increasingly hard erection. His hand in her hair kept her head tilted for his pleasure.

She was held and ravaged. Oh, the man could kiss.

By the time, he released her, she was flushed and aroused—and the vegetables in the sauté pan were ruined.

At the scorched scent in the air, she ran to the stove and yanked the pan off the fire. "Mother of *cats!*"

"Sorry, nymph." He grinned. "How about we take a shower?" The heat in his gaze said he planned more than that. "Then try breakfast again."

"Deal."

SAWYER ALMOST TRIPPED over the pup and barely caught his balance on the rough wood of the boardwalk. They should have practiced this heeling shit more at home.

Apparently, Achilles hadn't received the memo that a dog was to walk *politely* beside his owner rather than herding him. Unable to get his way, the pup took the leash in his mouth and tugged. *I'll lead.*

"Not happening, Achilles." Sawyer waited for the puppy to settle before starting again. He had a list of supplies to fill and a counseling session to endure, but there was no urgency to this Monday morning.

First stop was the feed store.

The feed store owner saw Achilles and smiled.

His smile faded when he looked at Sawyer. No surprise there. In the past, the short, wiry owner had always remained politely distant.

"Ware. I was hoping to see you." With a measuring stare, the owner leaned on the counter. "The drug buy you interrupted? My grandson was one of the boys. Seems he wanted to impress Simmons's girl, Jasmine, so he was hanging with the gang wannabes and acting macho. Real macho to get busted buying meth."

Oh, hell. Sawyer eased back a step. How pissed off was the feed store owner? "I'm, uh…" Couldn't honestly say he was sorry, could he? "That's a shame."

"Not to my mind."

Sawyer stared. "What?"

"Best he get a hard lesson now than a fatal one later. Meth? Jesus fuck, he'd have been addicted in a New York minute." The man's leathery face creased in a smile. "Thank you for breaking up the buy."

Sawyer relaxed into the warm feeling. "Just happened to be in the right place at the right time."

"Someone else might not have stepped forward or would've gotten spitted on a switchblade. Navy SEAL, right?" The old guy held his hand out. "Terry Breton—Green Beret in 'Nam."

Well, damn. The Vietnam snake-eaters were fucking famous. "Tough duty. I'd take desert over jungle any day."

From the strength of his grip, the vet hadn't lost much muscle over the years. "What can I do for you, frogman?"

"Morgan Masterson said you can handle large orders of hay and grain. Starting next spring, I plan to supply trained trail horses to guide businesses. Might lease to outfitters as well, if they're interested."

"No shit?" Breton considered. "Providing stock isn't a bad plan, especially since Mac retired and closed down the Sierra Pines Outfitters last year. You could well fill the niche. And some guides might add horse-packing trips if they don't have to deal with stock upkeep and training—and wintering."

"That's what I'm hoping."

The old guy frowned. "You sure you know what you're in for? Your place on Kestrel Mountain has excellent pasture, but it'll be under snow soon enough."

"My younger brother bought land in the foothills. I plan to overwinter the horses there."

"Smart…although transportation of stock is a pain." Breton scratched his chin. "You might make a horse drive though. Could even be profitable. Tourists pay good money to 'help out' on working drives."

Sawyer snorted. "I like working with animals; people—not so much."

The man's laugh sounded like rocks rubbing together. "My brother's the same way. Here's a thought. Hire the Mastersons to deal with the people while you wrangle the stock. You'd both profit."

Sawyer stared at him. "That's a…damned…good idea."

"Yep. Merely self-interest on my part. You bring in more tourists, we all benefit." He opened a drawer and pulled a paper from a file. "Here's the going price list for feed. Although it'll change by spring, it gives you ballpark figures. If you can, give me some notice, and I'll work out a delivery schedule."

"A puppy!" The squeal of delight came from the back of the feed store. A girl in the indeterminate age range between five and ten charged up to Sawyer and took his hand. "Can I pet your puppy?"

Taken aback, he stared at the mite: big brown eyes, short hair like a pixie, too fucking cute. After squeezing her hand—tiny, tiny fingers—he turned to Breton. The gangbangers would destroy this pixie. "Tell me she doesn't get this familiar with…everyone."

The man grinned. "I like you, Ware. Didn't think I would, but I do." He smiled down at the child. "Since she might inherit the store someday, she's allowed to talk with her future customers in here— although I didn't notice a proper greeting. This is Mr. Ware, Emma."

"Sorry, Grandpa." The girl's freckles disappeared under a bright blush, and her pink-sneakered foot rubbed against the hardwood floor. She looked up at Sawyer. "It's good to meet you, Mr. Ware. Can I pet your puppy…please?"

In full agreement, Achilles whined.

Caught between two pairs of pleading eyes, Sawyer chuckled. "Go for it. His name is Achilles."

The youngsters, canine and human, met in a happy tangle on the floor.

"If you have errands to run now, we've got a fenced area behind the store, and Emma would be happy to dog-sit. She's good with animals," Breton offered.

"Yes, yes, yes." The girl nodded enthusiastically.

Sawyer looked down. The pup's tail was going a mile a minute. "Achilles would sure prefer playing with your Emma rather than sitting quietly. Thanks." He handed the leash over to the beaming little girl.

Stepping out onto the boardwalk, he headed toward the other end of Main Street. His counselor, Jacob Wheeler, had offices on the second floor of the realty building with several other professional businesses. Atticus's woman, Gin, had joined the counselor and specialized in children and family issues.

Sawyer climbed the outside stairs and walked in. The blue and gray reception room was formal, although a built-in salt-water aquarium added a note of tranquility. Credentials and diplomas hung outside of each counselor's office, along with a photo. Gin had a photo of her in the kitchen making cupcakes. Jacob's photo was of him fly-fishing. Humanizing the counselors, Gin had told him.

Chatting with the receptionist, Gin turned with a smile. "Sawyer, it's good to see you." When she'd been his counselor in prison, he hadn't wanted the sessions, but sure as hell had liked hearing her slow Southern drawl.

"Gin. How are you?" Actually, he could see she was doing well. For a good month after she'd been kidnapped, she'd been jittery and wan. Now, she glowed with health.

"I'm doing just fine, thank you. I wanted to catch you before your appointment, since Atticus and I hope you'll come to supper tonight. He has a craving for steak."

His brother could grill a fine steak. However… Sawyer hesitated. Would Mallory want to make their relationship public? Although she saw him differently, most of the town saw him only as a convict.

He frowned. Would the town judge her for being hooked up with an ex-con? Surely, such a reputation wouldn't be good for her. And yet, although the nymph might note what others thought, her own opinion of herself and her actions held priority. If she was comfortable being with Sawyer—and she was—she wouldn't fret over what anyone else said.

And, *admit it, Ware*, these were his own insecurities, not hers. Only a handful of townspeople remained who looked at him and saw simply "convict".

In fact, for all he knew, the nymph had already told her buddies. "Would you mind if I brought Mallory?"

Gin didn't even blink. "Of course not. We'd love if she could join us. Say around six or so?"

"We'll be there."

After a quick heads-up text to his woman and getting back a text: *Tell Gin we'll bring dessert*, Sawyer headed into Jacob's office.

Two tall windows facing snow-topped mountains provided light.

The wall behind the walnut desk was covered with bookshelves, unfortunately, filled with psychology texts rather than fiction. Oversized photographs of quiet forest streams hung on the wood-paneled walls. A dark red and blue Oriental carpet warmed the hardwood floor.

Mallory would have approved of the tall plant in one corner. Much like her home, this office conveyed a sense of comfort.

"Sawyer." Jacob rose from behind his desk to shake hands. "Coffee?"

"Sure, thanks."

An old golden retriever rose from his dog bed and padded across the room.

Sawyer bent down. "Hey, Freud. How're you doing?"

The dog had dark, calm eyes—much like Jacob's. As Sawyer ruffled the soft fur, he got an interested sniff followed by a reproachful look. *Where's the puppy?*

"Sorry, boy. Achilles got dog-napped by a little girl." The two dogs had made friends the last time Sawyer had come.

"Have a seat." Jacob handed him a heavy mug of coffee, black, as Sawyer liked it, and refilled his own.

The corner farthest from the door held a rich brown upholstered armchair and matching couch. Sawyer was grateful for the warmth from the adjacent small brick fireplace. No matter the temperature, damned if he didn't feel cold every time he walked into the office.

As Sawyer tossed his hat on the table and took the well-cushioned chair, Jacob settled on the couch, moving aside the golden pillows and blanket.

"Does anyone ever lie down on your couch?" Sawyer asked, voicing a question he'd wondered about since the first day.

Jacob grinned. "Now and then. If someone wants to cry, it's nice to have a place to curl up. Fewer people use it now Virginia's taken on our younger clients."

Gin did love kids.

One end table held a bowl of small, rounded river rocks. The other had a bowl of various sized squishy balls. Sawyer chose a green squishy ball and tossed it from hand to hand. "Gotta say, sometimes this feels like being back in a SERE—survival school—interrogation."

An amused glint in Jacob's eyes warned Sawyer. "Today, you might well feel that way, Captain. It's time to look further back in your life."

Sawyer stiffened. "What?"

"Let's talk about your stepfather."

AFTER PUTTING THE cake she'd baked into the carrier, Mallory leaned against the counter and studied Sawyer. He'd returned from town in an odd mood—somewhere between sad and angry. "Sawyer?"

"Mmmhmm?" He pulled on his jacket and looked over.

"Are you all right?"

His brows drew together. "I'm fine. Why?"

"You have flickers of gray in your aura."

No smile, although his lips tilted slightly. "Is gray a bad thing?"

"It's...hmm...it can be a sign you're unhappy. And your aura was lovely this morning. Did something happen today to upset you?"

He stiffened, and the deep blue of his eyes darkened. "You really can see something? An aura?"

"Yes. I know it sounds strange to you. It's normal for me." It was easier not to talk about her talent, but seeing the increased pain in his aura meant she had to speak. His reaction told her something *had* happened. "Will you tell me what's wrong?"

He put an arm around her and murmured against her hair, "You are something. If I said no, you wouldn't push me. Or even get upset."

"No." She rubbed her cheek against his hard shoulder. He'd showered on coming back and smelled of clean, piney soap. "I'd be disappointed, but you wouldn't deny me without a reason."

"I don't have a good one to give you. Dammit." She felt his chest expand with his long breath. "At my counseling appointment with Wheeler. Well. He...I...*we've* worked through the shit, the

PTSD from when I was deployed. Trouble was today, he wanted…"

She felt his body tense. "Something else?"

"Yeah. Seems if a soldier was—how did Wheeler say it?—subjected to trauma as a kid, he runs into more problems with PTSD after battles. Like a double-whammy."

"Sounds logical." She realized Sawyer almost never talked about his childhood. She looked up at him. Although a deadly man now, as a child, he'd have been all shaggy brown hair, big blue eyes, and adorable. "You mentioned your mother had been abused. Did he hurt you, too?"

Darkness washed through his aura. "Yeah," he said and released her. "We'd better get going, or we'll be late."

Oh, Sawyer. The thought of him being hurt set anger simmering inside her.

"All right, let's go." She touched the side of his face and stepped away. She wouldn't push. Her job was to give him all the stability and warmth and love he could absorb. The rest she'd leave to Jacob Wheeler.

"I stopped at the store and picked up wine, beer, and soft drinks. It's all in the truck," Sawyer said. "If you get the dessert, I'll grab Achilles."

After a minute's drive down the lane, they arrived at Atticus's house and parked the pickup.

Mallory slid out and opened the small rear door so Achilles could jump out.

When Gin's black Labrador, Trigger, dashed into the yard, Achilles went into a frenzy of circles. *Oh boy, oh boy, I get to play with a big dog.*

Laughing, Mallory detoured around the chaos and up onto the porch.

Gin gave her a hug. "Come on in. The dogs will be fine out here without us. Trigger doesn't stray."

In the house, Mallory set the triple-layer chocolate cake on the counter and grinned at the excited high yips from outside. "By the time Achilles finishes greeting Trigger, he'll need a nap."

Atticus and Sawyer stopped in the door to watch the dogs.

"Trigger's teaching him how to play chase. I'd say they're both going to be exhausted." Atticus walked into the kitchen and gave her a careful smile. "How are you, Mallory?"

Mallory frowned at the change in his usual easy manner and then realized she and Sawyer had never appeared together as a couple. *Oh, sun and stars, I have a lover.* She stared at her man. *My* man. She was in an actual relationship—and in love—and somehow it all hit home.

Ignoring everyone else, Sawyer bent down and touched her cheek with careful fingers. "Is something wrong, nymph?"

She let her breath out, realizing she'd been holding it. "No. I just had one of those moments when the entire world seemed to move beneath my feet." A nice moment, actually.

"Moving worlds?" His eyes filled with laughter. "There are times I wonder if we speak the same English."

"You got it right, bro." Taking beers out of the six-pack holder, Atticus shook his head. "You're male. She's female. Two entirely different languages."

"No wonder I get confused." Sawyer planted a hard kiss on Mallory's lips and accepted a beer from his brother.

Atticus's expression—and aura—held a dawning approval of a Sawyer-Mallory couple.

Gin didn't bother to hide her grin. Opening the fridge, she pulled out two plates of appetizers.

Mallory leaned against the island. "Can we help with anything?"

"Everything is prepared," Gin said. "Atticus felt like grilling steaks—and has informed me the grill is his territory—so all I had to do was make a salad and toss potatoes in the oven."

"Mallory, beer or wine?" Atticus asked.

"Wine, please."

Sawyer tipped his head. "See, there's another one. Sometimes beer, sometimes wine?"

"Beer is for a hot, I-had-an-exhausting-dirty-construction day. Wine is for civilized conversation."

"That makes sense." He considered her. "Although it's a little scary you know yourself so well."

Meditating aided self-knowledge. He'd find out himself…because he hadn't missed a morning. In fact, he was up to twenty minutes now, and saying he liked it.

Carrying a plate of appetizers and the container of marinating steaks, the men went out to trade arcane grilling secrets.

Selecting a cheese and cracker tidbit, Mallory nibbled as she watched Gin set out the salad bowl and tongs.

Atticus's house was what she'd call modern cowboy. A red, brown, and white geometric patterned rug on the hardwood floor set the tone in the living room. The brown leather couch and brick red armchairs were oversized, sturdy, and looked comfortable. The lamp bases were wrought iron horses. A stone fireplace looked as if it saw good use.

In contrast, in the dining area, the cobalt-colored stoneware on a dark red tablecloth with a red and blue runner, floral napkins, and multi-sized white pillar candles were all Gin. Despite the feminine touches, the deep colors would undoubtedly satisfy Atticus's strongly masculine personality. "I love the way you two have blended your lives together."

Gin's gaze followed hers, and she laughed. "It took me a while to realize he's fine with 'fancy' as long as nothing is too delicate. I've had a lot of fun, especially since he enjoys entertaining almost as much as I do."

Mallory glanced at the two men out on the back deck. The brothers were much alike in their strong and protective natures. Alpha guys—or as Becca would say "Dominants." However, Atticus had an outgoing personality, whereas Sawyer was more difficult to know. More reserved. Edgier.

Darker.

Gin's aura held blue shades for a loving, generous personality. Like Sawyer, Atticus had a red aura—strong, realistic—but with some playful, optimistic yellow. After Atticus and Gin had fallen in love, their auras had brightened. They were very good for each other.

In fact, they'd meshed their lives so sweetly, she felt a touch of envy. She and Sawyer were farther apart in some ways. Her gaze on the red tablecloth, she said absently, "I wonder what Sawyer thinks of my home. There's not a hint of cowboy in it."

"Maybe you should ask him."

"How did I know you'd suggest a communication solution, Miz Therapist?"

Grinning, Gin acknowledged the hit. "Still, it's better if—"

"Five-minute warning, li'l magnolia," Atticus called out.

"Magnolia?" Mallory choked on a laugh.

Gin rolled her eyes. "I can't believe he says I still have a Southern accent. He's so full of it."

"Mmmhmm," Mallory answered, as if "it" hadn't been stretched to two syllables. "What could he be thinking?"

▲

AFTER THE GREEN salad, tender steaks, and baked potatoes had been devoured, Gin waved them into the living room to enjoy after-dinner drinks—and the cake Mallory had baked.

Mallory handed Atticus a slice. "I was going to make something exotic, when Sawyer saw this in my recipe box and made his preference clear."

"Chocolate cake and vanilla ice cream is a classic for a reason," Sawyer said, completely untroubled at bearing the blame.

"Mmm. Mom used to make this for your birthday. At least, before..." Atticus trailed off.

Gin walked in from the kitchen with the bottle of wine and refilled Mallory's glass. "Before what, honey?"

"Before Mom married an asshole." Atticus glanced at Mallory. "We had four years of living with the abusive bastard before he ended up in jail for assault."

Mallory pulled in a breath. "Assault?"

Sawyer's face had gone stone hard, and gray twined through his aura.

"I'd like to have had a crack at him. He was going to throw hot oil in their mama's face." Gin's expression turned proud. "Atticus was barely twelve, and yet, he stopped him."

Oh, Mallory wanted to learn more, but Sawyer had tensed. Time to change the subject. "Have you two seen—"

"I had help stopping him." Atticus took a swallow of his beer. "Sawyer called the cops and then charged the bastard."

With a dark frown, Sawyer shook his head. "No, I didn't. When Reuben knocked you down—kicked you—I froze, and he swatted me across the room into the woodstove. I did shit to help."

"What?" Atticus stared at his brother.

SAWYER STARED BACK as a cold sweat broke out on his skin. Fear sweat. As the ghost of their shabby living room formed around him, he could hear his mother's high screams. Feel Hector's small hand clutch his shirt. See Reuben draw back a huge fist and punch Atticus.

Skinny, twelve-year-old Atticus.

Sawyer was nine—and Reuben was a giant. As Att screamed and fell, Sawyer jolted forward—and froze. *Help Att. Run away. Hide Hector. Save Att.* His feet wouldn't move, and the phone dropped from his hand as he...just...stood there. Like a fucking coward.

Atticus hit the floor with a nasty thump, and Reuben kicked him. Right in the gut. The sound his big brother made... Everything inside Sawyer recoiled.

"Bro." Att's voice was soft, then sharp. "Sawyer."

Sawyer's head jerked up. *Shit.* He swiped his forearm over his damp upper lip and shook the voices—the memories—from his head. "Sorry. Been a while since I thought about that day." *A while, right.* All of several hours...since Jacob Wheeler had dragged the subject of his stepfather into their counseling session. Damn shrink. "This isn't a conversation for a dinner party, Att."

He glanced at Gin and saw only sympathy. Didn't she realize Sawyer had just stood there while her man—his brother—was kicked half to death?

"You don't think you helped? You got it wrong, bro." Eyes narrowed, Att leaned forward. "Come to think of it, the doctor mentioned you might not remember everything."

"Why would Sawyer forget?" Mallory asked softly.

"Because..." Atticus took a hefty drink of his beer. "See, when I smashed into Reuben and knocked the pan of chicken away, he punched me."

Sawyer nodded. "And I did nothing."

"True enough." Atticus's eyes went distant. "Until the big bastard kicked me. I was curled up, not even able to fucking breathe, and my little nine-year-old brother came out of nowhere, yelling bloody murder, and attacked Reuben like a fury." His gaze met Sawyer's, steady—and grateful. "You got a few good punches in, too, bro, before he managed to throw you across the room. Right into the woodstove."

"What?" Sawyer shook his head. Everything after Att getting kicked was buried in a fog. *Call the police. See Att get punched and kicked.* Then nothing. "I...don't remember anything after I saw him kick you. Actually, I don't remember him throwing me."

"You hit your head against that fucking cast iron stove. Jesus, Sawyer, you didn't wake up for a couple of hours. Scared the hell out of Mom. And me." Att's eyes met his. "The doctor said people don't always remember the minutes—or days—prior to a concussion."

Sawyer couldn't get past one thing. "I attacked him?"

"Yeah, bro. You were all of nine."

Huh. The pride in Att's expression was like a balm over the seeping wound in Sawyer's soul.

He hadn't been a coward.

For those long four years, Reuben had called Sawyer worthless. Scrawny. Chickenshit. Stupid. When Sawyer'd let Att down, it had confirmed everything Reuben said was true. He *was* worthless, scrawny, stupid...and a *coward*, too.

Only he wasn't.

He still couldn't remember those lost minutes, but knowing he hadn't let Att down? The revelation changed...everything.

An arm circled his waist before Mallory pressed against his side, her warmth and concern given so freely, his throat tightened. After a quick squeeze, she quietly asked Gin and Att their plans for Thanksgiving, generously moving the conversation to different subjects.

Letting him think.

The way she supported him felt like he had his SEAL team back, taking his six.

For a few minutes, he let things settle in his mind...and then slowly released the past.

Lifting Mallory, he set her on his lap.

His woman was even more warm and snuggly than her fuzzy cat. Even better, she wasn't embarrassed by his actions. She simply settled comfortably against him and kept talking. In fact, she even pulled his arms more tightly around her waist.

Acceptance.

Love.

The knot in his throat grew bigger. Blindly, he reached for his beer to wash the constriction away.

Gin's smile was understanding. In prison, she'd been his counselor before Wheeler had taken him on. She knew his past and knew this was a revelation. A smile quirked at the corners of her mouth as she asked, "I've been wondering, oh macho cowboy, what do you think of Mallory's home?"

Mallory made an exasperated noise, and Sawyer almost laughed. Sounded like some female discussion he'd missed. However, when the nymph turned in his arms to look at him, he knew his answer was important.

Fair enough. He glanced at his brother. "I like the western look here, Att. Feels a lot like home. The parts I liked the most."

The little body in his arms tensed slightly. Mallory loved her home.

Fortunately...so did he.

He touched her jaw, so strong and so feminine. "Your home though... I've never felt more comfortable or more peaceful anywhere. Ever." He could hear her small sigh of relief. "The furniture is big enough for me and damn comfortable. I'm not going to break something if I pick up a dish or sit down hard. And the house is so filled with light that, even on cloudy days, it feels as if the sun will appear at any moment."

When she tilted her head into his hand, rubbing her cheek on his palm, he only smiled. Because no matter how beautiful, her home was a mere reflection of the peace she carried and shared with everyone around her.

Chapter Nineteen

S AWYER FELT HIS wristwatch vibrating to relay a notification from his phone. Since Mallory was curled up beside him, he carefully eased away before sliding out of bed. As he stretched silently, he glanced at the clock. Three a.m.

Achilles jumped up and danced. *Time to play?*

Sawyer sighed. Did pups require no sleep?

Dammit, if he left the dog, Achilles would wake Mallory.

Silently, he took the dog out to Mallory's great room before pulling up his phone app. The map displayed the locations of the GPS trackers he'd put on the Aryan Hammers' vehicles. Yep, the assholes were on the move and not toward the highway. Looked like their target was somewhere at the east end of Main.

Welcome to Friday night in Bear Flat. Only maybe he should call it Saturday morning. Dammit, dressing and driving into town were low on his list of fun things to do. Why the hell hadn't the bastards pulled up stakes by now? Their membership was down to less than a handful—too small to survive here. They needed to rejoin their buddies in L.A.

Guess they hadn't gotten the memo.

Good news was the Mexican Mafia offshoot gangbangers had given up and left.

Bare-ass naked, Sawyer stepped outside, and cold, drizzling rain spattered over him. He'd gotten out of a warm bed for this? Snarling under his breath, he pulled his gear bag from the truck, pulled on baggy jeans, black running shoes wider and longer than his own, a black T-shirt, a Kevlar vest, and a bulky black leather jacket. His new skin-tight latex mask was in the jacket pocket.

Achilles, having finished pissing, joined him.

"C'mon, boy. I can't leave you here. Let's drop you off quick."

He swung by his house, left the pup in the cabin, and took a minute to make his license plate unreadable.

As he headed into town, adrenaline started through his system, driving the last of the sleep away.

He checked the GPS tracker again. The Aryan Hammers' vehicles had stopped on Gold Dust Avenue. Looked as if they were in the motel parking lot. Maybe they were meeting someone there?

Or...the motel was next to the gas station. This late at night, the pumps and minimart would be closed, since Roger Simmons was keeping reduced off-season hours.

In case a Hammer was keeping watch, Sawyer drove past Gold Dust Avenue, turned down Riffle, and parked in front of a secondhand store.

Before getting out, he donned the facemask. The tight latex was a bitch to get on, but turned him into a fucking realistic-looking old bald guy.

After flipping off the overhead so no light would show when he opened the door, he got out.

He jogged down the side of the secondhand store building to the back. Went past their storage building with piles of used clothing and appliances. Grimaced at the six-foot fence dividing the property from the motel and scrambled over it. At least they hadn't used barbed wire.

As he eased through the hedge surrounding the motel parking lot, he saw the lot was quiet, not even half-full. The motel rooms were dark. The only sound was the patter of the light rain.

Then a *thunk* came from the next-door gas station.

A-huh. His gut tightened. The mini-mart would be quite a lure to a gangbanger.

Sawyer headed quietly toward Simmons Gas and approached from the side.

There they were. Although someone had busted the gas station's lot lights, movement was discernible around the station's minimart. With a low sound of victory, they forced the front door open.

Animal entered the store first. Sawyer recognized the one who followed, as well as the third Hammer, who remained in the doorway. A quick recon showed no one else on the property.

From yesterday's surveillance, Sawyer had confirmed four Hammers were left in Bear Flat.

During break-ins, they always left one person at home, probably to do a pickup if things went south, or to provide bail. Thus, he had three-to-one odds here, and he was unarmed. His gut tightened, his instinct for danger making the hair on the back of his neck rise. *Pushing your luck, Ware.*

But if he got them now, they'd be done. To hell with the odds; this was worth the risk.

Flattened against the side of the building, he checked around the corner. The gangbanger in the door was watching for traffic coming from downtown—the wrong way. Perfect.

Silently, Sawyer eased up to him, jammed a forearm against the guy's larynx to silence him, and knocked him out with a punch to the temple. As he let the guy drop, he stomped down and busted the man's tibia.

As usual, his stomach turned over at the snap of bone. The sound...

Focus. Swallowing hard, he set his mind on the mission.

One down. Two to go. They'd spot him the minute he entered.

Keeping low, he lunged through the doorway and skidded to a stop behind the canned goods shelves.

"He's here, Animal!"

The two sets of footsteps charging toward Sawyer sounded like a stampede.

Fuck. Grabbing cans from the shelves, Sawyer crouched. The first bastard came around the shelves.

Sawyer threw—and the can hit the man. He went down.

Sawyer nailed the next one as well.

Animal staggered back, shaking his head.

A sound came from behind Sawyer. From someone charging through the door. Who the hell was that?

Sawyer dodged to the right as a pistol barked. The bastard was *armed.*

Turning, Sawyer dove straight through the gas station's display window, rolled, and scrambled to his feet. Three *more* gangbangers converged on the station. He could see even more coming from a van in the motel parking lot. Not a vehicle he recognized.

This had been a *setup.*

A burning pain sliced through Sawyer's hip, and he staggered.

"Kill the fucker!" The half-crazy voice was Animal's.

As the new gangbangers fired their weapons in a roar of sound, Sawyer dove toward the corner of the station. Bullets sent sparks flashing off the concrete.

Scrambling up, Sawyer rounded the corner. A bullet seared across the back of his arm.

Jesus fuck. Zigzagging, he sprinted through the darkness behind the station and dodged into the hedges behind the lot. Every jolting footfall sent pain stabbing into his hip.

His mouth tightened as he kept going.

The firing diminished as the Hammers lost him in the shadows. Shouts of anger, threats, curses came to his ears.

Far too many shouts.

Rather than abandoning Bear Flat, the Hammers must have brought in their brothers from Los Angeles. Like a dumbass, he'd walked right into a trap—one set to take out the vigilante. *Him.*

He'd never anticipated them adding to their people here. *Way to fuck up, Ware.*

Lights were coming on in the motel, although no one had come out. Undoubtedly, the cops were being called.

Anger at his stupidity drove his pace as he made his way from shadow to shadow until reaching his truck on the parallel street.

Painfully, he eased onto the driver's seat and—unable to tolerate the claustrophobic feel—yanked off his latex mask. His face was drenched in sweat.

His arm and hip burned—and from the wetness, were bleeding

like hell. He tied a quick bandana around his arm. After pulling some clean fast-food napkins from the glove compartment, he made them into a compress inside his jeans to put pressure on the hip wound. No time to do more now.

In darkness, he drove to the intersection before flipping on his lights. He could feel the internal shaking from the adrenaline and the fear.

As he turned the corner, a car sped toward him from the end of Riffle.

Ah, hell. The headlights spotlighted him—and his pickup.

Stomping on the gas, Sawyer sped away. In the dark cab, his features hopefully hadn't been recognizable. And his license plate couldn't be read.

After a second of hesitation, the other vehicle raced down the street toward the gas station. Maybe a cop?

Talk about a major clusterfuck.

On the way home, as if to add insult to injury, the light rain turned into sleet, forcing Sawyer to keep both hands on the steering wheel. With every movement of the wheel, the gunshot graze on his arm, shallow as it was, hurt like hell, and he used every swear word he knew. Pain management through profanity.

Rather than returning to Mallory's, Sawyer pulled into his own place. This was *his* mission—and his disaster. He'd keep her out of it entirely.

Inside the cabin, the pup was barking his little head off, so Sawyer climbed the steps and let him out. After a frantic greeting, Achilles started an unhappy-puppy whine, unnerved by the stench of blood and pain.

"Yeah, I know," Sawyer muttered, feeling like whining himself. He flipped the interior light back on and hastily cleaned his blood off the seat.

At least the sleet would cool the pickup off quickly. A few seconds with a screwdriver, and the light over his license plate worked again. A swipe returned the unreadable, mud-covered license plate to readable.

With Achilles at his heels, Sawyer headed into the stable,

stripped down, and left his gear in one of the improvised storage areas beneath a stall floor.

In the house, a quick shower took care of the blood and sweat. He bandaged the gouge behind his left arm as well as the one along his left hip. An inch over, and it would have shattered his hip socket. How could he not have anticipated the Hammers bringing in reinforcements? Even worse, the out-of-towners were heavily armed.

Failure was a heavy weight as he fell into bed—because the bedroom was where he needed to be if he got a visitor. On top of the quilt, Achilles made a circle and settled down, his muzzle over Sawyer's shin. And damned if they both didn't find the contact comforting.

Not that he was going to fall asleep anytime soon.

An hour later, lights flashed on his bedroom windows.

Yep, here were the cops. As was common in the country, a polite honk announced company.

Sawyer rolled over and turned on the bedside light. As Achilles jumped down, Sawyer carefully pulled on his jeans over the bandage. The heavily-lined wool shirt he donned would hide the bandage on his arm. "Let's go make nice to the police, Achilles."

The pup yawned and stopped at the top of the stairs. It would take the dog a while to reach the bottom since he took each step, one by one.

Shirt half-buttoned, Sawyer flipped on the outside light, saw Virgil Masterson, and opened the door. "What the hell?" He shot the questions out quickly, "Is there a problem? Is Atticus all right?"

Masterson scowled. "Your brother is fine. Where were you tonight?"

"Bed." Sawyer glanced behind him and saw the pup had stalled out most of the way down the steps. "C'mon, Achilles. You can do it."

After an *ooo-ooo-ooo* of protest, the puppy started up again. *Jump. Stop. Survey the step. Jump. Stop.* After achieving the last step down, Achilles scrambled across the room and bounced around Sawyer and Virgil to celebrate his victory.

Virgil laughed and bent to pet him. "Good job, buddy."

Straightening, he looked at Sawyer. "Now—"

"Hold on a second." Sawyer picked the dog up and set him outside on the grass. Probably didn't need to go, but on a normal night, the puppy's bladder would be bursting by now.

Leaving Achilles in the yard, knowing he wouldn't venture outside the circle cast by the porch light, Sawyer trotted back up the steps. His hip hurt like hell. "Now, what's up? Is this a Masterson stock problem or a Masterson, the cop, problem?"

When Virgil's mouth tightened, Sawyer knew the reminder about caring for their horses had scored.

"I'm here as a cop." Masterson folded his arms over his chest. "Someone broke into Simmons Gas tonight."

"Simmons. He's the guy who's always bleating on about getting the convicts out of town?" When Masterson nodded, Sawyer snorted. "I can see how he'd make a great target. Nonetheless, I'm not hard up for cash, thanks."

"Several people were involved. And there was a gun battle."

Sawyer allowed himself to stare at Masterson before shaking his head. Here he could be honest. "Although I'm allowed, I don't own any firearms, Masterson."

Achilles trotted in, fur drenched, leaving a trail of wet behind him.

"Jesus, I own a drowned rat." Grabbing the towel by the door, Sawyer knelt to dry the pup off. "Fair warning, Masterson. The minute I have horses on the property, I'll be buying a shotgun." Thank fuck his lawyer had pushed "mitigating circumstances" like PTSD to reduce the conviction to a misdemeanor and not a felony.

After a long, unhappy silence, Masterson sighed. "Yeah, well, living out here, having a shotgun is a good idea."

Sawyer looked up.

The cop's face illuminated by the porch light was hard. And tired. "Roger Simmons saw a pickup driving away. Says the driver looked like you."

Sawyer let his exasperation show. "For fuck's sake, Masterson, half the men in town look like me. More than half drive pickups. You know, no matter what your crook looked like, Simmons would think I was involved."

The lieutenant's expression said he knew it.

Sawyer tossed the towel onto the hook and ruffled Achilles's ears. "All done, champ. Let's find you a chew toy before you decide to eat the cop's boots."

The pup politely accepted a bully stick and settled down at their feet.

Sawyer turned back to the interrogation. "Anything else?"

After a second, Masterson sighed. "I don't think you tried to rob the place. In fact, I got a feeling you might've been trying to stop it. That isn't the way, Ware." Without waiting for an answer, Masterson turned and left. He ran his hand over the pickup's hood, checked the back license plate, shook his head, and kept walking.

Sawyer grinned. Masterson was a damn good cop. He hadn't been fooled.

As Virgil drove away, Sawyer's smile faded. Fuck, he hurt. Must be getting old. At one time, a couple of bloody gouges wouldn't have slowed him down. Now, all he wanted was a couple of pain pills and to fall into bed.

With Mallory.

No. Absolutely not. He'd give her a call in the morning.

Sawyer frowned at the stairs leading to his bed. Too damn far. With a grunt of pain, he picked up the dog and the toy, settling onto the couch. Achilles licked his neck and curled up in Sawyer's lap to play a sleepy tug-of-war with the stick.

Hip aching like a mother, Sawyer tipped his head back and watched the dark rain lash the window.

Roger Simmons had been in the truck on Riffle. Made sense he'd live fairly close to his station. And didn't it just figure— Sawyer'd been ID'd by the most prejudiced, mouthiest man in town. After having his ass handed to him by the Hammers.

But what had the cockroaches crawling around in his gut was having more Aryan Hammers in town than when he'd started.

Way to go, Ware. You were so fucking effective, they brought in reinforcements.

What with Simmons pointing his finger at Sawyer, by tomorrow, the Hammers would know who'd been fucking up their business, which meant an increased risk to anyone around him.

His chest contracted with fear. What if the Hammers went after Mallory?

No, that wouldn't happen. Aside from Gin and Att, no one knew he had a woman. The tightness in his chest loosened slightly.

Right now, Mallory was putting in long hours to finish up a job before the snows came. She wasn't going out.

Nonetheless, he needed to tell her. Somehow. Only how the hell could he explain without putting her at risk for collusion...or whatever knowing about a crime and not reporting it was termed?

Chapter Twenty

A S MALLORY DROVE up Kestrel Mountain Road, she could feel
steam coming from her ears. What a messed-up morning.

Last night, she'd gone to sleep, snuggled in the arms of the man
she loved…and woke to an empty bed and an empty house. No note
or anything. When she'd walked out on the porch, she'd seen his
pickup at his place and smoke curling from his chimney.

She'd worried then. Had she done something wrong? Was he all
right? Before she could call, she'd received a text: *Had to check
something out before you were awake. Sorry I didn't get a chance to wake you in
a better fashion. See you tonight.*

Of course, it had been a shame to miss out on being woken up
in a "better fashion." Although evenings and weekend mornings
were reserved for slow, sensuous sex, on a workday, Sawyer would
resort to energetic quickies. Having discovered her stash of bedside
table vibrators—and having added to them—he'd use them to
ensure they were both sated. He always made sure she got off, as if
he found her climax as rewarding as his own.

He was so…

Her mouth firmed. Neither of them had enjoyed fast or slow
sex…because he'd left during the night. Not a good start to a
Saturday, and it had gotten worse.

All morning, she'd worked on the bathroom add-on in Nancy
Jenkins's little house. An hour ago, the elderly widow had run into
town for groceries…and returned to regale Mallory with all the latest

news: the gas station break-in, the gunfight, and Roger Simmons's assertion of Sawyer's involvement.

No way would Sawyer have robbed Simmons Gas. On the other hand, he sure might have been there. Might have *died* there.

The fear curling in her chest made her breath come short. Made her even angrier.

Turning off the road onto Whiskey Creek Lane, she drove past Atticus's house and slowed at Sawyer's property. His pickup was parked by his house. *All right, then.* Pulling into the drive, she tried to tamp down her anger. Unsuccessfully.

As Achilles charged out of the stable, Mallory shut off the engine and jumped out, avoiding the puddles from last night's rain. "Hey, baby."

The puppy acted as if he hadn't seen her for weeks as he spun in circles around her, licking her hands, and collecting pats.

A muscular arm closed around Mallory's waist, turned her, and she was flattened up against Sawyer's solid body.

She planted a hand on his chest. "Sawy—"

He yanked her to her tiptoes and took her lips in a rough, demanding kiss. When her arms went around his neck—oh, she couldn't help herself—he pulled her closer, kissing her as if they'd been separated for years.

When he lifted his head, she couldn't remember what she'd started to say.

His cheek creased. "I missed you. But did you come out for a reason?" His black cowboy hat shadowed his features. Unusually, he hadn't shaved, and the dark stubble gave him an edgy, dangerous look.

"Ah…" Her brain clicked back on, and she glared at him. "You."

"Me, what?" He tilted his head, looking at her as if she'd lost the last tool in her toolbox.

"You didn't leave me this *morning*—you left in the middle of the night. And went to town."

His brows pulled together. "Listen, Mallory…"

"Were you at the gas station doing some…some vigilante

thing?"

"I thought you didn't have a problem with me acting against the gang."

Her head felt as if it would explode. "You said if you saw someone doing something illegal you had to intervene. Witnessing something isn't the same as *going looking* for trouble."

The hard expression on his face said going looking was exactly what he'd done. "Mallory, I—"

"Sawyer, how did you know someone was breaking into Simmons Gas?"

He stiffened. "You don't need to know how."

"I don't?"

His jaw tightened. His aura was dark with unhappiness, and there were murky colors she couldn't interpret at all. "Mallory—"

"You were out there all alone, and you didn't have a"—she searched for the word—"a backup, did you?"

Sorrow streaked like black lightning through his aura. "No. I don't have a team anymore."

She didn't approve, yet she couldn't let him walk into danger alone. "Let me—"

"No." His grip on her upper arms tightened, and he gave her a shake. "Never. This isn't in your skill set. Isn't anything you want to do. You will stay the fuck away from this gang."

"All right. But Sawyer, talk to me."

"No."

His answer was like a blow.

"I see."

"Mallory, there are more gang members in town, more than there were before. They're extremely violent. I want you far, far away from them. I don't want you going anywhere alone."

His gaze was focused, his worry obvious.

"All right." No, it wasn't all right. However, this wasn't the time to argue. She needed to cool off and take the time to think. They'd discuss it all tonight and arrive at something. A compromise and a way to keep him safe. She sighed. "I need to get back to work."

He leaned down and kissed her cheek. "Of course. Remember,

nymph, be very careful."

She kissed him lightly and drove back to town, her heart aching.

SCOWLING, SAWYER CONTINUED fixing the stalls, since, hell, there was nothing else he could do.

Before this, he'd considered himself an open, honest person, and even so, he'd evaded her questions. Shut her down. Closed himself off from the woman he loved.

Realizing he was stripping the screw head on the gate latch, he tossed the screwdriver in the toolbox.

She was hurt at his silence. Nevertheless, telling her everything would be wrong. His mouth firmed. He'd done the research earlier. If she knew for a fact he was breaking the law—and face it, infringing on the gang members' privacy was the least of his crimes—if she knew and didn't turn him in, she could be culpable.

It would be best if she could honestly say she didn't know anything.

In addition, if the gang found out how much he cared for her, they'd go after her. Which meant he needed to stay away from her. He kicked the toolbox lid shut. Doing the right thing made him feel like shit.

In the adjacent stall, Achilles yawned and looked at Sawyer. Then he tilted his head and scrambled to his feet.

A second later, Sawyer heard the hum of a vehicle. "Okay, tough guy. Let's go see who it is." His heart lifted. Had the nymph returned?

He yanked the leash from his pocket and clipped it to the pup's collar. "Let's work on those manners, while we're at it. Heel." Keeping Achilles in position, he walked out of the stable.

His momentary lift of spirits slid right back downhill.

The Chevy Tahoe was Atticus's unmarked vehicle—and from his brother's expression, he was in a piss-poor mood.

One guess why.

As if from guilt, Sawyer's hip and arm wounds started to burn.

Wasn't that fucked up? No longer in the mood for training, Sawyer unclipped the dog's leash.

The pup charged forward.

Atticus bent and ruffled his head. "Look how you've grown."

The puppy's short tail wagged furiously.

Sawyer shoved his hands in his jeans pockets. Might as well get this over with, so he could go take more ibuprofen and suck down another cup of coffee. "What brings you out here, bro?"

Atticus sent him a hard stare. "You know what."

"Because Masterson woke me up wanting to know if I'd shot up the Aryan Hammers last night?" To hide everything else, Sawyer let his anger show. His cop brother could read a suspect faster than most people read a newspaper. "You know fucking well I don't own any weapons."

"Are you saying you weren't there?"

Sawyer scowled. "Sure, I was. I woke up in the middle of the night and decided to check out the gas station—because me and Simmons are such good buddies. Seriously?"

"Goddammit." Atticus looked pissed enough to chew bullets. "Yeah, you were there. Jesus, Sawyer, you barely got your ass out of jail, and now you're pushing to get locked up again."

"Getting arrested is the last thing I want." Sawyer pulled in a breath. Pissed off or not, Att needed to know he had more trouble on his hands. "Att…forget about the station and listen. I don't know if you noticed, but the Aryan Hammers brought in reinforcements. I figure there are at least ten members here in town now. Well-armed."

"From the noise and shells, we figured there were more. At least ten? Hell." Att sighed. "Bro, I know you were a SEAL and can walk on water; however, this job belongs to the police force. Stop now, before it goes too far." His voice rose. "Are you hearing me, dammit?"

The pup's tail went under his belly, and he backed away.

Att's anger hit Sawyer like a blow, compressing his ribcage. He kept his voice even. "I hear you."

"Good." Att spun on his heel and got back in his SUV. The tires spat mud as he left.

MORGAN MASTERSON HAD heard all the yelling even before he came through the pasture gate. As he walked around the stable, he saw Atticus Ware's SUV roaring down the lane.

Now what?

Sawyer's shoulders were slumped. He stood in place, staring after his brother.

Well, hell. Morgan knew all about how battling a sibling felt. He cleared his throat. "That sure sounded like the fighting me and my brothers do."

Ware spun, saw him, and his blue eyes turned cold. "What're you doing here?"

More welcoming by far, the puppy dashed forward, all dark eyes and wagging tail. Morgan crouched to pet the little mite. Maybe it was time to get a dog. Fuck knew, the house felt damn empty these days. "Hey, mutt. He got a name?"

"Achilles." Anger visibly draining, Ware scrubbed his face. "Sorry. Been a hell of a morning."

Morgan snorted. "Been a hell of a night, too, from what I hear."

"Yeah? What'd you hear?"

"Simmons insists you were with the gangbangers who busted into his gas station." In fact, Roger had been frothing at the mouth and would've rounded up a lynch party if Virgil hadn't shut him down.

"I heard. Did the cops catch anyone?"

Morgan gave the dog a final pat and rose. "Got two of the Aryan Hammers. One has a busted leg...and insists he tripped while out walking. He doesn't know anything about how the gas station door was kicked open."

"Of course not."

"The other has a concussion."

Ware's lack of reaction was telling.

Morgan nodded to himself. Virgil had shared that a can of peaches had been lying nearby—and the dent in the asshole's head had matched the can's rim.

The SEAL had taken out a bad guy with peaches.

Chuckling, Morgan said, "I don't know if Atticus ever shared, but using veggies for weapons is a time-honored Bear Flat tradition. Gin and Summer held off some assholes with canned goods last summer."

"Did they now?" Sawyer snorted. "I'll have to feed Red some wine and get the story."

Smooth. The man wasn't admitting to shit. Morgan grinned in appreciation. "I figured it was you who derailed the robbery last night. Nice job."

Ware's expression shut down. "You came by to share the gossip?"

"No, I walked down to let you know I was back and to thank you for tending the horses. They look great. Virg was impressed, too." Ware had done a damn fine job. The horses' coats gleamed, and the stable was impressively clean. He'd even conditioned the tack. "We owe you."

"Nah. I enjoyed it."

"The other reason I came…" Morgan stroked his mustache and considered. This was bad timing, right after Atticus had reamed his bro a new one. Nevertheless, the SEAL needed to know he had backup. "If you need someone to cover your back while you're…playing with canned goods, call me."

Ware looked surprised, and then something in his face relaxed. As if it was a relief to know he wasn't alone.

These days, Morgan knew the feeling too well. So he ventured farther down the trail he was carving out. "The Hunts have a rifle range out back of Serenity Lodge. I'm heading up there to get in some practice. Want to join me?"

"I don't own firearms."

"So Virg said. I have plenty, from a classic Marlin to an old Mauser." He grinned. "My latest baby is a GA Precision Gladius."

Ware's eyes lit. "Snipers have a fondness for that."

Yeah, Ware knew his weaponry. "If you have a need for backup—or equipment—in the future, you come to me. This is my town, too," he said. "Meanwhile, let's go do some shooting for fun." He held out his hand.

After a long moment, Ware shook his hand. "You're on."

Chapter Twenty-One

ARLY SUNDAY EVENING, Mallory walked down the boardwalk in Bear Flat. Although she needed groceries, she'd procrastinated leaving. Not wanting to see anyone.

Because Sawyer wasn't talking to her.

Her chest hurt, as if something she'd swallowed had stuck partway to her stomach, making an uncomfortable lump beneath her ribs. Had she been foolish in thinking she and Sawyer had something special?

Since Dark Haven, they'd slept together every night…until last night. Last night, he'd called before she'd left work to say he and Morgan were having a Saturday night out. He'd sleep at his own house…and maybe catch her today. Even though he'd called from Morgan's house, the distance between them had felt more like a continent than a few acres.

She took a slow breath of the chilled air. Although she was pleased he and Morgan had found some common ground, Sawyer hadn't called her at all today.

"Hey, Mallory!"

Mallory turned.

With her husband, Jake, beside her, Kallie came down the boardwalk. Her short black hair was tousled, and her smile was wide. Barney, a giant logger who'd been a schoolmate, followed her. Kallie insisted the man was related to the purple dinosaur.

Mallory gave Barney a warm smile and turned to the other two.

"Did you have a good vacation?"

"It was great." Kallie frowned. "At least until we came back to all the stuff happening here. When did we turn into a crime-ridden city rather than a little mountain town?"

"I know what you mean," Mallory said.

Barney frowned, his gaze on someone across the street. "We know where the problem comes from. From people like that guy."

Mallory glanced over.

Sawyer was in front of the Bärchen Bakery, talking with Morgan. Sawyer. In a black cowboy hat. His denim jacket made him look even more muscular. How could she feel as if her heart was being stabbed, even as it did a *there's-my-man* happy dance?

Morgan looked over and saw everyone, slapped Sawyer's shoulder, and crossed the street. Jumping up on the boardwalk, he greeted Jake, "Hey, cousin-in-law. Welcome home."

Jake grinned. "Good to be back."

Morgan smiled at Mallory. "Sorry if I messed up your plans with Sawyer last night."

Puffing up his massive chest, Barney glowered. "Sawyer Ware's a convict. Mallory wouldn't have anything to do with him."

Oh, honestly. "Sawyer is—"

Interrupting, Morgan snapped out, "That guy is *Captain* Ware, who spent a decade serving a country that did shit to help him when he got out. He fell asleep at the wheel after two whole drinks, and his best friend died. Yeah, he fucked up. And he paid for it. *Jesus*, he paid for it."

Barney blinked, then looked shocked. "I didn't know."

"Yeah, neither did I, until he took on a gang to save old Verne's ass. I started asking questions. Talked to his brother. And Gin, too."

Mallory smiled. Morgan was the youngest Masterson brother and usually let others lead; however, no one—even Wyatt—could budge him once he'd decided something was right. "Did Sawyer do well with your horses?" She couldn't imagine any different.

Barney sputtered. "You let him near your horses?"

"Yeah, Barney." Morgan's tone hardened. "I had a fishing group to guide. Wyatt's in Africa. Kallie took off on vacation. Who was supposed to look after our stock?"

Kallie frowned. "But, Morgan, Virgil was planning to—"

"Virgil's a cop and working his ass off. Have you even looked at him recently?"

"Oh. Oh, no." Appalled, Kallie put her hand on his arm. "Jake and I wouldn't have left if—"

"No blame, cuz." Morgan patted her hand. "Atticus is putting in as many hours as Virg, so I didn't ask him, but he said Sawyer's even better with horses than he is."

"Really?" Kallie turned a speculative gaze toward Sawyer. "Wouldn't it be nice…"

"I had him over to see how he did." Morgan grinned. "Atticus is right—the guy's got a gift. Even dumbass Dodger acted like Ware was cubed sugar."

"This afternoon, I noticed how clean the barn was," Kallie said. "And the horses are super mellow, like they'd all been exercised recently. How much did he charge us?"

"Nothing. Said he appreciated the way we'd kept up the fences between our pastures." Morgan snorted.

Mallory nodded. Yes, that sounded like Sawyer.

"How nice of him." Kallie looked at Sawyer and nodded slowly. "He'll be a good neighbor. I know Mallory thinks he's okay."

"He's a good man." Mallory managed to smile. She so didn't want to talk about Sawyer—not when her heart was already aching. "Gotta go—I need to talk to Mrs. Reed."

Popping into the pottery shop, she chatted with Mrs. Reed and put in an order, hoping to help make up for the glassware the older woman had lost. Once back on the boardwalk, she headed toward the grocery store.

"Mallory."

At the sound of her name, she stopped.

"Hey, little bit." Virgil walked up and put an arm around her shoulders. "Have you seen my woman?"

Mallory leaned her head against his hard bulk. Why couldn't her mama have given her a couple of brothers? Or cousins. "Nope. She's probably found herself a puppy or baby to cuddle.

Virgil's smile was tender. "Probably." The way Sunny adored babies of any kind, the couple wouldn't wait too long before starting their own brood.

The thought set up a yearning inside Mallory, which she shook off with difficulty. "Be careful. Lisa and Bart's cat had a late litter of kittens."

"God help me, I'm not up to kitten antics. Not these days."

Mallory frowned. Virgil's face was drawn; dark circles ringed his eyes. "You look exhausted."

"Been a long month." His hazel eyes were unhappy. "The neo-Nazi bunch—the Aryan Hammers—were already escalating, and now they have more people."

"What's there to escalate? Bear Flat isn't that big."

"Break-ins are up. Muggings. Even worse, they're dealing—and recruiting—at the school."

Mallory stared at him.

Obviously overhearing as he walked past, Roger Simmons stopped. "By God, those bastards the prison brought in are taking over our town." His face darkened as he told Mallory, "They robbed my gas station."

"I heard," Mallory said.

"Jimmied the door right open. The motel called me when they started shooting up the place. When I got there, they ran like the chickenshits they are." Roger's jaw tightened as he noticed three gang members swaggering down the boardwalk.

"I heard some were caught?" Mallory asked hurriedly.

Virgil nodded. "Two were injured and unable to run."

"One ran right in front of my truck—saw him good. Masterson threw his ass in jail." Roger's face turned almost purple. "Would you believe the bastard threatened me? Told me I'd pay if I testified against him?"

Virgil said, "Roger, look, this—"

Roger thumped his burly chest. "I told him, bring it on." He turned and motioned to the gang members, his voice rising to a shout. "Yeah, bring it *on!*"

Although the Hammers jeered at him, Mallory could see their

auras darken with threat.

She put her hand on Roger's arm. "I'm so sorry this happened."

He deflated. "Yeah. It's costing me money. Insurance went up, and I'm gonna have to get bars on the windows and doors, and new locks. A security system. When the prison shut down, I'd hoped all this would go away."

"We think it will." Virgil's voice was even. "But it takes time."

"Wouldn't take near as long if we ran them all out," Roger muttered. He glared across the street.

Mallory realized his stare was directed at Sawyer.

Roger spat on the boardwalk. "You know I saw him that night, too. Driving away. He's one of the bastards."

"No, he's not," Mallory said firmly. "He'd never steal or break into your place."

"You're blind, girl." Roger glared at her, his voice rising to a shout again. "You dally with the bastard, and your customers'll find a new contractor."

Virgil folded his arms over his big chest. "Enough."

"More than enough." Fury made her want to wallop the narrow-minded idiot upside the head. "You're wrong about Sawyer—and you're going to end up eating your words."

She turned on her heel and walked across the street directly to her man.

He was watching her, his stance casual, but his face was tight, and the clear red of his aura had filled with shadows.

At his unreadable expression, she remembered he hadn't been in her bed last night. Hadn't called her today. Her heart sank.

Good going, Mallory. See what getting angry with Roger has led you into?

Nonetheless, she forced a smile as she stepped onto the boardwalk. "Hey. I could use a hug right now." Without waiting, she started to wrap her arms around him.

He stepped back hurriedly.

His action struck deep, a sharp slice right across her heart. She pulled in a breath and winced when she heard the small shudder of her inhalation.

Don't cry. No, no, no.

Another breath, and another, and she managed to push the pain and frustration away. A girl didn't get to be a construction worker—or a contractor—if she couldn't control her emotions. "Sawyer."

"Mallory, listen. I—" Like the snap of a rubber band, his entire body suddenly went taut—and he took another step away from her.

"What?" She looked up at him.

"Nothing." His gaze was fixed on something behind her.

She looked over her shoulder and saw the three Aryan Hammers. One of them—a huge skinhead with a forehead tattoo—had such an evil gray aura, it turned her stomach.

When the massive Hammer's gaze met hers, he leered, making kissy noises.

Mother of cats, what a disgusting person. Turning back to Sawyer, she kept her tone light. "So, what're you doing in town?"

"Nothing important." His voice sounded raspy. "Just lookin' for a good time."

His dismissive tone scraped painfully over her already frayed emotions. She forced a smile and tried again. "Would you like to come over this evening? Gin gave me a recipe for southern fried chicken."

"Nah, thanks, babe. Got things to do." His cocky grin didn't reach his eyes. His aura was dark with unhappiness and anger and so much else that she couldn't understand what was going on with him at all.

"I see." She pulled in a breath. No, this wasn't right. Emotions shouldn't be covered up like Aslan covered his messes in the litterbox. "Actually, no, I don't see. Sawyer, what's—"

"I think our fun's run its course, pet. I need more excitement in my life and…" He shrugged, as if he didn't realize the effectiveness of the words he'd used on her.

Or didn't care.

Defeat swirled like a dark fog around her. Hadn't she worried that she wasn't the kind of woman he needed? That he'd eventually want someone more stunning, more exciting, more vivacious—not a quiet bookworm who meditated and liked to work with her hands.

"You take care, girl." Indifferently, he turned away, swatting her ass as he walked past as if to say: *Done here, moving on.*

She spun to yell at him, but he was off the boardwalk and in the street.

As she watched, he crossed to talk to Candy, a slender, platinum-blonde beautician from the local salon.

The woman stepped right up to Sawyer, flattened her hand on his chest, and gave him a flirtatious look through her very black false eyelashes.

Laughing, Sawyer yanked her into his arms—and kissed her, hard and long.

By the time he finished, Candy was draped all over him.

No, he's mine! Only he wasn't, was he? Mallory turned her head away, trying to wipe the sight of the two together from her mind.

Well, that was…that. Slowly, Mallory unclenched her hands and walked away from the store where she was supposed to buy groceries.

Why hadn't she seen this coming and prepared herself?

All too often in the Sierras, an avalanche would break loose, crushing everything in its path. Ripped up by the roots, trunks broken, the tall, strong trees would be buried beneath massive boulders.

Did trees cry when they were broken?

SAWYER TRIED TO bury the memory of the pain in Mallory's eyes. Tried to tell himself it'd been necessary to hurt her. Fuck knew, she'd stay far, far away from him now, which meant she'd be safe. Nothing else was as important.

Animal had seen Mallory start to hug him.

Sawyer couldn't rewrite history. However, he could make it clear Mallory wasn't anyone important.

In fact, he needed to show no female was particularly important to him. Not Mallory. Not this one, either. Smiling coldly, he hid his irritation at how the blonde was running her hands over his chest and arms.

Act like a murderer, Ware. Be what this one wants. "Gimme your name."

Her pupils dilated, and she rubbed her breasts against his arm. "Candy."

Right, she'd told him her name a couple of times last summer. He fisted her hair, yanked her head back, and watched her pant with excitement. "See you around, Candy."

Releasing her, he sauntered down the boardwalk. He didn't want the Hammers targeting any female...so he needed to appear as if he'd pick up anyone.

Three of the few remaining tourists saw him. When he grinned at them, the women flocked to him to conduct a light flirtation.

He felt the stares of the Aryan Hammers. By the time he left the women, he'd ensured the gangbangers would believe he was single and looking to score.

What a dumb fuck he'd been. He should have told Mallory that Roger Simmons's loud mouth had painted a target on his chest, and she needed to avoid Sawyer in public.

Trouble was, she wouldn't back down from a threat. Not *his* woman.

Now Mallory was hurting because of his actions...when all he'd wanted to do was love her. Because he did. Yeah, with all his heart. It had taken all his willpower not to join her last night.

At least now the Hammers would figure he was just a dawg, enjoying any woman he could get, and no one woman was special.

And he'd hurt the nymph badly enough she wouldn't speak to him again. She'd write him off and leave him alone. The stabbing pain of her loss almost took him to his knees. But this was the right thing to do.

He'd do whatever it took to keep her safe.

Chapter Twenty-Two

ON THURSDAY EVENING, Mallory filled the bird feeders outside the sunroom. It was the season when the feathered ones would have trouble finding food…and by staying on this side of her house, she'd not be tempted to look toward Sawyer's place.

Maybe she should have taken Kallie and Jake up on their invitation to supper. Unfortunately, she hadn't wanted conversation, especially about what had happened last Sunday. At least her all-guy construction crew didn't demand discussions of relationships or feelings.

On the other hand, she was a woman, not a man.

Frowning, she paused in pouring sunflower seeds into one feeder. She'd been avoiding her friends rather than letting them comfort her, which wasn't wise. Had Sawyer's tendency to retreat when unhappy rubbed off on her?

She huffed a sad laugh. No, she'd always done the same thing.

They were a lot alike, really. She hung up the feeder with a grumpy sound. Maybe it was best they weren't together. They'd probably stay home all the time, content with each other's companionship.

Sometimes it was better if an introvert teamed up with an extrovert.

But…she'd liked staying home with Sawyer, even if they did nothing more than watch TV or read. They'd discuss—or argue about—the news or history or even silly things like the best desserts.

His view of the world was oriented to life being fair. He wanted to pay favors back and keep things balanced. In contrast, she walked the overly generous path. Their take on things made for some good discussions.

She missed him.

Stop thinking about him, all right? The directive was impossible to follow when his absence was an unending ache under her sternum. Even Aslan was sulking, pining for the entertaining puppy and the extra attention from Sawyer.

Aslan's insistence that a seated human meant an available lap always amused Sawyer. Then again, not much disturbed Sawyer's equilibrium.

Again, stop.

Mallory hung the last feeder before checking her garden. Her cover crop had sprouted nicely in the empty beds. She should cut the asparagus down and mulch the ground…and keep herself busy for a while. After retrieving her snips, gloves, and weed tote, she cut off the long feathery stalks and trimmed them for the compost heap.

As she worked, her phone rang. She pulled it out, checked the display, and sighed. *Sawyer isn't going to call,* she told her heart. *Stop hoping.* "Hey, Becca. What's up?"

"I wanted to make sure you didn't forget the End of Season party on Friday. Tomorrow night. You *will* show up, right?"

She *had* forgotten. Would still prefer to forget. The last thing she wanted right now was a party.

Feeling a pat on her knee, she looked down into Aslan's green-gold eyes and took in the cat's chiding expression. Cats were perfectly content with solitude; however, humans were designed to live in a tribe. It was time to stop moping and go see her friends.

"I'll be there." She smiled at Aslan ruefully and gave him a scritch behind his ear. *Thanks, King.* "Thank you for caring, Becca."

"That's what friends do." Becca sighed. "Actually, I'd have been on your doorstep last night, except Ansel has an ear infection and is running high temps. Since yesterday, he's been glued to my lap, and we've watched a thousand episodes of *Baby Einstein*. My brain might explode."

Envisioning it, Mallory laughed. "Is he getting better?"

"The antibiotic is kicking in. Finally. He'll be back to his usual hundred-miles-an-hour speed tomorrow."

"Poor Ansel—and poor mama. Is Logan helping?"

"We were taking turns until one of our lodge guests got mugged outside of the ClaimJumper last night. Logan went to town with him today to fill out the police report."

"Mugged? Seriously?"

"I don't know what's going on this week—it's like there's a crime wave. The principal told me the Aryan Hammers are giving the kids free drugs and inviting them over to their house."

"No." Mallory's growl had Aslan staring at her. "Just no."

She remembered her first day in the Bear Flat School. After attending San Francisco schools, she'd fallen in love with how safe the little high school had felt. "We're going to fix this, Becca. Now."

A HARD HAMMERING on the front door startled Sawyer and made Achilles yip in surprise. The pup scrambled to greet whoever might be there. Less enthusiastically, Sawyer shoved out of his big armchair and stalked to the door. Hell of thing when a man couldn't sulk in peace.

Morgan Masterson waited on the tiny porch.

He handed Sawyer a brown grocery sack and a six-pack of beer, then bent to pet Achilles. "Who's growing fast, huh? You're gonna be a great guard dog, aren't you?"

Up on his hind legs, Achilles waggled his whole body in agreement…and Sawyer found his first smile of the day. Then his crappy mood returned. "Is this a celebration?" Because he'd never felt less like celebrating anything.

"Nope. It's Thursday, and the Broncos are playing the Jets." Morgan walked into the house without waiting for an invitation.

Stymied, Sawyer shoved the door shut and leaned against it. "Are you this pushy with your brothers?"

"Yep." Morgan tugged a beer from the six-pack Sawyer was

holding. After opening it and taking a drink, he reclaimed the sack. "Given an opportunity, Wyatt could argue a grizzly to death. I learned not to give him the opening."

Wyatt must be the direct opposite of Morgan. "Your brother sounds interesting."

"You'd probably like him"—Morgan's mouth flattened—"if he ever gets his ass back here." From the sack, he pulled a massive bag of chips and a large container of dip. Everything went onto the coffee table before he dropped onto the couch.

Happily, Achilles joined him.

Sawyer was treated to two pairs of expectant eyes.

Jesus. Resigned, he took himself a beer, put the rest in the fridge, and settled into his chair. "You pissed at your brother?"

"Yeah. Some." Brow furrowed, Morgan drank some beer. "He just up and left. Right in the middle of the season."

"You two have a fight or something?"

"No, we didn't fight." Morgan tugged on Achilles's ears. "You know, Wyatt and I were there when your brother rescued Gin and the other social worker from the convicts."

"I heard—and I know Wyatt killed one of the bastards. Considering the way Aryan Hammers have targeted Att, I'm glad your brother is out of reach."

Morgan froze, his hand on the pup's head. "I never thought about reprisals. *Hell.* I've just been pissed off about him leaving."

"Understandable. You've run your ass off keeping up with your business. Wyatt left because...?"

"He'd never killed anyone before; it fucked with his head."

"Ah." Sawyer took a sip of his beer and glanced at the label. *Coors Original.* Not bad, but it wasn't Bud. "Takes some men that way."

"Not you?"

At Sawyer's silence, Morgan glanced over. "I doubt SEALs escape battle, Ware. You've killed before."

"Yeah. It was rough at first." He'd puked his guts out after his first action. "It's easier when there's a distance." Knife work was the worst. Feeling the punch of the knife through skin, feeling the body convulse, the stench of released bowels. The change in...everything...with death.

He thought of the way Morgan had phrased the comment about Wyatt. *Never killed anyone before.* "You killed a man, Masterson?" Morgan rolled the can between his palms. "Couple times." His jaw tightened. "The first when I was sixteen and helping Pa with a fishing trip. Man found out his wife'd fucked his buddy who was also on the trip. He went berserk. Pa tried to talk him down and got shot. And...I put a bullet into the bastard's head. Then, three years ago, Virgil busted up a bar fight, and a logger went for him with a knife. I punched the logger...too hard."

Morgan looked down at his hands—powerful, working-man's hands—as if he still couldn't believe he'd killed someone in such a brutal way. "But I didn't lose too much sleep over it."

"You saved lives. The lives of the good guys." Sawyer shook his head. "Your brother will see he did, too. Hopefully before you're worked into the ground."

"The Hunts helped out with some trips—but it's a relief tourist season is over." Relaxing, Morgan smiled. "And I got the interesting trails Wyatt might've grabbed, so it wasn't all been bad."

Sawyer looked at him. Wyatt might be the bigger brother, but it was doubtful his little brother caved in on anything essential. Morgan reminded Sawyer of...of himself. Back before he'd been deployed. Easy-going on the outside. Also reserved, careful, and competent.

Morgan picked up the remote and turned to the game. "Don't forget, I'm available if you need help out there, Ware."

"I won't forget." After watching him shoot on the gun range, Sawyer figured this quiet Masterson was probably the most deadly of the three.

Chapter Twenty-Three

VEHICLES FILLED THE Serenity Lodge parking lot, the sides of the driveway, and overflowed down the road. Bear Flat's End of Season party had never been this well attended, even when they'd held it in town. Bemused, Morgan crossed the wide porch and walked into the massive two-story log building.

"Welcome, Morgan. I'm glad you could make it." Becca Hunt stood beside Logan at the reception desk. Standing in a playpen, Ansel waved his red rubber hammer in greeting. Thor, their big German shepherd, stood in front of the playpen, guarding *his* toddler. Making it clear than any overly familiar stranger would have his throat ripped out.

"I didn't have a choice about coming." Morgan scratched Thor's neck and waited for the required tail-wag of approval, before ruffling Ansel's soft black hair. "Mallory said she'd wallop me if I didn't show up at five o'clock. Left me terrified."

Logan snorted.

"Women who use nail guns are scary, sure enough." Bart Holder, the owner of the hardware store, clapped Morgan on the shoulder and made his way into the room.

Morgan looked around. The main room of the rustic lodge was packed with Bear Flat locals—business owners, stay-at-home moms, retirees. People jammed the sitting areas, leaned on the walls, and stood talking in groups. Aside from Ansel, no children were present.

"Have you spoken with Simmons recently?" Morgan asked Logan. "Seems he's saying Sawyer's corrupting women—including Mallory—and getting them to hang out with criminals and gang-bangers."

"Corrupting Mallory? I'd like to see the day." Becca's eyes narrowed. "If I hear anyone say anything nasty about my girl, I'll slap them spitless."

Well, fuck, Logan's redhead had quite the temper. Morgan glanced at her husband.

Despite the anger in his eyes, Logan smiled. "I'll help, sugar. I don't know Atticus's brother, but Mallory wouldn't be deceived by a liar. After running a construction crew, she's no starry-eyed teenager, and she reads people even better than Gin."

"True. Whether or not they're a match, I don't think Sawyer's a bad man." With a sigh, Becca leaned against Logan. "She told me his aura is beautiful—a lovely clear red."

"The woman is scary sometimes." Morgan glanced at Logan. "I don't suppose you're serving beer."

"Mallory didn't think alcohol was a good idea for this meeting. We have iced tea or water." Becca winked. "And there might be cookies left."

"Now you're talking. Thanks." Morgan made his way toward the rear, exchanging greetings as he went. With the exception of two women and a young man, he knew everyone in the room. As he stopped to talk every few feet, he realized he was enjoying himself.

Maybe he wasn't as outgoing as his brothers, but he liked people. Gin had told him he was a perfect balance between extrovert and introvert. His lips quirked. Talking with social workers would warp a man's brain faster than drugs.

"Morgan, how's your brother doing?" At the back tables, Mrs. Reed poured him an iced tea and got one for herself.

Morgan snagged a couple of cookies and handed her one. "He doesn't have internet or phone service there, so we don't hear from him often. During his last call, he sounded good, although he's been taken aback by the poverty. Said kids have starved to death." Morgan couldn't imagine losing children from a lack of food. *Jesus.* "He's teaching villagers how to handle stock. Land's poor, although it can support grazing if managed right. He helped dig a well, too."

"And he's feeling better?" Mrs. Reed had known them for years.

"Yeah. I guess he made the right decision for him." Living with strangers sure wouldn't have been Morgan's choice. When he felt troubled, he headed for the mountains and solitude.

Mrs. Reed patted his arm. "Although you grew up in each other's pockets, you aren't the same. For all his gruff bluster, your brother has a sensitive soul. You, my dear, have a very stable personality."

Morgan almost grinned. Be fun to tell Wyatt how sensitive he was.

"But no matter how well balanced, you'd do better if you were married. It's past time." Mrs. Reed nodded. "Vanessa and I will consider who might suit you."

Before Morgan could find the polite words for *fuck, no*, the bookstore owner had rejoined her covey of businesswomen.

The season might be over, but it was clearly time to schedule some long guide trips. Starting immediately.

WITH KALLIE AND Sunny for company, Mallory waited to one side as the room filled. "A record crowd."

"It wasn't this busy an hour ago," Sunny said. "Who all did you instruct to show up now?"

"Basically anyone in charge of anything." Mallory nodded toward one cluster of people. "Priests and preachers." Another cluster. "The school board and committee leaders." One sitting area. "The daycare owners." A group near the back. "Head of the rancher's co-op, the biggest ranchers, the chamber of commerce people. And the neighborhood leaders—the bossy ones."

Sunny grinned. "There are a lot of those."

Many of the younger adults were only here for the party. Some were teachers, some clerical, some beauticians. Spotting Candy, the woman Sawyer had kissed, Mallory flinched and looked away.

The time with Sawyer was over; she needed to let her hurt and anger go, as well.

Logan walked to the front of the room, and his gravelly voice rang out. "Thanks for coming. Mallory wanted to say a word or two."

As he stalked back to Becca, Kallie snorted. "There's a nice, long introduction."

Jarred out of her somber mood, Mallory laughed and took the designated speaker's spot. As she looked at the crowd, her smile died. Could she make them see how important this was? Her words strangled in her throat.

Eddie Nilsson crossed his arms over his chest. "Speak loud, girl."

The rancher's disrespectful tone was the spur she needed. Her spine turned to steel as she said in a voice that carried to the back of the room, "I'm used to yelling orders over the noise of demolition. I run a construction crew, *boy*."

She waited for the ripple of laughter to die. "People, our town has a problem. Gangs moved in when the prison came—and not all left when it closed. They like having uncontested territory and, even better, a police force ill-equipped to handle them."

Noise broke out in the room, and she grimly waited for people to settle down.

"We aren't a big city. We can't afford a big city taskforce for gangs. After all, we live in a small town because we love the sense of community. Our size is our strength. Let's use it."

"How? You going to pray over them?" The sarcastic voice came from Eddie again.

There was always one loudmouth in every crowd. She tilted her head toward the church delegation. "I'll leave prayers to our churches. What I have in mind is an extreme version of a neighborhood watch."

Silence.

"In a neighborhood watch, residents patrol an area and call the police if there are problems. In cities, the watches have proven effective. I do think we should institute our own neighborhood watches—and include the downtown area. However, let's consider going one step further."

Her *one step further* was why she hadn't invited law enforcement to the meeting, although Sunny and Gin would inform their husbands. But absent cops couldn't take "official" notice of what might skirt the edge of the law.

She pulled in a breath. "I propose we also watch the Aryan Hammers. Watch their house. Watch them when they leave. Trail them wherever they go."

The noise rose as people started talking. Arguing.

"Are you going to assign people to watch over your lover, Sawyer Ware, too?" Roger Simmons's voice was loud.

"Oh, Roger, if you want to sit in front of his house and watch him, you go right ahead."

When a few people snickered, Roger scowled.

Mallory continued, keeping her voice strong. "The decrease in tourists has affected the Aryan Hammers' income. So now they're recruiting—and dealing—at our school."

The news definitely got a reaction. When someone questioned the statement, the PTA president said loudly, "Mallory is correct."

The church leaders' appalled expressions matched those of the ranchers.

Onward. "If we're visibly present wherever the gang goes, they can't make sales. Can't break into houses or businesses. We can learn which children are being recruited and step in. We will shine a spotlight on everything they do."

The local auctioneer grinned. "I have a bullhorn. If you want your assigned observer to announce a drug buy to the world, y'all are welcome to use it." He made a megaphone of his hands and yelled, "Drug buy between little Joe Smith and a gangster puke going on now. Come and see."

The room filled with laughter.

Considering expressions followed.

"I like the plan, Mal." Even without a bullhorn, the auctioneer's voice carried as he shouted, "Who's in?"

The roar of agreement filled the room.

Trying to keep from crowing in delight, Mallory folded her arms over her chest. "When you leave here, please tell every local you know about our plans. We'll get a schedule coordinator appointed and set up a watch list. Bear in mind, we're not trying to be sneaky. We're openly watching and following. We'll make it impossible for them to commit any crimes…and we'll drive away their customers."

With the PTA president beside him, the head of the school board planted his feet. "We'll call a meeting of the parents immediately."

Mrs. Reed stood. "The businesses are in. In fact, Vanessa and I volunteer to manage the schedule."

"You're on. Thank you." Mallory breathed a sigh of relief. Mrs. Reed had been the CEO of an international company before pursuing her dream of owning a bookstore. She could totally handle the volunteers.

When a stampede of agreement followed, Mallory waved Mrs. Reed and Vanessa forward and let them take over.

Success.

Mallory headed for the drink table. By the sun and stars, her throat felt as if she'd swallowed a mound of sand. Spotting Sunny, Kallie, Gin, and Becca at the dessert table, Mallory pantomimed drinking to let them know where she was headed.

"Well, if it isn't the carpenter girl." The ugly tone made the term an insult.

Startled, Mallory turned.

Three beauticians had approached, and it was easy to see which one had spoken. Candy's dark brown aura was so filled with negativity and selfishness, the sneer on her face was redundant.

Mallory picked up a glass of tea and started to move away.

The blonde blocked her path. "It was hilarious when Simmons gave you grief about Sawyer. Why didn't you just tell him Sawyer kicked you to the curb?"

No. Don't start a fight. Besides, she *had* been kicked to the curb, hadn't she? Mallory lifted her eyebrows and waited for the ill-mannered woman to say something worth listening to.

At Mallory's silent response, Candy flushed, glared, and walked away.

Her friends hurried after her. One said something about a bitch, and Candy laughed loudly.

"Talk about rude." Becca stepped up beside Mallory. Frowning after Candy, she crossed her arms over her chest.

Looking back, the three beauticians caught the full force of Becca's annoyed stare. One turned red, then paled.

Becca growled under her breath. "I think it's time to get my hair and nails done in Groveland from now on."

Mallory shook her head. "Don't get carried away. They're just young and—"

Hannah interrupted. "Actually, I'd say they're your age." Boston born and bred, the owner of Hannah's Hair was in her forties. Her short brown hair was perfectly razor cut, and her nails matched her cobalt blue suit.

Mallory sighed. The problem with crowds was there was always someone to overhear. "Hannah, if you want to instruct your beauticians about the ramifications of obnoxious behavior on their future income, it's your prerogative. But for me, I've already let this incident go. Becca will also." She gave Becca a nudge.

After a stubborn second, Becca caved. "I suppose. I do love your salon, Hannah. Can you recommend a different beautician though? Someone not a lackey of Candy's?"

"Absolutely. I'll change your appointments to Sadie." Hannah smiled. "I think you'll like her. She's from San Francisco, is very current—and she's truly a lovely person."

Becca brightened. "Excellent."

"Thank you. And thank you, Mallory, for your compassion." Like Aslan spotting an unwary rodent, the salon owner stalked in a direct line toward her beauticians.

Kallie appeared beside Mallory, her black eyes snapping with anger. "I'm going to knock that woman into next week."

"No, honey, you can't start a fight here." After patting Kallie's arm, Gin handed Mallory a cookie. "Sweetie Pie, you deserve a reward. I loved the way you took the wind out of Roger's sails."

Next to her, Sunny giggled. "You realize Roger picked on you only because if he picked on Sawyer, he'd get flattened." Moving Kallie aside, Sunny put her arm around Mallory.

The image of Roger Simmons trying to face down Sawyer was

almost amusing.

Kallie scowled at Gin. "Sawyer can have Roger—and vice versa. I totally should be allowed to flatten Candy."

"No." Gin's brows drew together as she turned back to Mallory. "I'm having trouble believing what Kallie told me—that Sawyer went from you to making out with Candy. On Main Street. At our barbecue, that man was into you, Mal. Completely."

The memory of him kissing Candy still hurt. "I—"

"You're the most stable person I know, so you didn't change. And he saw you very clearly." Gin held up her hand, forestalling interruptions as she worked through her reasoning. "When young, Sawyer went through women like I go through potato chips."

"Whoa, that's a scary thought," Becca muttered.

"However, Atticus told me Sawyer lost interest in shallow women, years and years ago." Gin pursed her lips. "Now I do hate to say it, but that Candy is shallower than a muddy puddle, bless her heart."

Sunny gave Mallory a squeeze. "I agree. In the clinic, Sawyer was way protective of you. And he was a gentleman. Breaking up or not, is such spiteful behavior like him?"

"No. Actually, it's not like him at all." He'd never been mean. "But why would he go out of his way to hurt me?"

Becca's laugh was unexpected. "Do you remember when I came over, pouting about some rudeness of Logan's? After you fed me cookies and tea and tons of sympathy, you finished it all off with, *'Unless you talk with him and ask, you'll never know why he acted that way.'*"

As the others grinned, Kallie murmured, "She's used the *talk to him* line on me, too."

Becca examined her nails, then gave Mallory an evil smile. "So, girlfriend, right back at'cha. Unless you talk with him and ask, you'll never know why he acted that way."

Well, honestly. Mallory scowled. "Although I believe in recycling, you've gone too far. Good advice shouldn't be returned like you would a...a soda bottle."

Her friends broke into laughter.

As the others talked about the neighborhood watch, Mallory nibbled on a cookie and considered. Talk to Sawyer. *Oh, boy.*

Still, the damn *vigilante* needed to be warned about the Town Watch. And while she was there, she'd talk to him. Really talk.

Only…she so, *so* didn't want to hear again how she wasn't exciting enough for him.

THE AFTERNOON CLOUDS had blown off, leaving a clear twilight sky. The tang of frost was in the air.

Overheated, Sawyer tossed his shirt to one side. Picking up the maul again, he swung. With a satisfying crack, two pieces of firewood flew apart.

Splitting wood had been his mother's sovereign remedy for teenage troubles. Fumbled the football? Go split some wood. Got a penalty in calf roping? Go split some wood. Fought with the girlfriend? Go split some wood.

As a kid, he'd spent hours working off his anger on the woodpile. Later, in the Navy, morning PT had served as an adequate substitute but, he had to admit, a mounting pile of wood added extra gratification.

Over the past few days, his firewood piles had grown to towering heights.

A whuff of warning came from Achilles, who was tied up at a safe distance from the flying wood.

"What?" Sawyer looked around and stiffened at the sight of Mallory's pickup.

The calming effects of splitting wood vanished, and an ache filled his chest. Again. Dammit, he missed her. For two weeks, they'd spent every free minute together, and rather than growing bored, he'd fallen more and more in love.

It was a wonder he'd managed to mask his emotions enough that she'd fallen for his performance with the blonde bimbo.

Achilles whuffed again, and Sawyer stared as the pickup pulled up to his house.

What the fuck? After his behavior on Main Street, no ex-girlfriend should speak to him again—especially one as strong as

Mallory.

She walked over, carrying a piece of paper. "Hey." Her gaze took in the healing bullet graze on his arm.

"Mallory." After sinking his maul into the stump, he freed Achilles and watched the pup greet her with frantic circles and whines.

Smiling at the puppy, she knelt to dispense pats and scratches.

She hadn't smiled at Sawyer.

Before, every time they met, she would give him that smile, the one he'd noticed was all his. A soft glimmer would start in her wide eyes, like sunlight on a forest lake, then a dimple would show, just at the corner of her mouth, before her beautiful smile would appear.

Today, her smile at Achilles's antics hadn't reached her eyes.

The black cloud settled more firmly on his shoulders. He'd made her unhappy. And if she didn't leave quickly, he was liable to lose his resolve and beg her forgiveness.

"What can I help you with, Mallory?" His voice came out brusque. With luck, she'd figure he was impatient.

"I'm sorry for interrupting your evening," she said softly. "At the End of Season party today, Bear Flat decided to start a town watch to deal with the increase in crime. I wanted you to know."

He nodded. A town watch? He'd have to be extra careful, for damn sure.

She continued. "Also... Along with the neighborhood and downtown patrols, we'll be openly observing the Aryan Hammers. We plan to follow them wherever they go and spotlight their activities."

Sawyer stared at her as cold horror streamed into his veins. "You're talking about a shitload of civilians taking on a violent gang? Putting themselves at risk?" He struggled to control himself and not scorch her ears with a whole new kind of vocabulary. "Who the fu— hell thought of this disaster?"

Because whoever dreamed up this clusterfuck would be the next one targeted by the fucking gang.

Her chin came up. "That would be me."

Fury spiked inside him so hard and fast his entire world went red. "*You?*" Gripping her shoulders, he started to shake her...got control…and glared instead. "I broke us apart to keep you safe, and now you've strolled right back into the kill zone. Jesus *fucking* Christ. I should spank you. Will spank you."

"Spank me? You…you—" Her green eyes snapped with anger, and then her expression went blank.

Oh, damn him, what had he said?

"Gin was right. You deliberately, publicly dumped me." She yanked loose and walked in a circle, staring at the ground. "You made a show of kissing Candy—which isn't like you—to make sure everyone in town knew we weren't together."

She glowered at him and made another circle.

He had hoped like fuck she wouldn't get past angry and start to think—but thinking she was. And she was one of the smartest people he knew. Dammit.

"You didn't want people to know we were together because…" Her hands hit her hips, and her eyes narrowed.

No man would ever want that unforgiving expression directed at him. Sawyer felt his balls shrivel.

"…because the skinheads are out to get you. You worried they might target your girlfriend. Me." She gave a satisfied nod, even though he hadn't said a damn word.

Maybe he didn't…totally…believe she could see auras, but she could sure read him like a book.

He cleared his throat. "Baby, it isn't safe to be around me. The Hammers would go after you just to hurt me." Then he remembered why she'd come to the house, and his blood pressure mounted like a volcano about to blow. "But that doesn't matter, does it?"

His voice rose. "You had to go and set yourself up as a whole separate target. Jesus, are you *crazy*? I lov—Do you know what it would do to me if they…" He couldn't even find the words.

Her lips curved. She actually fucking laughed—the brilliantly beautiful sound that brightened the entire world. "You…Sawyer Ware…you *love* me."

His head really did explode. "Fuck, yes, I love you!" When Achilles skittered back, he realized he was shouting.

The woman was going to kill him. Stone dead. Nonetheless, he cranked back the volume. "I love you. Now, will you stop being suicidal and go live in Europe for a month?" He hauled in a breath. "*Please.*"

Suddenly, his arms were filled with a soft, sweet woman, and she was kissing him—and still laughing.

And some dumb fucks said there were no more miracles in the world.

A FEW MINUTES later, Mallory wasn't sure how they'd arrived upstairs in Sawyer's loft. Instantaneous travel through space and time?

With firm hands, he stripped her naked, taking a long kiss between each article of clothing.

"Much better." Already shirtless, he picked her up and tossed her onto the bed as easily as he would a pillow. With decisive movements, he unzipped his jeans—and his cock sprang free.

Coming down on her, he flattened her into the bed with his weight and took her mouth in a rough, incredibly sexy demand that set her whole body on fire. A second later, he yanked her arms over her head and pinned her wrists with one big hand. "I'm taking you now, nymph. Hard."

He cupped her pussy. His eyes glinted in satisfaction as he found her already wet, and with no other warning, he shifted over, settled his cock at her entrance, and ruthlessly penetrated her in one hard thrust.

She gasped, her back arching at the wonderful, shocking possession. Oh, she'd missed him.

Pausing, seated as deeply and intimately as possible, he pressed his forehead against hers. "I'm sorry I didn't talk to you about my concerns." His lips brushed hers. "I love you so fucking much, Mallory McCabe."

With his whispered words, she felt the last of her anger die. Oh, they had talking to do—lots of talking—but he was protective right down to his bones. He'd thought the Hammers would hurt her—

because of him. Of course, he'd do what he thought necessary to keep her safe.

The idiot.

"I love you, too, Sawyer Ware." She pressed her lips against his, and then he took such complete control of the kiss—of her—that her mind emptied. As his tongue teased hers, his cock hammered into her, hard and fast.

"You'd best catch up, nymph." Releasing her wrists, he lifted his torso up far enough to use his hand on her clit. Firm fingers slid over the sensitive nub, and he laughed as the upward jolt of her hips drove his cock in farther.

The feeling of his thick, rigid shaft inside and his merciless fingers teasing her clit sent shudders through her, melted her insides, and a second later, she was climaxing, coming hard, pleasure rushing through her with each spasm.

"Put your arms around me." Pulling her legs up and around his waist, he surged into her, deep, deeper, and came with a low growl that reverberated through her.

"I missed you." She kissed his hard shoulder and tasted the salt on his skin.

"Me, too. You have no idea." Holding her pinned against him, he rolled them over, still embedded inside her. Right where he belonged.

Chapter Twenty-Four

A SOUND WOKE Mallory from her drowse, and as she sat up in bed, Sawyer entered the room. Shirtless and in clean jeans, he was toweling his short hair. Although the healing wound on his arm had given her a rough moment when she'd first seen it, now she could look past it and appreciate the way his solid biceps flexed with each movement. His powerful shoulders tapered to a lean waist. Still pumped up from splitting wood, his chest was simply amazing. His jeans hung low enough to see the angled line just above his hipbones.

She'd missed touching him.

"I brought you some water." He handed her a glass of ice water and set a coffee mug down on the bedside table.

"Thank you." After drinking half the water, she realized he was studying her, his gaze...dangerous. "What?"

"How much do you trust me, little contractor?" His voice had deepened.

"I trust you." The answer was easy. Automatic. Anyone seeing his aura would trust him. The clear, rich colors said this person was solid to the core.

"Good to hear." After setting her glass on the bedside table, he pulled wrist cuffs and rope from the drawer.

She frowned. Although she couldn't see the contents, the nightstand drawer looked fuller than it had the last time she'd been here.

"Wrists, please."

At the controlled heat in his eyes, a shiver of excitement ran through her. "What are you planning?"

"A little pleasure, a little pain, a little fun." His slow smile made her heart skip a beat. "Wrists. Now."

Her hands were in his before she thought about obeying him. "You're such a good girl."

The approving words pattered over her like a warm spring rain.

He buckled a fleece-lined black leather cuff around each wrist and checked the fit with his usual care. For a moment, he regarded at her silently, his eyes darkening. "You always look incredibly sexy dressed only in my cuffs."

Her nipples turned to hard peaks. He'd restrained her before, and each time, it was...special. Different. Intensely hot.

He flattened her onto her back and loosely roped her left wrist cuff to one headboard post, and the right wrist cuff to the other post.

After attaching ankle cuffs, he smiled at her. "You're used to being tied up now, so I'm going to add some new things."

He selected Apocalyptica's haunting "Farewell" tune and turned the music low, then removed a strip of leather from the bedside table. "Your safe word is now three hoots."

"But why—"

He pushed the strip of leather between her teeth and tied it behind her head. "This is why." He met her stunned gaze with determined blue eyes. "Tonight you have a safe word—and nothing else."

Sun and stars. She wouldn't be able to talk. To tell him what she was feeling. The knowledge was frightening, yet her body simmered with heat and need, as if he'd tossed a pine log into her inner fireplace.

"Nod if you understand."

Her breathing was faster than normal, but she nodded.

"Good. You'll have lots of time to get used to being silent." He pulled her downward on the bed, until her butt was near the foot-boardless mattress edge and between the six-foot-tall bottom bedposts.

After tying a rope to one bedpost at chest height, he lifted her right leg and secured the rope to her ankle cuff. After a second of consideration, he shoved a pillow under her bottom to elevate her hips.

"Better." He restrained her left ankle in the same way.

Her legs were now raised and spread in a wide V position, and her pussy was totally exposed. Her arms were not completely restrained, which was good, wasn't—

At the head of the bed, he tightened the ropes attached to her wrists, until her arms were drawn into a spread-eagle position.

Taking something else from the bedside table, he sat beside her and ran his hands over her breasts, stroking her gently. "I'm going to do things to you, Mallory. Lots of dirty things." His big hand caressed her cheek. "And you won't be able to stop me unless you give three hoots."

Eyes wide, she nodded. Her heart was thumping along...a little too fast...but not in flight mode. She'd come a long way from the night at Dark Haven. And she'd learned it was amazingly freeing to be tied up and unable to make any decisions.

Still...not being able to talk? A tiny flutter of anxiety ran over her skin.

"Good. I'll add one more thing to increase your sensitivity." He set a wide, black satin blindfold over her eyes and tied it behind her head.

She couldn't see anything. Couldn't speak. Couldn't move. "Uuuuuh," she protested instinctively.

His palm against her cheek was warm. Reassuring. "Easy, nymph. I'm here. I will not leave you for even a second, and I'll be talking to you as we play." His dark, quiet voice was measured and sure. "Take a breath and give me a nod when you're calm."

Okay, okay. She was all right. As she pulled in a breath, she realized the way he'd removed all her control, from sight to her ability to move, raised the simmering hunger inside her to a boil. After a second, she gave him the nod he was waiting for.

"Aren't you a sweet little nymph," he murmured. He nuzzled her cheek below the blindfold, and she felt the rough stubble on his jaw. His fingers played with her breasts, plucking the nipples gently. "I love your breasts. They're as sweet to look at as they are to taste."

As he caressed her breasts, he slowly kissed along her jaw, her neck, and down to her chest. When he started to use his teeth and tongue on her nipples, her breasts swelled to a throbbing tightness. He lifted his head, and cool air wafted across her wet skin. Her nipples gathered into achingly sensitive peaks.

"Beautiful."

Something brushed over the hard nubs. The backs of his knuckles?

"I'll be back to do more to these beauties after I torment some other areas. Isn't it nice that, with the way you're tied, I have access to everything I'm interested in?"

For the love of cats, the more he talked, the hotter—and more nervous—she got. A whimper escaped her, and he chuckled, low and masculine.

The music changed, grew more ominous. Ordo Rosarious Equilibrio's "Let Me Show You, All the Secrets of the Torture Garden".

Something rattled—he was rummaging in the bedside dresser again, and she stiffened. His warm hand stroked down her stomach, then he ran his hands up and down her inner—widely spread—thighs. "I love having your cunt and asshole wide open to me, pet."

His fingers explored her pussy where she most ached. One lone finger circled her clit with unerring precision, slick and sure, and a sharp stream of pleasure shocked through her.

ENJOYING THE FUCK out of himself, Sawyer smiled. She was soaking wet, and each time he ran his finger around her glistening clit, it engorged further.

When it poked out from beneath its hood, he inserted a finger in her entrance and curved it up to rub her G-spot roughly. Nice and spongy, showing her excitement. Mallory was always responsive, but bondage pushed her right to the edge.

But...he wasn't going to let her climax. Not for quite a while. In fact, a nice Dom might warn a helpless subbie. So he did. "Just so you know, I've got a lot of frustration saved up—and I'm going to take my time. Lots of time."

When she quivered, her breasts jiggled.

Yeah, very nice.

First, sensation play…which was always more fun when the submissive couldn't see what was being used. He dipped his fingers in the mug on the bedside stand and found the coconut oil was still hot. Rubbing it between his palms, he ran his hands over her torso and up to her breasts.

She jumped at the unexpected heat of his hands, then relaxed as he massaged her. Shoulders, arms, and…those sweet breasts. Oil-slickened, swollen, sensitive breasts. Oh yeah. And if he took some extra time teasing his favorite bits, she could hardly stop him. Gags were damn useful.

When she'd obviously drifted into a warm glow, he plucked an ice cube from her glass of ice water and ran it in a circle around one nipple.

The color in her face went bright red, and the ropes slapped the bedposts as her arms jerked. "*Mmrk.*"

Good thing—for her—he couldn't decipher what she'd called him. Suppressing a laugh, he moved to her other breast.

As he'd warned her…he mercilessly took his time.

Hot and cold gave way to alternating soft fur and sharp claws until she was tensing more and more in anticipation of what he would do next.

Gripping her long, sleek hair, he pulled, tilting her head back and increasing her sense of being helpless. The color in her cheeks deepened, and when he brushed his lips over the side of her neck, he could feel the hammering of her pulse.

More.

He picked up a silky makeup brush…and a strip of sandpaper. This time, he'd start at her feet and work his way up.

Between each slow circuit of sensual toys, he teased her pussy, keeping her aroused and needy—but never letting her get off.

He fucking loved the combination of sensual torture and edging.

Her skin reddened. Her nipples jutted into long peaks.

Smiling, he picked up the next toy. Long and thin, it looked like a marriage between anal beads and a thin dildo. Even better, a button on the wide end turned it into a vibrator. He covered it with a condom, lubed it, and took the time to tease her rim with the slick tip. With his other hand, he played with her clit.

When she was squirming and heading toward an orgasm, he firmly slid the ball-studded shaft into her anus.

Her whole body went rigid. "Mmmph!"

Maybe he did have a bit of sadist in him. Watching her wiggle as she struggled with the sensation of having her ass penetrated was almost as much fun as seeing how the plug increased her arousal.

He was harder than a rock, but, hell, he could keep this up forever.

HE'D SHOVED SOMETHING up her *butt*. Mallory couldn't believe what he'd done. Damn him. Every time she moved, the thing sent odd zips of pleasure through her—and she couldn't seem to stop wiggling.

Her whole body shivered with excitement. Her skin had grown so sensitive, she could feel the heat of his body as he bent over her.

"Let's try something new." His voice was steady. Firm. In control.

Oh, no. She couldn't see his face, but knew his jaw would be determined. When a shiver ran through her, he chuckled.

His fingers stroked around her pussy again, as he'd been doing since they started, keeping her so aroused, her center throbbed with need. "Some women—even ones who don't like being flogged—enjoy increased sensation on their pussy. Let's see if you're one of them."

What did he mean? She made a questioning sound and got no answer. What did he *mean*?

On her pussy, he tapped her labia lightly with his fingers, tiny slaps that were like hot little explosions. The slaps grew harder, imparting a slight sting.

Then, one finger tapped the top of her *clit* in almost the same way, making her jump and suck in air.

Oh no, he wouldn't.

Thankfully, he stopped.

She pulled in a slow breath of relief as he kissed up her stomach and licked over her breasts. Down below, her pussy was tingling, as if shocked awake. Her breasts throbbed in time with her heart as he sucked each nipple, biting very, very lightly.

The toy with the sharp claws lightly scraped down her belly, followed by the gentle warmth of his palm as if to smooth out the edgy sensation.

Her heart was thumping fast, and her body was damp with sweat and need. Every inch of skin was awake and aroused, her entire lower half a molten lake of need. Her clit thrummed.

Moving down, he slapped her wet folds again, lightly, harder, a soft *smack, smack, smack*. His fingers circled her entrance, setting off a desperate hunger for something inside. For his cock.

With a finger, he circled her swollen clit long enough to get her right to the edge of orgasm…then he stopped and slapped her labia again.

Smack, smack, smack.

Her pussy lips swelled, thick and sensitive and burning. He moved to tap her clit with one finger, and each time she jumped at the alarming sensation.

Somehow, somehow, she grew even more aroused.

He kissed her breasts, his hands warm as he pushed them together for his mouth and massaged the slick skin roughly. Gently. He bit her shoulder, teeth digging in just short of pain, before kissing the stinging spot. He suckled her breasts.

Waves of heat traveled from her toes to her head.

She had a few seconds with nothing happening and pulled in a slow breath. Was he done?

His palm struck her pussy…and this time, the bottom of her clit. Her *clit*.

Smack, smack, smack.

Even more blood surged into her labia and clit, and the throbbing burn was so intense, her hips bucked. How could something hurt and feel incredible at the same time?

"Someone likes having her pussy slapped, I think." His voice, so rich, smooth, and controlled, pulled her deeper, yet kept her safe, like arms around her in a scary world. Another contradiction.

His tongue ran in a circle over her stinging clit...sending her up and up, almost to coming before he retreated.

She moaned.

His hand slapped her...higher...right over her clit this time.

Smack, smack, smack.

Each slap was a burst of sensation, like boiling fireworks. When he stopped, her swollen pussy pulsed, burning with heat.

His hot, wet tongue circled her clit, making her tense at the amazing sensation.

He chuckled...and slid something with ridges into her vagina. It filled her, cool and hard, and together with his teasing tongue on her clit, sent her to the precipice.

And *over.*

Her insides convulsed around the hard objects in her pussy and anus, and staggering pleasure ricocheted through her system. His tongue slid over her clit, and with every stroke, she spasmed again. "Uuunh!"

As his tongue slowed and lightened, he slid the dildo in and out, then removed it.

Ohhhh. Her heart was thumping hard, her skin damp with—

Smack, smack, smack.

The shocking slaps hit right on her pussy and clit, and the appalling—*exquisite*—pain exploded through her. Her back arched in protest and delight.

Suddenly the plug in her anus was vibrating. The dildo slid in, hard and fast. A mouth closed around her clit—sucking.

She came again—so very hard—and all she could hear was the roar of blood in her ears. Her entire pussy was huge, swollen, and her heart was hammering like a wild thing.

He didn't turn the anal vibrator off.

The vibrations shook her sensitive backside, and she squirmed.

He pulled back on the anal plug, and each rounded section

stretched her rim between the narrower sections. So many bumps. He pushed it back, slowly running it in and out, driving her crazy with the unfamiliar sensations in such a sensitive—private—place.

She made a sound, some sort of sound, and he laughed. *Laughed.* "I'm not through with you, nymph."

The anal plug went back in, still steadily vibrating. She heard his jeans zipper.

"I want to feel you around me. Come hard, this time." He must have been standing at the foot of the bed as his hands ran up and down the insides of her legs. Then his shaft touched her entrance.

Her head moved back and forth as his cock pressed in. She had that thing in her butt—and he was so large—and she couldn't move away.

Mercilessly, he entered her. So thick, yet the heat and smoothness were glorious. Nothing had ever felt as good as he did.

Still sensitive from her climax, her vagina clamped down on the intrusion—and he gave a hum of enjoyment. "You feel fucking amazing."

When he was deeply inside her, he paused.

Needing more, more, more, she tried to move, to make *him* move, but her legs were restrained, and she had no leverage. The frustrated sound she gave made him chuckle.

When she wiggled, his balls bumped against her ass cheeks...against the anal vibrator. *Oh, the feel.*

His fingers ran over her clit, and she sucked in air so hard she almost choked.

Something new buzzed.

"Come for me, Mallory. Let me feel your cunt squeeze me." A vibrator came down on her clit, hammering the nub hard and fast. As the other vibrator in her ass buzzed away, his cock started moving, driving in, long and deep.

Within one second—just one—the pressure inside her built, coalesced, and ignited into a deep internal pulsing release. A tidal wave of pleasure hit her so hard that, behind the blindfold, her world went white.

Gasping, whimpering, and drenched in sweat, she tried to recover her senses, but the entire world was swathed in gauze. Her body had gone limp and boneless, even as little twitches made her quiver. The vibrator lifted from her clit. "Hang onto your ropes, nymph. I'm going to take you now." His cock slammed into her.

She moaned. The slapping had made her folds fat and sensitive and tightened her entrance around him, so every thrust pulled on her clit. Her very, very sensitive clit. This time, the need grew from inside her, steadily increasing like a hand tightening around her center. The pleasure increased with each hard plunge of his shaft.

"One more time, nymph."

She shook her head, pulled out of her foggy clouds, realizing she was teetering at the edge again, not as much in need as just…inevitability. He felt so, so good.

One hand was under her ass, lifting her for each stroke. The vibrator pressed against her clit again, and this time, the vibrations were erratic. *Rrr-rrr-RRRRRRRR.* Somehow, he timed his thrusts to the pattern, gliding in with each short *rrr*, pounding her during the long wave.

And she was coming again. *Again!* The climax filled her center with hot waves of pleasure, overflowing and pouring through her nerves and veins and cells to every finger and toe. Her anchor snapped, and she drifted free in the warm ocean.

His heavy shaft was inside her, pressing deep, and filling her with even more heat. The vibrator was gone, and he'd curved both hands under her bottom; his strong fingers were holding her up and tightly against him.

Possessing her. Using her to take his own pleasure.

As she drifted away completely, she wished he'd removed the gag so she could tell him how much she loved him.

THE LITTLE NYMPH had gone deep. Sawyer smiled as he removed everything and released her. After cleaning up, he rolled her tightly in a fuzzy blanket to continue giving her the sense of being restrained.

Once Achilles had a quick break outside, Sawyer tossed the pup onto the foot of the bed and pulled his cocooned submissive into his arms.

She roused enough to look at him with glazed, utterly beautiful eyes. Realizing he was holding her, she didn't even try to struggle. Instead, she sighed, rubbed her cheek on his shoulder, and was out.

Trust. Even though she couldn't move her arms, she'd seen him—and known she was safe.

He'd never been given a finer gift.

Chapter Twenty-Five

T HE NEXT MORNING, Mallory had dragged Sawyer back to her house and made them both breakfast. As expected, Aslan had complained vociferously about being abandoned overnight...until Sawyer had sacrificed a piece of his bacon.

Felines were wonderfully bribable.

Mallory smiled toward the back of the house where Aslan was undoubtedly taking advantage of having an extra lap available again. Her cat had missed Sawyer.

So had she.

Finished filling a new stoneware jar with dog biscuits, Mallory put it next to her cookie jar. She smiled down at Achilles who was watching her with hopeful eyes. "You don't think Sawyer will get this confused with the cookie jar, do you?"

Imagining Sawyer chomping down on a beefy dog snack—and what horrific language would follow—made her grin. She picked up a biscuit. "Achilles, sit."

A little butt hit the floor.

"Perfect. You're a very smart dog."

Achilles fielded the treat she tossed him and spun in a circle, delighted with himself.

Mallory laughed, leaned on the counter, and savored the peaceful start of the day.

She might have taught Sawyer to meditate—which, to her amazement, he had continued—but he'd taught her to love Sunday mornings. Sleeping in was nice. When it was followed by long, lazy lovemaking? Even better.

Feeling relaxed and happy, Mallory made her tea, poured coffee, and carried the tray into the sunroom where Sawyer was reading the paper.

The early sun streamed in through the windows, warming the room after the icy November night. Around the valley, all the mountains were now capped with snow. Soon the snow would extend to the foothills and valleys. Would blanket her garden and the pastures.

"Here, Ware. Have some caffeine to go with your news." After handing him a cup, she set her tea tray on the coffee table and joined him.

"Thanks, nymph." Smiling, he pulled her closer.

Having followed her in, Achilles considered the empty spot beside them, and then curled up next to Aslan on the sun-warmed tiles.

"Anything interesting?" Mallory asked. Bear Flat's weekly didn't usually contain anything exciting.

Sawyer set down the paper. "The usual social events. Some places to donate food for Thanksgiving deliveries to shut-ins. Some unhappy shit—like the housing market is still depressed, and unemployment is bad, especially now the seasonal logging and tourist jobs have dried up. Robberies, pickpocketing, car thefts, and burglaries are all up. Graffiti has gotten worse, too."

Wasn't it amazing how his strong body next to hers could relieve unhappy news? "Hopefully the Town Watch will have an effect on the crime." She tensed, thinking of how Sawyer had almost been killed when he took on the gang alone. "Are you going to slow down? Or maybe help with the Town Watch?"

He didn't pretend to misunderstand what she was asking. "Babe, I'm not comfortable with civilians putting themselves in danger. Protecting them is my job."

She understood his need to protect—and knew there was no way to keep him safe.

He looked down at her, his blue eyes unusually sharp. "I won't be slowing down, either. Not since everyone knows you were the one to start the Town Watch. Killing off the leader of the resistance is a time-honored tradition, especially for gangs. If Animal gets to you, he wipes out the Town Watch—and me." He closed his eyes for a moment. "I'm not sure how I'd react if you were hurt, Mallory."

The idea of the gang coming after her was terrifying. And fully as frightening was the thought of them getting their hands on Sawyer. She frowned. "Who exactly is Animal?" Just the name evoked a primitive fear response.

"He took over the Hammers when the previous boss, Slash, was imprisoned."

Atticus had killed Slash. Now she knew what had goaded Sawyer into taking on the vigilante role. With a frown, Mallory took his hand. "If they're after Atticus, isn't Gin in danger, too?"

"Att warned her. Jacob always walks her to her car when she leaves the counseling offices. She's vigilant about staying safe." Sawyer ran his hand over her hair. "I know you promised me you would be, too. Maybe now you understand the danger better?"

"I do." However, knowing how frightened she was wouldn't help Sawyer worry less. On the contrary. She drank her tea to wash away the tang of fear. "I promise I'll be extra careful."

"Thank you." He cupped her cheek in his hand. "Stay around other people at all times. Be aware of who is near you, even in busy places, and also when you're driving. Keep your phone easily at hand. And…do you have any firearms?"

"Actually, yes."

The way his brows went up was rather nice. "My New-Ager has weapons?"

"Gramps owned a couple of rifles and an old revolver."

"Where are they?"

"There's a hidden panel in the closet."

He looked impressed. "I didn't notice. Must be a pretty fine job."

"Thanks." She grinned. "It was one of my first woodworking projects. The one that taught me to measure twice and cut once."

He chuckled. "Screwed it up a time or two?"

"At least."

"When's the last time you shot any of those weapons?"

"Uh…maybe high school." She gave him a level look. "Back when I decided I wasn't the type of person to ever want to hurt or shoot anyone. Or even own a gun."

"What I thought." Sawyer pulled the phone from his pocket. "Masterson, any chance you could talk Hunt into letting us use his range? I want to see how well Mallory can shoot."

Sipping her tea, Mallory eyed him as he totally arranged her day. Without asking her. Her bossy, overprotective, demanding lover.

How in the world had she ended up with a real-life version of Éomer, the horse lord?

No wonder his sister, Éowyn, had so often looked as if she wanted to kick him in the family jewels.

HALFWAY AROUND A mountain, the Hunts' gun range was a good hike away from Serenity Lodge—probably to buffer the noise of firearms. Despite the cold mountain air, Mallory was toasty warm by the time she, Sawyer, Morgan, and Logan Hunt arrived.

As Mallory stepped through the fence gate and into the clearing, she tried one more protest. "You know, Ware, shooting isn't my thing."

"You don't have to like it, nymph." Carrying Gramps's range bag, Sawyer glanced at her. "I just want you to be able to hit anything you aim at."

Joining him at the line of stumps topped with seasoned wood that served as shooting benches, Logan and Morgan grinned. Their expressions of agreement said she was outnumbered.

"I suppose the way things are in town, it's wise to be able to shoot." Her mouth firmed. If any of those Aryan Hammers came to her house looking for Sawyer, she'd pull the trigger.

Probably.

Logan strolled out to attach paper to the various wood-backed torso targets.

Morgan set three rifle cases down on a T-shaped bench and started to unpack. "I brought my baby this time, Ware. You said you wanted to see it."

"Oh, yeah."

Mallory pulled Gramps's revolver out of the range bag and laid it on the bench she'd be using.

Logan walked over, and his eyebrows went up. "Nice piece. Colt .45's are popular with the older ranchers around here."

Sawyer grinned. "That old Peacemaker might not be fast to fire, but if the nymph shoots someone in the chest, he'll be pushing up daisies."

Mallory flinched. "I don't want to kill anyone. How about I aim for the arm or leg?"

"Unless you're a damn good shot—and not in a hurry—you aim for the center of the biggest mass." Logan slapped his chest.

"Load, pet." Sawyer handed her the box of 45s.

Well, it was what she was here for. Silently, Mallory loaded the six chambers.

"Weapons are live, Masterson," Logan called, alerting Morgan to stay behind the firing line of benches.

The range had a variety of targets, from stumps with mounted head-size metal plates, to tall arches with dangling metal targets.

After putting on ear protection and safety glasses, Mallory took the two-handed stance Gramps had taught, picked a close paper target, cocked the hammer, and emptied the revolver.

Sheesh, she'd forgotten how loud the gun was, even when muffled.

Sawyer put his arm around her shoulders and studied the bullet holes. All were in the chest area. "You're better than I thought you'd be. Let's try for more distance. I want you to work your way, target by target, to 25 yards." He pointed to a man-sized target way too far away.

"Seriously? I won't even be able to see the holes." Mallory reloaded the revolver.

Helping Morgan set up, Logan looked over. "That's why the distant targets are metal and mounted on springs. You'll hear a hit and see the target rock."

Picking a metal disk farther away and taking her time, she took another six shots. Not too bad, considering how long it had been.

Sawyer nodded. "Your grandfather taught you well—you have excellent form; just need more practice. Keeping going, nymph. I want to know you'll nail anything you aim at."

She raised an eyebrow. "That sounds rather dirty."

He grinned. "Do it anyway."

"Sir, yes, Sir."

At his silence, she looked up...and saw the hunger in his eyes. He ran his finger over her lower lip. "Right now, I have the damndest urge to haul you off to bed." He glanced around. "Or fuck you against a tree."

She flushed as heat lit in her core. "Bad Ware. Go play with Morgan's toys."

When Sawyer snorted, she flushed. "Okay, that sounded bad, too." She made a brushing-off motion. "Shoo."

As he walked away, she could only think how she'd never, ever grow tired of hearing him laugh.

Over in the "guy" section, Logan was using one of Morgan's rifles and aiming at something a long, long, long way off. The ring of metal sounded once out of five shots. "Damn."

"Nah, you're getting better," Morgan said. He was flat on his belly in the scrub grass, a rifle balanced on some two-legged mount. Sawyer stood nearby with binoculars. Morgan aimed and went utterly still.

A shot. *Clang.* A shot. *Clang.* A shot. *Clang.*

As Mallory reloaded her revolver, she eyed Morgan's rifle, something he was calling a Gladius. The weapon reminded her of a photographer's super-deluxe camera—huge with all the bells and whistles—except this was a rifle. And as with fancy cameras, the other men were drooling.

Men and their technological envy.

"That's a hell of a weapon," Sawyer said. "And you're a damn good shot, Masterson. Better than most of the snipers I worked with in the sandbox."

"Target shooting is a fun hobby." Morgan's lips curved. "If I'm actually hunting, I use a bow."

"You and Wyatt are a pair." Logan glanced at Sawyer. "Wyatt loves black-powder rifles. And throwing hatchets."

Sawyer grinned. "I look forward to meeting him."

"Ah, right, speaking of my brother's continued absence..." Morgan rolled up on an elbow. "We'll take you up on your offer to buy our stock and lease it back."

Sawyer went still. "I thought Wyatt made those decisions."

"He did, and might well again." Morgan's mouth went flat. "But it seems my brother wants to stay in Africa another few months. While he's there, *someone* has to tend the business."

Seeing the simmering anger in Morgan's aura, Mallory winced. Wyatt was going to have some fence-mending to do when he got back.

"I'd be a fool to turn you down," Sawyer told Morgan. "When you're ready, we'll talk prices and contracts."

"You got it."

As Morgan turned back to shooting, Sawyer returned. "Good job, nymph. You shoot well, even if it has been a while."

She set the revolver down beside him. "Take a turn, Captain. You know you want to."

He hesitated, then grinned and loaded it. After hefting the weapon for a second as if to check the weight, he aimed and put all six shots in the head of the most distant pistol target.

Wow. She knew he'd be good, but...wow.

He reloaded, and clang after clang came as he worked on the more distant *rifle* targets. Almost reluctantly he set the Peacemaker down. "Back to work for you." He bent to give her a sweet kiss. "Thank you."

After finishing off a box of cartridges, Mallory was through. Her wrists hurt, her arms were tired, and her accuracy was steadily decreasing.

Taking her revolver, she settled at another log "table" to clean it again...and watch the boys and their toys.

After his military service, Logan had suffered from PTSD, and gunfire used to bother him. In the last couple of years, he'd gotten better. And he certainly did all right when he was hands-on.

Sawyer was obviously enjoying himself, completely at home in the company of the other two.

Although Morgan and Logan were both rough and dangerous outdoorsmen, Morgan made an effort to be approachable. Logan didn't—and a lot of people found him daunting.

Sawyer fit well with them both.

"You Hunts going to be here for Thanksgiving?" Morgan asked Logan.

"Nope. After our last vacationer at the Lodge checks out, we're leaving for Oregon until Friday." Logan added for Sawyer, "It's my parents' turn to host us for the holidays. Back when, they'd whine if Jake and I didn't visit. With Ansel, their demands to see us have gone off the scale."

Mallory completely understood. Everybody loved the little toddler. "How about the Mastersons? Are you all staying home?"

"Nope," Morgan said. "Summer's parents put in a demand to see their daughter, so she and Virg are flying to Iowa tomorrow to spend Thanksgiving there."

"Are Kallie and Jake going to Oregon, too?" At Logan's nod, Mallory frowned at Morgan. "You'll be alone here." Alone for Thanksgiving?

He shrugged. "Not a big deal."

Yes, it was. Especially with Wyatt in Africa. "You'll be at our place, then—say around noon. Atticus and Gin are coming, and dinner is at one."

Morgan stared at her. "Mallory, you don't have—"

"Forget it, Masterson." Sawyer shot her an approving grin. "You don't argue with a woman about shit like this. A guy might win a battle about firearms. Holidays? Not a chance."

"I stand corrected." Morgan turned to her with a grateful smile. "And thank you. I'll be there. Uh…"

"Relax, I've tasted your cooking. You bring the alcohol." Smothering a laugh at his relief, Mallory turned back to cleaning her revolver.

Chapter Twenty-Six

THE AROMA OF roasting turkey had filled the house for hours. And the wait had been worth it.

Replete, Sawyer surveyed the remains of the Thanksgiving feast. "You make a damn good turkey, nymph." He wasn't lying, either. If she wanted, the general contractor could hang up her hammer and cook for a living.

"*We* made a good turkey," she said, smiling at him and Morgan.

He grinned. Much like the way she ran her construction site, she'd drafted him and Morgan into chopping and boiling and peeling. The woman could create order from any amount of chaos.

A chorus of agreement came from the guests around the table—his brother, Gin, and Morgan.

With his muzzle on Sawyer's boot, Achilles shifted and grumbled at the noise. The pup had "assisted" in the kitchen, cleaning up any spills, and despite Sawyer's standing orders, was treated to far too many tidbits.

Aslan hadn't been neglected and had retired to the back of the couch to clean his greasy whiskers.

Leaning back with a sigh, Sawyer eyed the pumpkin and apple pies Gin had brought. "If I sit for a while, I'll manage to free up a corner for dessert."

The counselor gave him a laughing look. "It's good to see your optimism has returned."

"Some of us know how to pace ourselves. I have room for pie,"

Morgan said with a smug smile. "And if I didn't say this before, thank you for the invite, Mal."

"I'm glad you could come." With Sawyer's hand in hers, she smiled at Morgan. "We'll have to do this more often. We can call it the Kestrel Mountain Gathering or something."

That sounded good. Sawyer could almost feel his roots extending into the soil. Family and friends. Neighbors. *Their* mountain. He couldn't think of anywhere he'd rather be right now.

Mallory rose to fill everyone's wine glasses. "I'm sorry Hector had other plans; I was looking forward to meeting your brother."

"You'll like him," Att said. "But after working his ass off to sell the ranch and transport stock to the new one, he was due a sunny vacation."

"Can't get more tropical than the Caribbean. Who's tending his horses?" Morgan asked.

"A couple of the hands stayed on. They'll babysit the place while Hector chases women," Atticus said. "With the way he downsized, they're not working too hard."

"It's good to have time to kick back a bit." Morgan glanced at Mallory. "Who's babysitting our Town Watch today? Or are you hoping the gang won't be out and about?"

"If anything, this would be the time they cause trouble," Mallory said. "The neighborhood watches are covering their own streets. Gustaf volunteered for the downtown. He thought his college-age kid would get a kick out of patrolling with him. Three of the single guys are taking turns watching the gang house. They'll call in for help if there is any action."

"Sweet." Morgan lifted his wine to Mallory in a token salute.

"I still don't like it," Atticus protested—which he'd been doing since he heard about the Town Watch. "The neighborhood watch makes good sense, Mallory; however, having civilians monitor the gang house doesn't. It's too dangerous."

"Just living in this town is dangerous." Mallory lifted her chin. "Our people have been assaulted and mugged. Houses and businesses have been robbed and damaged. There's graffiti everywhere. Our children are being pressured to join the gang and sell drugs. And our police are exhausted. You guys can't do it all."

"Doesn't matter," Att growled. "That's our job."

"It's also ours. This is our town, Atticus, and it's right for us all to defend it." She smiled slightly. "As for your 'civilians', do you know how many veterans live here? They come for the mountains—and the peace. Men like Logan Hunt."

Sawyer'd tried arguing with her—and lost.

Atticus wasn't quitting. "Not all of them are veterans."

Across the table, Masterson straightened, and his brows drew together. "No, not all of us are veterans, Ware. Nonetheless, maybe we've picked up a few minor skills. I grew up in this wilderness. Trapping and hunting. Surviving." As his sense of humor returned, Morgan grinned. "Even occasionally helping the cops catch bad guys."

Sawyer snorted. The tale of how the Masterson brothers helped Att rescue Gin and her colleague was already a town legend.

Morgan had a point. This *was* his town. And Mallory's.

And mine. Somewhere along the line, he'd come to care for the people on this mountain—and in this little town. This was his place and his people, whether some of them ever accepted him or not. "I think you lost this battle, Att."

"Oh, he did." Gin giggled and ran her hand down Att's arm. "Morgan got you by the short 'n' curlies, Atticus."

"Yeah, I know." After a grumpy second, Att grinned, then shook his head. "Still… Having people actually watching the Aryan Hammers…"

Mallory interrupted. "Although the Town Watch uses almost anyone who volunteers, only certain people watch the gangsters themselves—mountain men like Morgan, ranchers, loggers, hunters, or veterans." Mallory's gaze was steady. "We're doing our best to make sure no one gets hurt."

"All right." Surrendering, Att sat back and put his arm around Gin's shoulders. "In some ways, I agree with your plan. If the bastards can't recruit or make money, they'll probably move away. But there might be a backlash. If the Hammers hope to join one of the big L.A. gangs, they won't want to look like losers when they go back. Tell your crew to be prepared."

"I will." When Mallory took Sawyer's hand under the table, her fingers were icy cold. She talked a good talk...during the day. During the nights, she'd confessed how frightened she was that one of the watchers would get hurt.

He had the same concerns. Before, he'd worried for her, Gin, and Att. Now his fears had grown to include the entire town.

My town.

Chapter Twenty-Seven

W ELL AFTER MIDNIGHT on the Saturday night after Thanksgiving, the ClaimJumper crowd had thinned out considerably. Mallory smiled at the people remaining at her table. There were her Thanksgiving guests—Sawyer, Morgan, Atticus, and Gin—as well as Jake and Kallie. A few minutes ago, Logan and Becca had left, since they didn't want to impose on Sunny and Virgil, who were babysitting Ansel.

Becca had told about Virgil getting down on the floor with Ansel and letting the toddler bounce on his stomach. Mallory grinned at the image. Virgil would make an awesome father.

So would Sawyer.

Sipping her beer, Mallory watched her man. He was laughing at something his brother had said, his aura so brilliant she couldn't believe others didn't see it. Although traces of grief from losing his SEAL team and his best friend remained, most of the darkness was gone.

Atticus and Gin's auras mixed beautifully, and she loved how they unconsciously turned toward each other. Jake and Kallie did the same.

When Mallory and Sawyer had arrived at the tavern, Morgan had been with a couple of women—as usual. The Masterson brothers never lacked female company. Although Wyatt might be more outgoing, just as many women were drawn to Morgan's quiet confidence. The ladies had certainly been unhappy when the muscular wilderness guide abandoned them to join Mallory's group.

"So what are your plans for the winter, Sawyer?" Morgan asked, tipping his hat back. "You heading for the tropics like your brother?"

"Nope, I'll be here or at Hector's new ranch." Sawyer eyed him. "I take it you, Kallie, and Virgil read over the contract for the horses?"

"Great. First Mal reads auras, and now you read minds?" Morgan scowled. "Yeah. We talked—and signed. We'll keep our personal mounts, and you'll buy the rest. They'll be happier wintering somewhere not buried under waist-high snow."

Sawyer smiled and held out his hand to Morgan, then Kallie. "It'll be good doing business with you."

After the handshaking was concluded, Kallie asked, "How are you doing with the other guide services?"

"Three are on the fence. One is in. Another one is adding horses to their services and will lease from me, but they're starting small." Sawyer shrugged. "I'd hoped for better; still, considering my background and newness to the area, it's not surprising."

"Takes time," Atticus agreed. He glanced at his watch. "We probably should head home."

Gin leaned into him. "Can we dance first?"

The big detective smiled. "Absolutely."

Before he could rise, his cell rang with the ringtone that Mallory knew was for the police station. A hand on Gin's shoulder, he pulled it out. "Ware."

Mallory recognized the loud, frantic voice of a young patrol officer. "Thank fuck I got you. A Town Watch guy called. He says the Aryan Hammers set fire to Simmons's house—and is still there. The family's trapped inside."

"Fuck." Atticus glanced at Sawyer. "Get the women home."

"Aye."

Atticus kissed Gin hard. Barking orders into the phone, he ran out the door.

After a second of stunned silence, Morgan rose and turned toward Sawyer. "The bastards will be armed, and we don't have many cops on this weekend. The rest aren't close enough to get here fast."

He was right. Mallory felt the blood drain from her face. She turned to Sawyer. "The fire department has only a few volunteers. What if the gang shoots at them?"

Sawyer's jaw turned tight. "Bet that's their plan. The Hammers want the cops to show up."

Gin gasped. "What?"

"It's a fucking trap. With people in danger, the cops have to respond."

Mallory's hands clenched. Sawyer would feel he had no choice either. He could get hurt. Killed. Her skin went cold. "Sawyer."

He was already rising to his feet and slinging on his denim jacket. She took his hand, held him back. "Don't go alone, my Captain. Let the town help. Tell us what to do."

He stared at her.

"She's right, Ware," Morgan stated. "I got your back, but we're still outnumbered."

She could see Sawyer's conflict, his fear that *civilians* would get hurt. Would die.

"You can't do it alone, Sawyer." The push he needed was obvious. "Simmons has a teenaged daughter and a seven-year-old. Take the help you need to get them out."

"Fuck." Her man tugged absently on his hat brim, then, no longer in doubt, stepped up onto a chair. In a voice that had commanded men in war, he yelled, "Listen up!"

My turn. Mallory stepped up onto her own chair and amped her volume to band saw strength. "The Town Watch is called to action."

Someone yanked the plug from the jukebox.

People stood to see what was going on.

Sawyer continued. "Your Town Watch called the police. The Aryan Hammers set fire to Simmons's house."

"Son of a bitch!" Men started moving toward the door in a rush.

"Stop!" Sawyer's voice could have cut steel.

The crowd stopped.

"The bastards are out for blood. Anyone with weapons, get over here. If you don't have a firearm, hang back until we clear the way."

Sawyer jumped down and swung Mallory down, too.

A surprising number of people flowed toward the table. Then again, with the rise in crime, more locals had been going armed.

"You can't give us orders, Ware." An ex-corrections officer named Romero rose with a scowl. "Who the hell do you think you are?"

Mallory glared. "Sawyer is—"

Morgan's loud voice drowned her out. "Who the hell do you think has been the vigilante in this town? Who kept the bastards from ripping off the vet clinic? Stopped drug deals? I know it wasn't you, big mouth." Morgan gave Romero a dismissive look. "Our vigilante is the Navy SEAL. A captain."

"A SEAL? Well, damn." The owner of the convenience store, Mark Greaves, gave Sawyer a respectful nod.

More stunned murmurs came from the surrounding crowd.

"Ha!" Terry Breton from the feed store grinned at Sawyer. "I *figured* you were the one fucking them gangsters up. What are your orders, Cap?"

Sawyer nodded to Terry, and the colors in his aura took on a deeper hue as he assumed the responsibilities of command.

He glanced at Morgan. "What's Simmons's place look like?"

"It's on Riffle Avenue, which dead-ends to the north. Roger's is the last house—a two-story on the left." Morgan stroked his mustache and considered. "Front yard is grass. There are two houses across the street, both heavily wooded. Roger's backyard is forest all the way to Gold Dust, the next street over. There's lots of cover, except in the front yard."

Sawyer scowled. "We'll get slaughtered if we drive up Riffle, which the cops and firefighters will do. So, Gold Dust is to the west? Pay Dirt Avenue parallels it to the east?"

"Affirmative, Cap. Closest cross street is Argonaut." Terry yanked out a pen and showed Simmons's house at the end of Riffle with the nearest two parallel streets.

"We can land a team on Gold Dust." Sawyer pointed to where Simmons's backyard would meet the street. "And here on Pay Dirt. If we cut through the backyards, we'll have cover."

Terry nodded. "That'll work. No time for anything more elaborate."

"If the gang got their revenge and ran, we're golden. If not"—Sawyer motioned to the people on his right and held up the napkin—"You're going to drive down Gold Dust without lights, park at the end, make your way through Simmons's backyard and to each side of his house. Use the cover of the trees. If the police are pinned down—and I'm betting they will be—we'll have to open fire on the gang. The goal is to drive them away so the firefighters can get the family out."

Sawyer's jaw tightened. "People, be sure of your target and what's behind it. We don't want good guys killed by friendly fire, yeah?"

When he studied the feed store owner, Mallory remembered Terry had been a Green Beret.

Sawyer said to Terry, "In the dark, our best bet is a pincer movement with an overwhelming assault. Otherwise, the gangbangers could target individual shooters by the muzzle flashes. So wait for my order and make sure your team fires together."

Terry saluted casually. "You got it, sir."

The Aryan Hammers would be shooting at…everyone. At Sawyer. Mallory swallowed hard.

Sawyer pointed to Terry and told the group of people on his right, "You are the Gold Dust Team, and here's your leader. He is in *charge*, am I *clear*?"

A chorus of agreement sounded: *Aye-aye, sir; Affirmative; Yes, sir;* and a couple of *Oorahs* from the Marines.

Mallory heard Sawyer mutter, "This is going to be a clusterfuck." He turned to the people on his left. "The rest of you, you're with me. We're the Pay Dirt Team, and we're heading for Pay Dirt. Same directions. We'll gather on the street, make our way through the backyards approaching Riffle, and assess the situation. If needed, we'll open fire together. No shooting until my command. Clear?"

Same chorus of agreement.

"Move out."

He looked at Mallory. "You stay put, nymph. Stay safe."

Jake was giving Kallie the same orders—and Kallie nodded obediently.

Mallory put her hand on Sawyer's arm. "The Colt is under the seat in the pickup. Take it with you."

He hesitated, then nodded. "I will. Thanks."

Reaching up, she kissed him quickly. "I love you—you be careful."

Bracketed by Morgan and Jake, Sawyer jogged out of the tavern. She heard Sawyer ask Morgan, "Your baby in the truck?"

"Yeah. Let's take my ride."

As they disappeared, Mallory felt fear rising inside her. A trap. Her friends—and Sawyer—were walking into danger. Could be shot.

She stiffened. "The firefighters are also the paramedics, and there aren't many in town this weekend. Not enough for…for…"— if things went badly.

Gin stared at her for a second and rose. "I'm going to wake up Doc Vickers. We'll get the clinic ready, just in case."

"Good." Mallory met Kallie's gaze. "I've had first aid training." And a lot of experience on construction sites. "There's a big first aid box in the pickup."

"Training I've got." Wilderness guides would. Kallie nodded. "Let's go."

Gin was grabbing her purse. "You two be careful."

Most of the cars were already gone from the parking lot as they turned the corner. Mallory jumped into the pickup as Kallie got in the passenger side. Sawyer's hat was in the back seat—and the space under the driver's seat was empty. He'd taken the Colt. Good.

As they turned the corner onto Pay Dirt, Mallory switched off the headlights and parked behind a line of other vehicles.

There was sporadic gunfire coming from the west. *Sporadic* would indicate the gang was shooting at someone, right? Mallory's stomach clenched. As the noise roused people, lights in the neighborhood houses were flickering on.

With Kallie beside her, Mallory jogged through the darkness between two rental houses, across a backyard, stepped over a low fence, and into the next backyard. They moved alongside a small house surrounded by Douglas firs. Smoke was thick in the air, scratching her throat with each breath.

Ahead of them, through the trees in the front yard was Riffle Avenue, which dead-ended into forest.

Firelight flickered through the trees.

"The house really is on fire," Kallie whispered.

Anger flooded through Mallory's veins, driving back the fear. Those evil people had set fire to a house with children in it.

Ahead of them, Sawyer's group was flitting from tree to tree in the forested front yard. Kallie beside her, Mallory followed, staying well back. She stopped when she could see Simmons's house across the street.

It was madness.

The downstairs windows had been broken out, and flames raged in the living room. Burning trash was piled in front of the doors and windows like giant bonfires. The family was trapped inside. Even if they got through the flaming barricades, the gang waited outside.

Her mouth tasted like metal.

Was this what a war zone was like?

The gang's vehicles, a black SUV, a battered Ford four-door, and a red Dodge Charger, lined the curb directly in front of Simmons's house.

Near the center of the street, a black and white patrol car was stopped, lights still flashing. At its bumper was the volunteer fire truck, headlights still on. Angled behind it, not quite to Simmons's house, Atticus's Chevy Tahoe had obviously skidded to a stop.

At least two, maybe more, Hammers had taken cover between the vehicles and the burning house. Another was behind a big maple, the sole tree in the front yard. A crash of glass—and a shout of glee—indicated more gangbangers around the sides of the house.

Roger's workshop, close to the edge of the forest, wasn't on fire, but Mallory could see figures running between it and the house. One turned, and she saw the muzzle flash as the handgun fired.

Heart galloping wildly in her chest, Mallory ducked behind her tree. The Hammers were still shooting. She pulled in a breath and tried to push the fear away.

"Mal." Kallie was crouched low, staring toward the street. "Levi and William are hurt."

Mallory edged out.

Behind the black-and-white, illumined by the fire truck lights, one police officer was sprawled face down on the pavement. Pale blond hair—William.

Next to him, Levi was slumped against the front tire, his hand against his chest. Blood blackened the gray pavement. Atticus crouched beside him, helping put pressure on the wound while occasionally firing toward the Hammers.

His shooting was all that kept the gangbangers from rushing the car, Mallory realized.

Sawyer had been right—it was a trap.

Levi and William, the two patrol officers, were young. They'd have fearlessly driven down the street, piled out, and been sitting ducks. The gang would have shot at the fire truck—and the firefighters had probably dived under the dash.

Atticus would have arrived—and had no choice but to rescue his men.

The Aryan Hammers were still at the house…because they wanted to kill Atticus and everyone else and return to L.A. with a victory. Their yelled curses and taunts came from the wooded areas adjacent to the house. There were an awful lot of them.

Mallory turned to look at Sawyer.

The Pay Dirt Team—hers and Sawyer's team—was across the street from Simmons's house. Sawyer stood behind the tree closest to the police car. Jake Hunt was behind another tree. Morgan wasn't in sight. Behind the other trees were Sawyer's volunteers. And, Mallory realized, with the fire so bright, neither the gang nor the police realized the townspeople were there.

Sawyer's voice rang out, "Pay Dirt team, take cover!"

At the police car, Atticus spun around. Unable to see anything, he yanked Levi down and flattened himself on top of both officers, covering them.

As Sawyer's men stepped behind trees, he yelled, "Gold Dust team. Fire!"

Mallory tucked herself tightly behind her tree. Kallie was

hunched behind hers.

In a horrendous blast of sound, Terry's entire team fired from the sides of Simmons's house. Mallory cringed at the screams and yells of pain. Moving silently from the rear, Terry's group had taken the gang by surprise.

The wave of firing stopped. Random gunfire—much less—came from one side of the house. A man's hoarse screams came from the other side.

Edging out, Mallory saw bodies lying next to the Charger. The gangbangers using their vehicles for cover had been totally unprotected from the gunfire behind them.

"Gold Dust, take cover," Sawyer yelled.

Five of the Hammers were dashing toward their vehicles, firing at Terry's group in the woods around the house.

Sawyer yelled, "Pay Dirt, fire."

The Hammers fell.

WITH MALLORY'S COLT in his hand, Sawyer crossed the street. Despite the bitingly cold air, sweat trickled down his back. He quickly checked his men. All moving, thank fuck.

And his brother was alive.

With a grim smile, Att looked up at Sawyer, nodded, and returned to caring for the downed men. From the skidded car at the rear, Att had arrived too late and had charged in to keep his boys from being slaughtered.

What a goatfuck.

Sawyer called to the four men closest to him, "See if you can clear the fire away from the door."

Raising his voice, he shouted to the rest of his team. "In teams of two, search the grounds. Remember the bastards are armed. Capture them and take them to the cops. Take injured gangbangers to the fire trucks with a guard. Gold Dust team is near the back, so be careful."

As the men went to work, the firefighters jumped out of their truck. One ran to assist Atticus with the injured patrol officers.

Sawyer's men had cleared a gap in the trash fire at the front door, and two firefighters headed into the house.

A pumper truck pulled up.

In the wavering light from the fire, Sawyer checked the front yard. A glance established three Hammers were dead. How many were left?

He considered and didn't call Morgan in. Instead, he turned to Jake Hunt, who'd taken up a position at his side. "Can you take charge of the group searching the left of the house? I'll check the right."

"Will do."

As Jake moved away, someone else took his place—a huge logger whose hands made his 30-aught shotgun seem like a toy. Hadn't this guy plowed into him at the ClaimJumper months ago? With a grim nod, the man waited for Sawyer to continue.

Sawyer moved on.

And stopped dead at the sound of a voice that should *not* have been anywhere near a bloody action.

"Leroy, I've got this bleeding stopped, but he needs stitches. Take him to the clinic." It was Mallory, using what she called her band saw voice, giving orders as coolly as if she were in the middle of a construction site. "Francis, that Hammer is dead. Leave him and help put out the trash fire."

Despite his fear—and anger at her risking her neck—he felt a surge of pride. That was his woman, bringing order out of chaos. And she thought she was quiet? *My ass.*

He returned to his own task.

One body was being hauled to the front by two men. Another gangbanger, cursing and struggling, was pinned to the ground by a cluster of Terry's men.

No one else. Looked like the teams had cleared the area nicely. Any gang member who'd made it out of the area was probably still running.

"Looks good," Sawyer told the silent logger beside him and headed back toward the front.

The trash piles had been shoved away from the house or put out, and the flames inside were dying down. The firefighters might be able to save the frame—but the building was a fucking mess.

Simmons and his wife stood near the patrol car along with a teenaged girl. Sawyer frowned. Hadn't Mallory said there was a little boy?

Followed by his logger escort, Sawyer walked into the front yard.

A firefighter was helping a kid out of the house. "Heath, next time, you leave when your parents say leave. It's our job to get your pets out."

Sawyer couldn't keep from smiling as the scolding continued. Heath had apparently gone back into the fire to save his cat. Brave kid.

Clad in pajamas, the boy needed support to walk—but the cat was in his arms.

"Sawyer, down!" Mallory's scream was unmistakable, and Sawyer dove for the ground. The logger followed—and the crack of a handgun sounded through the night.

A man dropped out of the maple tree, knocking the firefighter away from the boy. The skinhead hauled the shrieking boy up in front of him and shoved his semi-automatic against Heath's head. "Move away from my car, or he's dead!"

It was Animal. *Fuck*.

"Teams, hold fire," Sawyer shouted. Even if someone killed Animal, the bastard's dying twitch would blow the kid's head off.

From the ground, Sawyer eyed the line of fire from Animal to the workshop roof. There was a chance, but only if the bastard didn't have his weapon against the boy's head.

Make him move it, then.

Sawyer shoved to his feet.

The skinhead was almost to his Charger.

Revolver pointing toward the ground, Sawyer shouted, "Look at the *animal* running away with his little tail tucked between his legs. What a fucking *pussy*."

The skinhead spun around, gun still pressed to the boy's temple. He saw Sawyer and his face darkened. "You cocksucker."

Sawyer laughed. "All of L.A.'s gonna hear how you abandoned your gang. Didn't avenge shit. Just ran like a yellow dog. *Ooo-ooo-ooo*."

Sawyer imitated Achilles's yelps of fear.

"*Fuck* you!" Animal turned his pistol toward Sawyer. Even as he fired, Sawyer dove for the ground.

Pain ripped through Sawyer's arm.

A split second later, the crack of a high-powered rifle split the night.

Rolling over, Sawyer jumped up. Dammit, he shouldn't have gotten hit. *Getting slow, Ware.*

Animal was down. One head shot.

The youngster was alive and was snatched up by his hysterical mother and father.

Taking his first good breath in minutes, Sawyer turned—and Mallory slammed into him so hard, he lost the last remnant of oxygen in his lungs. Trembling like a leaf, she hugged him until he couldn't restock his lungs.

She shook him, actually shook him. "Don't you *ever* do that *again.*"

He took himself a long hard hug, breathing in her fresh, clean scent. Peace in the midst of chaos.

"Jesus, Sawyer." Atticus appeared, face tight. "You scared the fuck out of me."

"Me, too," Mallory's voice was muffled against Sawyer's chest.

Att ripped off Sawyer's sleeve and examined the bleeding graze across his deltoid. "Not too bad."

After pulling in a shuddering breath, Mallory stepped back—and bandaged him up using gauze dressings she was carrying in her pockets. Damn, she was something.

"Who took the shot?" Att asked.

"Hold on." Sawyer checked the area, turned toward the work-shop, and yelled, "All clear, Masterson."

A minute later, Morgan appeared, his Gladius in one hand. Si-lently, he walked over to look at Animal's body. His chest rose and fell. After a long minute, he approached Sawyer, saw the rough bandage, and dismay appeared in his eyes. "I'm sorry. I couldn't risk a shot with the asshole's barrel to Heath's head."

"No, you couldn't. You did everything exactly right." Sawyer released Mallory to give Morgan a one-armed hug. Poor bastard was shaking with the release of adrenaline.

So was Sawyer.

When Sawyer stepped back, Mallory wrapped her arms around Morgan and gave him a hug that, from experience, Sawyer knew would make Masterson's world feel like it had spun right again.

Morgan's arms tightened until Sawyer could hear the little contractor's ribs creak.

Giving the man time to get his emotions back under control, Sawyer turned to check the field of battle.

The giant logger was still guarding the flank, and Sawyer released him with a nod and smile of thanks.

Simmons stood near the police car in front of his family. His gaze met Sawyer's, and the gratitude in his eyes said everything. *War was over.*

Behind Simmons, his son was on his mother's lap. When his sister knelt and put his pet in his arms, the boy pulled the cat close—and cried.

Feeling his own eyes burning, Sawyer turned away.

"Nice shot, cuz." Kallie ran over to hug her cousin.

Returning to Sawyer, Mallory put an arm around him. "Well-executed rescue job, Captain Ware. I suppose you need to check your troops before we can leave?"

"I do." Sawyer pulled her closer before scowling. "What the fuck are you doing here anyway?"

Although the darkness of violence and death lingered in her eyes, she smiled at him. "They may be your troops; however, I recruited them—and thought there might be too many injuries. Kallie and I had to help."

He sighed. Yes, she would see it that way.

She was tensing for a fight. A fight that wouldn't happen. Her sense of honor was just one of the things he loved about her. He smiled. "I understand. For my peace of mind, stay close now, soldier."

She grinned and touched her index finger to her forehead in a mock salute. "Yes, Sir."

Brat. He pulled her in for a firm kiss and whispered, "You'd better figure on saying '*Yes, Sir*' over and over tonight, nymph, right along with '*Please, Sir, please.*'"

When she melted against him, he took her mouth again, feeling the zing of adrenaline that said he was alive, she was alive, and they needed to celebrate in the best way possible. The house fire felt like a warm day compared to the lust heating his blood.

As he lifted his head, he heard shouting behind him. "Go, Captain." "Attaboy, Ware!"

What the fuck?

Keeping one hand on his woman, Sawyer turned and…froze.

His "troops" were waiting on the street, grinning at him, and when he looked at them, damned if they didn't all salute, and then raise a cheer loud enough to wake the entire town.

Chapter Twenty-Eight

S PRING HAD COME to Bear Flat.
        Although the higher elevations were still snow-covered, in Mallory's valley, poppies and lupines brightened the meadow. Near Sawyer's cabin, Mallory breathed in the sun-warmed air and glanced at the text that had just come through on her phone. *"Almost there. What's with all the cars?"*

Almost there. *Yes!*

She tilted her head, hoping to hear horses, but the rushing creek was filled with spring run-off and drowned out any noise from hooves. Shielding her eyes from the bright sun, she looked toward the south where the winding trail there met up with another coming from the west.

Last winter, Sawyer and the Mastersons had worked out a route from Sawyer's mountain ranch down to Hector Ware's new spread in the foothills where the horses had wintered.

There. She saw movement. A flash of metal. Finally, a long string of horses and riders emerged through the blooming white dogwoods at the forest's edge.

She shouted, "Here they come!"

As everyone turned to look, the horses splashed through the shallowest part of the creek. The cluster of children playing there yelled in welcome and held open the gate to the pasture.

Mallory could see the surprise on Sawyer's face. Halfway back in the line of riders, Kallie and Jake gave loud whoops. The rest of the riders—guests and hands—were perking up and beaming. Riding drag, Morgan pulled off his hat and waved it.

Picking up the excitement, the horses broke into a trot, heading for the stable. The riders shouted with glee.

Cheering and welcoming yells came from the people in the yard and crowding the fences.

Oh, how she'd missed her man. It had been far too long. Unable to wait any longer, Mallory swung over the fence and ran across the grass.

Catching sight of her, Achilles gave a delighted *ooo-ooo-ooo*, broke away from his very important task of leading the drive, and charged across the pasture to greet her.

Mallory crouched to greet the frantically whirling dog. "Did you take good care of Sawyer and the horses?"

During the exchange of hugs and kisses, Achilles assured her he'd done an excellent job of supervising.

Laughing, Mallory rose and realized the line of horses had reached the stable and the center of the milling crowd.

Sawyer jumped off his gelding and handed the reins to someone in the crowd. Eyes on Mallory, he started across the yard toward her.

A second later, she was pulled into his rock-hard arms.

Burrowing as close as she could get, she rubbed her face against his shoulder and inhaled the scent of leather and sweat and man. "Oh, Sawyer."

"Fuck, I missed you." Sawyer pulled her tighter, his big frame hard and amazingly real.

She pulled his head down for a long, wonderful kiss. And another. "Oh yes. More." She rose on tiptoes—and he took control, molding her against him, as he devoured her mouth.

The ground disappeared right out from under her.

When they came up for air, the last of the riders had moved past. By the stable, the townspeople were helping unsaddle and water the horses before turning them out to pasture.

Sawyer looked around at the cars parked up and down the lane, at the people milling around the cabin. "What's all this?"

"Bear Flat wanted to celebrate the town's first annual spring horse drive." She grinned. "Your place has been commandeered for a town barbecue."

The disbelief in his gaze was simply wonderful.

WHAT THE FUCK? Sawyer could only stare.

The wooden half-barrels beside his porch and the driveway entrance were overflowing with bright red and white tulips. Had Mrs. Reed and Vanessa decided his yard was too boring for a celebration? Good thing the eight-foot bush—had Mallory called it a lilac?—beside the cabin was in full, fragrant bloom.

Three barbecues were set up near the cabin, and the aroma of grilling meat made his stomach growl. Close by, picnic tables covered in red-and-white tablecloths were loaded with food.

Blankets, lawn chairs, and picnic baskets dotted the lush grass a little distance away. People everywhere… Families with babies and toddlers, clusters of men in flannel shirts and jeans, older locals in lawn chairs, young men and women flirting… "Is the whole town here?" he asked, feeling gut-punched.

"Maybe not everybody, but close." Mallory smiled, her eyes a vivid green in the sunlight. "The business owners appreciated how you timed your arrival before the tourist season starts—and on a Sunday—so they could come."

He and Morgan hadn't "timed" anything. "Have I mentioned Bear Flat people are crazy?"

She grinned. "You fit right in, Captain."

He couldn't argue.

She laughed at his disgruntled look. "Go finish your duties. I'll be waiting for you over there." She motioned to the swath of picnic blankets covering the grassy area, well away from the stable and corrals.

"But…" Fuck, he didn't want to let her go. Only, she was right; he had responsibilities. "See you soon."

After a worried look between them, Achilles trotted after her, obviously deciding his duties were over, and it was time for food.

With a burning hunger for his woman simmering in Sawyer's blood, the end of the trail drive seemed to take forever, even though people appeared from everywhere to help.

Leading away one of the horses, Att had stopped to give him a hard hug. Saddle over one shoulder, Logan had nodded on his way past. Virgil was helping one of the younger riders groom his horse.

It hadn't taken long before the horses were turned out to pasture and the tack put away in the stable. After learning the town had set out blankets and chairs for the guest riders, Morgan and Kallie had guided them there. Everyone was getting fed.

Sawyer looked around the empty stable and grinned. Work done. Time for food and drink.

As he walked toward the barbecues, trying to spot his woman, Barney stopped him.

"Hey, Cap." The massive logger who'd been beside him at what the town had labeled "the Simmons Fire" handed him a beer with a thumping slap on his arm that almost knocked him over. He pointed to the right. "Mal's over there."

"Thanks, Barney." Weaving through the maze of blankets and chairs and groups of people, Sawyer exchanged greetings, handshakes, hugs, and finally reached his target.

Mallory was on a blanket, Atticus and Gin on her right, Virgil and Summer on her left.

Sawyer dropped down beside his woman, close enough to breathe in her clean fragrance. Wrapping an arm around her, he took himself another long, satisfying kiss, and the rough edges inside him settled into place with a contented sigh.

"I love you," he whispered against her lips, then remembered they were in the middle of a crowd. *Damn.* Pulling upright, he glanced around.

Hell of a lot of smiles were now directed at him and Mallory.

"Your drive looks like fun, bro. I wish I could've gotten the time off. Next fall, I'm in." Atticus glanced down at his little redhead. "You want to come?"

"Riding all day?" Gin's little nose wrinkled. "I wouldn't be able to walk afterward. However, I do believe Trigger would be happy to join you."

Sawyer followed her gaze and saw Trigger and Achilles playing tag around the blankets.

"Must be nice to be young," Sawyer said. He'd loved the drive...and was going to be fucking happy to be in a soft bed again.

With his woman in his arms.

Smiling, he took a sip of his drink and felt it dissolve the dust in his throat.

"Mr. Ware, I got food for you." Trotting up to the blanket, Roger Simmons's little boy handed him a plate filled with two burgers, potato salad, beans, and a massive piece of cake. The plate was accompanied by a worshipful look.

"Looks great. Thanks, Heath."

The kid grinned and ran back to a herd of youngsters.

"It's good to see him acting like a kid." During the winter, the boy had been unnaturally quiet. Looking around, Sawyer spotted Simmons's pretty teenager, who had also seemed subdued. "Both kids look perkier."

"Heath's resilient," Virgil said. He was sprawled on the blanket, his head resting on Summer's thighs.

"Jasmine probably had it rougher. She understood how close her little brother came to dying." Mallory grinned. "In addition, Terry's grandson *finally* caught her attention. These days she's thinking of other things than death and violence."

A young man had his arm around the girl, his stance protective. With a shock, Sawyer realized the tall, strong teen was the blond boy he'd caught buying drugs. "Was Jasmine the girl he was trying to impress when I caught him in the alley?"

"Mmmhmm." Mallory smiled and leaned her head against Sawyer's arm. "He learned a man shouldn't give up his integrity for a woman. And she realized a macho swagger doesn't guarantee a good character."

"I don't think I learned those lessons until well past high school." He studied the young couple and smiled at how they leaned against each other. Young love. Nice.

Sawyer kissed the top of Mallory's head. His own love had a rare understanding of people. Sometimes it seemed as if she could read his mind. And she possessed another uncanny talent. "Last night..."

"You're frowning at me, Ware." Without him asking, she took his beer so he could dig into his food. "What happened last night?"

"I was sitting by the campfire. Did you know when your eyes are dazzled by firelight, it's impossible to see up into the tree canopy? To see anything higher than head-high?"

She wrinkled her nose quizzically. "And?"

"At Simmons's fire, you yelled for me to get down." He could still hear the panic in her voice. "How did you see Animal in the tree? He wouldn't have been visible."

Laughter filled her eyes. "I've told you before—auras are easier to see in the dark."

She'd actually seen Animal's *aura*. He shook his head. "You are the most amazing woman."

AS HE APPROACHED, Morgan heard Sawyer's comment and had to grin. Ware sometimes reminded him of Wyatt. Neither one wanted to accept any shit he couldn't see nor touch. Smirking, Morgan dropped down on an empty blanket. "Told you she could see auras."

Sawyer gave him a dirty look. "You're not helping, Masterson."

Grinning, Morgan accepted a food-filled plate from Heath and saw the huge wedge of pie. "By damn, that's Vanessa's cherry pie, isn't it?" His favorite pie in all the world.

"Yessir. I told her to make it big cuz everybody knows how much you like cherry pie."

"You're a good kid. Thank you."

Beaming from the compliment, the boy ran back to the cook area. He looked great. Healthy.

Alive.

Because Morgan had killed a man for him.

After the Simmons Fire last November, Morgan had headed up into the high country for a few weeks. At that elevation, the air was so crisply cold, it felt as if it would snap. The trees had been a stark black against the pristine snow.

Camping in the snow, he'd lived from moment to moment, concentrating on survival. Far away from the soggy, clinging emotions of people, he'd come to terms with the shot he'd taken. No matter how sickened he was at killing another human, he'd done what needed to be done. He'd protected a child—one of his tribe. When it came right down to it, all creatures lived by the natural order—life and death, kill or be killed...and protect the tribe.

When he'd returned, wind-burned and gaunt, Sawyer had pushed him into seeing the local counselor. Talking with Jacob Wheeler had been interesting, but Morgan hadn't needed the psych dude. He was doing all right. When the counselor agreed, that had been the end of it.

As Morgan lounged on the blanket, he listened to the conversations around him—and enjoyed the hell out of food he hadn't had to cook. Especially the pie. Oh yeah.

After the last bite, he sighed and looked up. "Hey, Mal, I heard from Wyatt. He'll be back in a couple of weeks."

"Good news." She grinned. "Just in time to put him to work."

"Exactly." There would be some battles coming as well. With Kallie's agreement, Morgan had made more than a few improvements to the business.

Might even say he'd done the same to himself.

"Speaking of work..." He glanced at Sawyer. "Since the drive is over, your job is done. The Mastersons and Hunts will assume responsibility for the clients."

HALLELUJAH. SAWYER GRINNED. This was probably how Achilles felt when the leash came off. "I stand relieved. Gotta say, I am fucking pleased to have your outfit handling the two-legged critters."

Morgan huffed a laugh. "We noticed." He glanced around and noticed Kallie was escorting the older clients toward the parking area. "Speaking of which, I better help before she gets pissed at me for sitting on my ass."

As Morgan headed for the guests, Sawyer watched Kallie. The tiny brunette was like a herding dog, filled with energy, keeping her guests happy, and enjoying the hell out of herself in the process. Mallory had good taste in her friends.

Sawyer kissed the top of his woman's head and smiled down into her clear green eyes. "What's the plan for the afternoon?"

"We eat and drink and talk. We all want to hear about the trail ride—feel free to exaggerate; the bigger the tale, the better. Once everyone leaves, we can have our own celebration."

"Can't ask for better than that."

The afternoon progressed with, as Mallory had said, food and drink and talk. The townspeople not only made the clients from the horse drive welcome, but coaxed stories of the experience, which led to a round of tall tales from the Bear Flat old-timers.

As the sun lowered behind the still white-capped mountains, the Hunts and Mastersons shuttled the clients up to Serenity Lodge, and the townspeople cleared away all evidence of the celebration.

Then a stream of cars headed down the mountain, leaving Sawyer and Mallory waving farewell in front of the cabin.

"C'mon, Captain." Mallory took his hand. "Let's go home."

Taking her hand, he walked with her down the lane and up the hill to the farmhouse.

Aslan was perched on the porch railing, having monitored the gathering from a safe distance. With a welcoming purr, he accepted a chin rub, then jumped down to greet the pup.

Tail wagging frantically, Achilles bounced around the solemn cat, sharing all his puppy adventures in high yips and whines.

Grinning, Sawyer opened the front door for Mallory and glanced back over his shoulder.

His horses were grazing peacefully in the green meadow where the rushing creek glinted in the last of the sunlight. The little cabin—which Hector would use when he came to visit—sat waiting for its next occupant. Mallory's farmhouse—now their farmhouse—seemed to expand in serene welcome.

This was where he belonged. To this land. To this town. And above all, to this woman.

"Welcome home, my hero," Mallory said softly and rose onto tiptoes to give him a kiss.

As peace filled his soul, he wrapped his arms around her.

Yeah, he was home.

~ The End ~

Want to be notified of the next release?

Get an email when a new book is released and hear what's planned for the future.

Sent only on a release day.

Sign up at:

www.CheriseSinclair.com/NewsletterForm

Have you tried the Wild Hunt Legacy series?
Hour of the Lion

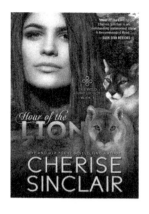

Available everywhere
Get Hour of the Lion now!

Winner of The Romance Reviews' **Best Book of 2011** *award ~ There's a reason why Cherise Sinclair is on my auto-buy list: she writes fantastic erotic romances with great stories and wonderful characters. So, when I saw her newest release, I was intrigued that it was a departure from the kind of books that she normally writes. But, I am happy to report that she's done it again. Hour of the Lion was simply amazing. Hot hunky shifter men, a strong and sassy heroine, a gripping story, and some oh so lovely ménage action are just the tip of the iceberg in this phenomenal read!*

~ The Romance Reviews

First a Marine, then a black ops agent, Victoria Morgan knows the military is where she belongs…until a sniper's bullet changes her life. Trying to prove she's not washed up, she rescues a young man from kidnappers. When the dying boy transforms into a cougar—and bites her—she learns of an entire hidden society. He begs her to inform his grandfather of his death and to keep the secret of the shifters' existence. She can't refuse, but what if the creatures pose a danger to the country she swore to protect?

As guardian of the shifter territory, Calum McGregor wields the power of life and death over his people. When a pretty human female arrives in their wilderness town, he and his littermate become increasingly concerned. Not only is the little female hiding something, but she is far more appealing than any human should be.

While investigating the shifters, Victoria begins to fall in love with the werecat brothers and the town as well. For the first time in her life, she might have a real home. Her hopes are crushed when a deadly enemy follows her from the city, and the shifters discover she knows their secret. Now nobody is safe—least of all Victoria.

With a fantastic heroine, two yummy heroes and a whole host of fun side characters (I've already asked for a certain bear and wolfie to get books) this slick paranormal romance came at me out of nowhere and knocked my socks off.

~ Scorching Book Reviews

Excerpt from
Hour of the Lion

IGNORING THE WOOD pixie chittering angrily in the oak tree, Sheriff Alec McGregor silently stepped onto the porch, coming up behind the burglar. He tried not to laugh as the criminal squirmed like a paw-pinned mouse.

It'd been a boring week so far. The last excitement was a good four days ago when old Peterson, having indulged in rotgut tequila, tried to demonstrate how to tap-dance on top of Calum's bar…which he did about once a month.

At least a pinioned burglar had the dubious distinction of being unique.

He rubbed his chin, feeling the rasp of stubble. He'd noticed—being as how he was a guy—what was wiggling was a very fine, nicely rounded ass in tight jeans.

And being a guy, he felt the need to see the front of this dangerous perp who had one leg inside the window and the other outside. He moved silently across the porch and checked out the criminal's front side to see what else the evening might hold.

Evening is going well. Hair, the rich color of dark walnut, rippled across her shoulders, and her purple T-shirt was tight enough to reveal amazingly lush breasts for such a compact body. Since she was too occupied to notice his arrival, he could study her assets without being considered a macho pig. *Abundant.* Yes, that would be the word. He'd heard the *more-than-a-mouthful is wasted* saying, but when it came to breasts, he was a bit of a glutton.

Concentrating on freeing her leg from something, she was oblivious to everything else.

He thought for a minute and decided to speak up. And hey, he needed to see the color of her eyes—for the report and all.

"My jail is empty today," he remarked sociably. "In case you wondered."

She froze like a mouse hearing a fox. When huge copper-colored eyes met his, everything inside him came to a halt, like the day he'd been chasing a rabbit and got his leg caught in a steel trap. A hard painful grip, only this time it was his chest being squeezed.

The sound of her breath whuffing out, like she'd been pounced on, cleared his mind. *Cop—I'm a cop.* And she was a burglar. No pouncing on this little prey allowed...and wasn't that a damned shame?

"Oh, hell," the lady perp said, obviously having recovered fast. She now looked more pissed-off than concerned, and that just wasn't right. "Listen, I'm really just—"

He leaned his hip against the porch railing and crossed his arms. "It's called breaking and entering," he offered helpfully.

Her mouth dropped open. "No way. Hey, I talked to the realtor this morning and—."

"Um-hmm. It's good you've done your homework. Shows a certain pride in your work."

The sparks in those big eyes almost did him in. "I am not a burglar, dammit. I'm here to rent this place. Amanda Golden is supposed to meet me."

He studied her for a minute. She had the realtor's name right—
'course it was there plain as could be on the rental sign.

A wisp of scent drifted past him. Blood. Fresh. "You're bleeding."

She blinked at the change of subject, and he noticed with pleasure how her thick lashes feathered down against skin tanned almost
as dark as her brown eyes.

"I'm bleeding?"

Herne help him, but she really was lovely—and he shouldn't let
that pretty face suck him in. She probably wrapped every male she
met around her *ringless*, delicate finger.

Besides, she was human. Some shifters enjoyed sampling human
females, but he'd never understood the attraction.

He pointed to where a nail had snagged more than her clothing,
and blood darkened the leg of her jeans. "Looks like the previous
renter overlooked a few nails from last season's Christmas lights. Let
me get you down from there before I start on some serious interrogation."

Her eyes narrowed, then she leaned forward. Reaching out, she
obviously intended to steady herself on his forearms, but the
opportunity was too good to ignore. With a smooth move, he
dropped low enough that her hands settled on his shoulders instead,
and he grasped her around the waist. His fingers curled around
surprisingly hard abdominal muscles—the female must work out
regularly—and he lifted her up.

She gasped as he swung her onto the porch. Her grip tightened
on his shoulders, lean hands, not soft, yet they felt very, very good
on his body. Her hands would probably clutch his shoulders—just
like that—as he slid inside her, filled her.

He shook his head. Where the hell had that image come from?

Her eyes were huge, and she smelled of pain and fear. He released her immediately. She was frightened. And he could tell it was
more than just worry about being arrested. No, she was scared of
him. The idea was insulting.

"Um. Thank you." Her voice was husky.

"My pleasure." After all, honesty was the best policy, and he'd enjoyed the hell out of getting his hands on her. Was looking forward to enjoying more, but…she was scared of *him*?

On the street, a white Taurus pulled up behind the Jeep. Amanda Golden slid out, briefcase in hand, hurried up the sidewalk, and onto the porch. "Hello, Alec. Ms. Waverly? I'm sorry I'm late. I got hung up at the title company."

"That's all right. I've been kept entertained," his ex-burglar said dryly.

"Well, damn, guess I have to let you go." And she would have decorated his jail cell so nicely too.

She shot him a nasty look, her appealingly full lips tightly compressed.

When she started to move, Alec tucked a finger under her belt to halt her. "Let's make sure you aren't hurt too bad," he said. "Nails can be nasty."

As he leaned forward, he realized the faint scent of blood wasn't just from the nail; it came from multiple places. She had dark red-brown spots on the back of her T-shirt. The gasp when he'd lifted her from the windowsill—had that been from surprise or pain?

He studied her closer. Meticulously applied makeup covered a bruise on the side of her face. There was maybe a lumpy dressing on her shoulder under the T-shirt, and something more than a bra wrapped around her sides.

Now, all that damage might be from a car accident. But that wouldn't explain why she was scared of him, the most likable fellow on this planet. So. He could be wrong—frequently was—but he picked the most logical explanation.

Someone had beaten the hell out of her.

"Where else are you hurt?"

Why would the big sheriff ask that? Vic wondered, feeling a chill. She'd covered the blood and bruises adequately. Had her description and injuries been on an APB?

Dammit, he'd already given her one scare. For a nasty moment, she'd thought Swane had hired him until it became obvious he was just a small-town cop having himself a good time.

"Don't be silly," she said, deliberately misunderstanding. "A little nail scrape doesn't warrant all this concern."

Nudging his arm away, she shook hands with the realtor. "Ms. Golden, nice to meet you."

"Just call me Amanda." Tall, blonde, wearing silky black pants with matching jacket, she was the epitome of a refined style that Vic had never mastered. After giving Vic's hand a firm shake, the realtor frowned at the cop. "Is there a problem?"

"You got here just in time," Vic said. "Your policeman was about to arrest me and haul me away."

Amanda's snicker wasn't at all businesslike. "Ah, yes. If his jail's not overflowing with criminals, Alec feels he's not doing his job." She leaned forward and whispered loudly, "Of course, it's only a two-cell jailhouse."

Vic smiled and glanced over her shoulder to see how the sheriff took being taunted. With one hip propped on the railing and a lazy grin on his tanned face, he didn't look too upset.

When his focus shifted from Amanda to Vic, his gaze intensified, as if he were trying to see inside her. She felt a quiver low in her belly, but from worry or attraction—she wasn't sure. Probably worry.

Towering six feet five or so with appallingly broad shoulders that narrowed to a trim waist, the man moved like a trained fighter. Not all spit and polish like a soldier though. His golden-brown hair brushed the collar of his khaki-uniform, and he'd rolled his sleeves up, revealing corded wrists and muscular forearms. She remembered how easily he'd lifted her, how those big hands had wrapped around her. He was damned powerful, despite the easy-going manner.

Yeah, the quiver was definitely from worry.

But then he smiled at the realtor, and a dimple appeared at one corner of his mouth. The laugh lines around his eyes emphasized a thin blue-tinted scar that angled across his left cheekbone as if someone had marked him with a pen. His voice was deep and smooth and slow as warm honey, and she felt her muscles relax. "You have a mean streak, Amanda," he was saying. "I'll have to warn Jonah."

"He wouldn't believe you," the realtor said as she worked on unlocking the front door.

The sheriff turned, letting that should-be-a-registered-weapon grin loose on Vic, and her temperature rose. "So," he said, "Ms. Waverly, will you be staying in Cold Creek?"

He was gorgeous, and he looked at her as if she was something tasty. "Um..." she said and his smile increased a fraction, just enough that she realized what an idiot she was. *You're losing it, Sergeant.* She scowled at him. "A while."

And the sooner she left this damn town, the better.

The breeze whipped his shaggy hair "Well, while you're here—" he started.

"I need to get my stuff," she interrupted. Anything to escape. Odd how the scare from the sheriff's appearance had wiped out her need to pee.

To her annoyance, he followed her down the steps. "You're going to enjoy Cold Creek," he said. Before she could dodge, he slung an arm around her shoulders, and she felt his fingers trace the thick gauze dressing covering the cat-bite.

"Thank you, but I can manage," she said, smoothly enough despite the way her heart was pounding. Then she looked up.

Dark green eyes the color of the mountain forests narrowed, and he studied her as if she were a puzzle to be solved. A quiver ran up her spine as she realized the laidback manner and slow voice camouflaged a razor-sharp intelligence. Knives tended to come at a person in two ways: dark and hidden, or out in the open, all bright and shiny. A bright and shiny blade could still leave you bleeding on the sands.

She pulled away. "I'll be fine."

"Well then, I'll take myself off so you can get settled in." He waved at Amanda Golden and smiled at Vic, but this time the smile didn't touch his eyes. "I'm sure we'll run into each other again, Ms. Waverly. Cold Creek's a small town."

Cordial, polite. And Vic heard the threat underneath.

Get Hour of the Lion now!

Also from Cherise Sinclair

Masters of the Shadowlands (contemporary)
Club Shadowlands
Dark Citadel
Breaking Free
Lean on Me
Make Me, Sir
To Command and Collar
This Is Who I Am
If Only
Show Me, Baby
Servicing the Target
Protecting His Own
Mischief and the Masters

Mountain Masters and Dark Haven (contemporary)
Master of the Mountain
Simon Says: Mine
Master of the Abyss
Master of the Dark Side
My Liege of Dark Haven
Edge of the Enforcer
Master of Freedom
Master of Solitude

The Wild Hunt Legacy (paranormal)
Hour of the Lion
Winter of the Wolf
Eventide of the Bear

Standalone books
The Starlight Rite (Sci-Fi Romance)
The Dom's Dungeon (contemporary)

About Cherise Sinclair

Authors often say their characters argue with them. Unfortunately, since Cherise Sinclair's heroes are Doms, she never, ever wins.

A *New York Times* and *USA Today* Bestselling Author, she's renowned for writing heart-wrenching contemporary romances with devastating Dominants, laugh-out-loud dialogue, and absolutely sizzling sex.

With fledglings having flown the nest, Cherise, her beloved husband, a far-too-energetic puppy, and one fussy feline live in the Pacific Northwest where nothing is cozier than a rainy day spent writing.

Connect with Cherise in the following places:

Website:
CheriseSinclair.com

Facebook:
facebook.com/CheriseSinclairAuthor

Facebook Discussion Group:
CheriseSinclair.com/Facebook-Discussion-Group

CPSIA information can be obtained
at www.ICGtesting.com
Printed in the USA
BVOW03s1052300717

490635BV00001B/91/P